Pennyweight Flat

Books by the same author:

Our Hollow Sofa (2004)

Ants in My Dreadlocks (2005)

Stinger in a Sugar Jar (2007)

Couscous Threads (2008)

Bad Grass (2009)

My French Barrette (2012)

Driftwood – poetry collection (2010)

Pennyweight Flat

CYNTHIA ROWE

Pennyweight Flat
Published by Cynthia Rowe

This is a work of historical fiction. Please be aware that this novel is set in the Australia of the 1850s when times were different regarding attitudes to the Chinese and towards the treatment of the Indigenous people of Australia. This book seeks to reflect the lives of the people during the Gold Rush in Victoria at that time. It does not represent the 21st Century views or the opinions of the author.

The author asserts her moral rights.

ISBN 978-0-9874554-5-1

Cover design by Alli Spoor
Text Typeset by Mercier Typesetters Pty Ltd, Granville NSW

Author Biography

Cynthia Rowe has a degree from the University of Melbourne and has taught French and English for most of her working life. She has also spent time in France and the French Territories and was awarded a *Diplôme Approfondi de Langue Française* by the French Ministry of Education. She is a Writing Fellow of the Fellowship of Australian Writers NSW.

Cynthia's short stories have appeared in magazines and been broadcast on National Community Radio. Her poetry has won many awards and can be read in numerous literary journals internationally. She is Editor: Haiku Xpressions; President: Australian Haiku Society; Past President: Eastern Suburbs Branch (Bondi Writers) Fellowship of Australian Writers NSW.

Dedication

This book is dedicated to my great-grandfather, on whom the character of William Bass is based.

Acknowledgments

Special thanks go to Allan Dry, Chewton archivist and historian, who provided me with references to the Red Hill Hotel and Assembly Hall as they had appeared in the Mount Alexander Mail during the Gold Rush period, dating from 1854.

The Chewton Domain Society's collection at the Chewton Town Hall was invaluable, particularly concerning my grandfather, William Low, proprietor of the Red Hill Hotel and Assembly Hall during the Gold Rush, whose involvement with the local community of Forest Creek turned out to have been considerable.

My thanks go to the historian at Sovereign Hill for giving me valuable insight into life in the 1850s goldfields. Also, thanks to The Castlemaine Historical Society; State Library of Victoria; National Library of Australia; The Sovereign Hills Museums Association.

I am grateful to Arthur Mitchell for passing on material in the form of daguerreotypes, photos and family correspondence during the Gold Rush period, together with his written reflections on that time in Victoria's history—particularly his knowledge of childhood diseases in that era.

Sincere thanks go to Catherine Hammond for her wise editorial comments; to Chris Headford, webmaster extraordinaire; to the staff at the Waverley Library for their on-going assistance.

I am indebted to my husband, Bruce, for his input and for his willingness to traipse through the goldfields areas of Victoria with me.

1

Forest Creek, November 1854

Inside the Red Boulder Hotel the atmosphere was thick with brogues and the patois of many nations. Yann's throat was as dry as the landscape outside, but until he was paid he had no shilling for a sour beer. A drink of water would have to suffice, a clean one that didn't bring on dysentery. First he had to find William Bass, the innkeeper—and his employer.

The barman slopped Old Tom gin into a smeary glass.

"Is Monsieur Bass 'ere?" Yann shouted above the din, lowering the neckcloth over his face to reveal dust-thickened lashes. "I 'ave somesing for 'im." He stroked the tail of the Tonkinese cat perched on his shoulder.

"Oh, the great Napoleon's grandson, no less … although some mightn't believe it." Barnaby jerked a forefinger in the direction of the cellars. "Down below!"

Ears burning with indignation, Yann Sauvage scurried down the steps. He was the grandson of the former Emperor of France, on his mother's side, and his father was also well-bred. Jean-Paul Sauvage had been a lieutenant in the great man's army before deserting.

Upstairs in the bar, a fiddler started up and Yann could hear raucous shouts, snatches of song. Diggers commiserated with each other for having failed to unearth anything that day, consuming alcohol to make them forget the toil and the dashed hopes. Homesickness? Yann, too, suffered from *mal du pays*.

Cyrano's claws dug into his shoulder. The animal oozed tension, shivers of apprehension. Cyrano knew something was afoot in the multipurpose cellar. Like Magali, Yann's mentor, who had accompanied him on the long voyage to the Colony of Victoria, the Tonkinese cat had the sixth sense.

The sole of Yann's shoe caught on the splintered wood of the last step, threatening to catapult him into the dankness. Little light shone down here. Water dripped. A candle flickered in an alcove carved into the sandstone wall, forming shapes like the ghosts of the day's burning. Ignoring the pain from his blisters—worse than usual after the trek from the newspaper office—he regained his balance. The flame sputtered from the wick, slowed and then surged again. Yann could hear raised voices, one of them William Bass's.

His employer rarely argued. Bass was an even-tempered man who read poetry in his spare time. Yann had seen him count syllables with his forefinger, the tip of which had been severed by a machete-wielding digger. So why was William Bass annoyed? It took a lot to push him into a temper. His rage was usually reserved for the fortune hunters who unlawfully wielded a pick in the grounds of the Red Boulder Hotel.

The noise seemed to be coming from the vault where the gold was stored.

"I am 'ere for the nugget. You must 'ave it."

The speaker had an accent, a French accent, and a frisson ran through Yann. He should have been glad to hear the familiar tones of a countryman, but he had learned to be suspicious of others' motives. He lived in fear of the Saint-Simonians, whom he suspected of having murdered his mother. Some said Yann's father had fled to the Colony of Victoria to escape the clutches of the Saint-Simonians. Others said Jean-Paul Sauvage was heartbroken by the death of his wife and wished to be as far away from France as possible. Yann had vowed to track his father down, and discover the truth.

He cringed back into the alcove, pushed his body behind the flame to ensure he could not be seen if the Frenchman emerged. A thought shot through his mind: *Would it be more prudent to retreat, go back up the stairs?* His sheathed dagger, its handle carved with the Napoleonic eagle and weighing against his waist, reminded him that he was well-protected should he have to defend himself. And just last week, Magali had presented him with a cut-throat razor. An added weapon, if necessary? If he'd had sufficient coin, Yann would have purchased a pistol. Or a rifle. Most men on Forest Creek carried a rifle.

Doubts whirled in his head as the argument continued, louder now, the words more strident. Yann attempted to blend into the pale rock. If only his hair was not so dark. Even the sooty points on Cyrano's off-white body—ears, nose and the socks of his feet—were more pronounced in the stuttering light.

A shout came from upstairs in the bar: "There's a new Bagatelle Table in the gaming room, delivered today! I'll wager an ounce of gold to the first to 'ave a go !"

The vault became quiet. Only the faint tap of carpenters putting the finishing touches to the Concert and Assembly Hall on the west side of the Red Boulder Hotel could be heard. Yann went to move down the passage.

Cyrano gave out a low growl. Yann shrank back.

Thwack. Another thwack. Cyrano's tail thrashed. His claws were now embedded in the fabric of Yann's jacket. .

"*Ça va!*" Yann attempted to quell the thrashing tail. "It's all right."

The aggressor burst from the vault. As he bolted past, Yann saw he was clad in a striped maillot, tight, like the sailors' shirts back home. He wore a scraggly beard, as did all men on the Diggings, but he had one identifying feature. A patch of hair the size of a shilling glowed white on the crown of his head.

The cat parted its teeth, preparing to spit. Yann clamped his fingers around Cyrano's snout. The pair merged as one into the hiding place while footsteps pounded up the steps. The man paused, made as if to turn back, but continued on. The sound of his boots faded.

Was it safe to investigate? Yann wondered.

But that meant passing the morgue, and the idea of dead people sent spasms of uneasiness down his spine.

2

No sound came from the room in which the gold was stored. Had the man with the accent killed Yann's employer?

Heart churning, Yann crept towards the vault and found the innkeeper lying on the ground. Mr Bass's mutton-chop whiskers were in disarray and his limbs formed the shape of a starfish.

"Monsieur William? Monsieur William?" He grabbed William Bass by the frockcoat and gave it an apprehensive shake.

"Oh, there you are, Yann." Bass groaned and pushed himself up on one elbow. "You have returned from Castlemaine?"

"Is you all right, *monsieur*?" As Yann heaved the well-built frame into a sitting position, a prisoner rattled the bars of the adjacent lockup, banged on the wall and hollered, the blare echoing through the cellars.

"I am fine, no bones broken." William Bass inhaled a raspy breath. "Take no notice of the kerfuffle next door, Yann. The fellow prospected without a licence. The Native Police will be here tomorrow to pick him up. We'll be rid of the rascal soon."

"I 'ear you argue."

"Don't worry about the other, ah, altercation. That particular chappie was demanding his nugget back, but it's already being transported to Melbourne on the government Gold Escort. I should have waited for the private escort, but I find that Studs de Wolf feller not as reliable." He set his teeth in a smile. "Did you pass on my instructions?"

"*Oui*. I place your announcement in journal as you request." He handed over the editor's note.

"Very well then, I must pay you." William Bass pointed his blunt forefinger at Yann's feet. "You could do with a new pair of shoes, young man. Those girlie things might be fine for the footpaths of Paris, but they're no good for tramping about the Diggings!"

"But …" An ant burrowed into the sole of Yann's bespoke Parisian shoe, now detached from its upper; he resisted the urge to scratch.

4

"You need boots, m'boy!"

"But …" Should he admit he needed food more than he needed boots?

The innkeeper snaked two fingers deep into his pocket. "My god, it's gone!" he roared. "That rascal stole my chapbook!"

"I no understand."

"My poetry, he robbed me of my little volume!"

"I saw zis man. I will find 'im, take it back." Yann wondered how poetry could be more important than one's personal safety.

"Quick, that book is important to me!" A sigh billowed from the innkeeper's chest. "I do not know what will become of us on the Diggings. I should be grateful my hotel has not been burned to the ground! Bentley's Eureka Hotel in Ballarat was destroyed by fire just last month!"

Uninterested in burning hotels in Ballarat, Yann asked, "What *couleur* is zis book?" His palms were moist at the thought of confronting the man in the striped maillot.

"It's slim and has a, well, its cover is magenta. Oh, I don't know, boy. Just get on with it!"

Magenta? A bright colour should be easy to find.

Yann ran for the stairs leading up from the cellars. Cyrano sprang from his shoulders, and by the time Yann had reached the steps the Tonkinese had already leapt to the landing in one bound. The bell at his neck chinked as he gathered speed.

Two stretcher bearers edged past, lugging the body of a fallen digger down towards the morgue. Yann swallowed back his dread. Emerging into the street, he expected to find the cat waiting but could see no sign of him. Shreds of cloud had formed a blanket over the sky. A bank of storm, a roiling mass of energy, erupted over the landscape, turning the heavens black. Lightning zigzagged. Had Cyrano run away, terrified of the squall?

Thunder rumbled, deafening and ominous. The sky cracked open. Giant rain squirted into the dust and diggers scampered for shelter, seeking refuge inside the Red Boulder Hotel, or heading for their tents. A dog roamed up and down the highway, baying and howling. Yann sidled past the remains of a horse whose hindquarters had been hacked away by hungry miners, his eyes scanning the crowd for the man in the striped shirt. Had he fled into the bush, to the banks of Forest Creek? Or would he return to the scene of his crime?

Yann considered going back to the hotel, but rejected the idea. He flailed along the now treacly road, a pea soup of gunk sucking at his feet.

Rain sheeted down. His toe collided with a bullock's head half-buried in the sludge. As he went, he shouted: "*Où es-tu*, Cyrano? Where are you?" Still no trace of the Tonkinese.

William Bass's chapbook slipped his mind.

Where was Cyrano?

3

Horses whinnied. Dogs barked. Having searched for Cyrano without success, Yann approached the slab hut he shared with Magali. His legs ached like those of an old man.

Cooking smells came from the surrounding tents and his mouth watered at the thought of food—*ragoût*? He felt like stew. *Ragoût de mouton*—lamb stew? Or kangaroo haunch. He didn't care too much, as long as it was tasty.

The blue, white and red tricolour of France hung limply above the hut, and he was surprised to see no hint of smoke. Magali had never promised to stay once they reached their destination. Had she taken off, decamped without telling him? Yann had almost no money and Magali, having spent the bulk of her fortune on the passage to the colony, was also running short.

He passed diggers drinking brandy-punch from a vat. As he pushed open the canvas door he half-expected to see Magali bent over the hearth, but the fire was cold and the one-roomed dwelling empty. The griddle, leaning against the mantelpiece alongside the candle mould, was unused and there was no fat around the rim. Magali had done no cooking and would be making no candles from the tallow. In the leech barometer, the slimy creature sank back into the phial, indicating the storm was over.

Yann's footwear was wet. The cuffs of his redingote dripped and, numbed from the chilliness brought on by the rain, his fingers fumbled with the buttons of the double-breasted coat. The gold cross around his neck swung as he slung the coat over the back of a chair.

He shook his hair free. Magali's duty was to keep the fire burning, while he earned money to enable them to move on to other Diggings in their search for his father, Jean-Paul Sauvage. So where was she? Looking for a toad, perhaps? Yann had seen her talk to toads. He knew miners who spun mischief, claiming she was a witch. Some crossed themselves at the sight of her, spreading word around the Diggings that she was a heretic. Untrue. Magali kept a crucifix nailed to the wall above her bed. She read the cards, though. And many believed Magali had the gift. She certainly helped people, acted as midwife to their babies and cured the sick with her herbs.

The embers in the grate had cooled. Yann put his lips together and gave a hopeful blow. No flame surged. He plucked a handful of twigs from the wood basket and placed them in a crisscross pattern. His eyes swept the room, looking for paper. Seeing none, he sprinkled eucalypt leaves over the squiggly structure instead. He snaked his fingers into the front pocket of his redingote and pulled out a silver vesta. Prising open the lid, he discovered only two matchsticks.

"*Zut!*" he swore.

Reminding himself to be careful and not waste them, he struck one of the matches across the ribbed base of the holder. An explosion of sparks and toxic gas rose into the air.

He reeled back, coughing.

The flame fizzled out. The second and final matchstick flared. Yann kept still until the flame took hold. Singeing the pads of his forefinger and thumb, he held the burning taper against the twigs and leaves and waited for the blaze to warm his bones.

Phut.

"*Merde!*" he cursed again as the fire died.

Hearing a scratching at the door, he rushed to open up, expecting to see Cyrano there. His cat would make him cosy in no time. He peered around. No Cyrano. With a sigh he kicked away the dead branch that had been thrown against the hut by the wind.

"*Où es-tu, mon pote?*" he shouted into the night. "Where are you, mate?"

Placing his fingers in his mouth, he gave a piercing whistle. Only a cacophony of barks rose from the dogs guarding the miners' tents.

Yann had a sudden thought. Had Cyrano snuck in without his realising? Was the cat curled up asleep? He thrust aside the calico drape around his bed. The sapling and hessian bunk on which he slept was as he had left it that morning. The patchwork quilt and blanket were thrown back. The accordion he liked to play lay alongside his pillow. In the boxed frame on the wall which served as a shelf, the daguerreotype of his mother sat propped in its usual place. Beside her photo was a separate shot of a rakishly smiling Jean-Paul Sauvage.

Yann wondered if he should go to the Holmes-Lacy General Store and Post Office to buy some matches. But what if Cyrano turned up while he was gone? What would the cat do then? Panic? Run off into the bush?

His mind churned at the notion of confronting the storekeeper's daughter. Clemency Holmes-Lacy's uppity manner made him resentful, made his gut turn squeamish. Just that afternoon, glowering, he had watched Silas Holmes-Lacy jerk the reins, watched the two-wheeled dray rattle off, thrashing around tree branches, potholes and a dead cow with its legs in the air. Flaxen curls bobbing, the storekeeper's daughter had twisted in her seat. The smirk on her lips told him all he needed to know. Even the dimples in her cheeks exuded arrogance. She thought him no better than the dirt upon which he walked. How wrong she was about his heritage.

As he stood there thinking, a blob of water landed on his shoulder. He brushed the rain away, lifted an iron saucepan off its hook and positioned the pot beneath the drip. The marble clock on the mantel gave out a tinkly chime to indicate the half hour. Already half past six, and still no sign of Magali. Had she been kidnapped? But why would anyone kidnap her? Neither she nor he had much money. He gave a caustic laugh. Any person attempting to make off with Magali would soon regret it.

He went to the stained dresser and wrenched it open. He sucked in a breath. The food was gone. The salt pork, the dried peas, and the pickles were not there. Diggers who arrived on the goldfields with no money often went hungry to the point of starvation. Had a ravenous digger broken into their hut and raided their larder?

Magali's dried herbs, the ones she used for healing, still hung from the ridge pole overhead. The culprit had left those, but Yann could hardly make a meal of them. His fingers hovered over a small piece of bread. He picked it up, but found green mould crawling along the edge. The thief had also left a fragment of cheese. Yann's gaze ran over the claw marks streaked across the creamy surface. Were these the signs of a marauding rodent, a bush rat? His hunger pangs were growing by the minute. Should he risk it? Unlike cheeses from his own country, English cheeses had a habit of sticking in his throat.

He noticed that Magali's bottle of absinthe was almost empty—it had been three-quarters full this morning. Near the bottle was the slotted absinthe spoon through which she poured water, over a sugar cube, into the liquor. She called her favourite drink the 'Green Fairy' and forbade Yann from tasting it, claiming the absinthe would drive him insane, make him hallucinate.

"Although," Yann muttered, "*she* drinks the stuff and with no ill effects."

He spied a sack of semolina, also left by the intruder, and became excited. If only he had hot water he could make couscous for his dinner. He swallowed. That meant he had no choice but to buy matches.

He ran a comb through his locks, flicked dust off a ribbon, and secured his hair at the nape. Pulling the door to, he set off, wending his way through the rabble of shanties and canvas, calling for Cyrano.

"Cyrano! *Où es-tu?*" he bellowed.

A digger boiling his billy over an open fire looked up as he passed. "Wotcha want, Frenchie? Lost something?"

"I 'ave lost my cat!"

"Someone prob'ly ate it!" He poked at the unleavened bread—called 'damper'—within the ash-covered coals, muttering, "Why don't yer get a dog, like everybody else! Far more use to ye."

Passing the Newspaper and Agency, Yann saw notices attached to the annex. Beside 'Gold Bought Here' signs, others had tacked 'Lost' signs on wooden poles. Should he place a notice, asking if anyone had seen Cyrano? Would there be a charge? If so, he would not be able to afford it.

"Cyrano!" he called again, scanning the trees.

Diggers trudged towards their tents with picks slung over their shoulders. Dogs on leashes panted behind them. Dogs were everywhere, sniffing and growling, keeping guard outside the canvas hovels, tied to the flagpoles. Most were big dogs, ugly dogs, whose task was to protect property. Feral dogs also roamed through the encampment. Was Cyrano quivering in a tree, too afraid to come down?

"Cyrano!" he yelled again. "*Où es-tu?*"

"Oh, shut yer face!" a voice shouted through the gloom.

Yann came to a butcher's shamble where legs of lamb and pieces of steak hung from hooks, swaying over blood-stained chopping blocks. Four animal skins lay drying on a rack outside. Despite the stench, Yann's eyes devoured the meat.

The butcher called out, "Wanna buy, young man?" His apron dangled almost to his boots, and he hoicked at the fabric.

"'Ave you seen my cat, *monsieur*?"

"Naw, never seen no cat, but oi've some lamb cutlets, freshly killed. Very tasty. Loik some?"

Flies blurred in a purple haze around the open stall. The rank smell of gore and giblets permeated the air. Yann eyed the grubs wriggling on a greasy rump and the sight of the scrawling mass almost took away his hunger. He shook his head. He needed matches before he needed meat.

10

Alcohol was forbidden on the Diggings, yet Yann recognised a sly grog shop disguised as a restaurant. The canvas dwelling was tricked up with large letters on the side: 'Soups, Meals, Coffee and Other Drinks'. Yann knew the coffee cups would be filled with rum; William Bass complained about it often.

"*Mon Dieu!*" He slapped his forehead.

In his anxiety about Cyrano, and his concerns about finding food for himself, he had forgotten about the stolen chapbook. As he walked into the Holmes-Lacy General Store and Post Office, he remembered that William Bass had not paid him. His pockets were empty.

Dare he ask for credit?

4

The store swarmed with miners purchasing loaf sugar, preserved red-herrings, candles, cotton reels, picks and calico. Some paid in coin, others in ounces. Studs de Wolf, operator of the busiest private Gold Escort on the Diggings, was stocking up with sacks of potatoes and onions, flour, loose tea and various other supplies. As if he were planning a long journey.

Viola Holmes-Lacy said, "Will that be all, Mr de Wolf?"

Running his fingers through his turbulent hair, he grunted assent.

"And your enterprise is doing brisk business, I imagine, with the Diggings so lucrative in the current environment?"

He grunted again, pulled out a roll of money and paid her. "I'll pick this lot up on the morrow, early," he said. "I'll collect me mail now and that'll do me." Dirt spattered from the soles of his calf-length boots as he stomped into the nearby canvas-covered space.

Silas Holmes-Lacy could be heard: "I am sorry, Mr de Wolf, yer mail didn't reach the Diggings from Kyneton this week. The Argus gentleman had a burial to attend."

Studs de Wolf stormed out, muttering, "What're newspapermen *for*, if not to carry the mail?"

Eyeing a jar of treacle, Yann wondered again: *Should he ask for credit?*

He could see no sign of Clemency and felt a surge of relief.

"Farewell, Mr de Wolf!" Viola Holmes-Lacy's eyes shone from her apple face like cloves in a freshly-baked pie. She turned to serve Yann. "Can I help you, sir?" Pushing her curls back into the cap, she adjusted her shawl so it covered her plump stomach.

"I need m-m-matchsticks for my fire, madame," he stuttered, feeling himself grow hot with shame as he added, "but I 'ave no money. Monsieur Bass, 'e owe me two shilling."

"Shiiiilling-sssss!" She shoved her tongue behind her teeth and made a whistling sound.

Yann jumped back. "*Pardon?*"

"Sssssss!" she repeated. "It is grammatically correct to say shilling*s*!"

"I am very sorry." He felt the blush rising.

"I am sorry, too. We do not extend credit in this establishment."

"But I cannot boil water when my vesta is emptied. I 'ave no matches."

"That is not my concern, young man. We are not a charity! Get your money from Mr Bass ... although he may not feel so flush since my husband delivered his new Bagatelle table this afternoon."

Yann felt a rush of air as Clemency Holmes-Lacy burst past.

Hauled along by a scowling British bulldog, she cried, "Oh, Mama, Princess Albert sank her teeth into three miners' legs, all at the same time, well, one after the other. They were very angry. She will have lost us *all* of our custom!"

"Nonsense, my love, we have the best provender on all of Forest Creek and that will keep them coming." Viola Holmes-Lacy emerged from behind a pile of tea chests and boxes. She flicked a cockroach off a loaf of bread and fixed her attention on the dog. "You are a naughty, naughty Princess Albert!" she cooed, leaning to pat the slobbering creature.

Clemency turned to Yann. "Can I help you, sir?" she asked, securing a frilled apron around her waist.

"I, I need ..." He could feel his mouth lose shape as he struggled to find the words.

"He needs credit for his matchsticks," snorted Viola, "but he'll certainly not get it from me."

Relieving her daughter of Princess Albert's leash, she disappeared into the back of the shop. Snuffling sounds could be heard as she tied the dog up. She bustled through into the Post Office at the side and began to sort packages with her husband.

Yann turned to leave. With a start, he spied a grosgrain ribbon with a brass bell attached to it lying on the far end of the counter. His heart missed a beat. Was that Cyrano's collar?

"Where did zis come from?" he pointed. "It ees my cat's collar?"

"You have a cat?" Clemency locked her gaze with his. "Never! It's a monkey I've seen perched on your shoulder as you go about your business!"

"'E is a cat."

"No cat would sit on a person's shoulder, not like he does!"

"'E is a special cat, a Tonkinese." Yann simmered with frustration.

"Is a Tonkinese a hybrid of the two breeds ... making it a *monkey* cat then?"

"Ah, *non*, he is called Cyrano and 'e is missing."

"Cyrano? Why do you call him that?"

"I name him for 'is long nose which is, ah, a little like Cyrano de Bergerac."

"Who is Cyrano de Berger-whatever you said?"

"'E was a very famous playwright and a swordsman."

"Perhaps Mr Bass will arrange to have one of this Cyrano what's-it's plays performed in his new Concert and Assembly hall?" She pushed her mouth into a bow shape. "Do all monkey cats have long noses?"

Yann was more concerned about his rumbling insides, not to mention his missing pet, than this ridiculous conversation with Mademoiselle Clemency Holmes-Lacy.

"The Tonkinese breed 'ave dark points on the nose, ears and paws … on colder parts of 'is body." He made a gesture with his hands. "I suppose this could make 'im seem like, er, not like a normal cat."

The store was now emptied of customers and Yann was surprised to see Clemency's face no longer wore its arrogant expression. "I am *so* sorry you've lost your monkey cat," she whispered.

Her mouth turned down at the corners, and Yann saw she really cared. Had he been wrong about her?

"I know how badly *I* would feel if Princess Albert strayed," she continued.

A rustling. Viola Holmes-Lacy swished from the Post Office into a room to the rear of the store.

Clemency raised her voice. "I heard you say Mr Bass owes you money. If it's rightfully yours, then ask him to pay you!"

Yann was confused by her sudden change of mood. Once more, he was about to leave when he felt her reach into his pocket. She slipped matches inside, snatched her fingers out and went a fetching shade of pink.

"Sshhh! For your fire." Her topaz eyes were huge.

He experienced a strange sensation in the pit of his stomach.

She placed a finger on her lips. "Don't let Mama know!" Pause. "Have you thought of carrying a flint pouch? All you need is a piece of grass, rub the two together and whoosh. Much easier … and you don't have to be concerned with the quantity of matches in your vesta."

"I 'ave n-n-never used a flint before," he stuttered.

"I could show you, but not tonight." She handed him the cat's ribbon. "This was left behind by a man with an accent like yours." She added, "He had a mark upon his head, white, like a wound. He has been in the store before. His name is, ah, Victor. He is the Count of Cor-something."

"Victor, Le Comte de Corbeau?"

Yann could feel his heart race. Le Comte de Corbeau was the most fanatical of all the Saint-Simonians, a man who believed in the abolition of the right of inheritance, which was the reason members of Yann's family could be in danger.

Clemency's voice intruded. "I cannot imagine how the Comte de ... Cor-beau? ... came to have your collar. He seemed quite pleasant about it though. I understand he found it lying on the ground."

Yann was not convinced by the count's explanation. "And was 'e wearing a sailor shirt?" He ran Cyrano's ribbon over the pad of his thumb.

"Sailor shirt?"

The bell on the cat's collar jingled as Yann traced horizontal lines across his chest.

"I think so, but I'm not sure ...?" She lifted her eyebrow.

"My name is Yann, Yann Sauvage." Pause. "My complete name is Yann *Bonaparte* Sauvage."

"After the famous general?"

"Exact." The matchsticks rubbed against his thigh.

"You can call me Clem."

"Clem? But zis is name of a boy?"

"I suppose it is."

"I 'ad a friend in Paris called Clément."

"Was he a very close friend?"

Yann shrugged. "*Non*, just a friend."

"Sometimes I even don moleskins." The dimples grooved in her cheeks. "I wear them after dark when I venture out, because the men stare lustfully at ladies on the Diggings." She took a breath. "Even those of virtue are not exempt, so it is safer that way." She pointed at his shoes. "You need some boots, Yann. I can sell you sturdy boots, left by the cobbler this morning."

"I 'ave no money, not until Monsieur Bass pay me." He paused. "I sink you 'ave discovered much gold? I see your dray go to ze 'otel," he said, recalling how angry he had been that they refused to carry him on his way.

"Oh no, the Holmes-Lacys have not struck it rich. We transported no gold to Mr Bass's vault today. I was simply there to help Da deliver the new Bagatelle table to the Red Boulder Hotel."

Yann gave a brief, embarrassed nod. "*Au revoir, mademoiselle.*"

"Goodbye, sir." She raised her voice. "I hope you find your monkey cat!"

As Yann left he heard Silas Holmes-Lacy say, "Stop making eyes at the customers, girl!"

5

The cradles no longer roared. The doors of most dwellings were ajar to let in the cool night air. Making his way to the Red Boulder Hotel, Yann passed a digger with suppurating wounds on his skin. Liver spots dotted the man's hands and face, a sure sign of scurvy. Fresh fruit and vegetables were rare at Forest Creek, and Yann was amazed miners didn't raid the market garden adjoining Johnnie Lee's restaurant in the Chinese quarter.

Inside the tavern, the click of stick against ball rang out as a miner attempted to knock down a ninepin in the game of Bagatelle.

In the bar, Barnaby grabbed a Tipperary Boy by his neckcloth. "You owes me money for yer drink, ye scoundrel!"

The digger's eyes bulged. "Ye can have it back then!" A spray of grog erupted from the Tip's mouth, careening down Barnaby's face in a narrow brown stream.

"Is Monsieur Bass 'ere?" Yann yelled through the din.

He was determined to let William Bass know he had been unable to find his stolen chapbook. He would ask for—no, demand!—his money.

"He's left, gone home for a spot of high tea before they do post mortem on t'digger ... or maybe they'll be cuttin' him open tomorrer." Barnaby pointed to the cellars below and then ran his shirtsleeve across his right cheek. "He was in a right temper, said someone stole his chapbook and 'e wants it right back."

Yann mused: *If Monsieur Bass was in a 'right temper' would he pay him?*

Exiting the hotel, Yann skirted the stables where the odour of hay, horse manure and the privies to the rear assaulted his nostrils. A rat shot out from the chaff box in the corner. The groom, whistling tunelessly, gave a feeble swipe with his broomstick.

Yann climbed the steps to William Bass's house.

Hemmed by a spreading veranda, the house overlooked the Red Boulder Hotel. Chandeliers glowed through the windows. Shadows thrown by the candles danced across the walls. The sight of the taffeta curtains, tied back with tasselled cords, reminded Yann of how his own life had changed. In France, he had slept between silk sheets. On the goldfields of Victoria he either shivered, or sweated, under a rough blanket. The patchwork quilt prickled his skin; the straw-filled mattress made his body itch.

Magali had said: "When you find your father, he will have made his fortune, the Saint-Simonians will have turned around and you will be able to go home. Until then, these small discomforts will help you to become a man."

"I am a man."

"A mature man."

Was becoming a 'mature' man meant to be so difficult? he wondered, lifting the knocker, ashamed to be asking for money.

William Bass opened the door, revealing a brightly lit entrance hall. A gold-leaf mirror with console was positioned against one wall of the tessellated entrance. A leafy aspidistra rose from a jardinière perched on a pedestal.

The hotelkeeper held a damask napkin in his hand.

"Good evening, *monsieur*," said Yann.

"My boy, there you are! Did you recover my chapbook?"

"I am sorry, *monsieur*. I cannot find zis person." Yann averted his gaze.

William Bass's brows drew together in a knobbly frown. He ran the serviette across his lips. "That chapbook is important to me."

"I 'ave tried, *monsieur*. But ze storm make it difficult."

"I need it!"

Yann's nostrils flared at the smell of roast chicken. "'Ave you seen my cat?" he asked, attempting to divert William Bass's anger.

"Your cat? Whoever worries about a *cat*, for heaven's sake? There are household pets all over the Diggings, mostly dogs, and many of them with rabies, I'll be bound. Friend of mine died of a monkey bite in India, and I believe your beast looks as though he could well be a carrier of that disease." William Bass gave a threatening pause. "No, sir, I am far more concerned about my chapbook!"

"You owe me two shilling, *monsieur*." Yann forced his lips into what he hoped was a beguiling smile. "I need money to buy food."

"I am sorry, lad. Find my chapbook and I will pay you your money."

In the drawing room to the left Yann could see William Bass's sister, recently arrived from England, chatting to guests while a maid in a starched apron poured tea from a silver teapot. They drank from fine china cups, sank their teeth into chicken wings—no kangaroo haunch or kookaburra pie for them!—and cucumber sandwiches. The bread looked springy and enticing from where he stood.

"*Monsieur*, I need some boots as well." Saliva welled up in his mouth, his indignation with it. "Please," he added, using the English word through clenched teeth. He knew he would get no satisfaction unless he remained polite.

"Find my chapbook!"

The door clunked shut.

Yann threaded his way back through the tents, pug dwellings and slab huts with canvas roofs held together with lengths of rope. The sky above was high, wide and navy-blue, clear after the storm. Crickets chirped, but his heart was leaden as he eyed the unfamiliar stars. The smell of eucalypt permeated the countryside, and everywhere he went fires burned, giving out a reek of alien leaves and twigs. The wild limbs of the trees gesticulated. An ounce of gold a day would be enough to survive, but Yann had no gold, no coin. Would he be forced to dig on the sly, without a licence, dodging the inspectors as best he could? William Bass had reduced him to this. But to dig he would need boots.

Picking his way through tents, Yann took care not to tumble down any shallow mine shafts. The air seethed with the sparks of open fires, the odour of charred meat and damper. The soles of his shoes flapped with dried mud and he tripped on pieces of quartz.

Had he collided with a nugget without knowing? he wondered.

Muck squelched in his holey stockings. Prising his toes free of the gunk, he called in a low voice, "Cyrano, *où es-tu?*" He followed up with a piercing whistle.

On a branch, high in a straggly melaleuca, he heard rustling and his heart paddled. Cyrano? The moon broke from behind a cloud and he saw the possum's eyes, red pools staring at him. His shoulders slumped. Cyrano's eyes were blue and almond-shaped.

Surprised, he heard a voice hiss through the darkness.

"Hey, Frenchie!"

6

"*Quoi* … what?" Yann slewed around. "Oh, ees you, Barnaby."

The barman moved towards him, hands deep in his pockets. "Are ye looking for that beast ye carry around on your shoulder?"

"Cyrano 'as r-run away," Yann stuttered.

"Ye won't get far in those shoes. You need boots."

"I 'ave no money for boots." Yann shrugged. "Monsieur Bass, ah, 'e did not pay me today."

"The boss is a bastard like that. Held back me wages last week because I gave credit to a Cornish digger." Pause. "He can be kindly, though, I seen it with that Paddy family whose tent went up in flames. Did a benefit for 'em, didn't he?" Barnaby gave out a sniff. "But, y'know, the tavern gets to me sometimes. It's the blasted ghosts."

"Ghosts?"

"They tear at me mind."

Yann raised an eyebrow.

"You know, them post mortems they carry out at bottom of the cellars. Reason I quit early, let the other bloke take over for a while."

The cellars scared Yann, too, but he wasn't about to admit it.

"Y'know there's a place you c'n get boots for nuffinck."

"For no money?"

"Yes, a digger, feller won't be needin' his for a while."

"I cannot buy."

"Who says anythin' about payin'?" Barnaby sniggered.

Yann ran his tongue over his lips. Was Barnaby suggesting he should rob someone? Did he look so desperate that he needed to steal?

"Digger's an invalid, injured in a fall. Johnnie Lee give him a dose of opium to knock him out." Barnaby gave another sniff and wiped his sleeve across his nose. "Half a mile along, near the big River Red Gum down by the creek."

"Are you saying I should *steal* ze boots?"

"They're for the takin', Frenchie, and I don't need 'em." His eyes swivelled. "I know things are tough for ye, and your ma helped mine when

19

she were laid low … gave her Calendula, Catnip and, from memory, Chaste Berry… She knows a thing or two about healin' does your ma."

"Magali is not my muzzer."

"If you say so." He pointed towards Forest Creek. "Git, make haste before someone beats ye to it."

Barnaby mooched off, retracing his steps to the Red Boulder Hotel.

Hesitantly, Yann headed for the towering eucalypt. He came to the tent where the snoring digger lay with his legs poking out. The miner's dog, tied to the flagpole, snored in unison, as if he too had been given a dose of opium. Crutches lay on the stony ground, and beside the digger's crutches sat a pair of boots. The leather was shiny, the laces waxed, and a delicate layer of dust dulling the toes indicated that they had barely been worn. The boots seemed to cry out: I am yours! Barnaby is right, please take me!

Yann's heart pounded faster. Should he grab them and run? He had never stolen anything before. He was no thief, not under normal circumstances. He was no *bagnard*, not like the convicts transported to the French colonies for being light-fingered.

Then again, conditions on the goldfields were not normal. On the Diggings, it was every man for himself. If someone gave you a push along to help yourself, as Barnaby had done, why should he not do so? Just last week, Yann had heard Welsh miners brag about stealing gold dust and nuggets from the Chinese. The police were corrupt, too, for the most part former convicts from Van Diemen's Land. They pocketed half the money taken in fines and frequently arrested innocent people. Had the *flics* turned a blind eye to the Welsh miners' crime, greased their own palms with the stolen gold?

Yann assessed the leg of lamb hanging from the tent pole. *Should I steal that, too?*

Or just the boots?

An insect twitched on the dog's snout. Still dozing, the animal slapped a paw across its nose. The paw flopped back. The invalid digger continued to snore, an unbroken stream of rumbling and grinding of teeth. Yann's hand stretched to pick up the footwear.

A shot split the night and he whipped around, heart jiggling in his chest. *The police?*

A bearded digger in the distance reloaded and discharged his rifle, for the fun of it. The digger's friends joined in and their smoking gunpowder filled the sky with grey, dotted with a spattering of fireflies. Traces of sparks rained down on the landscape, like the Bastille celebrations in France, like crackers on the 14th July.

The invalid digger snuffled in his sleep, but didn't wake.

The dog gave a soft woof. Terrified the man would wake up and catch him in the act, Yann bolted. He zigzagged through tents and mine shafts and cradles. He zoomed past puddling machines, buckets and pickaxes. He sped by windlasses where the ropes around the barrels were sticky from the rain. The canvas windsails, created to send relieving gusts down the shafts, hung limp. But his heart lurched like never before.

Mon Dieu, I nearly became a thief! I nearly became a thief! The words tumbled over and over in his mind. The horror of it hammered as he made for the hut with the blue, white and red flag drooping from the flagpole.

"I almost stole from a poor man, like a base robber!" he said out loud. "I am no better than the rest of this lowlife."

The cross at his neck swirled and swung as he scooted for home.

7

Using one of the precious matches Clemency had given him, Yann lit the fire and waited for the water to heat up.

His hands shook as badly as they had on the *Red Jacket*'s voyage to Australia. On the ship he had endured similar trembling for much of the time, sometimes from exhilaration when he screamed into the gale, sometimes cringing with fear as the clipper lurched and groaned from Liverpool to Melbourne.

He poured the boiling liquid over the semolina, spilling some of the precious fluid onto the hearth. "*Merde!*" He watched the stain spread.

In Forest Creek clean water was expensive, a shilling a bucket, because most of it was carted in from other places, from distant creeks. Here the stream meandered through the Diggings. From Golden Point to well past the junction of Barker's Creek, an unbroken chain of diggers nine miles long, a ribbon of human beings desperate for instant wealth, washed their tin pans. Now, it seemed, he was about to join their grubby chain.

Yann shovelled forkfuls of couscous into his mouth, gulping it down. Rather than comfort him, the semolina sat in his chest and settled. Yann was still on edge—from having contemplated theft, and from worrying about Cyrano—and he was desperate at the thought of having no money. And where was Magali? Had his mentor met a man, fallen in love? She had been engaged to marry once. Had she found a new beau? If that were the case, would Magali still want Yann hanging around? Or would he now be a nuisance? Would she forget the promise to help him find his father?

Yann stopped worrying about Magali. He decided to turn in, and hunt for Cyrano in the morning. The light would filter through the linseed-soaked canvas of the window above his bed soon enough, and then it would be time to make decisions about his future.

He drew the prickly blanket up under his chin and waited for sleep to come, but the memory of the invalid digger and his flea-raddled dog rolled around in his mind. He could not relax. He tossed and sighed. He couldn't wipe away the vision of the snoring digger, no matter how hard he tried.

Should he go back? The man's feet had been bandaged. He was unable to walk. What use could boots possibly be to him?

Yann pushed himself up. No, he would not be tempted. He reached for his accordion and settled his shoulders against the wall. His fingers pressed the buttons. He squeezed the instrument back and forth. The music vibrated through his body and the rhythmical motion helped make him forget. He sang:

Sur le pont d'Avignon
On y danse, on y danse
Sur le pont d'Avignon
On y danse...

Through the words, he heard an unexpected sound and ceased singing. He held still. Was that a skittering outside?

Probably just possums, he told himself. Or any one of those strange nocturnal creatures he spied at night with babies clinging to their backs. All these marsupials peered at him with eyes that glowed in the dark. They leapt through the branches with extraordinary agility and sometimes made him feel ill-at-ease. He recommenced:

Sur le pont d'Avignon
On y danse, on y danse
Sur le pont d'Avignon
On y...

More skittering.

Or was he imagining it?

A pebble jumped over the canvas and slid down his window. Then another. Had the food thief returned to see if the hut was unoccupied? Should he open up? But ... there wasn't much left to steal. He continued with his song:

Les beaux messieurs font comme ça
Et puis encore comme ça.
Sur le pont d'Avignon
On y danse, on y...

A hail of pebbles rained down his window, a cascade of disquieting noise that he did his best to ignore.

A voice hissed, "Psst. Are you there?"

Was this Barnaby come to warn him that the police were on his trail? But he hadn't actually stolen anything; he'd just been tempted. Surely it wasn't a crime to wander about the Diggings at night, admiring others' possessions and thinking about gold and wealth, the comforts of life?

More words followed. Words which might be a trap.

"I have some important news about Cyrano!"

8

Curiosity overcame caution. Yann released the window strap and rolled up the canvas. As he squinted through the opening, he spied a boy in moleskins and a leather cap standing outside.

"'Ow do you know ze name of my cat?" he called, doubtful.

An impatient sigh. "You *told* me your monkey cat's name! Don't you remember, in the store?"

"I 'ave never seen you before."

"Of course you have, Yann!" Clemency Holmes-Lacy pushed her cap back from her forehead. A fair curl slipped out. She shoved the tress back with finely-shaped fingers.

"Oh, er … I do not …" he mumbled, confused.

"Are you normally so dopey when people ask you questions, or did that song I heard you play addle your brain?"

"I am sorry, Clem-enc-eee?"

She gave an exaggerated shudder. "Call me Clem! I *hate* Clemency. I never forgive anybody for anything! It's a ridiculous name to be lumbered with!"

Yann leaned out further. "Sank you very much for ze match. I was able to boil some water, make food."

"Well, now we've established that your appetite has been satisfied and that, being of French nationality, you probably have a very good table, are you interested in finding your monkey cat?"

"You 'ave found Cyrano?"

"For heaven's sake, Yann, aren't you going to invite me in?" Clemency looked thoughtful. "On reflection, you should come outside. We have no time to waste."

"*J'arrive* … I am coming."

Yann tied the window shut. He slid his dagger into his belt, pulled on his battered shoes and slipped his cut-throat razor inside his pocket. He found Clem seated on a log beside the hut with her chin in her hands, drumming her fingers on her face with impatience. Up close, he saw she had a smear of dirt on her cheek.

"*Bonsoir*," he said, wondering if he should tell her about the dirt, or even offer to wipe it off.

"How formal you are!"

Yann shrugged.

Clemency jumped up. "Well, are you interested in getting your monkey cat back?"

"Of course. I 'ave been very worried. Where is 'e?"

"He's in a cage behind the butcher's shamble."

"In a cage?" Yann's eyes grew round.

"Please don't repeat everything I say! It's very annoying." She took a breath. "I'll explain. He's locked up because the butcher plans to sell him."

"Sell 'im? To …?"

"To the Chinese, to Johnnie Lee."

"Why do Chinese want my cat?"

"To eat, silly! They will chop your monkey cat up, and fry him with onions and with bean curd!"

"*Mon Dieu!*"

"Quick! Follow me!"

"Shall I bring lamp?"

"No, we need to be stealthy."

Clemency set off. Her boot-clad feet flew around tents. She dodged cook pots on hot embers, dogs on leashes, exhausted diggers asleep beside their fires.

"Ouf!" Yann almost collided with the handle of a cradle; he swung around and ricocheted off a row of clothes hung on a tent line. "Will we 'ave to *buy* Cyrano back?" He wrestled the sleeve of a flannel shirt from his throat.

"Buy? That monkey cat is rightfully yours! We'll *steal* him back!"

Once more, Yann was being encouraged to thieve. "What if ze *boucher* … I mean *but*cher … catch us?"

"You have a weapon, a pistol, a knife? You must have. Every person has a weapon on the Diggings."

"*Oui*." He thrust out his chest. "I 'ave a dagger." He pointed to his waist and then patted his pocket. "And I 'ave a razor."

"Then stab the fellow where it hurts, cut off his cods, whatever it takes!"

Yann had never heard a *demoiselle* talk like that before. "But …"

"Shush." She held a finger to her lips.

Tiptoeing, she made for the rear of the shambles. The smell of blood, mud and offal was overpowering. Yann reeled from the stench. In the muck lay an empty whisky bottle, alongside a jumble of cages containing rabbits and hens, pheasants and suckling pigs. A lamb on a leash stood passively, waiting to be slaughtered.

Yann ran around frantically, peering through the gloomy wire. "I cannot see 'im!"

"Not so loud. Keep looking. Your monkey cat was here before." She paused. "Oh, dear…"

"We are too late?" Yann's heart thudded in his chest. "Oh, *non, non …* ees not true. 'E has been eaten?"

He heard a miaow at last, low and long. Cyrano was pleading to be released. Together they thrust aside wire contraptions, crates with holes cut in the sides. Other animals squealed and grunted, but he couldn't rescue them all. Splinters of wood and rough metal tore at Yann's fingers. He laboured on.

"Shush! You are making too much noise." Clemency waggled a finger at a nearby tent. "You'll wake the butcher."

"*Où es-tu*, Cyrano?" Yann's chest heaved. "Where are you?"

Again, the cat made a plaintive sound, muted as if he were ashamed. From beneath the pile, Yann edged out the cage containing the Tonkinese. Blue eyes, huge with fright, met his gaze. The butcher stirred in his tent.

"Quick! We should go!" hissed Clemency.

"But I must free Cyrano!"

"Just carry him as he is and run!"

"But 'e is used to being free."

"Your monkey cat should be glad to be alive." She grabbed at a gap in the wire. "I said ruuuuun!"

Lugging Cyrano, they fled. Behind them a man roared, his shouts followed by gunfire. The bullets spurted into the ground around them.

9

Snuggled against Yann's neck, Cyrano wore his grosgrain collar again. He did not purr, refused to drink from the bowl of water at Yann's feet and remained still. The three of them sat on the log outside the hut.

"Your monkey cat has beautiful fur." Clemency ran her hand lightly down Cyrano's back. "How strange!" She ceased stroking and sniffed her fingers. "He has an odour, as if …" She sniffed again. "Someone has poured lamp oil over Cyrano, as if they had planned to set him alight!"

Yann buried his nose in the cat's coat. "You are right." Horrified that anyone should do such a thing, even in this unrefined place, he muttered, "*Salaud!*"

"Was that a curse, a French curse?" Dimples formed question marks in her cheeks.

Yann gave an imperceptible nod.

"You are right to curse. The butcher is an evil man, but I cannot imagine …" She hesitated.

"What are you thinking?" Yann still felt awkward calling her by a man's name. "Ah, um, Clem?"

"Well, the *butcher* probably didn't steal your monkey cat."

"What do you mean?"

"Some other person must have exchanged Cyrano for coin. Or for gold dust."

"And how you know butcher not take 'im?"

"Because the man … I *refuse* to call him a gentleman considering he tried to kill us for taking back what is rightfully yours … is always minding his shambles."

Yann had a sudden thought. "Did you not say ze man who left Cyrano's collar in store wear a maillot?"

"Yes, I did say that. Who is this person and why would he want to steal your monkey cat?"

"Zis is an evil man, a Saint-Simonian who would kill me. He knows Cyrano is important to me."

"The Comte de Corbeau?"

"*Oui.*"

"Why would he want to kill you?"

"'E wishes to abolish right of inheritance and I am grandson of Napoléon."

"Napoleon's grandson?" She inhaled. "Yes, I have heard people say this." And then: "But I think you are fibbing, Yann."

He looked at her, startled.

"I studied French history … just a little, with a private tutor, but enough to know that the Emperor only had one son. Your name would be Bonaparte if that were the case. You would not be called Sauvage."

"My muzzer is, I mean *was*, 'is daughter."

"Your mama. Oh, I see." Thoughtful pause. "You said 'was'. Has she has passed?"

He gave a curt nod.

"I still don't understand. How could she be the Emperor's daughter?" Clemency's eyes were huge.

"She ees born wrong side of … blanket, I sink you say in English."

"Oh!" She frowned. "And that means?"

"Napoléon Bonaparte never marries my grandmuzzer." A mixture of pride and shame flooded through Yann.

"Oh, oh, I see." She lowered her gaze and then looked up at him. "Do you have any brothers or sisters?"

"I am a single child."

"And how did you come to be here?"

Yann explained how he and his mentor had set off from Melbourne in a lumbering overloaded cart, how they had stopped at Digger's Rest on the first night and travelled through the treacherous Black Forest to Woodend the following day, then headed up Mount Alexander Road to Forest Creek.

"No bushrangers emerged from the undergrowth waving pistols?"

He shook his head. "But ze cart become bogged. Passengers must dismount and push."

"And you found it humiliating to be seen pushing a cart?"

Yann nodded, reflecting that his Parisian friends would have laughed if they had seen him sweating and shoving. "Dead horses were on roadside, baggage left behind. People are crazed by a fever to make zere fortune."

"So you were astonished to find the streets of Forest Creek were not paved with gold?" She took a breath. "The gold is there, though."

"You 'ave siblings?"

"Three brothers and a sister." She sighed. "Mama is with child again. We are hoping it's a boy!"

"Again a boy?" A smile quirked at his lips. "Your family must be veee-ry noisy."

"On the contrary, it's very quiet, and I get lonely sometimes." She fiddled with her hands. "But I visit them every Sunday without fail."

"Visit?"

"I go to Pennyweight Flat Cemetery, place flowers on their graves, talk to them. I have begged and begged for proper headstones but Da says it's a waste of good money." Her mouth turned into a bitter line. "They are interred in a bleak place, rough ground chosen for being worthless, so hard to dig that the burial plots are shallow. No fear of grave robbers there. And not even any gold in the soil around them to make their days more cheerful."

"I am sorry… and from what did zey die?

"Oh, they died from diphtheria, dysentery, um, diarrhoea, pneumonia … and oh, maybe whooping cough … certainly fevers, terrible fevers with their eyes big as pennies. They passed from the things tiddlers seem to catch on the Diggings. Sometimes I cry myself to sleep over it." She placed her chin on the heel of her hand. "They were uncoffined, too, with not even a grocery box to protect them." She paused. "Unless there was one to spare in the store."

"Your brozzers and sister are buried in naked ground?"

Yann turned to stare at her, remembering his mother's brass-handled coffin, the polished wood, her marble gravestone inscribed with gold leaf, the flowers and elegance of the Père-Lachaise Cemetery in Paris. Yann had lain on his mother's grave and sworn that he would find his father. Shivers ran down his spine to think of the Holmes-Lacy children buried with dirt stuffed in their nostrils, worms eating their bodies.

"Yes, poor things. And we even have fresh vegetables. We grow our own so none of us will come down with the scurvy and, oh I remember now, one of the boys took to his bed with typhoid but I can't recall if that's what …" Abruptly, she changed the subject. "How old are you, Yann?"

"Ah, I am nineteen springs."

"Springs? Oh, well, I can see you have led a cosseted life, but you are old enough to know you need proper boots!" She pointed to his shoes, covered in glutinous muck with the soles dangling from the uppers.

"I 'ave no money."

"But you still have a job?"

He nodded.

"Well, Mr Bass will pay you. I know it's not easy on the Diggings and you are unused to making do, but you must be patient."

Would he tell Clemency about the invalid digger, how he almost stole the man's boots? "Barnaby know someone …"

"Do not trust Barnaby," she interrupted. "I have heard things, that he dips his fingers in the takings. Da and Mr Bass were discussing whether the barman was of dubious morality just this afternoon, wondering, to put it bluntly, if he was a thief!" She leant across and touched Yann's hand. "I have an idea. Why don't you pan for gold to supplement your income?"

"You no understand." A hint of annoyance crept into his voice.

"I do understand! You are worried about the cost of a licence, and thirty shillings a month is difficult enough *without* the government planning to double the fee. Many are unable to pay, but they come flooding to Forest Creek just the same."

Yann chewed his lip.

"Pan without a licence!" Her look was piercing, and he felt that strange feeling in his stomach again. "The police have ordered twice weekly checks and there is unrest all over, but *I* know a place where the licence inspectors won't find you!" She gave his arm a light tap; a frisson ran through him. "There's a bend. I could meet you on Sunday."

He forced himself to concentrate. "But it is breaking law to seek for gold on Sabbath."

"Do not bother about the law! All the diggers shout 'Joe! Joe!' when the inspectors are around, so you will have plenty of warning."

A voice called out in the distance, getting closer.

"Where are you, daughter?"

10

"Clemency, where *are you?*" Silas Holmes-Lacy sounded angry. "Answer! I know you are there!"

"I must go," she hissed. "If Da comes here, tell him you haven't seen me." Pause. "I'm glad you got your monkey cat back." On the point of leaving, she turned. "If you're interested in panning, leave a note under the headstone. It's just a piece of ordinary old rock, on the fourth grave to the right inside the entrance gate of the cemetery."

Before he could reply Clemency gave a little wave, adjusted her cap and darted off between the tents, moving furtively and making almost no noise. Yann watched her fade into the distance, heading for the Holmes-Lacy General Store and Post Office.

Silas Holmes-Lacy ceased calling her name.

Yann crossed his fingers, praying that Clemency had managed to avoid being reprimanded. He pushed himself up. What a strange evening this had been. He stroked Cyrano, who revved up his engine and began to purr.

"Clemency Holmes-Lacy is not so bad, after all," he said, addressing the cat in French. "She is rather vulgar, though, flaunting herself about the Diggings in men's clothing. However, she has a kind heart and needs our sympathy for her many lost siblings." The cat's purr turned to a slaggy dribble. "But, alas, the young lady is not too intelligent. She fails to understand I *cannot* dig for gold without boots!"

Inside the hut, Yann stoked the fire before climbing into bed.

His bones ached and he longed for sleep, but Cyrano's claws pricked his skin like a thousand needles and the smell of the lamp oil under his nose made him feel nauseous. He was unable to erase the thought of Clemency's brothers and sister buried, uncoffined, in stony ground without even a gravestone. What sort of parent would deny their children a coffin, even one made from rough-hewn pine? Or refuse to give the smallest sign on the ground above to show they had ever existed?

He pushed the cat away. Almost immediately, Cyrano edged back up. Soon he was wedged beneath Yann's chin, drooling and flexing his claws.

"Aïe, aïe!" Yann shoved him away again, more roughly this time.

He thought about Clemency's suggestion, rejected the notion, and then considered her suggestion once more. Was she right? Did she really know a place where he could search for the elusive ounce without a licence, and without being caught? Should he leave a note, let her know he was willing to try panning for gold illegally?

Yann nudged the cat away, yet again. Clenching his hand into a fist, he banged it against his forehead as he thought. He needed boots. Without boots, he would never be able to do the work. Within the dried mud, his shoes were almost shredded.

Should he go back and plead with William Bass, point out that it was impossible to look for the man who had snatched his chapbook without decent footwear? He could hardly move around the Diggings barefoot—aha, unless he had a horse. No, Yann rejected the idea. Stealing a horse would be worse than stealing boots. He would surely be hanged by the neck if he did that.

His heart beat faster as he wondered: Should he return to the River Red Gum, grab the footwear from the invalid digger? By now, he was in a lather of sweat. His long johns were clammy and his shirt was clinging to him.

He decided to sally forth and assess the situation. He dragged on his trousers, flicked up his braces and eased on his redingote. He patted his shoulder. Cyrano jumped up and settled into his usual place—against Yann's neck.

Stubbing his toe on the saucepan, which was still on the floor, Yann opened the slab hut door and peered around. Most fires had dimmed to glowing coals. Horses grazed quietly. Someone sang a final rendition of 'Campdown Races'. A mouth organ squeaked out 'Jeanie with the Light Brown Hair'. The joke telling stopped and a hush fell over the Diggings. Even the dogs no longer barked.

And then Yann heard words, spoken in perfect English.

"Where are *you* off to?"

11

Yann started. *"Tu parles pas f-f-français avec moi?"* he stammered, sounding as childish and guilty as he felt.

"Very well, I will talk French with you if it makes you feel less homesick." Magali sighed and gave him a *bise*—the kiss on each cheek in the custom of their country. "We will speak in our mother tongue."

His mentor, who spoke seven languages including Berber Tamazight, without the slightest hint of an accent, had returned. She pushed her way into the hut, lit the oil lamp on the mantel and dumped the satchel containing her medicines on the table. Placing a hand on one hip, she eased herself onto a chair. "You haven't answered my question," she added over her shoulder. "What were you doing creeping about at this time of night?"

"I-I-I was taking Cyrano for a walk to calm him down," he lied, not daring to admit he had been planning to steal from an indigent digger.

"Why does he need calming?"

Yann subsided onto a rickety seat near Magali and explained about the Tonkinese disappearing, about how he had been snatched by the Comte de Corbeau during the storm and sold to the butcher.

"I see," she murmured. "The Saint-Simonian is here, in Forest Creek? Well, well."

"It frightens me."

"The Saint-Simonians say they are interested in setting up railways in Australia, though that could be a ploy, a diversion. Maybe Le Comte de Corbeau is here for that? I hope he is less intent on abolishing the right of inheritance in France. Your life could be in danger."

"Even if every descendant of Napoléon were to be struck dead, apart from me, I would not want to be Emperor."

Her face softened. "I cannot imagine it."

Yann locked his gaze with hers. "I was worried. Where have you been, Magali?"

"I have been tending an infant with diphtheria. I have blown Flowers of Sulphur down the boy's throat but I fear the mite is destined for Pennyweight

34

Flat, a miserable place to end one's life." Her grey eyes were thoughtful. "His father has been working Donkey Gully farther along that road … without success, even though the ground has produced many ounces. The poor children wear flour bags for clothing."

"I thought you had left without telling me, gone off with a prospector who'd struck it rich. Gold digging, they call it!"

"Yann, do you believe me to be so shallow? I made a promise to your mother to guide and protect you." The drawstring bag filled with herbs and crystals at her neck rustled as she pushed wisps of hair back into a tortoiseshell comb enhanced with cabochon garnets.

His voice rose. "I can care for *myself.* Young men my age go to war, it's just …"

"I made a pledge to watch over you *until you are reunited with your father.*" Her words rasped, as if she were exhausted. "*Voilà.* After that, it's for you to decide if you wish to go your own way."

"You still have no idea where *Papa* is?"

"I know Jean-Paul Sauvage is on the goldfields somewhere. Some diggers say he was seen at Ironbark Gully, near Sandhurst." She placed the deck of tarot cards face down in a neat pile. "He was certainly here, in Forest Creek, three years ago, and in a big uprising. The cards indicate that."

"What big uprising?"

"The Monster Meeting of 1851 was held on the site of the shepherd's hut near Golden Point. Twenty thousand people protested under the Miners' Flag, at the proposed increase in the price of a gold licence."

"And?"

"I believe your father was among them. As I go from dwelling to dwelling I ask, and show the photo I carry with me. People assure me he was here." A smile tugged at the corners of her mouth. "His force of character, his charm, makes him difficult to forget."

"Where is he now, do you think?"

"Maybe Jean-Paul has become politically involved with the diggers, or even sported a red ribbon in his hat in defiance of the law in Sandhurst, and perhaps helped storm the police camp? With his military experience he would have been invaluable, and to die for a cause is the most beautiful of deaths." She took a breath. "I am certain he will have taken up the cause."

"To keep the cost of licences down, or to abolish them entirely?" Yann hoped it was the latter; he could pan freely then.

"If mining licences no longer existed miners would be elated, their troubles all but over. They come here with nothing, put up their tents, find nothing and leave empty-handed, moving on to the next alluvial field. They follow the rumours." She glanced around their dwelling. "At least you have a solid home, even if we do sleep under a canvas roof."

"Solid?" Yann gasped. "You call this slab hut solid?" He pointed at the saucepan on the floor, no longer collecting drips.

"*You* have a bed to sleep on," Magali continued, "unlike those who lie on bare ground under sheets sewn together, with bush wood and leaves over the top to warm them. Even then, they become drenched to the skin when a thunderstorm unleashes its fury."

She heaved her body up, gave a loud yawn. She opened the glass cover of the mantel clock, inserted a small key in the porcelain dial and wound slowly.

"I do not like living like this! I am better than this!" Yann recalled his privileged childhood. "I suppose when I do go back to France everything will have changed. Napoléon III will have completed his grand projects. Baron Haussmann will have finished constructing the boulevards and Paris will have changed forever."

"Perhaps." Magali replaced the key on the mantel. "I think you need a friend, Yann, someone your own age." She picked up the poker and prodded the embers. "With a handsome appearance like yours, you should make friends easily, particularly with the young ladies!"

Feeling his face grow warm, Yann decided not to tell Magali about Clemency Holmes-Lacy. He had been surprised to find the storekeeper's daughter wasn't at all uppity, amazed she had helped him find Cyrano. 'Clem' wasn't as bad as he had imagined. In fact, she was not too bad at all.

"They're a motley group on the Diggings, all bearded men and rough," he said.

"On the contrary, I have seen children panning." Magali replaced the poker.

"Well, I am not a child and I do not have a licence!"

Magali continued on as if he had never spoken. "In this place, you are no better than the others. Never forget that. Here, everyone is equal. You are on the same footing as these people. Like you, they eat foods containing the graves of many insects. Their biscuits are laced with ants. And, if they are lucky, they will have gold dust in the plum pudding for Christmas."

"They eat gold dust in food?" He scowled. "Well, we have nothing save a bag of couscous and your healing agents." He glanced at the dried herbs hanging from the ridge pole. "Somebody stole our salt pork and pickles … and the dried peas!"

"You forgot to mention the eggs." Pause. "Yes, desperate people do steal things and, alas, I had little in the way of fresh fruit and vegetables so sorely needed by this stricken family. I had only the esculents I purchased today from a Celestial horticulturist on Fryers Creek, that species of cauliflower with a heart not much bigger than a walnut. The Brassica is highly spoken of ... but, yes, it was *I* who donated our food!"

"I was hungry!"

"You weren't *too* hungry. I see grains of couscous." She indicated the empty bowl. "I shall pray for the boy." She pointed to the crucifix above her bed. "And then I plan to indulge in some well-deserved rest." She yawned again. "Tonight I shall have no need for tisane to make *me* sleep." She crossed herself and extinguished the flickering candle.

Not daring to mention that he badly needed new boots, Yann decided to turn in. In no time, Magali began to snore. At the end of the bed, Cyrano narrowed his gaze.

Yann attempted to sleep too, but again sleep refused to come. He fidgeted and wriggled under the prickly blanket, but was unable to stop thinking about the invalid digger drugged with opium. The man's footwear begged to be taken. *If he didn't nab the boots, someone else would.*

He threw the covers off.

12

Magali ceased snoring and started to grind her teeth. Doing his best to be stealthy, Yann opened the door and crept out. Cyrano settled into the usual position on his shoulder and they headed off through the tents and scrubland.

Wide awake and alert now, Yann passed the sly grog shop which was still doing business. Diggers lay sprawled on the lumpy quartz ground, unconscious from the drink. Women in grubby crinolines giggled and pointed at Cyrano, displaying toothless gums. He was repulsed by these people. He would never have been subjected to such a sight in the elegant *quartiers* of Paris that he used to frequent. Clemency Holmes-Lacy was a princess in comparison to these people. She was a princess in moleskins, a navy flannel shirt and with a cap on her head.

Did she often dress up as a boy? he wondered.

A smile seeped across Yann's face and he began to relax. Clem's teeth were nice, he told himself, as white and even as the pearls Madeleine, his mother, used to wear when dressed in her finest. Yes, he liked it when Clem smiled.

A late carriage rattled along the road behind him. Yann could hear laughter and shouting coming from the Red Boulder Hotel. A piano tinkled 'Dixie'. "I wish Oi was there!" yelled a patron. William Bass had a night licence. Apparently the customers were playing Bagatelle on his new table while drinking rum, whisky, or the brew from his beer engine.

The moon shone, making it easier for Yann to pick his way through tents and rigged-up shelters. Dogs on watch snoozed. A brindle bulldog, not unlike Clemency's Princess Albert, opened one eye, gave a low woof. In one canvas and slab dwelling a bawdy group of diggers yelled and screamed while slurping champagne from a pudding tub. "Eureka!" they shouted. Had they struck gold? If so, he envied them.

Yann almost collided with a black horse with four white feet and a blaze down its nose. The soles of his shoes clicked and flapped as he stumbled over fallen branches, logs and an axe handle. He edged past the butt of a double-barrelled rifle beside a sleeping digger and continued to make his way down towards the creek.

As he approached the River Red Gum, Yann passed a group of fortune hunters cracking jokes around a roaring fire. They ignored him. *Had they noticed him*, he asked himself, *and would they be able to identify him if the digger reported his footgear missing to the Native Police?*

The invalid digger's tent came into view. The man still lay on his back. His clotted beard was awry and he remained asleep. Strangely, his dog was no longer there. *Just as well*, thought Yann, *otherwise Cyrano might have panicked.*

Circling the tent, he took a long look. He needed those boots. They could be the start of his bid for self-reliance. No longer dependent on Magali, and with sturdy footwear, he could find William Bass's chapbook and pan for gold in Clemency's secret location. With his newfound wealth, he could search for his father on his own.

As if on cue, a cloud wrapped itself around the moon. Feeling his way, Yann stretched his hands out to find the boots. The miner snorted in his sleep and Yann snatched his hand back. He waited a moment and then slowly tried again. He eased the right boot into his possession. It felt odd somehow, not as he expected. The laces were coarser. When he had first spied the laces, they were glossed with wax. These ones were rough cord. The leather was also rougher than he had imagined, not shiny and smooth and covered in a fine layer of dust. Were these the same boots? The digger certainly seemed to be the same man.

Yann barely noticed the horse tethered nearby. Without warning, a rustle of leaves impinged on his consciousness, as if someone was pushing their way through.

A shout: "You are under arrest, sir!"

The invalid digger sat up, yawned and laughed. Yann's heart plummeted and he let the boot slip from his fingers. Cyrano spat.

A lantern shone in Yann's face. The trooper's uniform was marked with sweat and food residue. He wore a revolver in his belt. His teeth were stubbled, stained brown, and his breath reeked of stale whisky.

"*Monsieur*, I do not steal. I look! I admire zese boots." Yann felt sick. His body trembled. His palms were slippery with perspiration.

The cloud floated away from the moon and, as if in a bad dream, Yann saw Cyrano's claws, curved and highlighted in the blue-white haze, shoot out. The Tonkinese tore at the trooper. Droplets of red formed along facial scratches.

"Bastard!" The lawman clutched at his wounds.

"Run, *mon pote!*"

Yann jerked his shoulder. Cyrano leapt off and streaked away, stomach to the ground, melting into the gloom.

"You'll pay for this, Frog robber!" The trooper hauled Yann towards a log. He wrenched Yann's hands behind his back and began to uncoil a length of rope. "This is temporary, mind, until I get my manacles. But I, Nathaniel Clovis, is a dab hand wiv knots, so ye'll be tied to this stump of wood for a while … days, maybe … until the ants eat ya and the mosquitos drive yer insane 'cos yer mitts are tied."

As the trooper spoke, Yann noticed a dark shape push away from a spindly eucalypt. He knew that person well. What was the barman doing here?

Had Barnaby set a trap?

13

The digger scrambled up. Showing no sign of a limp, he strolled across to the barman and they began to compare notes.

"Two tonight, not a bad haul. Ye gives me half of *your* half of the five quid, means two pounds ten shillings each. Easier'n a day pannin' in the hot sun," said Barnaby, "or me sloppin' beer behind a bar."

Raucous laughter.

"Lyin' here makin' money on me back is my idea of the best job on the Diggings!" the miner chortled, pointing a calloused finger in the direction of the overhead branches of the majestic River Red Gum.

"But what if 'e gets thrown into the lockup, permanent like, and then off to Melbourne? There won't *be* any fine." Barnaby's voice became a whine. His brow furrowed into deep lines.

They began to argue.

"*Zut!*" Yann cursed at his foolishness for having been so easily duped. Clemency had been right when she'd told him not to trust Barnaby.

Behind him, the trooper continued to fiddle with the rope. "Eh, stop yakkin', fellers! Could one of ye 'elp me? Me rope's in a tangle."

Barnaby and the miner continued to argue. From the corner of his eye, Yann saw movement in the scrub. A possum leapt up through the branches of the tree sheltering the miner's tent and he thought of Cyrano. His cat had had a bad night of it, but at least he had escaped these rogues. At least he had managed to get away.

Yann started. Like a flying fox, Cyrano leapt from the tree. Hissing and spitting, he landed on the law enforcer's head. Claws sliced as, with bristled fur and slitted gaze, he began to tear at the man's flesh. His movement was frenzied, but his bell made no noise. Nathaniel Clovis dropped the rope, which curled across the ground like a cut snake. He screamed and clutched at his face, moaning and whimpering.

"Oh, my Gaaaawwd," he shrieked. "Heeelp me! A blurry marsupial has blinded me now. I can't see a fing, I'm bliiiind! It was a quoll, wiv a sooty snout! Never seen such a devil before!"

Barnaby and the miner ignored the trooper's pleas and began to trade blows. Throwing punches, they grunted and wrestled. They pushed and shoved, flailed and scratched. Collapsing into the dirt they kicked at each other's ankles. Back and forth they went, until they ploughed into a puddle. Mud flew in sticky splashes until their clothes were thick with the muck. Their faces were swollen with fury. Only the whites of their eyes showed.

Yann found it difficult to tell which one was Barnaby. They rolled and heaved and went on trading punches, sometimes striking air. He told himself it was only a matter of time before they drew weapons and began to shoot at him.

The trooper continued to scream: "I caaaan't seeeee!"

This was Yann's chance. With a jerk, he broke free. He snatched up the boots and took off, zigzagging through the scrub, bypassing the joke-cracking diggers. His dagger dug into his waist as he vaulted tent ropes. He skirted cradles and windsails, fallen branches, cooking ovens and a goat tethered to a tent line where a blanket was hung out to air.

The cut-throat razor in his pocket banged against his thigh and his shins glanced against tubs waiting to wash gold from the alluvium. He could hear gunshots behind him, the pounding of horse's hooves. Insane shouting. He dodged through bushes, leapfrogged the embers of dying fires and square ropes delineating ground to be excavated.

He thrust aside a bewildered Chinaman.

A rough hairy man, sitting on an upturned box quietly smoking his pipe, stared.

A massively large woman with a brandy keg strapped around her waist failed to negotiate the path back to her tent, tripped into a mine hole and screamed for help but was ignored.

Yann continued on. Soon Cyrano joined him. Streaking out of the undergrowth, the cat hurtled ahead, coat flashing in the dark as they headed for the safety of the slab hut. Yann's breath came in staccato pants. The muscles in his legs began to spasm. His chest heaved. He felt his innards rise up as if he were about to vomit. He blew through tightened lips, fighting the urge to throw up. He could hear the pounding of horse's hooves. Reaching the hut, he paused to catch his breath. He leaned against the outside wall and, desperate not to be seen, crouched down low.

Face etched with blood, the trooper galloped past grasping at his eyes and wailing, "I can't seeeeeee! Help me!"

Yann inhaled. "Please don't tell me you blinded that man, Cyrano? Please! I have enough problems without that!"

Cyrano stretched and yawned.

Yann gulped in mouthfuls of air to calm his skittering heart. He pressed his ear to the door, listening for sounds inside. Magali's snoring vibrated the walls and he relaxed.

He tensed up again, wondering if she would ask questions when she saw him wearing another man's boots. He was in deep trouble this time. He needed to cover the footwear with leaves and twigs, secrete them somewhere. He searched around for a hiding place.

Where? In the bushes?

14

Yann's hands had become sweaty and stained by the time he finished covering the boots with bits of bark and leaves. He examined his palms, thinking he would have to wait at least until Saturday before his next bath. Life in the Colony of Victoria was so basic that he despaired sometimes. Tears welled up and he blinked them back.

His eyelids drooped. The mantel clock chimed three dainty bell-like sounds. It was so dirty here, so very, very dirty…

He drifted off. In his dreams, he was a child again. His cheeks had been scrubbed until they were pink. He launched his toy yacht on a boating pond where it bobbed, leaving shiny wavelets in its wake. Nearby Madeleine, his *maman*, was dressed in a white gown decorated with lace and ruffles. Her raven hair was pinned up, piled high, with sweet-smelling gardenias scattered through it. Jean-Paul Sauvage, smiling and blue-eyed, the buttons of his uniform glowing in the afternoon sun, looked on with pride.

Abruptly, the dream turned brown. His life became an anthill of tents, overflowing with dust and mud. Animals lay abandoned on the side of the road and the stink made his stomach churn. Children were buried uncoffined. He could see their eyes glowing, feverish pinpoints beneath the earth, and he was buried with them. He felt the soil plug into his nose, tamp down until it was rock hard, and yet the soil oozed worms. The cold ground suffocated him and the devil laughed and laughed and laughed…

******

Kookaburras cackled, pulling Yann into trembling wakefulness.

He rolled over and dozed fitfully, until a voice speared through his brain. "Boots, I hold in my hand deadman's bounty!"

This time, his eyelids shot apart. Had Magali found the hidden footwear?

The cradles were already roaring streamside and his heart flittered like a moth against a windowpane. On his window, the leather strap made a

44

grainy mark against the light. Spirals of smoke wound beneath the drapes around his bed. His limbs ached as he pushed Cyrano off his feet. Throwing back the covers, he peeped through the gap in the calico.

"*Sacré bleu!*"

Magali was busy shining the boots he had stolen. Wisps escaped from the combs in her hair as she worked. Her arms swept back and forth until the toes gave out a subtle lustre. The laces were different, though. Yann could have sworn they had been of rough cord last night. Now they were shiny with wax. He pulled up his braces and emerged, assuming an innocent expression.

"Look what I discovered whilst gathering faggots for the fire, Yann!" She held up a boot. "Someone left these, probably stolen off a dead digger's feet. People will take anything in this place! But no matter, I found them beneath a bush!"

A blaze crackled in the grate. Her face was rosy.

"A bush?" Beside him, the cat stretched.

"By our slab hut."

"Really?" He wondered if she could hear his heart beating and did his best to look uninterested.

"I have replaced the laces with new ones I had." Magali indicated the iron-banded steamer trunk at the foot of her bed with her chin.

He gave a brief nod.

"You don't look very excited at our unexpected windfall."

"*C'est bien,*" he said. "It's good."

"I think they are your size, maybe a touch big, so I have stuffed the toes with bandages." Pause. "Unfortunately, this destroyed the spider's home."

"Spider?" His eyes widened.

"A jockey spider ... black with a red stripe on its belly ... had set up its dwelling in one boot. I know this particular spider. It has a very pretty web of fine strong silk, but can kill with one stroke of its venomous fangs. Somewhat like the black widow of North America." She gave a giggle. "Did you know the female consumes the male while mating?"

"Erm, no, I didn't." He swallowed. "Has it been there long?"

She shrugged. "I removed all egg sacs, as far as I can tell. If you feel a scuttling over the next few days, there could be cause for concern, or maybe not ..." Her voice trailed off.

"Was it *really* big?"

"The belly was shaped like a pea, with long legs. Quite beautiful!"

"Did you kill this, ah, female jockey spider?" He cleared his throat, praying she would say yes.

"*Mon Dieu*, of course not! You should know better than to ask."

"Then where is this, this poisonous creature you talk about?" An icy block of fear grabbed at his gut.

"She is back in the undergrowth where she belongs." Magali's finely arched brows drew together in a frown. "You know I never kill any of God's creatures."

"Are you mad?" He padded to the fire in his stockinged feet.

"You should be grateful I found you new footwear … broken in by someone else, too. They will not pinch. You can walk around Forest Creek in comfort. Don't complain. It does not become you."

"And be killed in the process by a spider?"

"You will not die!"

"I'm glad you are so confident." A note of sarcasm crept into his voice. "I suppose you reasoned with it?"

"Do not give me tongue, Yann!" Her face softened. "One needs to converse from time to time with God's creatures."

"I have seen you chatting to toads, and so have others. People talk about you on the Diggings."

"They are happy enough to ask for my help when they are ill." She held out the boots. "Try them, see if they fit."

"I hate having old boots, any boots. I hate it here!"

"Your situation is better than Napoléon's when he was exiled on Elba."

"He escaped."

"You are not captive, Yann. You can leave freely, unlike your grandfather, who was thrown back onto St Helena and poisoned with arsenic."

"Do you think they poisoned *Maman* with arsenic?"

"I prefer not to talk about it." Pause. "To more pleasant things, I have prepared semolina dough. You are having galettes for your breakfast, served with poached stubble quail eggs I discovered in a nest."

"Was there a spider in the nest as well?" He smirked.

Sighing, Magali rolled the dough on a makeshift board, cut round shapes and tossed the galettes into a pan. She filled a saucer with grated cheese for the cat. Soon cooking smells filled the room.

Yann eased his right foot cautiously into one boot. He inserted his left into the other and tied both laces. He pushed himself upright and began to pace. These boots were solid, comfortable and more suitable for tramping around the quagmire of Forest Creek than his other shoes. Even the bandages in the toes added to the comfort. *Mon Dieu*, how pathetic his life had become. He was reduced to living like a peasant, wearing second-hand boots, scratching around for a living.

Magali dished up the galettes and quail's eggs. She slid them onto a glazed Limoges plate with a small chip on the rim.

"Eat before it cools!" she said, placing his breakfast on the table. "You will need your strength in order to work. Mr Bass is a hard taskmaster, but we need his money. I have only a small amount of coin left." Returning to the fire, she added over her shoulder. "We must find your father soon."

Shovelling in the food, Yann mulled over the situation. Should he admit his employer had threatened not to pay him unless he found the missing chapbook?

"Why don't you ask the people that you help to cure for payment?" he said.

"I cannot do that. The diggers are unable to afford it. The rich travel by coach to Melbourne for medical treatment because the doctors here are more interested in finding gold than caring for the sick. Others walk, and by then it is too late."

"Then why don't you SELL your potions, set up a business on the Mount Alexander Road?"

"And what would the poor do then?"

"Have you thought about telling fortunes with your tarot cards, putting up a tent somewhere?"

"For heaven's sake, I would be drummed out of town as a witch, burnt at the stake. I knew a woman in Algeria who was stoned ..."

"It's not like that here. The diggers are tolerant." The words burst from Yann's mouth, surprising him.

"I don't care how tolerant they are. I cannot take money from people who are indigent."

"The ones you think are struggling might get lucky, might find a nugget. It happens all the time." If only *he* could stumble on a nugget, he told himself, his dilemma would be solved

Magali swept her eyes over his clothing. "You are not wearing your redingote today?"

"It's too hot. Anyway, people stare at me. A waistcoat is enough."

"But you look elegant in it!"

"Everyone here wears shirtsleeves. I shall invest in moleskins as soon as I have enough money."

A knock at the door.

Cyrano's fur rose.

15

Setting the kettle down on the hob, Magali opened up to find a bearded digger, clad in slops and Wellington boots, standing there.

"Ma'am, is you the one what heals people?" He lifted his battered hat.

"I do my best."

"Me missus asked me to come urgent, like. She's unable to piss proper." He sniffed.

"Infection?"

"First came on when she was busy picklin' home-killed mutton in saltpetre, and it's never gone away since." He ran the back of his hand over his inflamed nostrils.

"Is she with child?"

He shook his head. "Nah. If she is she ain't said nuthin' to me."

"Then I'll give her agrimony." Magali scrabbled in her bag. "A diuretic and de-obstructant. Does she have scrofulous sores upon her skin?"

"I don't think so, ma'am, just this terrible pain in her belly and not able to normally piss." He jiggled his hat back into position

"Is there blood?"

"She didn't say, ma'am, she were just cryin' and moanin'." He plunged his hands deep into his pockets and shuffled his feet.

"I will come with you, *monsieur*, and consult with your wife." Magali plucked yellow flowers from the herbs on the ridge pole. "We shall try acacia as well to coat the urinary tract. The Arabic gum is good for dysentery, should she also succumb to that problem. The Dja Dja Wurrung Aboriginal people in the area follow this belief. Did you know that, sir?"

"Nooo, I did not, ma'am."

"I discussed it with one of their elders, very knowledgeable. And the Jaara, those worthy Aborigines, tell me their own people are classified as 'fauna' by the authorities? Is that not incredible?"

"Really, ma'am?" he murmured. "They look like human be-ins to me."

Yann finished his galettes. He dropped the quail's egg to the floor for Cyrano to gobble up and pushed back his chair. The boots felt solid on his feet.

He knotted a handkerchief around his throat and went to pass Magali. "Well, I'm off." He gave her a kiss on each cheek. "*Salut!* Bye!"

"*Bonne journée.* Have a good day," she said. "The chickweed leaves are open and the leech has curled up at the bottom of its water so the weather should be fine, at least until this evening."

Yann gave a brief nod.

Magali tweaked another weed from the ridge pole.

"*Allez viens!* Come!" Yann gave his shoulder a tap and the cat leapt up. Instead of settling into the usual position, Cyrano remained on the alert.

"If you're headin' for the hotel, mate," said the miner, fixing him with a sly smile, "the innkeeper is in a right temper this mornin'."

Yann nodded again, then strode off.

"I saw an advert for a brickmaker," Magali called out. "You could always apply for that if Mr Bass should become too difficult!"

"*Mon Dieu!* I have no intention of stooping so low as to make bricks!" he muttered and kept on walking.

As he trudged up the road, wheelbarrows jostled him sideways. Dogs snapped at his heels. Cyrano spat at passers-by who laughed and made comments. "Think 'e's got rabies?" mused one old man, crossing himself.

Yann stroked the cat to calm him down.

Mount Alexander Road had become a dust track again. Yann inched his neckcloth up over his nose and continued past a hotel that was in the process of being erected.

A sign announced 'The Majestic Saloon, under construction.' A carpenter extracted nails from between his teeth and hammered a wooden plank onto the framework. His offsider handed him a second length of wood. Another tradesman turned over the surrounding ground with a pitchfork, as if to ensure no gold would be buried under the building. The new tavern seemed to grow before Yann's gaze.

Forest Creek was changing daily. Yann passed even more hotels: the Hibernia, the Dalrymple. Buildings were popping up everywhere. If William Bass continued to withhold his pay, maybe he could get a job in one of the new inns.

Near the creek, a puddling machine squeaked and thumped. The horse dragged the harrow inside the round trough, plodding in never-ending circles, moving the clay and water. The horse went round and round, making Yann dizzy with the boredom of it.

A blacksmith pulled a horseshoe from his fire and tapped it into shape. Farther on, an axe grinder worked the blade against the wheel. Water sluiced over his hand, turning the earth at his feet to mush.

Merchant outlets sparkled in the morning sunshine, having sprung up overnight like brightly coloured toadstools. An Indian hawker in a covered wagon sold spices, perfumes, fabrics threaded with silver. At another open stall a vendor offered humbugs and boiled sweets for sale, brushing away blowflies.

A midget, waddling along inside a sandwich board that advertised a juggling competition in Castlemaine, kicked at a heap of empty bottles sprawled against a tree stump until they went zapping in all directions.

Yann wriggled his toes inside his stolen boots. Had they belonged to someone from the other side of the world in search of a better life? He only hoped the footwear hadn't been lifted from a dead man.

He felt a sharp nip on his left toe.

"Nom de Dieu!"

Had Magali failed to locate yet another poisonous spider?

16

The skink, an inch in length, blinked and scuttled off into the grass. Yann, relieved, was left holding the tiny reptile's tail. He grabbed Cyrano by the scruff of the neck. After making sure the dotted creature had negotiated a safe getaway, he pushed the bandages back into the toe of his boot and continued on.

A carriage waited outside the Red Boulder Hotel. The Percherons flicked flies with their uncropped tails. A drunken digger sprayed a stream of urine on the rear wheel, coursing yellow dribbles along the spokes. Nearby, a miner in a coolie hat wielded a pickaxe. He hacked at the ground, prising up bits of quartz. He examined his find with a furrowed brow.

Yann was stunned to see the Chinaman searching for gold on William Bass's land. He was certain the innkeeper would be enraged. Gold seekers were brazen in their fossicking, and it was asking for trouble to dig in the grounds of the Red Boulder Hotel. Coolness washed over him when he entered the inn. A soothing sound of tapping came from the almost finished Concert and Assembly Hall.

A maid in a starched apron scuttled up the stairs clutching a pile of clean sheets. She pounded along the passage, making for the guest quarters. A man in morning suit and top hat with a lady on his arm also headed for the stairs. A bulky steamer trunk sat there waiting to be taken to one of the ten bedrooms and Yann prayed no one would order him to convey the luggage. Subservience disturbed him. He found it humiliating to carry the belongings of others and, having been used to tipping the help in his home country, he felt the urge to hurl it back whenever a patron tossed him a coin.

A smell of cigar smoke buffeted the morning air, giving out an overlay of richness and largesse. Voices seeped from the private sitting room where William Bass conducted his business.

"My good man, I cannot inform you of their names. My rouseabout lost the blessed chapbook …" Bass's voice dropped to a murmur, and then rose again: "I will be forced to take refuge in the law, sir!"

A muttered comment.

"No, I did not say I would take the law into my own hands! However, those ruffians have no right to invade my property! I shall invoke the aid of the appropriate authorities! Now the Chinese are at it and I will not have them taking my gold from under my nose and shipping it off to their unregenerate ..."

Yann edged into the bar.

The twang of the 'forty-niners'—diggers from California—slapped at him. Cousin Jacks, the staunchly united Cornishmen, discussed their luck wielding a pick.

"How be it with you, Jawn?" A fellow with muscles bulging beneath his shirtsleeves slurped at his whisky.

"Aye, it baint no better, where it be, there it be, and where it baint there be I," John complained in response.

Yann was surprised to see Barnaby in his usual place, after the scam he had tried to pull. *Did he have no shame?* The barman concentrated on the beer he was squirting into a glass. His eyes were black-rimmed. A bandage decorated his forearm. He was conversing with a digger in stained moleskins and the usual navy slops who leaned on the bar. The digger's braces were frayed. His rolled-up sleeves revealed a tattoo of scars along his arms. On Yann's shoulders, Cyrano stiffened and thrashed his tail.

Was this the miner with whom Barnaby had set up the boot game?

Shivers ran up and down Yann's spine. His heart began to paddle and he decided to make himself scarce. Hoping Barnaby would not clap eyes on him, he eased past miners jostling and pushing inwards for a drink.

The barman's voice hit him like a punch in the back: "Eh, Frenchie, that fleabag you cart around, wearin' like a necktie, has blinded a blurry trooper, and he's comin' after ya!"

Yann turned. "You exaggerate. I, ah, do not believe you. You are telling lies, you are always telling untruths."

"That devil on yer shoulder, looking like a monkey, did just that. At the time, the joe figured it were, like, a marsupial." He picked at his teeth thoughtfully and added, "However, I might've let trooper know different, eh?"

"You are not honest man!"

The babble went quiet. People were eyeing him.

"Well, Frenchie, ye'd better pray good and hard that Nathaniel Clovis doesn't get 'is sight back, or ye'll be thrown in the lockup."

"But zis is not fair!" Yann shouted. "You trap me! You put me in a very bad situation!"

"If you was a man of integrity, you would've said no in the first place! Y'are no better than a common thief!"

"Ah, get on with the servin', Barnaby," grumbled the digger in the stained moleskins. "Yer little game didn't work with 'im. Ye got one sucker. Forget about it!"

Cyrano gave out a low growl.

"You are immoral persons, *messieurs*." Yann felt the anger rise up. "You are evil!"

He found himself trembling. Indignation competed with shame in his mind and confused him. He felt as though the boots on his feet were aflame, as bright as a pair of glow worms in a cave. Luckily, he was hemmed in. No one was able to see his stolen footwear.

"The joe's comin' to get ya!" Barnaby didn't let up. "He's already got a rag over one of 'is peepers but I reckon he'll catch ya. He will, he'll tear ya apart for what ye did to 'im …"

Yann didn't wait to hear the rest. Dodging the trunk, he darted up the side passage, heading for the door into the Concert and Assembly Hall.

Behind him, he heard William Bass calling, "My boy, I've been wondering where you've been! Have you found my chapbook? I need …"

Yann ignored the innkeeper. The man with the French accent, whom he was convinced had sold Cyrano to the butcher after attempting to set the cat on fire, had disappeared and could well have left Forest Creek by now. And it was obvious that William Bass had no intention of paying him until he retrieved the chapbook. What to do? He needed to work out a plan of action.

17

In the Concert and Assembly Hall, the odour of oil paint and cut wood wrapped around Yann like a comforting cloak.

Francis Angus, in a plaid jacket with a velvet collar and leather on the elbows, stood pointing at the proscenium. "The panels representing the Muses are quite perfect, Mr Murphy," he informed the smock-wearing artist. "And I do so admire your portrait of Shakespeare. I see the Corinthian scene by sunset is coming along, too. Will it be completed for the Gala Ball?"

Murphy wiped a brush on an oily rag and nodded.

A second artist murmured, "The Red Boulder Hotel will be the envy of all in the Colony of Victoria, sir."

"Well done, men!"

Francis Angus's manner was genial and he smelled of shaving soap. In fact he smelled unusually clean, as if he had recently bathed. Was he so rich he could afford to purchase an endless supply of good water? Yann eyed the repairs on the man's jacket. Or did these patches indicate Monsieur Angus was short of money? Perhaps the leather elbows were an Anglo-Saxon fashion statement? Sometimes Yann found it hard to work out the cultural subtleties and differences.

His gaze swept the room. They said this hall was sixty feet long, twenty-five feet wide and with a ceiling twenty feet in height, that it was the largest building yet constructed in Forest Creek. Yann was accustomed to thinking in metres, litres and kilograms and had difficulty adjusting to feet, ounces and pints. Just the same, the space he stood in was impressive. The walls were covered in a rich satin paper, as was the ceiling. The ventilator in the centre kept the room cool and a stage fit for dramatic performance was set at the upper end. He felt at home in this elegant Concert and Assembly Hall, where dust motes danced in the sunlight beneath windows reaching almost to the ceiling.

Cyrano stretched. He leapt onto the polished floor, landing gracefully. He arched his back, strutted to the stage and mounted in one bound. He proceeded to examine each colourful panel as if assessing its craftsmanship. From time to time he sniffed, before moving on.

"Your animal has good taste, young man." Francis Angus turned to Yann.

"'E is a Tonkinese, *monsieur*, an aristocrat!"

"And a Tonkinese is …?"

"A rare cat, a special breed of cat."

"Ah, delightful." Francis Angus smoothed his moustache. He pulled a pipe from his pocket, lit and began to puff. "The creature is most unusual. I've never seen one like it before. Did you bring him with you to the Colony of Victoria?"

"'E was a gift from my *maman*, just before she die and I find I cannot leave 'im in France."

"You must be very fond of him?"

"'E remind me of my past life." Yann took a breath and said, "*Monsieur*, I 'ave been looking for a man who take a book of poetry from ze innkeeper, but wisout success. Why is a chapbook so important to Monsieur Bass?"

"Ah, I am not entirely sure. But yes indeed, poetry does mean a great deal to William."

"But I no unnerstand, *monsieur*. Cannot 'e purchase as many books of lovely verse as 'e wishes? It is not so difficult, I think?"

"I really cannot say." Francis Angus took a meditative puff on his pipe. "Words cannot always be replicated in another volume of poetry."

"Is zis some special verse?"

"Well, all I know is the hotelier has plans for a better life for all of us. There are thirty thousand people in Forest Creek alone, with growing unrest on all the Diggings. William Bass finds this disturbing."

"*Oui*, I 'ave 'eard of Monster Meeting in 1851. Will it 'appen again? Will people rise up in Forest Creek?"

Would angry citizens bay for the blood of those more fortunate than themselves? Yann wondered, consoling himself with the knowledge that, as he was poor and of no threat to anyone, he had little to fear.

"Shall we say a movement is afoot of a more violent kind?" Mr Angus took a reflective puff of his pipe. "Feelings have been running high. There is a build-up of troops in the town of Ballarat as we speak."

"Will zere be civil war?"

"Perhaps, and the Asian problem is escalating as well. The Chinese in Forest Creek now outnumber us white folk by four to one." Pause. "And they send their ounces back to China rather than invest their money in the colony. Some even dig in the grounds of the Red Boulder Hotel, knowing William Bass discovered gold when excavating the cellars. The earth around this inn still contains riches for the taking."

Yann's eyes grew rounder.

"Oh, yes, there are quantities of gold in these Diggings we can only dream about!"

"Monsieur Bass is a wealthy man?"

"Of course, on the one hand William has a personal fortune and is concerned to protect it. On the other hand, he is a fine fellow, determined to uphold order in Forest Creek. He maintains that the diggers must follow the regulations, or the forces of the law will bear down …"

"But 'e refuse to pay *me*, which is unjust."

"I am sure William has his reasons. He is always fair."

"But I need money!"

"I wish I could help you, young man. But I also depend on his largesse for my art and for the gold-washing machine I am developing. My invention will mean extracting the colour is more efficient for miners digging in clay." Francis Angus paused. "I am also developing the Angus Gun, my own canon which some call the Great Gun, of novel construction with a square bore and superior lightness."

From the direction of the bar, shouting could be heard.

The cries drew nearer.

"I'll have the bastard for this," cried a voice, "'im and that rabid animal, that monkey, and my sight all but ruined! Where is that Frog-eatin' so and so? I'll wring his neck …"

There was a crashing. Things were being thrown. Not only did the trooper sound angry, but he also sounded drunk. Or was the man's vision so badly impaired he was unable to walk straight?

Yann placed his fingers in his mouth and gave out a piercing whistle.

Cyrano came running.

"Is exit door unlocked?" He pointed an unsteady finger at the entrance on the north side of the Concert and Assembly Hall.

"Yes, but I don't understand …"

"Pardon, *monsieur*, but zis man will kill my cat and put me in prison if he find me 'ere."

"Put you in prison?"

"*Oui, monsieur.*"

Yann knew Trooper Clovis would sling him into the lockup beneath the Red Boulder Hotel without a second thought. His new boots shook the boards as he skidded to the door and wrenched it open. Cyrano streaked past, leading the way. They hurtled into the street past bullock drivers and coaches. They shoved aside walkers arriving at the Diggings, sent whisky bottles flying. Pickaxes snatched at Yann's clothing. Miners cursed as he tripped over their tubs. Yann and Cyrano fled down Mount Alexander Road, turned right and headed off across the paddocks.

18

Yann and Cyrano sat perched on a slope overlooking Mount Alexander Road. Yann was just able to make out the French flag fluttering over his hut.

A long stream of conveyances wound north into Forest Creek. Carts and bullock wagons, horsemen, water carts and simple walkers passed in one unbroken line. Southbound traffic, leaving the Diggings, was almost as thick. Had there been news of a strike elsewhere? Were the dispirited fortune seekers deciding to move on? Rumours flew thick and fast here, and diggers were able to take down their tents and be off within minutes.

Dragonflies darted and hovered. The sun bleached the landscape into a sea of movement. Yann plucked a piece of grass and began to chew as he gazed around. Interspersed with dirty green trees, spiky scrub and reeds outlined the creek course.

A sound like a pistol shot rang out. Studs de Wolf urged his Gold Escort team on, cracking his whip and swearing. The wheels, made from the thick end of a round log with a hole burnt in the centre for the axle, churned up the dust as the dray lumbered forward. Yann leaned back on his elbows. He closed his eyes, feeling the rays hot on his face. His limbs relaxed and, beside him, Cyrano rolled over to let the warmth caress his belly.

Yann's mind refused to stop going around in circles. He pushed himself into a sitting position and clasped his hands around his knees. Clemency had been right when she warned him not to trust Barnaby. And the trooper, Nathaniel Clovis, would continue to hound him as long as he had any sight left. Yann also knew that William Bass had no intention of paying him until he recovered the chapbook. He was left with one only option. He would have to fossick without a licence. He needed to contact Clem.

"*Eh bien*, Cyrano, we are going to Pennyweight Flat." Yann spat the grass out and stood. "*Allez viens!* Come!"

The cat yawned, stretched and sat up.

Yann set off down the hill towards the track off Mount Alexander Road which led to the children's cemetery. He followed the reeds and the gums outlining the creek's path. He dodged pan-shakers and the handles of cradles, noting that there were fewer dogs—probably left behind to guard the diggers' tents—here. Every now and then he tossed Cyrano onto his shoulder, but for the most part the cat scampered around alongside him, inspecting mine shafts, sniffing at windlasses.

Sweat coursed down Yann's face, but at least his feet were comfortable. He traipsed past fellows lugging buckets of stone down to the water to sluice away the detritus. Disappointment lined their countenances as they slogged back to their eight feet by eight feet plot to begin sorting dirt all over again. The clatter of activity made Yann's head spin.

One lucky digger screamed: 'Eureka! Yaaaaay! Eurekaaaa! I'll be purchasin' golden syrup for me puddin' tonight!"

Some sections of the creek were free of reeds. Had people yanked them out for weaving baskets? Yann wondered. The water was patchy, drying to a trickle and then flowing again. The bank on either side was crusty with trampled soil. The stench of blood from the butcher's shamble, the putrid rot of offal, effluent and dead animals assaulted his nasal passages.

The sun crawled across the sky and he saw children using tin dishes. Their clothing was made of hessian and they panned in the sludge with the adults. Did Magali know these ragged mites? They coughed, paused to wipe the slag from their nostrils with muddy fingers, and then went on panning. The horsehair petticoats of the women beside them swayed as they worked.

Three men toiled at a long tom. They shovelled dirt into the top of the sluice box, and then washed it down with water to separate the particles.

Chinese diggers jogged past. Their pigtails hung down in squiggly lines and the poles over their shoulders bent from the weight of the soil they carried. Their countrymen rocked cradles with the brims of their hats turned up.

Yann decided it was time to ask for directions. "Pardon ... can you 'elp me?"

The Chinaman ignored him.

He approached a miner wearing a formal English chapeau. "I am looking for Pennyweight Flat, a cemetery for children. Can you direct me?" He hastily added, "Please?"

The bowler-hatted man examined the blisters on his palm, thought for a bit and remained silent.

Cursing his French accent, Yann was about to repeat the question when the digger said, "There be a small knoll, with a rock wall all around. It be a sad place, and ye cannot miss it." He pointed a calloused finger towards the gently sloping hill. "Do ye have a relative there?"

As the digger spoke, a cry went down the line, "Joe! Joe! Joe!" The man plunged his smeary hands into his pockets as the words echoed along the creek. Fossickers hid behind rocks. Miners scrambled up trees and even burrowed like moles into the earth. The honest ones fumbled for the stamped piece of paper which had cost them the monthly asking price of thirty shillings.

Yann's palms became moist. What if this was not a simple licence check? What if Nathaniel Clovis was on his trail, bent on retribution for Cyrano having injured him?

He picked up his pace, and left the creek behind. His heart began to calm. Overhead, cockatoos screeched and swooped through the cloudless sky, forming necklaces of white against the blue. In a distant tree, parrots with pink chests chattered and picked at berries. Distracted by the birds, he forgot about Cyrano.

Soon Yann became aware the cat was no longer by his side. He swept the landscape with his gaze but could see no sign of Cyrano until, startled, he saw him dancing in the long grass. The Tonkinese stood on hind legs, his paws shooting out like a boxer sparring. The sun lit up the creamy fur, turning it golden so that Cyrano resembled a lion. Rampant. On the attack.

"Cyrano, *que fais-tu là*?" Yann repeated the words in English. "What are you doing there, Cyrano?"

He drew nearer and his heart lurched when he saw the snake's forked tongue flash, quick as lightning. Cyrano kept cavorting as if he had discovered a plaything. He feinted, sprang back, darted forward again. Backwards he went. He moved sideways. His body fluffed to twice its size. His claws were extended. Arcing. Striking.

"*Arrête!*" Yann shouted. "Stooopppp!" He gave out a shrill whistle.

Cyrano ignored him. His moves became even more frenzied and exaggerated.

Yann wrenched his dagger from its scabbard.

"*Écarte-toi!*" He advanced with measured step, moving forward, slow and deliberate. "Get out of my way!"

Cyrano hesitated, backed off for a moment, then launched again. He backed off a second time as the venomous fangs attacked, but continued with his taunting dance at a distance.

Finally the gap between cat and snake had sufficiently widened and Yann's fingers grasped the handle of his weapon. The pad of his thumb pressed down on the Napoleonic eagle. The steel blade flashed shards of silver. Concentrating, Yann felt nothing around him, heard nothing. No cradle roar invaded his consciousness, no scrape of gravel on tin pan. He experienced only stillness. He drew back, aimed, released. The knife sliced through the air.

19

The blade sheared past its target. Yann froze. He had missed the brown snake by a hair's-breadth.

"It's your fault, *mon pote*," he muttered to Cyrano, now watching from a distance. "If you had left the serpent alone, my friend, it would have simply gone away."

Knowing he must do something quickly, he whipped off his waistcoat and slipped his braces from his shoulders. Hoisting his shirt over his head, he tossed the fabric across the viper. The silk twisted, heaved and rolled.

Bare-chested and frantic, Yann rushed around searching for a weapon—anything—suitable for crushing the creature's skull. He snatched at the nearest branch but it broke. He grabbed another. The twig snapped. The next broke, too. He picked up a rock, lined his target up and threw. Missed.

"Merde! Merde! Merde!"

He watched helplessly as his shirt writhed and thrashed into a wonky bag shape. The shape edged across the ground in a circular motion until it rested, gently undulating, against a piece of metal. Yann peered. Was that an abandoned shovel lying there? If so, how to get it?

His face contorted as he thought: *What if the snake struck, shot venom into his veins?* Who would discover him away from the creek and the mine shafts? Would he endure an agonising death in the Colony of Victoria, in this muck and dust, this stinking hellhole, never seeing his father again, never discovering how his mother died?

The snake-filled fabric developed a rollicking motion, wavering away from the spade. Slowly. Slowly, then moving back again. Away. Back. Yann held out his hand, ready to snatch. The bag of deadliness slewed and slithered. Whenever he prepared to grab the instrument, the creature whisked back across the handle.

Yann bided his time. At the third try, he managed to sweep the spade into the palm of his hand. Droplets of perspiration dripped from his hair onto his face. He flicked back the sweaty curtain to better see and plunged the blade into his shirt. Again. And again. In its death throes the snake threw out a pungent, bitter smell, as if decaying before it had finally died. Suppressing the urge to retch, Yann kept going until the writhing had stopped and blood and pus seeped through the silk.

He crouched down, letting his wrists fall loose and taking long shuddering breaths. Eventually his limbs slackened and he regained his strength. When the feeling of panic had passed, he eased one corner of his ruined chemise aside to inspect his aggressor.

Its eyes now dull, the snake had partially thrown off its skin and created a second snake as a decoy. Blood streamed from one nostril and from the gaping maw. Yann traced a tentative finger over the scales, which curved in lacy brown swoops, an impeccable camouflage. The skin was almost delicate to look at, and impressive in the way it blended the reptile into the surrounding stones and wallaby grass.

"You are, or *were*, surprisingly handsome." Yann pushed himself up. "And you put up an excellent fight, a valiant fight unto the death. But I won the battle! As they say … *c'est la vie!*"

A breeze picked up, cooling his body. Icy spasms ran through him and he shrugged on his waistcoat. He plunged the steel of his knife into the oozing head, then draped the snake over the fork of a tree, removed and sheathed the blade and set off.

"*Allez viens*, Cyrano!" he called out. "Come! We are almost at Pennyweight Flat. It's time to leave a message for Clem."

They arrived at a small knoll enclosed by a rock wall, overlooking Forest Creek. A lopsided gate in one corner of a ragged post and wire fence opened into the cemetery. Yann pulled the gate to behind him. His eyes swept the rubbly space. Was this *truly* a cemetery? He sidled past tiny mounds of earth outlined with rock slabs, haphazardly placed. A pennyweight, one twentieth of an ounce and of almost no value, meant no quartz was to be found here. *Were these children of such little worth?* he wondered.

Jagged rows of unmarked graves lay among the grey-box trees. Magpie chatter filled the air, the warbling at odds with the bleak surroundings. Yann scratched his head. Fourth grave to the right? Was that what Clem had said? Or was it the third? He tried to count but found he was unable. The stones lay scattered as if tossed down by disgusted parents. As if these mourners loathed this place for taking their children from them. The hardness of the soil meant the graves were shallow. Uncoffined. Unrecorded. He inhaled. The sickly smell of death hung in the air.

Some had set rocks upright to create makeshift headstones, and Yann recalled the luxuriant white lilies heaped over his mother Madeleine's grave in Père-Lachaise Cemetery. So high you could barely see the marble. In this place, bits of bark and gum leaves settled between the burial plots.

Startled out of his reverie, Yann spied one traditional gravestone. The words were not etched with gold leaf as on his *maman*'s headstone, but he could make out an engraving. This headstone was curved at the top and wedged between russet rocks on either side. The rocks were stacked high, piled almost to the commemorative inscription.

Yann read aloud in hesitant English: "Sacred to the Mem-ory of Hugh James Brierley who died"—and he paused—"January 26, 1853, Aged 11 Months."

Moved by the simplicity of the epitaph, Yann's gaze swept the cemetery. Clemency's brothers and sister were asleep beneath this ground, in the most primitive burial place he had ever seen. He began to count again. One, two, three … was that a grave? Or was it a naturally occurring bump? No, it was a grave. The earth exuded the stench of death.

As he tiptoed between the mounds, his concentration was broken by a ruckus. Shouting. The sound of horses galloping below, along the banks of Forest Creek.

And was that gunfire?

20

Although curious, Yann decided to lie low. A shiver ran through him. Was the lawman, so bent on revenge for having been injured by a cat, firing and screaming? Doing his best to ignore the mayhem rolling along Forest Creek, Yann went back over the graves. He counted carefully: *un, deux...* Unnerved by the sound of shots, he started again, pointing this time: *un, deux, trois, quatre ...*

Uninterested, Cyrano sat as still as a sphinx on a hump of earth where an even-shaped rock did duty as the headstone.

"Are you sitting on *numéro cinq*?" Yann asked the Tonkinese.

Cyrano remained impassive. Apart from his nostrils flaring at the suffocating reek, he seemed almost bored. Was he trying to tell his master something? Yann counted again. Yes, he decided, this was the burial site Clem had mentioned. He pulled a stub of graphite pencil from his pocket, licked the tip and prepared to write. With a start, he realised he had brought no paper with him.

"*Ah, la vache!*" he muttered, telling himself anything would do, anything he could scribble on. Taking care not to step on the graves, he sidestepped his way along, picking up leaves and bits of bark and flat twigs as he went. Towards the edge of the knoll, beneath a grey-box tree he found a sliver of dead wood that was smooth on the underside.

Instinctively, he inscribed '*Oui*' on the surface. "*Non*, it should be 'yessss'," he said in a low voice. If only his written English were better.

Tongue curled at the corner of his mouth, he continued. 'I wish to ...' Unable to think of the word for search he inscribed '*cherche*' and then 'four gold'. After signing his name with a simple Y, he wondered: Would Clem understand his message?

Thrusting Cyrano aside, he wedged the piece of wood underneath the rock, leaving one corner jutting out enough for her to find it. As he straightened, a digger in a threadbare smock pushed back the gate and entered the cemetery lugging a pick and shovel. His wife followed, cradling a chaff bag. The bag was folded and wrapped, with a head-like shape at one end. Was the couple here to bury their infant?

Not wishing to intrude, Yann crept into the trees along the edge of the knoll. The couple was silent with grief. Yann listened to the thump of the axe, the screech of the shovel as the blade bit into the earth. The blows seemed to shear through his brain. On the banks of Forest Creek the din had abated. Yann slid down into a sitting position and turned his back to the bereaved people.

The digging and grunting went on. The ground at Pennyweight Flat was harsh, but the miner seemed to be expending more effort than was warranted for a child's grave. The sun moved to the west. Shadows lengthened. Yann heard a rustling sound and glanced over his shoulder to see the woman unfolding pages of the Argus newspaper. She lined the hole in the ground and then arranged the chaff bag inside, lovingly, as if she were putting her tot to bed for the night. She crossed herself.

Her husband began to spread dirt over the body. Plopping and whooshing, the pebbly clods resounded. The man's nose dripped as he filled the grave in and his smock, splodged with stains that resembled blood, billowed as he worked.

Watching the digger, Yann's skin became laced with goose bumps. The hairs on his arm rose and he resisted the urge to also cross himself. Their grief was none of his business. He had no right to be there.

The digger's wife called out, "Did you lose as well, dearie?"

Yann scrambled up. "*Pardon?*"

"Ye look so forlorn I wonder if someone close to you has passed. Be it your own child?"

"*Non*, I am, I am not marri-eddd," he stuttered.

"… a brother, sister?"

"*Non*, I 'ave no brozzer, no sister."

"Your accent … youse is French, isn't ye, dearie?" Her eyes seemed to shine with unshed tears as she spoke.

A stray sheet of newspaper blew across the scrubby earth and clung to Yann's trouser leg. He picked it off, shrugged. "*Oui*."

"Well, it's a long way from home, but at least ye haven't buried anyone. Or have you? Ye seem to be upset."

Yann straightened his shoulders. "My muzzer is dead, not very long ago."

"I am sorry, dearie. I hope it weren't from fevers brought on by the local waters. Terrible they are, from the dysentery."

"*Non*, she not die in Australia."

66

"Stop yakkin', Mother." The digger picked up his tools. "Leave the fellow alone, ye've got another sort of cradle to rock right now." His nose dripped some more. He wiped it with the sleeve of his smock and gave a raspy sigh. "And me hearin' tells me that mad trap has scarpered, so we can rest a bit easier."

Trap? Wasn't that English argot for trooper? Yann needed more than ever to contact Clem. He ripped a blank edge off the newspaper, held it out with his pencil.

"Could you write some message for me?" he asked, adding, "Please, *madame.*"

"Oh, nooo, neither me nor me better half never learned to read nor write, more's the pity." Her gaze scanned his clothing. "But you look like a real toff, even if y'are half undressed. I can't imagine y'ain't lettered. Ye should be able to put pen to paper yerself."

Cyrano strolled across. Yann lifted the cat onto his shoulder.

"And if ye can afford to feed a high-bred animal like that one … unusual strain, by the look of it … then ye can afford to pay someone to do your scribblin' for ya."

Yann gazed at his feet.

"Mother, ya comin'?" Hoisting the tools over his shoulder, the digger held the gate ajar.

"Keep your hat on, Jonas! I'm talkin' to this nice young man. He might be toffy but least he don' shout at me!"

Cyrano jumped down and wound around the woman's skirt until she brushed him away. As the pair disappeared down the hill their ragged clothing was highlighted by the lowering sun. Cyrano miaowed, the sound deep and long. A type of howling.

Yann turned to see him sniffing at the freshly dug grave. "*Arrête!* Stop! Do not dig up the grave! We are leaving!"

21

Yann tossed Cyrano out the gate and they set off down the slope. He could hear the racket of cradles in the distance, and he could see the tiny figures of the toiling diggers. And the upheaval he had heard? If the trooper had really been after him he had apparently given up, Yann told himself.

Without warning, his boot slipped on a piece of quartz. Yann tumbled into the spriggy grass and rolled down the hill, grazing his elbow and banging his head. He came to rest in the scrub, fading in and out of dizzy confusion until he felt Cyrano's tongue lick his face in long rough strokes.

"Aïe, aïe, aïe!"

Shoving the cat away, he groaned and pulled himself up on one elbow to examine the damage. His leather waistcoat was unharmed but his trousers were ripped below the knee. His shins bristled with scratches. He heaved his weary body up, gave his clothing a perfunctory brush and was about to continue on when he noticed a round object. Small and bright, the piece of metal glowed in the sun. A jolt went through him, a lightning bolt.

Is that a coin? he asked himself.

He leaned over to pick it up, paused. Blinked. Blinked again.

"*Mon Dieu*, I have discovered gold!" The nugget was small, but Yann snatched up the lifeline, inspecting his find with glee. "At last, lady luck has blessed me with her bounty!"

He danced a little jig. He was about to yell 'Eureka', and whoop and run around showing off his find to the barrowmen and puddlers along the creek, but he suddenly realised that the area he stood in was not roped off. Now he had enough money for a licence. Was this the beginning? Was he about to make his fortune through a chance finding? Others had. Were there untold riches in the ground beneath his feet? Another thought came to him. Had the earth been 'salt and peppered'? Had the nugget been deliberately dropped to suck him in, make him believe the particular area was awash with alluvial gold for the taking?

Yann decided to be cautious. He would purchase practical clothing with his money, and then go about the business of making his fortune prudently. He wrapped a handkerchief around the gold and pushed it into his pocket, feeling around to make sure there was no hole in the fabric. He would return that night with a lantern, after everyone was asleep, and hunt around. See if he had been blessed with good fortune.

He scratched his head. But all the countryside in the Colony of Victoria looked the same to him: bland and brown. He had no rows of neat poplars, nor barns, to guide his way. He could follow Forest Creek, but how to find the exact same spot in the dark? Eucalypt leaves and twigs would not help.

He had an idea. "Cyrano!"

The cat, busy rounding up a cicada, pounced and began to chomp. The insect continued to chirp while being chewed.

"*Arrête!* Stop that!"

Yann removed Cyrano's collar. He secured the ribbon to the soil with a pebble and, walking backwards, checked to see if it was visible. The bell gleamed softly and he prayed no one would be tricked into believing it was a piece of the precious metal.

"*Voilà*," he murmured. He would spy Cyrano's collar, and know this was the place to start fossicking.

He gave a sharp whistle. Cyrano dropped the cicada remains and followed him. Along the winding water course, Yann hummed *Frère Jacques*. He was flying high, ecstatic at his find, ecstatic at his ingenuity. He had trouble keeping a grin off his face.

One digger stopped panning. His hard eyes looked out from under a greasy fringe. "Find yerself an ounce or two, did ya?"

Yann shook his head. "*Non, monsieur.*"

The digger added: "You foreign fellas don't mind walkin' around half-naked neither, do ya?"

'Foreign fella?' Yann glanced down at his bare arms. His skin, freed of shirtsleeves, was turning to bronze. Did he really look so different? Did that mean the injured trooper would have no trouble finding him? He checked to make sure the buttons of his vest were done up.

Cyrano bounded ahead, slowing to inspect a straw hat that had flown off a Chinaman's head. A bucket of gravel dangled from a bamboo pole as the Asian made for the creek.

Yann snatched up the Chinaman's hat, jammed it on his head and lengthened his stride. This was the second item of clothing he had stolen, and this time, the straw smelled of jasmine oil and rancid perspiration, infused with a soupçon of pork. Keeping the brim turned up in the Chinese fashion, Yann plucked a piece of green spear grass, wound it around his hair to create a ponytail. Now he just needed clothing like that worn by everyone else on the Diggings. A flannel shirt and moleskins. He wasn't bothered at the prospect of being thought of as Chinese. He was determined to blend in, melt into the crowd if that's what it took to avoid being thrown into prison.

The Holmes-Lacy General Store and Post Office came into view. Yann knew Silas Holmes-Lacy disapproved of his garb. The storekeeper would disapprove even more now that he no longer wore a shirt. The sun was low on the horizon. He decided to circle the store and make his way to the rear where Viola Holmes-Lacy had her vegetable garden.

He would wait there for Clem to appear.

22

Yann positioned himself beside a eucalypt. Pulling the stolen hat down over his brow he let his gaze run over the rows of turnips, carrots and cucumbers. Eyeing the tomato plants tied to stakes, he realised he hadn't eaten all day.

Inside the store, he heard Princess Albert bark.

A mopoke hooted. Using Yann's shoulder as a springboard, Cyrano careered up the trunk, teeth bared, jaws juddering. Unable to find the owl, but alert for any edible nightlife, he crouched on the branch above.

Yann crossed one leg in front of the other. He leaned back against the tree, thinking: *What if Clem's father came out with his gun and threatened to shoot?* A feeling of unease ran through him.

The back door creaked open. Silas Holmes-Lacy? Yann edged into the shadows.

A voice called: "Raise your hands you ... you heathen scoundrel! Don't move or I'll shoot a bullet right through your cods so that you speak with a squeaky voice for the rest of your life! Back off from our *vegetable patch*!"

Yann tensed. Was that Clem brandishing the rifle? He saw the fair hair drawn back, the topaz eyes, and the tension ebbed out of him. This truly was his lucky day. Clemency Holmes-Lacy wouldn't shoot him. Confident, he pushed himself away from the tree. A cartridge whizzed past his ear, lodged itself in the trunk above his head and left a puff of smoke hanging in the air.

"Stopppp, Clem!" he shouted.

Clemency opened the breech. The casing flew out and she reloaded. Yann could smell the cordite as another bullet screamed upwards, aiming for the clouds. Was she insane? Yann had never seen *demoiselles* behave like this before. Had he been wrong to believe she was his friend?

"*Arrête!*" he bellowed. "Stop!"

She paused, as if surprised to hear a Chinaman speak in French. She brushed aside a wayward curl and lifted the rifle again. Hesitantly, this time.

Yann cringed, wondering if he should turn and run.

Without warning, Cyrano spurted from the tree. He scampered across a row of turnips and skidded to a halt beside Clem. Standing on his hind legs, Cyrano rested one languid paw against the crisp blue fabric of her crinoline.

"Oh, helloooo, monkey cat! What are you doing here?" Patting with one hand, Clem lowered her firearm and squinted through the gloom. "Am I mistaken, or is it … is it *you*, Yann?"

"*Oui*, it is I. Please do not kill me, Clem!"

"Why are you loitering about as if to rob us of our produce? I thought Johnnie Lee had sent one of his henchmen to steal our vegetables." She slung the gun over her shoulder and marched towards him, skirt slurring the feathery tops of the carrots. "If you had asked me nicely, I would have gladly given you a turnip or two…" She paused, ran her eyes over him. "Where is your shirt? And what happened to your trousers?"

"I kill a snake and I fall."

"Fall? Your arms are bare and you resemble a Chinese digger with your hat brim turned up." She sniffed. "You smell like a Chinaman, too, although they rarely devote their attention to any pursuit but mining. If it weren't for that cross at your neck, I would have thought …" Her gaze seemed to bore through him. "Why did you not come via the front of the store like normal people?"

Yann chewed the corner of his lip.

"Are you scared of Da?"

Yann noticed her bruised skin. "A leeetle." He gave a cautious nod.

"My da's not so bad really, although he does strike me sometimes."

Yann pointed to her cheek.

"Oh, you mean that?"

He nodded again. "*Oui*."

"Well, it was for my own good." She shrugged. "I thought you planned to leave a note for me at Pennyweight Flat Cemetery, under the headstone of the fourth grave." Thoughtful pause. "Or were the tombs too difficult to count? Sometimes even I have trouble remembering …"

"I do count," he interrupted, "and I leave a *petit mot*, a note. But I discover some nugget when I leave … only a small while ago!" Forgetting about Clem's problems with her father, Yann was unable to wipe the grin from his face.

"You found a *what*? Not *gold* in Pennyweight Flat Cemetery? Heavens, now the miners will start digging up the graves and that would be terrible!"

"*Non*, I find gold as I go down ze hill."

"Oh, you have been lucky." The dimples in her cheeks disappeared. "Then you won't be in need of my help if you've already tumbled upon your own colour."

"It is not much. I 'ave a *petit* ounce, or maybe two, I sink."

He pulled his handkerchief from his pocket. Unwrapping his find with care, he placed the metal in the centre of his palm and held it out.

"That's wonderful." Her smile faded; she sounded subdued. "Well, now you can purchase a licence to dig and make your fortune on your own. You won't have any need for me."

"Maybe not, but first I must 'ave new shirt and trouser."

"Surely you own more than just the things you stand up in?" Clemency pointed at his feet. "I see you have new boots. Where did you get those?"

He averted his gaze.

"As you won't be needing boots, I have some wonderful new shirts, recently arrived from a tailor in Melbourne. I can show you those, in soft creamy silk."

"*Non*, I need to wear same as everybody else."

"What do you mean? I cannot imagine why you would wish to look like everyone else on the Diggings."

He gave a brief shrug.

"If you entrust me with your find, I will weigh it on our scales and tell you what is available." She held out her hand.

He picked the gold off his palm with thumb and forefinger.

"Would you be so kind as to come into the store with me? You can choose from our range in there."

His eyes widened. "*Non, non*, I will wait 'ere an' you decide. It is not too complicated, I sink."

"Very well," she said.

Yann felt himself flush as Clemency Holmes-Lacy looked him up and down.

"You are tall-ish and reasonably slender, quite well-proportioned," she said, assessing him for size. "The usual navy flannel slops and moleskins, will they be suitable for your needs?"

Regaining his composure, he nodded. "Now I won't have to be brickmaker. Magali tell me she sees an announcement and I should apply for zis job."

"A brickmaker!" Clem paused. "I was under the impression you worked for William Bass at the Red Boulder Hotel?"

73

"I do work for 'im. But 'e not pay me until I find 'is chapbook, stolen by man in the striped maillot."

"Oh, you mean the Saint-Simonian who would have you killed, the rogue you said sold your monkey cat to the butcher? The Comte de …?"

"Le Comte de Corbeau."

Hearing the Saint-Simonian's name, Cyrano growled.

"Well, Da has even worse plans for *me*. He has placed a tender … the plans are available for inspection at the Red Boulder Hotel … for constructing a thirty by eighteen feet wooden store. Better than selling goods in a roadside hut, he says."

"You will be moving?"

"Not at all. We will still be living at Forest Creek, but more permanently." Clemency took a shuddering breath. "Da also says he's seen an advert for ovens and a bakehouse to let and has me, his daughter, in mind to run it. Can you imagine … me a baker, you a brickmaker?"

Yann gave a glum shake of his head.

"I would have floury hands and you would be covered in red clay." She gave a short laugh. "What a terrible life *that* would be!"

Silas Holmes-Lacy's voice rang out. "Clemency, is there a problem? What is keeping you?"

Clem hissed, "You know, if you are too scared of Da and wish to discuss your sudden fortune, you can still leave a note for me, fourth grave to the right in Pennyweight Flat Cemetery!"

The storekeeper's tone was of outraged annoyance. "Have you chased off that yeller thief yet?"

Clem hefted her rifle. Skirt swaying, she zigzagged her way back between the rows of vegetables. "Coming, Da!"

A battalion of butterflies beat in Yann's stomach.

He prayed Silas Holmes-Lacy wouldn't strike Clem on his account.

23

Yann hurried home, relieved to resemble everyone else on the Diggings. The trooper would find it more difficult to identify him now. His thoughts moved to Clem. Clemency Holmes-Lacy could have been mistaken for a young lady in her crinoline, if not for the rifle she carried and the robust words she used. He found it strange that they had become friends.

Cooking smells filled the slab hut. Cyrano headed for the fire where he entwined his tail in Magali's skirts. He pulled free and sprang onto the mantelpiece, hunched and began to drool. From time to time, his chocolate-coloured nostrils twitched.

"Are we having *tadjine* for supper?" Yann pointed at the steam spiralling from the hole in the conical lid of the Algerian casserole.

Magali dipped in a serving spoon and stirred. "This time I have made *tadjine* with kookaburra … a gift from a digger."

Feeling uneasy at the thought of dining on the laughing bird, Yann said, "Oh, well, that's one less to awaken me in the morning!"

"The bird was given to me by a grateful patient and I gladly accepted." She moved to the table, raised her glass of absinthe and ran her eyes over his apparel. "Did you steal those clothes?"

Startled, he stammered. "N-n-no."

Had she guessed he had stolen the boots? He was on the point of explaining how his outfit had been purchased with honestly discovered gold when her eyebrows drew together in a frown.

"Then why are you dressed in such a fashion? Did Monsieur Bass pay you before he left? And, if so, why did you spend your earnings on clothing?"

"Monsieur Bass has left?" he asked, thinking there was now precious little hope of receiving the money owed to him.

Magali's speech was slightly slurred. "The hotelkeeper has taken the Cobb & Co. coach to Melbourne to visit his lady friend, who resides in Spring Street … or so the goss-ship goes … and whom he plans to marry." She drew herself up. "You still haven't explained the moleskins and slops, which everybody wears so you cannot tell one from the other in this colony. Human beings are covered in dust, all with the same urge for instant wealth." She took another sip. "Was your Parisian attire not good enough for you?"

"I, also, wish to look like everybody else."

"Aha! Now we are arriving at the truth! Are you chasing anonymity because you are in trouble with the law?" Before he could reply, she went on. "You are becoming dark in spirit, Yann." She inhaled. "Like your Corsican forbears." She waved the cloudy emerald drink in his face.

Yann reeled back.

"A lawman with scratches, facial lacerations and a bloodied bandage over one eye, is hunting down a young Frenchman … yes, a Frenchman! … who carries a rabid … the lawman's word! … monkey on his shoulder. The man, who wears a revolver in his belt, has overturned tents throughout this 'bank till free to all' as the diggers call it. He is so enraged that I *know* it is you he is after! Honest people do not creep about at night as you have been doing recently!"

Yann's mouth felt as dry as ash. "And wh-what did you tell him?" His throat ached, his vocal chords knotted into a ball. He felt physically sick.

"Naturally, I said no young Frenchman lived here but I don't think he believed me." She pointed a wavering finger upwards. "Nathaniel Clovis still has one eye to see with and, after all, we do flaunt the tricolour on our roof. Not to mention that others have seen you come and go."

"Take the flag down!"

"I might do that." This time her sip was more reflective. "However, at the moment your appearance is almost Chinese, with your hair tied back in a pigtail. Is that deliberate? Are you seeking to change your identity?"

Yann was tempted to tell her the truth, but remained silent.

Magali gulped the dregs from her glass, picked up the slotted absinthe spoon and twirled it between her fingers. "You did not purchase that headwear smelling of pork and which you wear brim upturned in the Asian style, I'll wager!"

"You are right," he burst out. "I did steal the hat! I stole it from a Chinaman! Are you happy?" He strode to the calico drape around his bed, hoicked it closed and threw his body onto the patchwork quilt she had sewn for him.

On the other side of the drape, he heard the tinkle of fluid being poured. A fresh glass of absinthe? At least the alcohol would kill any germs, he told himself. Yann knew many on the Diggings who preferred to drink whisky rather than risk dysentery by swallowing the brackish water *she* was using.

"Are you planning to sample my *tadjine*?" she called.

Pretending he hadn't heard, he picked up his accordion and began to play, singing the words:

Alouette, gentille alouette,
Alouette, je te plumerai

Je te plumerai le bec,
Je te plumerai le bec,
Et le bec, et le bec,
Alouette, Alouette!
Ah! Ah! Ah! Ah!

He took a breath and continued:

Alouette, gentille alouette,
Aloutte, je te ...

"It's a kookaburra I have prepared, not a lark!" Magali shouted.

"I wish it were lark, lark pâté. I could do with some lark pâté for dinner, instead of kookaburra *tadjine*!" he shouted back. "I was feeling better about myself, feeling better about my life in this filthy place and now you have spoiled it!"

Magali's sigh was audible. "Well, continue with your song if that improves your view of the world. The eyes come after the beak ... and, yes, I did remove those ... and then the head and the neck." A pause as she thought. "I did pluck the back of the bird, tore off its wings." Another sip. "You haven't sung about the stomach, or the claws. And what about the tail, Yann? You are beginning to make me feel homesick, too, homesick for lark's tails, the tails of *all* passerine birds!"

Yann knew Magali was teasing, and a smile twitched at the corners of his mouth. Perhaps he *would* have some kookaburra *tadjine* for dinner.

He stopped playing the accordion. "Have you discovered further news of *Papa*?"

"As a matter of fact ..."

A knock at the door.

A panicky cry rang out. "Are you there, ma'am?"

"I shall be there in a little moment, just as soon as I make myself decent. I was resting!" she called, before swishing aside the calico drape around Yann's sleeping space.

Stray wisps of hair hung over her right cheek and she hissed, "You would be well advised to conceal your body beneath the bed upon which you recline!"

Yann slid off the hessian bunk and scrambled under the mattress.

At the front door, he heard her murmur, "Can I be of some assistance to you, *monsieur*?"

"There is a fire, ma'am, a terrible fire. Poor souls' tent is burnin' up the night sky," responded the digger. "Your healin' is much needed. Can ye help?"

24

Ashamed to be hiding like a coward, Yann crawled out from under his bed. He had not eaten since breakfast and cramps groped at his stomach. The smell of the *tadjine* made his head swirl, but first he needed to check on the racket outside.

He unfastened the canvas window. Flames sizzled and popped, and through the haze, he was able to make out a horse and cart laden with water clattering along Mount Alexander Road. Troopers galloped past. Storekeepers stood outside their premises, gawping. People milled under the veranda of the Red Boulder Hotel. Miners, nursing glasses of beer, sipped, and wiped the foam from their moustaches while they rubbernecked. Or bent their elbows, swigging from whisky bottles.

Diggers sat in the dirt rolling dice, barely bothering to turn their heads while, through the windows of the Red Boulder Hotel, Yann saw men playing games of chance. They continued to gaze at their cards, uninterested in the bedlam caused by the burning tent. If he listened hard, Yann could hear the click of cue against ball as customers played Bagatelle. The honky-tonk sound of the piano ceased, and then started up again.

The flames lessened, throwing out a few final defiant sparks. Smoke wisped skywards and the reek mingled with the stench from the slaughter yards. Two scruffy individuals lugged a stretcher, covered in a soot-spattered cloth. They joggled the litter down the hotel steps, making for the morgue below. Onlookers crossed themselves.

The crowd dispersed. Some trudged back to their tents, muttering and shaking their heads. Others moved on to the sly grog seller for a pick-me-up gin served in a chipped coffee cup. A few approached two outsized women, handed over their shillings, and waited their turn to drink from a tube connected to the side pockets of the women's dresses, beneath which brandy kegs had been lashed.

Yann secured the strap on his window and headed for his own fire where the food simmered. Death was commonplace on the goldfields and he wondered if the person who had passed was known to the inhabitants of Forest Creek.

Cyrano parted his jaws expectantly as Yann rolled up the sleeves of his flannel shirt to inspect the *tadjine*. Dipping in the serving spoon, he slopped kookaburra stew laced with carrots, chick peas and chilli pepper onto a plate. He slung his behind against the table and ate. The meal was spicy and surprisingly tasty—kookaburra was not so bad after all.

Reflecting on how comfortable his moleskins were—although, at this stage, they were too clean if he wished to blend into the crowd—he picked bones from the casserole and lobbed them onto the hearth for Cyrano. He wiped his plate clean with a doughy piece of Diggings bread and slid the dish into the bucket of washing up water where it mingled with the discarded vegetable peelings, olive pips and date ends.

Glancing around the room, he saw that Magali's bag was no longer there. Twigs and leaves from her herbs were scattered across the floor and, beside a sprig of sage, lay her tarot cards. Death faced upwards. A shiver ran through him. He gathered up the deck and put the card in the middle of the pack. The hairs on his arms stood up. Was this an omen? Did the Death card indicate that the trooper would find him and throw him into the lockup beneath the Red Boulder Hotel? Would he be put on trial for the loss of the man's sight? And, if so, would the magistrate consign him to a prison in Melbourne?

"Or worse," Yann murmured. "What if the trooper shoots us all in retribution for you, Cyrano, having clawed out his eye?"

The cat continued to bother the bones.

Endeavouring to stay calm and think only about the gold awaiting his searching fingers at Pennyweight Flat, Yann picked up his accordion. He settled himself on a chair and resumed playing:

Au clair de la lune,
mon ami Pierrot.
Prête-moi ta plume,
pour écrire un mot.

Ma chandelle est morte,
je n'ai plus de feu.
Ouvre-moi ta porte,
pour l'amour de Dieu...

As if in sympathy with the words, the candle started to sputter. Should he light another? he mused. Or should he turn in and get some rest before setting out after midnight to search for Cyrano's collar and the alluvial gold which had so far eluded him?

The candle gave a final phut. The fire had fizzled to barely glowing embers and Yann found himself enveloped by a darkness which, for no good reason, suffocated him. His breath was tight in his chest and he could see only shadows.

A soft plop hit the canvas roof and he started. His ears pricked at the rustling above the hut. He heard a brushing noise. Was that rain? Or was the wind riffling the branches of the trees, moving the leaves about? He sprang up, reached for the oil lamp. The lamp was not in its usual place.

Another plop. Was Magali rummaging around outside? Was she preparing to come in? Or was someone else in the scrub, waiting for him to come out? Something flapped and Yann whipped his head around. The strap tying his window closed had broken free. Now loose above his bed, the leather made a sketchy outline in the gloom.

Tap. Tap. Tap.

His heart slammed against his chest. Sweat ran down his arms to his hands.

Tap. Tap. Tap.

Had he secured the strap of the window properly in the first place? He was sure he had. Or was he mistaken?

Cyrano brushed past. The cat gave a throaty hiss. The hiss was followed by a deep and eerie growl, and Yann noticed his quilt undulating in the half-light. Something was beneath the bedding. Before his horrified eyes, the lump moved of its own accord, looping and lolloping. He fixed his gaze on the slithering motion beneath his covers. He searched around with his fingers until he felt the cold brass of his lamp, praying enough lard remained for him to light the wick.

His thumb and forefinger were stiff, refusing to work. Flexing his fingers, Yann edged forward and snatched a twig from the wood basket. Scrambling the kindling into his grasp he poked it into the fading glow of an ember. The twig seemed to take forever to catch alight. The lamp door winced as he finally thrust the makeshift match against the wick, forcing himself to remain steady until the flame took hold.

The wick reacted slowly, and then flared. Yann swung the light over his bed to get a closer look at the wriggling bedding. He threw back the covers and found a snake squirming and writhing in the place where he had lain only a short time before. Bigger than the one he'd killed that afternoon, at least seven feet long, the serpent had patterns on its pelt, darker bands contrasting against pale with a light underside. This creature was as ugly as any he had seen.

Yann stood there, rigid.

Cyrano spat.

The light threw misshapen shadows against the slab walls. Startled by the glare, the snake lifted its blunt head to strike. The forked tongue darted.

25

The poisonous fangs had missed Yann by a whisker. Clouds obliterated the moon and tremors ran through his body as he nailed the slain snake to the outside wall of the slab hut. His nostrils still carried the reek of decay thrown out by the viper in its death throes. He prayed that the sight and the stink of the dead creature would serve as a warning to whoever had tried to kill him, would alert them to the fact that the ploy had failed.

Had Nathaniel Clovis managed to open his window and drop the serpent inside while he was eating the kookaburra *tadjine*?

Cyrano pranced at Yann's side, outstretched paws toying with the now still tail, baring his teeth and making chattering noises. Yann yanked his dagger from the snake's gullet. He wiped the blade clean on the scrubby grass alongside the hut before sheathing it.

"Do not even consider eating this creature, Cyrano. You would be as sick as a dog from the poison … well, as sick as a cat." He grabbed Cyrano by the scruff, traipsed back inside and tossed him to the floor.

He checked to make sure the window strap was firmly secured. In the lamplight, his recently purchased clothing now looked far from new. His moleskins and both sleeves of his flannel shirt were streaked with serpent gore and unspeakable gunk which made him want to puke. He dampened a kerchief in the washing up water and sponged the blood and pus off as best he could. The muscles in his arms and legs began to spasm as images of the snake poised to strike flickered through his brain.

Would he be able to get some sleep before setting off to find the spot which had yielded his first lucky ounce? he wondered. Reptilian muck had pooled, right in the place where he usually slept, creating a patch of stinky ooze. The sapling and hessian bunk rocked and swayed as he turned the mattress over. Still shaking from his struggle with the serpent he placed the lamp on the shelf above the bed, unlaced his boots, kicked them off and sank back.

Cyrano perched on the pillow beside his head.

"*Bouge!*" Yann gave him a shove. "Move!"

The Tonkinese continued to make the same eerie chattering sounds. Exasperated, Yann pushed him to the ground. The cat sprang back. Keeping one eye open, he curled up at Yann's feet.

Another plop on the roof and Yann lurched upright. *"Mon Dieu!"* Had the trooper returned to find out if he were in fact dead? The plop was followed by another

A third plop hit the canvas. Soon rain began to slice across the roof and Yann relaxed. The storm slung sheets of wet on the canvas and he found the noise strangely soothing. His mind began to drift. The insides of his eyelids formed shapes and colours and he could feel himself move into the rhythm of a gentler dream.

Without warning, a different plop. Closer, this time. Yann's eyes sprang open. He heaved his body from the bed. Grabbing a saucepan from the fireplace crane, he positioned it under the drip and pulled the calico drape to. His eyelids began to close again to the steady beat of the downpour. He was no longer concerned by the odour of dead snake in his nasal passages, nor by the image of its gruesome goo. He had faced and overcome the certainty of an agonising death, been forced to fight for his life twice on the same day. But … two different snakes? What were the odds of that happening?

He began to count sheep, and then switched to counting snakes. He needed rest before gold digging on the ghostly slopes of Pennyweight Flat.

26

A wet and acrid smell, like the odour of singed clothing, pushed Yann's mind from gritty dreams into full consciousness. Was he imagining it, or did he hear children whispering nearby, inside his own home?

The whispers were followed by the deeper voice of a man, who seemed to be speaking in English. "Are ye sure we're not bein' an inconvenience to ya, ma'am?" he murmured. "Ye say ye have a lodger."

"It is my duty to help out. You have suffered a great deal and I am completely agreeable for the children to sleep in my bed, at least for tonight," Magali replied, her voice low, "until we are able to make more permanent arrangements."

"Are ye sure?" He sniffed.

"Quite. I'm only too glad to share my humble home with you. What a terrible experience you've been through, having your tent burn down and all your cherished belongings with it, not to mention …"

"It was the lamp, ma'am. The oldest of me nippers knocked over the lamp accidental-like and the tent went up like ye wouldn't believe and me poor wife …" He began to sob, great gulps of despair.

"There, there. I will help care for the children until you are able, and I am sure William Bass will be of financial assistance as soon as he returns from Melbourne. The innkeeper has been extremely generous in the past for folk in your situation, Mr Brisket, and I am confident he will not be the slightest bit different in your case." Pause. "Maybe he will even host a benefit in your honour?"

"I 'ope so. We could do wiv a change of luck." He began to sob again. "Oh, poor woman. Me missus never 'ad a chance."

Squeaks and bangs. Yann's nostrils were assailed by a tangle of elements. Water and fire were mixed with damp wool and mud, sweat and cinders.

"What's that blurry saucepan doin' on the floor, miss?" a child wailed. "I nearly broke me ankle."

"The saucepan has been placed there to catch the drips from our roof."

"Our roof never 'ad leaks, even if it were only a tent!" The child began to snivel. "And now we 'ave to sleep wiv leeeee-aks." Her snivels turned to wrenching howls of desperation. "An' it stinks in 'ere too!"

"There, there. Never mind, we'll find you a place of your own very soon." Pause. "Into bed you go, children, and be careful not to do *pipi* on my mattress. Would you like to say a prayer before you go to sl …?"

"I thought the French were heathens, ma'am, who never go to church," Brisket interrupted, his voice fierce with disapproval.

"That's not strictly true, *monsieur*. At any rate, to be precise, I am colonial French, a Pied-Noir from Algeria. In North Africa, we Catholics are devout and believe strongly in setting an example to the natives. And were there a church here, I should surely be a regular and devoted member of the congregation."

"Then why do ye dabble in the occult?" He snorted back phlegm.

"Occult?"

"Them cards."

"Tarot is a card game played in France, *monsieur*, a respectable parlour pursuit. However I occasionally do spreads for my own interest, you understand, to gain insight into current and possible future situations. There is nothing sinister in the cards at all."

The digger grunted. "Avoid intemperance as ye would the fiercest tiger."

Was Monsieur Brisket alluding to Magali's bottle of absinthe, Yann wondered, *or her tarot cards?*

Magali cleared her throat. "And now to the children's emotional and spiritual wellbeing." She murmured a few words about *le bon Dieu*, and then, in a louder voice: "Your father and I have chairs to rest upon. We will watch over you, and find somewhere more permanent and far more comfortable in no time at all. I promise."

"I want my maaa-maaa! I don't like livin' wiv a rich person."

"I am not a rich person … far from it."

"But you live in a hhhhouse!"

"This is not a house, it's a hut." Magali's voice took on a soothing tone.

"I want my tent back, a place wiv no leaks!" The child began to snivel again.

"There, there."

The snivelling subsided. Magali tossed kindling onto the fire. Yann heard her scrabble around in her steamer trunk for blankets.

Just feet from his ear, a raspy cough sawed the air. Yann crossed his fingers, hoping the stricken child didn't have diphtheria. But, wasn't the illness only transmitted between children? Surely he was too old to suffer from it? He could think of nothing worse than expiring from diphtheria on the goldfields of Victoria.

Soon a rumbling snore emanated from the fireside. Had the digger fallen asleep? Or was he weeping some more? The fidgeting no longer distracted Yann. He speculated whether to risk creeping out the front door, or take the safer option of exiting through his bedroom window beside the dead snake. Dead snakes, dead people … what sort of country was he living in?

Abruptly, the calico drape swished open. Hair awry, her eyebrows singed, Magali loomed over him. "When you emerge for breakfast in the morning, keep your mouth shut, wear your hat brim upturned and yet low over your eyes and pretend you are Chinese. Speak not a single word of English!" she hissed in French. Her breath smelled of absinthe.

"But I only ever talk to you in French, never in English!" Yann glared. "What on earth is going on? There are strangers in our hut. Do you plan to invite the entire Diggings into our home whenever a miner is forced to live with the consequences of misfortune or the clumsiness of his idiot children, who I heard whingeing and complaining about the state of our abode?" He jabbed a finger. "Not that I disagree with their opinion."

"Don't you say another word, Yann! Those mites have lost their mother this evening, a horrible tragedy. You will remain Asian under our roof, until this poor family has found shelter elsewhere!"

"Well, I'm going then, looking for another place to live! Don't forget I have lost my mother, too. I don't have to stay here." He took a breath. "Was Napoléon ever forced to pretend he was Chinese in his own home?"

"Not that I know of. But, on this occasion, his grandson must. So keep quiet and say nothing!"

"If I speak in French …?"

"You may speak in your mother tongue to me, but only if you have no alternative *but* to talk to me. And keep Cyrano out of the way. That animal is of a rare breed, and makes it far too easy for people to identify you!" She turned to leave.

"Pssst!"

"What?"

"Do you have any paper?"

"Paper to write on?"

He nodded. "Can I have a sheet?"

"Yes, of course." She ran her gaze over his clothing, sniffed and said, "Whatever is that terrible smell of decay in your bed space?" Before he could reply, she added, "And whatever happened to your new moleskins?"

"The trooper managed to drop a snake through my window and into my bed while I was having my dinner, eating your kookaburra *tadjine*. I was forced to kill the serpent, which made a mess ... and caused the smell." He took a breath. "The lawman tried to assassinate me!"

"You mean the man who storms around the Diggings with a revolver in his belt? He put a viper in your bed?" Magali's eyes, red-rimmed and smoky, popped. "Why would he do that?"

"Trooper Clovis blames Cyrano for scratching out his eyeball and blinding him. Isn't that reason enough?"

"It would be easier for him to pull out his gun and shoot you in the chest." She sighed. "This snake about which you speak could have entered of its own accord. In Forest Creek, they are everywhere, and Tiger snakes are nocturnal in hot weather. You are being fanciful, Yann. The Australian sun is addling your brain."

"Ma'am, is everything all right?" The digger was awake.

Magali switched to English. "Nothing of import, Mr Brisket. My lodger is simply feeling poorly. Since he's been on the Diggings, he suffers terribly from homesickness." She pushed a sheet of paper into Yann's grasp. "He has a deep-seated need to write a letter home to his family in China!"

"This has been a terrible night," the digger said. "I hate this cursed place, Forest Creek, and I cannot afford to take leave of it. Out of debt, out of danger, oh, ay."

"Things can only improve, *monsieur*." Magali gave a loud yawn, yanked the drape firmly closed around Yann's bed and settled back into her chair.

"The smell of burning flesh is worse than death," Yann heard her murmur. "Or even that of slain vipers."

"Aye," said the man. "'Tis that indeed." His voice trembled.

Yann stuffed the paper into the pocket of his moleskins and lay there until he estimated by their ragged breathing that Magali and the digger had fallen asleep. At the first solid snore, he pulled his braces up over his arms and dragged on his boots. He set his hat down over his eyes, lifted his lamp from the shelf and unstrapped the window. He tossed Cyrano outside and hoisted himself onto the sill.

Sliding down past the dead snake, he dropped to the ground and set off for the slopes of Pennyweight Flat.

27

Dodging windlasses, puddling machines and buckets of stone left lying unsifted, Yann made his way towards the place where he had found gold. Guided by the creek, he followed the same path to Pennyweight Flat as before. He stopped momentarily, realising he had forgotten to bring a bucket. Should he go back for it, he asked himself, and risk running into the bereaved Brisket family? He decided to move on.

Rushes sawed and jigged. The reeds beckoned, throwing a riot of feathery shadows over the honeycombed banks and making it difficult for Yann to be sure whether he was treading on solid ground or about to tumble down a mine shaft. The wet earth sucked at the soles of his boots. He no longer thought of his footwear as stolen. They were *his* boots and so far they had given him no blisters.

Cyrano, undeterred by the rough terrain, jumped down from his shoulder and scampered around diggers sleeping beside low fires. The men's beards were clogged with mud, and many lay snoring with a gun in one hand and a knife in the other. Dogs woofed and rattled their chains. Yann took no notice. He continued to skirt mine shafts, claggy mounds of soil, nodes of earth. The dogs' masters, exhausted, barely twitched as he passed.

Soon Yann had left the spackled area behind. Through the gloom he could see the stony knoll where the Pennyweight Flat Cemetery was situated. He knew he had almost reached the spot. Wispy clouds began to seep across the stars and he prayed the rain would hold off.

He swung the lamp around. Up, down and around he scoured the earth for any sign of Cyrano's collar. He kept moving, but saw nothing.

Cyrano, still bounding ahead, suddenly skidded to a halt. He began to make the same strange chattering noises he had made after Yann discovered the serpent in his bed. *Surely not another viper, and in the middle of the night*, Yann said to himself. Did these poisonous creatures never sleep? This time the cat sound seemed elevated, as if coming from the branches of a tree.

Yann raised the lamp higher. Cyrano sat perched in a tree fork. His tail, a bottlebrush of agitated fur, thrashed as he pawed at the brown snake Yann had killed that afternoon. He flicked, growled, flexed his claws and sank his teeth into the skin. Giving playful nips, he growled some more and continued with his game.

"*D'accord*," said Yann. "I agree. You are very brave, now your enemy has been conquered."

However, he pondered, at least he now knew they were close to the place where he had left the collar. He peered and probed, still unable to find his marker. He examined pieces of quartz, checking them in the dim light for threads of gold, chucking them away in disgust. He swung the lamp back and forth over the slaggy ground. His ears were assailed with the throaty hiss of possums, the skirmishing of a host of nocturnal creatures.

Yann snapped at shadows, lunged at dark shapes. He roved across the area in a frenzy of determination to locate the collar and thereby find gold, seek out his father and be free of this cursed Colony of Victoria. But … what about Clemency Holmes-Lacy? If he became rich, he would be leaving her behind. Did Clem's father really physically assault her? And what could he do about it, anyway? Lost in his thoughts, he noticed the ground begin to vibrate. A thunder of hooves rang out, and his heart stuttered. Sweat soaked the flannel of his new shirt. His skin was chilled with an icy perspiration. Was this the trooper?

He jerked his head up to see a riderless horse, its flanks flecked with foam, galloping past and he exhaled. He lowered himself onto a flat stone and pushed the gold cross back into position around his neck, tucking it into his shirt before heaving his body up again. When daylight came, he would be forced to stop looking. His fingernails were clogged with mud and bits of stone. He could feel blisters forming on the palms of his hands. His locks had burst free. Plucking another piece of grass, he re-tied his hair and continued his search.

Should he move on, stop mindlessly seeking until he found Cyrano's collar, he wondered, carry out the task methodically instead of scavenging randomly through the swells and undulations?

"*Merde!*" he swore. If only Cyrano hadn't injured the trooper he could look in full light, and without fear of being arrested.

The night became colder. He rubbed his arms, aware that morning was approaching. His lamp was low on oil and began to flicker. He shivered, watching the pre-dawn throw streaks knotted with pink chunks across the horizon. The sky was wide, the world so vast in this southern land, and sometimes the size of it frightened him.

He took a breath. Well, his search for Cyrano's collar had been fruitless. What to do? Should he leave another note for Clem at the cemetery? He had paper this time and it seemed the sensible course to take. Clem knew where he could pan safely without a licence. It was time to take up her offer.

How did one spell '*chercher*' in English? S-E-R-C-H? Surely she would understand, no matter how bad his spelling.

The kookaburras began to laugh and Yann knew he should leave.

"*On y va!*" he yelled at his cat, now sleeping on a low branch. "Let's go! We're off to Pennyweight Flat Cemetery." He placed his dirt-soaked fingers in his mouth. The soil was bitter on his tongue as he gave a piercing whistle.

Together, he and Cyrano headed for the stony knoll. They made for the stand of grey box trees rising behind the swells of earth where the bones of the children lay. Goose bumps ran along Yann's arms. Crows cawed. Wings flapped. A murder of ravens filled the lightening sky. He suppressed the urge to flee.

28

Back at the hut, Yann scrambled through his window and fell onto his bed. His clothing was stiff with mud, and his mattress was impregnated with snake blood, but he barely noticed. All he could think of were the crows at Pennyweight Flat. They reminded him of the ravens gathered on the roof in Paris just before his mother died, and the memory sent flurries of fear though his soul.

He drifted into a deep sleep. His dreams were brighter than his conscious thoughts, with lumps of quartz bounding around in cats' collars. Clem wore an upturned hat with a solid gold brim. She turned his note over and over, gazed at it upside down, sideways, and then tossed it away, unable to understand what he'd written…

The mantel clock struck nine. Yann's eyelids, sticky with tiredness, sprang apart.

A child's voice piped, "Your lodger is really, really dirty, ma'am. Oooh, dirtier'n my dad after a day of pannin'." Her voice caught in a sob. "Has me ma really gone to heaven, ma'am, 'cos she used to …?"

"But you haven't *seen* my lodger, dear," Magali interrupted.

"Yes, I 'ave too, I *pee*ked." The girl gave a long, moist sniff. "The man has yeller skin. He's all covered in mud and he looks like a wild animal wiv black hair, and 'e stinks of pork."

Another voice joined in. "I peeked, tooooo. And he does, he blurry stinks of pork!" Cough. "I hate pork 'cos pigs is dirty, all covered in muck and berks fings. Like the codger who's lyin' in there!"

"Now, children, I instructed you not to intrude on the Chinaman's privacy. My lodger is not well. In fact the man is so homesick for his country, so very homesick and this excruciating emotion, which can happen to anybody of a sensitive … or, perhaps one might say, at times, unreasoning? … disposition has rendered him quite ill."

Mon Dieu! Yann said to himself. Not only had he become Asian, but an extremely unwell, sensitive and at times unreasoning Chinaman who was black-haired and resembled a wild animal.

He could smell crêpes cooking and his mouth watered. If he were so sensitive and unwell, would Magali perhaps deliver him some breakfast to his bed?

With a start, he noticed Cyrano was no longer by his side. Was he tucking into crêpes near the hearth, while his master cringed behind the drape, praying the enraged trooper did not find him? Then again, Magali had expressly told him to keep the cat out of the way due to his unusual appearance. His heart began to strum. Surely his mentor hadn't killed the Tonkinese, wrung Cyrano's neck for safety's sake? She had preserved the life of the poisonous jockey spider in his boot, claiming not to believe in killing any of God's creatures. Would she be so kind to Cyrano? Or would she choose to preserve his, Yann's, life over that of his cat?

"Now eat up, children," he heard Magali say. "We must be off to the Red Boulder Hotel. Mr Bass is due back from Melbourne this morning on the Cobb & Co. coach, in time to host the Gala Ball tonight. We must speak to him about your plight before he becomes caught up in the final preparations."

A slag-filled cough rent the air.

"Are you wearing your red flannelette chemise as I instructed, dear?"

"Me ma sewed me into it, ma'am."

"Your mother sewed you into your chemise? Oh dear, I see, and what do you do when you wash?"

"You mean 'ave a bath? I don't like baaaths."

"Well, we will worry about hygiene later. Your father is off and panning, successfully, I hope. Mr Brisket tells me he has been clearing four pounds a week, a good wage by my reckoning, better than he would earn back in England."

"Are we gonna be *rich*?"

"With William Bass's help, we should have you housed quite soon in a new tent and with fresh garments to replace your damaged clothing."

"And a new flannie for me chest?"

"We'll see, *ma puce*."

"*Mon Dieu*," breathed Yann. Why was Magali calling this ragamuffin 'sweetheart' when she barely knew the child? Or *did* she know the child? Had she been having a liaison with Mr Brisket before the fire burned down his tent? Had Magali been complicit in Mrs Brisket's death?

Yann rejected the thought.

"Are we goin' to the ball, ma'am?" squeaked one of the children. "Will there be grand ladies …" This time, the cough resembled a dog barking.

"No, Gala Balls are for grownups."

The front door closed. Their voices faded.

Yann scrambled off his bed. He hauled back the drape, expecting to find a plate of crêpes waiting for him. Dirty dishes floated in the washing up bucket, but he could see no sign of food. Only a green choko lay on the table. He grabbed the vegetable and sank his teeth into the flesh. The taste was blander than he remembered. He sought out the seeds with his tongue and began to chew, enjoying their nutty flavour. Yann also knew chokos were a diuretic. He would probably be doing *pipi* all day. No matter, he was hungry.

The hut was strewn with singed clothing. Patched trousers flopped over chairs. Battered shoes were spread out to dry on the hearth. Jackets, fashioned from hessian and smelling rancid, hung from every hook and nail. Among the litter of garments a few charred ribbons indicated that the Brisket children were girls. One boot-button eye was missing from an armless rag doll with crispy hair.

The cindery odour made Yann's stomach churn. Still chewing on the choko seeds, his gaze lobbed onto a piece of paper wedged under the clock.

He eased the note out and unfolded it.

Le chat dort. Je l'ai mis dans la cage qui se trouvait à côté de notre maison.

"The cat is asleep," he read. "I have put him in the butcher's cage I discovered beside the house."

How could Magali be so certain Cyrano was asleep? he asked himself. Had she drugged him with herbs? Herbs like verbena, or wood betony— said to be good for warding away snakes? Or even rue, which had caused Yann's skin to form the most horrible blisters when he was having trouble sleeping as the ship lurched and heaved around the Cape of Good Hope on the voyage to Australia? Was Cyrano clawing at the bars right now, frantic to be free?

Edging open the front door Yann listened for terrified howls but could hear nothing, no sound of an animal crying out in anguish.

He peered around, wondering if it was safe to come out. The neighbouring tents were deserted. Dogs, tethered to tent posts, yawned and gave half-hearted barks. Drays churned past along Mount Alexander Road. Whips cracked, and along the creek, the cradles were roaring. He could see no sign of the trooper, but an ebony-skinned officer of the Native

Police loomed through the scrub and began wending his way through the surrounding dwellings.

Uniform buttons gleaming, he headed for a nearby tent.

29

Rather than risk being seen exiting the front door, Yann chose his window. Shinning down past the dead snake, he dropped to the ground.

Blowflies buzzed and he brushed them away. Ants crawled over the snake. Wriggling white worms, like maggots, oozed. Yann's dagger dug deep into his ribs. The cut-throat razor he carried knocked against his thigh. Should he skin the reptile, leave it to dry, display the remains beside his window as a trophy, and as a warning to others who would try to attack him? he wondered.

The air hummed with cicadas and the whirring of wings. A jewelled butterfly soared past his head. A haze shimmered in the air, precursor of another hot day which would soon turn last night's mud to dust. Yann pushed through the scrub, searching for the abandoned butcher's cage. He needed to find Cyrano before the cat expired from the heat. Or would Cyrano become terrified when he woke and found himself back behind the same bars? Would he believe he was once again about to be slaughtered?

"*Où es-tu?*" Yann kept his voice low, calling and listening for Cyrano's distinctive cry. "Where are you?"

He nudged aside brush, weedy tussocks and coarse grey foliage. He sank his hands into greenish-brown spikes, weeping grass and sombre bunya leaves. A bush rat scuttled past. The northerly wind gusted, and Yann thought he could hear a scratching sound coming from beneath the hut. He plunged to his knees, lifted a chaff bag tacked to the wall and peered under the slab construction. Leaves and bits of bark—more than usual—lay heaped among branches, together with the small chopped logs Magali stored for her fire.

Yann twisted onto his back. He slid his body under the hut and, grasping his knife, swept his arms back and forth, feeling his way through festoons of spider webs. Dust balls and litter filtered into his nostrils. Thinking he could hear footsteps, he pushed the chaff bag into its former position with his feet. A sneeze threatened to erupt. He held his nose with his thumb and forefinger.

He took a deep breath. The air outside smelled of manure and sour leather, indicating the intruder was a horseman. Yann's heart knocked against his ribs and he remained riveted to the spot. The horseman moved away, hesitantly at first.

The sounds—and the smells—faded.

Yann gave a final sweep in a last desperate effort to locate the butcher's cage. Through the kindling, leaves and scrubby twigs, his fingers at last touched on metal and he hauled. Creating a bow wave of bush debris, he inched the cage towards him. Whooshing away the camouflage with his spare hand, and swivelling his head sideways, he peered through the bars.

Cyrano was stretched like a skun rabbit, out to it, apparently unaware that he was back in the hated butcher's prison. Yann detected no movement and his heart froze in his chest. Was Cyrano dead? Had Magali, in her zeal to protect him from falling into the hands of the trooper, killed his cat? But then he saw Cyrano's ribs, highlighted by the pale fur, rise and fall almost imperceptibly.

His heart calmed. Wriggling open the cage door, he eased out the unresisting body. As he gathered the cat into his arms, his nasal passages inhaled a strange odour of alcohol. *Mon Dieu!* he said to himself: THE GREEN DRINK! Had Magali dosed Cyrano with absinthe? If the Green Fairy liqueur could drive grown people insane, what would it do to a highbred Tonkinese?

Clasping Cyrano to his chest, Yann manoeuvred his way out from under the hut. The sun bleached the sky and he blinked away black spots. His irises adjusted to the light and he slung Cyrano over his shoulder. Clambering up past the worm-ridden snake, his boots gripped the slab wall and he eased the cat down onto his bed.

As Yann hoisted himself back inside his home, Cyrano gave a loud, alcohol-infused yawn. He opened one eye and made a feeble effort to push his legs upright, sank back, yawned again and resumed sleeping.

What to do now? Yann desperately needed to know if Clem had discovered his note under the headstone at Pennyweight Flat Cemetery. What would her answer be? Would she agree to help him? He had a whole day to fill before he could return to the slopes of Pennyweight Flat to discover her response.

He picked up his accordion and played it softly, humming, not daring to sing out loud and thus attract the attention of passers-by. Every now and then, he heard the rustle of footsteps, a brief laugh as diggers sought their tents for a quick bite to eat or to plug their pipes with fresh tobacco.

The hut was like a furnace, hotter than any oven. The roof beams seemed lower than usual, oppressive, and Yann's mind drifted as he played. Would the snake really deter potential intruders? Certainly the head would. Yann knew the fangs were still dangerous and that 'dead' snakes had been known to strike. Perhaps he should skin the reptile, keep the skin as a souvenir to show his friends back in France, when he returned after finding his father. In the opulent salons, he could brag about how he had faced death and survived.

Yann pushed thoughts of salons in Paris out of his mind. He figured the snake's head alone would be sufficient warning should Trooper Clovis come looking for him. Had the horseman been the trooper? Had the dead snake scared him off?

He pulled the blade from his belt, rolled back the window and leaned out. Careful to keep his fingers at a distance, he sawed until the snake's blunt skull hung free. Holding the decapitated reptile in his left hand, he banged the body against the slab wall. Ants and maggots spattered the ground below. After the skin had been freed of parasites, he dragged the snake into his room and spread it lengthwise on the floor beside his bed.

Cyrano opened one eye, made a brief chattering noise, stretched and continued to doze.

Yann slid the cut-throat razor from his pocket. He made an incision down the centre of the belly, through to the stump. Beginning at the head end, he pulled the skin from the flesh, careful to avoid tearing it. Where the skin was tight and difficult to remove, he sliced the muscle attachments. He worked carefully until he reached the intestinal and urinary cavity, removing the skin with his blade.

Sweat streamed down his face. He flicked wisps of hair away with the back of his wrist and, slicing a final muscle attachment, eased the skin free of the flesh. He scooped the innards out, cut a final membrane and scrambled the surplus pieces of fat off with his thumb.

He sat back and surveyed his handiwork. The pelt was impressive. If he'd had spare water, he would have washed it down, but water was a luxury and not to be used lightly. He pushed back the drape and laid the skin out to dry before the fire, which was now reduced to embers.

Cyrano was awake, perched on the side of Yann's mattress, his fur raised in ferocious spikes of anger. The cat leapt down, scratched at the stinking pile of innards and attempted to cover it with his paws. He arched his back and made long and eerie howling noises, as if he were hallucinating. The hairs on Yann's body stood on end.

"*Arrête!*" he hissed. "Stop!"

At that moment, he heard a familiar rasping cough outside and knew the Brisket children were approaching. He wrapped his fingers over the cat's snout to silence him. Diving behind the drape, Yann secured the fabric around his bed.

30

Yann twisted off a piece of snake gut to keep Cyrano occupied. He shoved the cat beneath his bed, rolled over and pretended to be asleep.

"Come, children, change out of your good clothes. We will go down to the creek and tell your father the wonderful news," said Magali.

Bustling in the living room.

A loud, snorting sniff was followed by a child's voice, saying. "It smells funny in 'ere, miss."

"Does it, Dora? You can call me Magali if you like." Pause. "You may do so, as well, Bethany."

"Maggie?" piped Dora.

Yann could hear Cyrano chewing and purring beneath his bed.

"No, Magali is the correct pronunciation of my name. Three syllables. Ma-ga-li." Magali enunciated her name with care. "Quite simple, really."

"I loik Maggie better. Don't you, Dora?" said Bethany, and then filled the hut with a piercing shriek.

"Whatever is wrong, child?" Magali's voice was tinged with panic.

"A snaaaaake! There's a snaaaaake in the hut!" squealed Bethany.

"Where?" asked Magali.

"On the heaaaarth!" the girls shouted in unison.

"A snake?" cried Magali.

Yann thought she sounded unusually alarmed for someone who claimed to love all God's creatures. He decided it was time to shin out the window again. Soon the drape would be thrust open and he would be quizzed by either Magali or these odious children, and all the while he would be forced to pretend he was Chinese.

He grabbed the purring cat by the scruff, opened the window and slid down past the snake's head—which was now oozing pink pus. Slithering beneath the hut, he pushed Cyrano back into the butcher's cage and eased the bolt into position. The cat gave a feeble miaow, and then curled up and went back to sleep.

Yann lay sprawled on his back, listening to the sounds above. Another scream, different, rang out. *Was Dora kicking up a fuss this time?* he wondered.

"There's gooey fings, worms and blood and dis-gusting oooozy innards!" she screeched.

Yann sighed. The Brisket children had apparently discovered the snake's remains.

"Oh dear, yes." Magali's voice was calmer this time. "The Chinaman must have brought the offal home to eat for his dinner." She gave a loud sniff. "I shall certainly reprimand my lodger for his unsociable behaviour."

"Dis-gusting!" shrieked Bethany.

Yann could hear stamping feet, and galloping, overhead. The floor vibrated and bounced inches from his nose. Whatever were they doing? All he needed now was for the rough boards to cave in.

"Control yourself, Bethany!" Magali ordered.

Images flooded through Yann's mind. At this moment, he was a million miles from his home. The sun was searing his skin in a way his ancestors could never have imagined. The yellow grass and washed-out landscape made him feel insecure. Did Jean-Paul Sauvage feel the same way? Or had his father, like Cyrano, adjusted?

Cyrano relished the freedom of the goldfields. It was just as well Magali had fed him absinthe to calm him down. It seemed to be working, for the cat had not stirred.

Yann heard Magali toss wood onto the fire. The chimney was only feet from his head and the bricks gave out a scorching heat. Outside, the northerly wind had picked up. The snake blood on his moleskins was spreading with the perspiration. His new flannel shirt was dark with moisture and his braces dug into his shoulder blades. He swivelled his body in an effort to get comfortable.

Cyrano stretched and yawned. His breath smelled of alcohol mixed with raw snake meat.

In the distance, Yann heard Magali say, "Come, children, we have wonderful news for your father. He will be so pleased William Bass has agreed to hold a benefit for you."

The front door closed. Yann heard the chatter of children's voices disappearing into the distance. The cradles roared and his lids became heavy. He found it strangely soothing lying among the twigs, leaves and small logs scattered in an untidy heap about him. It would be safe to come out now, he reasoned, but he was starting to feel at home in this sweat box.

Magali had told him about the hammams in Algeria, the steam baths. He imagined a hammam would feel exactly like this. The logs and scrappy leaves broke up into disjointed images. The scent of the roses his mother used to pick seeped into his mind. On the long trip over, standing up on the ship's deck at night when he was unable to sleep, he used to trace the shape of his *maman*'s facial features with the stars, using his finger as an imaginary writing instrument. Cyrano continued to doze. Yann drifted off.

******

Sticky from sleep, his eyelids blinked apart. The sky was beginning to darken. The wind had swung to the south and a breeze lifted the chaff bag tacked to the outside wall. Nearby, scattered leaves skittered. Wrenching howls came from the butcher's cage.

Yann pulled back the bolt and Cyrano crept out, his aristocratic head swaying from side to side as if he were trying to clear his thoughts. All was quiet in the surrounding tents. The Brisket children had gone to join their father. He should get out from underneath the hut while the going was good.

31

Yann toss the innards, now covered in ants, out through the bedroom window. He brushed the remaining insects off his skin. Swishing his hands around in the washing-up water, he observed a clot of ant corpses floating and swaying amongst the dishes and vegetable peelings.

While he stood there wondering whether to scoop them out, his gaze latched onto an unopened jar of pickles. On the table amidst the stockings, chemises and other smoky bits of clothing, the jar sat beside an earthenware bottle he'd never seen before with WHISKY in large letters along the side. Did the whisky belong to Monsieur Brisket?

He noticed two extra sapling bunks, made of opened flour bags nailed onto a frame of bush poles, amongst the clutter. Two pillows, also from flour bags, smelled as if they were stuffed with gum leaves. Did this mean the Brisket family would be living here until they found somewhere more permanent?

Yann wrenched the lid off the jar. He picked out a pickle and began to eat it in quick bites, gulping the food down. What with all the subterfuge, the hiding necessitated by Cyrano having put out the trooper's eye, Yann could barely remember when he'd last had a decent meal. Still chewing, he ran his fingers over the snakeskin still spread across the hearth. It was drying nicely.

The cradles had stopped roaring along Forest Creek. Diggers were returning to their tents. Yann decided it was time to go back to his sleeping space before Dora and Bethany arrived. They might ask some awkward questions. Making sure his pigtail was in place, he popped another pickle in his mouth and grabbed the jar.

He jerked the calico closed just as Magali and the Brisket children burst through the front door, their clothes smelling of dust overlaid with smoke and perspiration.

Cyrano arched his back, fluffed up his tail and began to move sideways towards the drape.

"*Chut!*" hissed Yann. "You must be quiet, for both our sakes!"

"Now children, before preparing the evening meal I will mix up some herbs for you to take to ease your chests." The pestle ground against the mortar. "You first, Bethany."

"I 'ate 'erbs, Maggie!" Bethany stamped her foot.

Yann smiled. For once, he was unable to disagree with this odious child.

"I hhhhhh*ate* 'erbs, too!" chimed Dora. And then she uttered a long, "A-tishoo."

A whoosh and the front door opened. Someone stomped into the hut, jangling tools onto the floor. *Was this Monsieur Brisket, returning from his day panning by the creek?* Yann wondered.

"Me pick 'ad to be sharpened on *three* occasions by the blacksmith today … and me gad, too … yet I filled me matchbox with gold, ye'll be pleased to know," a man's voice announced.

"Why, that's wonderful, Mr Brisket! Would you like a drink before your evening meal?" Magali asked.

Yann heard water being poured into a metal container.

"I'll wash up first, and take me bucket outside," said Brisket, "before I sip a drop of me whisky if that's all right with ye, Maggie? Eat at pleasure; drink by measure is my motto."

Yann started. *Did the entire Brisket family now refer to Magali as Maggie? And for how long would they live in his home?* Permanently?

A smile crept to his mouth again. The word 'Maggie' reminded him of the magpie bird he'd seen picking up stray things to store in its nest. Magali also had a habit of collecting 'things': sick children, impoverished diggers, animals, herbs, poisonous insects. Where Magali was concerned, the list was endless. He heard pots being banged, water boiling.

"Somebody's stolen my jar of pickles," Magali called out, "Dora, Bethany, did you eat them?"

"No, Maggie. Pickles is dis-*gus*ting!" *That had to be Bethany*, Yann told himself.

Magali sighed, as if she too was tiring of Bethany's complaints.

Giggles erupted. Yann heard the clatter of knucklebones.

"Now 'scatters'!" shouted Dora.

"I'm not doing 'scatters', I wanna do 'dumps'!" Bethany's words were followed by the sound of sheep bones being flung across the floor.

Afraid Cyrano would bound out and join in the game, Yann held the cat firmly by the scruff.

"Stop squabbling, children!" called Magali. "What about 'thread the needle' or 'catching flies' … but, mind, you must remember to keep your palms down." Pause. "I used to play with goat shanks when I was an infant."

The girls went into a huddle of conversation.

Without warning, Magali swished back the calico drape. "I believe this is yours." She lobbed the snakeskin onto Yann's bed.

In her spare hand, she held a spatula with a dab of liquid on one end. She lunged for Cyrano, prised his jaws apart, slid the spatula along the cat's tongue and clamped Cyrano's jaws shut until he was forced to swallow.

"What are you doing? Are you feeding Cyrano more absinthe?" Yann sat bolt upright. "Leave my cat alone!"

In the background, knucklebones clicked again.

"You must keep Cyrano subdued or he will give you away!" hissed Magali. Wisps straggled from the combs in her hair.

"I will not have him go mad from the Green Fairy drink!"

"Would you prefer to languish in a Melbourne prison, for the sake of your animal?"

"He saved my life … helped me escape!" Yann decided not to elaborate, tell her about stealing the boots.

"And I think you should remove that gold cross. I know of few Asians who are Christian."

"I will not!" His mouth became a fist. "This cross was a first communion gift from my *maman*."

"You must learn to let go of the past, Yann." Her eyes homed in on the empty jar propped against his pillow. "So it was *you* who stole my pickles!"

"I was hungry."

Magali let out a long sigh. "Oh, forgive me, Yann." She enveloped him in a suffocating hug smelling of dust and dandelions. "But these children have lost their mother." Before he could protest, she added, "Madeleine would approve of my actions." She jabbed a finger skywards. "Up there, she knows I have your wellbeing at heart."

"Is everything all right, Maggie?" The digger was back inside the hut.

"My lodger is merely homesick, Mr Brisket."

"Sick in the head, more like," Yann heard him mutter.

Magali yanked the drape shut behind her. "I am serving couscous for the evening meal, Mr Brisket. I am sure you will enjoy the North African dish."

"Couscous, eh? Eat such things as are set before ye."

"St Luke, I believe?"

"Ay, a good dinner sharpens wit and softens the heart."

Yann took a quick peek through the gap, surprised to find Magali towering over a stringy man with a droopy moustache clad in battered moleskins. *Whatever did she see in such an unprepossessing creature?*

Soon he detected cooking smells. His mouth began to water, but Magali pushed no food through the drape, no steaming heap of couscous. Cyrano was back on his pillow, asleep again. Yann made up his mind to climb out the window and head for Pennyweight Flat as soon as they had all eaten and settled down for the night.

He heard Brisket pat his stomach and say, "What a wonderful meal, Maggie. Now I can relax with no more cradle to rock tomorrer. What are ye plannin' to prepare for the Sabbath? My dear late wife used to do a marrow roast of a Sunday." His voice caught and he paused for a moment. "Butcher used to give 'er a bone marrer real cheap."

"I think the children could do with some gruel. That should ease their chests."

"I hhhhaaaate gruel!" Bethany complained.

"I will add mace and a little lemon peel and you will find it quite delightful," replied Magali in a measured tone.

"My wife used to make Miner's Broth to 'elp ease our lassies' ailments."

"I h-h-hate Miner's Broth!" shouted Dora.

Yann started to feel queasy with all this talk of food.

"There has been an influx of flies and ants in our home. I think it's most probably the fault of Ya…"

Yann held his breath as Magali almost spilled out his name.

"What about some old style flypaper?" suggested Brisket.

"How is that done?"

"Ye boil linseed oil, add a small amount of ground resin until ye 'ave a stringy paste. Spread on sheets of 'eavy paper … I'll show ye how."

Yann let out his breath.

"Eat not the bread of idleness," Brisket murmured thoughtfully.

"Proverbs 31, verse 27, if I'm not mistaken?" said Magali.

"Quite right, Maggie, and no one could ever accuse ye of bein' a lazy bones."

The time passed slowly. The conversation became desultory, disjointed. The clock on the mantel chimed ten. As well as Monsieur Brisket's vague mutterings, Yann could hear the sound of music, a jig being played. Or was that a waltz coming from the Red Boulder Hotel?

32

The children fell asleep even before Magali had finished reciting their evening prayer. Everything remained quiet, apart from Mr Brisket's resounding snores echoing through the crossbeams.

Yann tied the snake pelt around his waist. He pulled up his braces and eased his arms into his leather waistcoat. He tied a red and white spotted neckcloth around his throat and ran his fingers over the daguerreotype of his mother twice, for good luck. If only his *maman* could see him—he was living in a way she could never have imagined.

Shaking Cyrano awake, Yann opened the window above his bed and tossed the cat out. He grabbed his lamp and shinned down past the snake's head.

The music was louder now and the sound, carrying through the night air from the Concert and Assembly Hall, was enticing. Flaming torches lit up the Red Boulder Hotel. Seeing carriages and drays and coachmen, Yann decided to go closer. If he stayed under cover of darkness, he could watch from a distance. It was a while since he had seen people dressed up in their finest and he was curious to find out what the inhabitants of Forest Creek wore on such an occasion.

Cyrano, crouched in the scrub at his feet, yawned and stretched. Yann slung the cat over his shoulder and strode off towards the hotel. He threaded his way through tents, cradles, tin pans and stray boots. *How did diggers manage to lose one boot?* he wondered. *Were they so drunk they tumbled into mine shafts on their way back to their tents late at night and never noticed the difference?*

A Chinaman trotted by with his possessions dangling on the edge of a long pole, showing not the slightest interest in the festivities.

Yann made for the Concert and Assembly Hall on the western side of the inn. An impressive array of carriages lined Mount Alexander Road. He counted one four-wheeled phaeton, several two-wheeled gigs, a couple of sulkies and a dray with oxen nudging at the grass. Horses were tied to the hitching rail. The coachmen stamped their feet and sipped whisky while they waited.

Standing in the shadow of a straggly gum on the opposite side of the highway, Yann had a clear view. He could see the gleaming instruments of the German band on the stage, and the food laid out in the London fashion along one side of the hall.

William Bass, resplendent in a maroon velvet jacket with quilted collar and cuffs, greeted people as they entered.

A mazurka started up. Merchants' wives and daughters whirled around the dance floor in the arms of local businessmen clad in their best frockcoats. Miners removed their boots and, handing their tickets to the doorman, slunk into the hall in their stockinged feet. The diggers huddled in a bunch, furtively tapping. Some sucked on clay pipes, talking from the sides of their mouths as if they had never seen such a sight before, had never rubbed shoulders with such glittering company.

Silas Holmes-Lacy stood chatting with Francis Angus. William Bass's sister, in oyster grey taffeta, tapped Mr Angus on the shoulder with her flower-printed fan. He turned, smiled, and drew her into the conversation.

Yann could see no sign of Holmes-Lacy's wife, Viola, but his eyes were drawn to a young lady. Her head was held high and her blonde curls were swept up into a wreath of pink heath. She wore a powder blue crinoline with a lacy shawl thrown loosely around her shoulders. Guided by a dark-haired, bearded man of medium build she threw her arms wide in the dance. As she laughed, dimples formed in her cheeks. She withdrew her arms, placed her hand over her mouth and began to giggle.

The buttons on her partner's jacket gleamed in the glow cast by the silver candelabras ranged along the middle, and at each end, of the table. With a jolt, Yann knew he was looking at Clemency Holmes-Lacy. She seemed so ladylike dressed like that. He had always believed she was younger than he. Had he been wrong?

Her dance partner looked suspiciously like a policeman. Or was he a trooper? He wore baggy trousers, but his short coat resembled that of a lawman.

Yann backed off until he was deep into the shadows. The trooper's eyes were intense and flashing. But … could Yann trust Clem not to betray him? He clenched his teeth, deciding he had seen enough. Once again, doubts began to enter his mind about Clemency Holmes-Lacy.

About to leave for the cemetery, he noticed a guest dressed differently from the others. This individual wore a striped maillot. He had a straggly beard and puffed on a cheroot. He lingered near the doorway below and to the left of the stage which led into the Red Boulder bar, the gaming room, the sitting rooms and the accommodation.

Yann's heart began to race. Should he enter the hall, accost the man—the Saint-Simonian—and demand that he hand over the chapbook?

Barnaby, carrying a tray of drinks and wearing a white shirt with a frilled placket, pushed past through the door to the left of the stage into the Concert and Assembly Hall. When Yann looked again, the man in the maillot had vanished.

"*Merde*!" Yann cursed. He had missed his chance to redeem the wages William Bass owed him.

The music swung into a jig. In the distance diggers began to fire off weapons, discharging and reloading their arms. Had someone struck it lucky? Or was this a deterrent to would-be thieves and assassins?

A shower of fireworks exploded into the sky. A mouth organ played 'Old Folks at Home' and the familiar ache in his throat of not belonging threatened to overwhelm him.

"*Allez viens*, Cyrano," he murmured, pulling his hat down low. "We are off to Pennyweight Flat Cemetery and let's pray Clem has not deceived us."

As he turned, two women from the sly grog shop further up the road ambled past gawping.

"Well, I never," said one, pointing a fat bejewelled finger. "Mr Holmes-Lacy is havin' a fine old time, enoyin' hisself, *and* his wife taken poorly." She gave a loud hiccup. "'Is daughter is wif 'im too."

"He's a *hard* man, Mr Holmes-Lacy," said her friend who wore a grubby gingham skirt. "Never gives credit, no matter what." She added, "He's probably got a business deal on the go. He's never one to let an opportunity pass to make a bit of lucre." She tugged on her cap. "What's wrong wiv 'is wife?"

"She lost 'er baby." An amethyst ring threw out a purple light as the bejewelled one brought her finger to her cheek in thought. "It were stillborn, I fink."

"I never had no time for 'er, not for that Viola Holmes-Lacy. Uppity she is, but ..." Pause. "'Ow many's that she's lost? Four mites or five?" asked the woman in the grubby skirt.

"Think it might be the fourth lad going off to the children's boneyard, and I fink there was a lassie too. Old Holmes-Lacy won't never pay for a decent burial, oh no! 'E just shovels 'em into that worthless piece o' ground and be done wiv it. And ... what wiv all those boy brats he's spat out! I even saw 'is daughter goin' about Diggings in trousers once when she thought no one was lookin'."

"How very bold!"

"Yeah, ain't it?" The bejewelled one sighed. "Wanna go inside? We could partake of some free nosh."

"Ain't free, ticket cost one pound five shillin' *and* wine at the usual rates. Too dear by 'alf." They kept walking up the road.

Yann asked himself: *As her mother was unwell, would Clem have left a note at Pennyweight Flat Cemetery?*

And more importantly: If she had left a note, could he trust her?

33

Inside Pennyweight Flat Cemetery, Cyrano stretched and stalked about. He pushed his nose into the stones encircling each grave. He stopped, sniffed and lifted his svelte head, making the same chattering noises he had made at the sight of the snake.

"Surely not another serpent?" Yann sighed. Did these creatures never sleep?

Without warning, the cat started to dig. Was this where the digger, Jonas, and his wife had buried their infant? Or was it another grave? They all looked the same. Lumps and bumps and bits of broken rubble.

Earth shot out between Cyrano's legs.

"*Arrête!*" Yann shouted. "Stop!"

The cat lost interest in digging. With one languid bound, he leapt into a grey box tree on the edge of the knoll. Encased in a nest of overhead stars, he settled down and thrashed his tail with contentment.

Yann threaded his way among the mounds, doing his best not to stumble onto any burial sites. Images of children cut down with diseases like diphtheria, pneumonia and dysentery filled his mind. Death by starvation? Shivers jiggled down his backbone as he swung the lantern, searching for the grave nominated by Clemency. Fourth to the right, he reminded himself.

In the flickering glow thrown out by the lamp he spied a pink ribbon poking from beneath the makeshift headstone—a rough rock propped upright and held in place by a piece of rusty wire. Was this the one? Had Clem placed the ribbon there to guide him? Only feet away the light picked up the disturbed soil of a freshly dug grave. The grave of Clemency's recently deceased sibling? he wondered. She had looked happy dancing with the uniformed man. Was death so commonplace for her and her parents that they no longer cared?

Yann berated himself for thinking such a thing. As obnoxious and uppity as Viola Holmes-Lacy was, no mother deserved to lose a baby.

The oil lamp on the ground threw out long shadows. Yann slid the tips of his fingers beneath the rock, taking care not to send it toppling onto the fresh grave. He pushed inwards until he felt the blunt edge of a folded piece of paper. He locked his pinkie under the paper, eased it out and unfolded it. As he began to read, the scudding clouds parted overhead. The paper was smudged with dirt and had a damp feel.

His fingers, unsteady, traced the words and he mouthed them to better understand what Clem had written.

I will meet you when the kookaburras first begin to laugh, Sunday morn on the banks of Forest Creek. Chinaman's Bend is situated right here. Follow the creek until the bend becomes a sharp U. The rushes are thick and shaped like a flugelhorn. You cannot miss it. C

A neat cross in green ink marked the spot.

"Shaped like a flugelhorn?"

A grin crept over his face. At last! He was about to make his fortune and, when he had enough money, he would set out to find his father.

His enthusiasm faded. Should he reply to her message? He tore off one corner of the paper, scribbled with his pencil: '*I see yoo too-morro*'. He folded the scrappy reply and inched it in beside the pink ribbon.

A breeze had picked up. The trees swayed. The night was becoming cold and goose bumps rippled his skin. He hugged his arms to his chest and pulled his hat down as far as it would go. A colony of bats flew over Pennyweight Flat Cemetery and Yann made up his mind to hurry back to the hut to get some sleep. Panning for gold was hard work. He would need all his strength in the morning.

"*Allez viens!*" He placed his fingers in his mouth and gave out a high-pitched whistle. "Come, Cyrano, we're leaving."

No response.

"*On y va!*" he shouted. "We're off!"

The box trees ruffled in the wind, but he could see no sign of Cyrano. He jogged across to the edge of the knoll and peered up.

"*Tu viens?* Are you coming?"

The cat was no longer there.

"*Zut!*" Yann spat in annoyance.

Had the cat wandered off unnoticed, his mind confused from the Green Fairy drink, while his master scrabbled around for the piece of paper? Was he now lost in the bush, afraid and disoriented? And what if the trooper stumbled upon Cyrano? He could wring the cat by the neck and toss the corpse away, without giving it a second thought. Or he might sell Cyrano to Johnnie Lee to be cooked with carrots and peas and advertised in his restaurant as the *plat du jour.*

Revulsion washed through Yann. And then he wondered: *Had Cyrano tumbled into an open grave and, groggy from the absinthe, been unable to climb out?*

He prowled around the cemetery, checking. He came upon the unmarked grave where the digger in the threadbare smock had buried his child, and swung his lamp back and forth. The flame flickered in the air currents, creating dark shapes: rabbits' ears and witches' hats, old crones with warts on their noses. Just like the games he had played on the silk-lined walls of his bedroom in Paris.

Despite these distractions, Yann was able to spot the scratch marks where Cyrano had been digging. The wind dropped and a sickly smell filled his nostrils. Had the miner not gone down far enough? Was his child buried in a too-shallow grave? Surely not. Yann had heard him work away for a long while with his pick and shovel. His toiling had seemed interminable. Yann shuddered and moved on. The whole cemetery seemed to reek of death and he felt the nausea rise up in his chest. He circled the edge of the knoll, calling the cat's name as he went.

"Cyrano, *où es-tu?*" He put his fingers in his mouth and whistled again.

Still no response. The moon went behind a cloud. Yann decided to leave the cemetery and search for Cyrano in the surrounding scrub.

"*Où es-tu?*" he called.

Making his way towards Forest Creek he collided with a long tom and almost lost his balance. "*Putain!*" He stubbed his toe on a puddling machine, cursed again. "*Merde! Merde! Merde!*"

Stumbling through the gloom, Yann knew he was nearing the creek by the stench of rotting offal seeping from the butcher's shamble. His hand brushed against something warm. Scuttling sounds filled his ears and he heard boots retreating through the long grass. He whipped around. The dim light caught the form of a man. Had he disturbed a fossicker raiding a successful digger's hole under cover of night?

Yann's shoulders slumped with resignation. Come tomorrow, he would be no better than such a man. Mining on a Sunday, which was illegal—and with no licence—was enough to have him chained to a log if he were sprung. Then again, he would only be panning for gold. Not stealing it. Night fossicking on someone else's claim was a greater sin than nicking items of clothing.

He continued to stumble around, calling for Cyrano. Inky shapes lunged. Stealthy digits rummaged. The whispering of trees and reeds

113

mingled with the hushes and shushes of human beings. Shapes merged with the night and disappeared. Yann was encircled by shapes, groped at by shapes. People with empty stomachs grabbled for colour, for the means to assuage their hunger. Some stopped and stared, their eyes ablaze with gold lust. Others moved on without a second glance. Shadows clung and shifted, but none of the shapes was Cyrano.

34

Next thing Yann knew a kookaburra was blasting its wake-up call in his ear, cackling on the branch of a tree right above the ground where he lay. He lifted his head from the spiky grass and prised his lids apart.

"*Chut!*" he yelled. "Be quiet!"

The bird took no notice. Yann's dagger was digging into his side and his bones ached. His hair, now loose, streamed over his right cheek.

"*Mon Dieu!*" he groaned, levering his body upright. What on earth was he doing here? Then he remembered Cyrano disappearing during the night. Not only that, but at daybreak he was due to meet Clemency Holmes-Lacy at Chinaman's Bend, on the banks of Forest Creek.

His fingers were stiff from the pre-dawn chill. He flexed them to restore circulation and plunged his hand into the pocket of his moleskins, searching for the plan Clem had left for him under her brother's—or was it her sister's?—gravestone in the cemetery. He eased the paper, still damp and smelling of death, out. Unfolding it, he traced the map of the creek with his index finger until he was certain he knew where to go.

Dawn was breaking. Faint rays peeped over the horizon. Soon the sun lifted the curtain of low clouds and a gilded haze spread across the countryside. He plucked a piece of grass, rubbed the spikelets off the stem and tied his locks back into a pigtail. He jammed his hat on his head and grabbed his now extinguished lamp. Following the reeds, he set off towards the bend in the creek which Clem had marked with a green cross.

The Diggings were silent. In deference to the Sabbath, the cradles were still. No one was about. Even the night fossickers had returned to their canvas hovels.

One bearded digger was sprawled in the open, sound asleep. A rifle rested in the crook of his elbow. He clasped a knife in his other hand. The embers of the fire were cold and an empty whisky bottle lay on its side nearby. Yann tiptoed past. Was the miner guarding his 'golden hole', or was it a claim he believed had the potential to become a 'jeweller's shop'? Or would the claim turn out to be a 'shicer', or 'duffer', producing nothing but dashed hopes? Would Yann's own hopes be dashed? If they were, it would not be for any lack of will on his part.

He pushed on towards the bend. As he went, doubts began to creep into his mind. What if Clem, enticed by the prospect of sharing a portion of the trooper's half of the £5 fine, had warned the uniformed man of Yann's intention to search for gold that Sunday morning?

He spied the area she had outlined in her note. The rushes bushed out at the top like the bell of an instrument, with wisps growing sideways along the stems. Were the wisps meant to represent the valves of the flugelhorn? Should he remain out of sight, see if Clem was truly alone before he approached? Concealing his body behind a straggly eucalypt, he waited.

Soon Clemency Holmes-Lacy appeared. She followed the course of the creek, lugging a voluminous carpetbag covered in brown tapestry swirls interspersed with leaves and pastel peonies. In her other hand, she gripped a dog leash. Princess Albert snuffled along behind, unusually reluctant. The dog stopped to inspect every hole, every stray barrow, every windlass.

Clem tugged on the leash. "Do get a hurry-on, Princess Albert, we are late!" The British bulldog immediately decided to squat. "Have you no self-control?" she sighed. "That's the fourth time you've urinated since we set out—*and* you've had nothing to drink since last evening."

Yann's shoulders relaxed. It didn't seem as though Clemency Holmes-Lacy had set a trap for him. On the point of emerging from behind the tree, he saw her glance about and the blood drained from his face. Was she expecting someone?

She placed her carpetbag on the ground, opened it and pulled out a pair of moleskins. She gave another quick look to see if anyone was watching before unbuttoning her gingham skirt. She let the clothing drop to the ground. Eyeing her slender legs, Yann felt himself grow hot. Her calves, pale as milk, were elegantly proportioned. Her feet were encased in ankle boots, and he flushed red as she inserted one leg, and then the other, into the trousers before hauling them up. She rolled her skirt into an oblong shape and stuffed it, together with her shawl, into the bag, then extracted a leather cap. She twisted her blonde curls into a knot and jammed on the headgear.

"*Oh, là!*" Yann breathed out.

Unlike his Parisian friends, he had never seen a *jeune femme* undress before, never seen any woman—not even Magali, despite their close proximity in the hut—remove her clothes. He had previously thought of Clemency Holmes-Lacy as a *gosse*, a kid. He had certainly never thought of her as *belle*. Hypnotised, he watched her tuck her smock into the waistband of the trousers. She pulled up her braces and yanked on the leash. Giving out a high-pitched squeal, the dog waddled after her.

"We are late, Princess Albert!" She turned and wagged a finger. "Yann will be waiting, so mind your manners and don't even look sideways at his monkey cat." She circled the clump of flugelhorn-shaped rushes, dragging the British bulldog after her.

Yann brushed the leaves and twigs off his clothing. He made sure his hair was neat, placed his hat on a jaunty angle. He could do nothing about the dirt beneath his fingernails, he told himself, skidding down the slope and onto the creek bank.

Clem looked up, startled. "Where have you been, Yann? I told you to meet me here at dawn!" She wore a frown on her face. Her topaz eyes were red-rimmed, as if she had been weeping.

"I am waiting up zere." He pointed.

"Aha! You did not trust me? You thought I might bring the law along?" Her tone was accusatory. "Do you really think I would betray you for a few measly shillings? I thought we were friends, Yann." A slick of tears washed over her gaze.

"But, ah," he murmured, "I see you dancing wis a trooper last night."

"So you have been spying on me?"

"I am sorreee." Princess Albert began to run a pink tongue across the toe of his boots and he shifted his legs. "You see, I am very afraid."

"I understand that." She sniffed. "And with good reason. Trooper Clovis has come into our store *twice* looking for you. He now wears a patch over one eye." Pause. "But I'm sure Robert O'Hara Burke is not the slightest bit interested in your misdemeanours."

"Robert O'…?" Yann frowned.

"The Irishman I was dancing with last evening. Mr Burke is gentry, you know. He resides in Beechworth and is the Ovens Police Inspector."

"Oh, *mon Dieu!* And he will arrest me?"

"You have no need to be concerned, Yann. Robert O'Hara Burke is far more interested in fighting in the Crimea. He even has grand plans to cross the entire continent of Australia from south to north, *and* he informs me he has a poor sense of direction. He even became lost once on the track from Beechworth to Yackandandah." She gave a scornful laugh. "Can you imagine how badly he will fare in this vast land?"

Yann felt a twinge of resentment that Clem should be so enthused about a man who could well throw him in prison.

She interrupted his thoughts. "Where is Cyrano?"

"'E 'as disappeared again."

"I am sorry. You must be distraught. On the other hand, perhaps it is as well. Your animal is too distinctive." She pushed the bulldog, who appeared deeply interested in the stink of snake blood, away from Yann's leg with her toe.

Did these clothes really smell so bad? he wondered.

"It's a shame," she continued, "for I am certain he and Princess Albert would have become firm friends." She bent, opened the carpetbag, and pulled out a small pickaxe. "You will have need of this."

"I thought I will be panning?" A hint of uncertainty crept into Yann's voice as he took the implement from her.

"Oh, no, it's far too dangerous for you to look for colour in the open." She strode to an area where the reeds had been woven into what appeared to be a mat, only a few feet from a shallow square mine. "You need to remain in hiding, in case the trooper comes looking for you."

Yann pointed at the claim. "But I cannot steal from anozzer man."

"You won't be digging in there, silly." She threw back the matting. "No, this is the place where you will make your fortune."

Yann found himself looking at a hole in the ground, as round as the one beside it was square, with a small windlass straddling the gap. The barrel and frame of the windlass had been manufactured from bush timber with a handle at one end. The rope around the horizontal cylinder was frayed and old.

"You are telling me I must search for gold in zere?" Yann was aghast, having imagined a pleasant Sunday morning panning for gold out in the open.

"Well, the situation is ideal for your needs. You can dig without worrying about the Native Police, or anyone else, arresting you."

Yann nudged away Princess Albert, who was now licking his trouser leg lovingly. "And zis mine, who she belong to?"

"The claim was originally worked by a Chinaman, a digger now gone from Forest Creek." She chewed her lip. "He may have died. I'm not sure." She clapped her hands. "Do please leave Yann alone, Princess Albert!"

Yann no longer cared about the dog licking his trousers. "You say a dead Chinese man? Is zis not bad luck?"

"Of course not! You could become extremely rich."

"And who will sift soil for ore while I am down in zere?"

"I shall." She opened her carpetbag wide.

Feeling ashamed at being more interested in his quest for gold than in the Holmes-Lacy family's loss, Yann took a breath. "I am sorree your muzzer lose her baby."

"Oh, I am almost becoming used to it now." When she looked up, tears trembled on Clem's lower lid. "Another one is gone to God, popped in an empty grocery box and shovelled into the ground at Pennyweight Flat Cemetery. Poor little Silas!"

"Silas?"

"Da names all the boys Silas, in the hope that one will grow up one day to carry on the family name. But I suspect that won't happen." She set her mouth in a straight line and changed the subject. "I could have sworn I brought a tin pan with me." She scrabbled around. "Oh, bother, it's not here. Mr Studs de Wolf was stocking up in the store for yet another trip and, in all the kerfoofle, I must have forgotten it." She scrabbled around some more, and then sighed. "Never mind, I shall find one."

Yann stared as she stuffed her skirt and shawl roughly back in. He was impressed at how well Clem coped with hardship. The girls he had known in Paris would have had a fit of the vapours if thrown into a similar situation.

Clem pulled out a candle in a wrought metal holder and waved it. "Well, don't stand there gawping!"

"What is zis for?"

"It's called a 'spider' in mining parlance and it's so you can *see*, silly. Just insert the spike at the base into the mine wall." She thrust the candle and a box of matches at him. "Don't forget, you will need to fill up with more oil later." She pointed at the extinguished lamp on the ground.

"*Merci.*" Yann tucked the candle in his pocket.

"You should climb down quickly, before the police come to check that no person is mining on the Sabbath."

"And you, Clem, what will you say to police?"

"I'll worry about that when the time comes. Now git!"

35

Yann slotted the pickaxe into his belt alongside his dagger, swung his legs over and lowered his body through the gap. Straining to see in the dimness, he was just able to make out chocks of wood jutting from the walls.

Using the chocks for footholds, he eased his way down the shaft. Through the gloom he could see a bamboo bucket dangling from a hook at the end of a rope. A dank smell filtered into his nostrils. Bits of stone and clumps of earth broke free. Using the rope to guide him, he kept edging down into the mine. His fingers cast about for handholds as he slowly made his way towards the bottom of the shaft. The soil turned from black, to gravel, to stone mixed with clay. Sweat ran down his neck. He continued inching through the darkness, past the drift and hard gravel.

A wave of relief flooded through him as his feet touched the ground. He was unable to see at first. After a few seconds, his vision cleared and he gazed up at the circle of blue light above his head.

Clem peered over. "Are you all right, Yann?" A blonde curl strayed from beneath her leather cap. "You are very quiet."

He shouted and waved, doing his best to sound confident. "*Oui*, I am very well. I 'ave now reached bottom." He prodded, ran his fingers over the surface. "Ah, and I sink I can feel quartz."

"Quartz? Why, that's wonderful. That means there should be gold!" Her voice echoed downwards, bouncing off the walls around him. "Now start digging! When your bucket is full, call out and I will wind it up and start sifting for colour. In the meantime, while you are at work with your pickaxe, I shall do my best to find a tin pan ..." Her voice trailed off as she moved away.

Yann felt suddenly alone. The walls closed in and his heart paddled. His shirt was drenched with perspiration and he hadn't even begun to dig.

Humming *Frère Jacques* to calm himself, he pulled the candle from his pocket. He reached for the packet of matches, opened it and swiped a match against his leather waistcoat. An explosion of sulphurous sparks and smoke filled the shaft. Pushing the flame against the wick, Yann suppressed the urge to cough.

When the air had cleared and the flame had taken hold of the wick, he took a deep breath and wedged the candle into a niche in the wall. He looked around. Apart from the bucket left hanging at the end of the rope, the mine appeared to be abandoned. Why had the miner left? Was it a duffer? Had it produced no gold at all, causing the digger to leave in despair? Or was there another reason? He unhooked the bucket.

Pulling the pickaxe from his belt, he began to chip away at the quartz. The pile of rough stone began to mount. Under the flimsy light of the candle, he looked around for a spade or other implement suitable for shovelling the pile into the bucket. He could see nothing, no tools left behind, but his eyes latched onto the beginnings of a cross passage branching off horizontally—a mine drive. He lifted the candle from the niche. The flame flared briefly to reveal what looked like a small cave. The drive entrance, littered with rough stones, showed no trace of any tool.

"*Putain!*" Why hadn't Clem thought to bring a spade? Or was she looking for one right this minute?

Yann had no option but to use his hands. He replaced the candle, scooped up the gravelled soil and dropped it into the bucket. He threw another handful in, and another. In no time, his fingers were rough and sore. "Aïe, aïe!" He shook them.

He could feel blisters forming on the heel of his hand and the bucket was only half full.

"Clem!" he called.

No answer. Untying his scarf, he pulled it from his neck and bound his right hand with the spotted cloth. He proceeded to fill the bucket to the brim.

"Clem!" he called again.

Still no answer.

Yann decided to climb back out of the mine, wind the dirt to the surface, ready to be panned as soon as Clem came back. If she had found a cradle as well, that would be even better. But a cradle would be noisy. The clatter would be a giveaway that he was fossicking on the Sabbath.

He hooked the bucket back onto the rope and rammed his hat firmly on his head. Using the chocks for footholds, he grasped at the walls with his hands. As he started to move upwards, his left boot slipped off. He wavered, swayed, wavered again. His boot knocked against the bucket and he almost lost his balance. Should he climb up the rope attached to the windlass? But the rope was frayed, he told himself, and weighed down by the fruits of his labour.

Floundering around, his toe found another foothold, sharper this time, like a piece of rough rock. Then his right boot slipped. He hung on with all his strength, managing to lasso the rope around his leg. If he tumbled back down the shaft and broke a limb, no one would know. He might lie there for days. Or even die, if Clem never returned.

His biceps were straining with the effort of holding his body upright. His hands were trembling. And was that blood coursing down his wrist? Yann took a deep breath, held it, and succeeded in getting both feet positioned. He kicked the rope away and continued up until his fingers felt the rim of the shaft. The sun hit the back of his hand through his neckcloth, searing the lacerated skin.

Heaving his elbows onto the turf, he clung to a tuft of spiky grass. He thrust his body up and out, onto the dusty ground. His hat flew off. Blinded momentarily by the shimmering haze, he turned his head to the left. To the right. His vision cleared. No one was there. Even Clem's carpetbag was gone. Had she deliberately left him, gone to bargain for her share of the fine, dobbed him in by telling the licence inspector he was illegally mining? Was she now directing the inspector to the spot? And where was Cyrano?

The Forest Creek stench, exacerbated by the heat, was pungent and he felt like gagging. Had the butcher slaughtered more animals early this morning? Was Cyrano one of them?

Cicadas rattled, and he wondered what he should do next. Search for a pan without Clemency Holmes-Lacy's help? Or unwind the scarf binding his hand, and sift for wash gold through that?

He let out a sigh. First, he needed to bring the bucket to the surface. He snatched up his hat and positioned the brim low to protect his eyes from the glare of the sun. The metal windlass, cooked by the rays, burned through the fabric protecting his skin but he kept winching. The bucket was old and he prayed that the bamboo would remain intact.

The device groaned and squealed. The rope became even more frayed. Would it hold out? Or would all the gravel he had worked so hard to get hurtle back down into the shaft?

He continued to wind, doing his best not to jerk the rope. His muscles ached in protest, but he struggled on.

Without warning, a cry rang out along the creek bank: "Joe! Joe!" He wasn't the only fossicker searching for gold illegally.

Worse, a licence inspector was about.

36

The ground thundered with the sound of horses' hooves—it seemed more than one licence inspector was moving along Forest Creek.

"Joe! Joe! Joe!" Another warning ricocheted through the reeds.

Yann's hand momentarily froze.

With a jerk, he let go. The lever whipped over and over, rotating in wild circles. He heard an ominous thump as the bucket hit the bottom of the shaft, and he prayed it had not shattered into a thousand pieces. He swung his legs into the gap and began to scramble down into the mine. Not daring to use the rope in case it broke, he groped for handholds. As if in a bad dream, his boots fumbled for the chocks of wood set into the walls.

His hat flew off again, floated downwards, swooping from side to side until it disappeared from view. Yann's throat was parched. He yearned for water and, by the time he reached the bottom of the shaft, his clothing was drenched with sweat. Gravel and dirt crunched beneath his feet but he had no time to check if the bucket had broken.

"*Il faut que je me cache!*" he said. "I must hide!"

In the niche, the candle still burned. Licking thumb and forefinger as best he could with a dry tongue, he extinguished the wick. His heart battered against his rib cage and, dropping to his hands and knees, he scuttled into the cross passage entrance.

Around him, everything was as dark as pitch. Even when his eyes had become accustomed to the gloom, he could barely see his hand in front of his face. He bent over to make his body as small as possible. Huddled in his hiding place he waited for the inspectors to shine their lamp.

"*Ah, la vache!*" he cursed, realising he had left his hat lying in the middle of the shaft.

Would the inspectors see the hat and know for certain he was there, mining illegally? The headwear was Chinese in style and Yann knew Asians were unpopular, resented for sending their colour back home to China rather than ploughing the gold back into the local economy. If the troopers saw the hat, would they believe he was a Chinaman and be even more incensed?

A wild screech interrupted his thoughts. Startled, Yann peeked out to see Cyrano flying down the shaft. The cat's claws were splayed out, pulverising the air, as if to break his fall.

"Sorry, monkey cat!" Clem, bits of hair wisping from beneath her cap, peered over. "Are you there, Yann?"

Yann exhaled. "*Oui*, I am 'ere," he said, relieved it was only Clem.

"Then conceal your monkey cat! I came upon him beneath a bush … or rather, Princess Albert did!"

"Where 'ave you been, Clem?"

"I was forced to venture further than I expected. I was almost at the cemetery when I came upon a pugilistic encounter, a fight between a Chinaman and a European digger on Pennyweight Flat over a disputed claim …"

"What about licence inspectors?" he interrupted.

Ignoring his question, she launched into a long explanation. "Well, then I saw Da and ducked into some shrubbery. That's how Princess Albert came across your monkey cat, and they fell in love instantly!" Sigh. "I was afraid Da would be furious to come upon me gallivanting around the Diggings and would insist I go home to help prepare the Sunday dinner. Mama is still poorly and we are partaking of Mock Venison, which is really roast leg of mutton!" Heavy sigh. "I loathe cooking and, oh dear, we are out of bay leaf and the marinade would not be as tasty …"

Yann grabbed the cat with one hand.

He massaged his own neck, stiff from gazing upwards, with the other. "Should you not leave?" he called. "Zey might catch you!"

"Oh, I'll spin them a tale. Just make sure *you* keep Cyrano out of sight. And, above all, keep him quiet! He makes such a terrible noise when he is annoyed, an awful howling!"

"But, but … zey might arrest you and chain you to a log!"

"Twaddle! I am now clad in my skirt again." She lifted her cap. "I simply need to doff this and tell them I am taking a Sunday stroll." Curls tumbled over her face. "Here is your pan." Yann ducked as a cylindrical object slewed down into the mine. "It has a few perforations, but is preferable to nothing."

The tin pan clattered to the ground, missing Cyrano, who was now perched on Yann's shoulder—flexing his claws in a mixture of contentment and terror—by a whisker.

"*Merci*, Clem." Eyeing bits of broken bamboo, Yann prodded them with the toe of his boot. "But I sink ze bucket 'as broken."

"Oh, bother! You have spilled your wash dirt then?"

"And I do not 'ave a shovel," he added. This whole gold digging exercise was turning out to be a disaster. He had never imagined working a claim to gain a living could be so arduous.

"Oh, double bother! Did you say a shovel? I never thought of that! I saw a shovel, too, on the slopes of Pennyweight Flat. I am not myself today. The Physician, Surgeon and Accoucheur was not available to help Mama, due to having departed for Melbourne. So… another Silas is gone to God, not at all fair!"

Princess Albert gave a sudden agitated woof. The bulldog's bark alternated between high-pitched and guttural. Yann could hear the clop, clop of horses' hooves as the inspectors rounded the creek and entered Chinaman's Bend. Grabbing Cyrano by the scruff, he scrambled back into the cross passage entrance.

"*Chut!*" he hissed at the cat. "Now be quiet!"

Cyrano held up a languid paw and began to lick. Yann noted that his breath smelled less of the Green Fairy drink than before. Was the cat now sober? He certainly seemed alert, and yet calm.

Above him, Yann heard voices.

"A good mornin' to ye, lassie. I hope ye're not tin pannin' on the Sabbath? Ye know it's breakin' the law."

"Panning on a Sunday?" Clemency gave a tinkly laugh. "Whatever gave you that idea, sir?"

"Ye've got dirt on yer boots. Have ya been puddlin' then?"

"I'm simply taking a stroll, sir, enjoying the fresh air."

"The Commissioner's arrived in Forest Creek and he takes a dim view of workin' a claim on Sabbath."

"I have no claim to work."

"Well, you're a handsome young lass, but handsome is as handsome does. How do I know ye're not committin' the terrible sin of blasphemy on the Lord's Day?"

Princess Albert gave a cautious woof.

"Git away, mutt!"

The bulldog yelped.

"Well, I think ye're lyin'!"

"I am not lying!"

Horse's hooves rang out as a second trooper arrived.

"Ye've just arrived in time, mate. I think we got us a felon. And a pretty lookin' felon she is too!"

Yann's heart rippled in his chest.

Cyrano pricked his ears.

"I've done nothing, sirs, I swear!" Clem was begging now. "Leave me alone!"

A choir of cicadas started up, making it difficult to hear. Yann was just able to make out the sounds of struggle in the scrub. A horse whinnied. What should he do?

A scream rang out. "Stop it! Leave me alone!"

"Give us a kiss, lass, and I'll forget all about it, yer lyin' and all. Just one kiss!"

"Get your hands off me! You are inebriated!"

Yann heard Nathaniel Clovis say, "I'll look the other way." The trooper gave a lecherous laugh. "Not that I wouldn't mind watchin'."

"You've only got one eye to watch wiv!" His fellow trooper hooted and slapped his thigh in amusement.

"And my one good eye tells me she's ripe for the pickin'!"

"Get away, you simpleton! The Ovens Police Inspector, Robert O'Hara Burke, is a close friend of mine. I will have you dismissed for harassment! And for drinking while you are meant to be working!"

Raucous laughter this time.

Cyrano stiffened. His ears pricked up, and he shot from the safety of the cross passage. He began to hurtle up the shaft, raking the walls as he rocketed towards the surface.

Clem's voice was muffled now.

Yann reached for his dagger with sweaty hands. Should he follow, risk being arrested all over again? He grasped the blade between his teeth.

Slipping and slithering, he started clambering upwards.

37

Hauling his body to the top of the shaft, Yann clasped his fingers on the rim. He steadied himself on a chock of wood and peered over to see Clemency, arms flailing, wrestling with a tow-haired trooper. Her curls were awry, her smock pulled low over one shoulder.

The man's uniform was ragged and a dirty kerchief covered his face. The second trooper, astride a horse and wearing a black patch, swung down from his saddle and stood by watching. A louche smile etched his grog-blotched face, as if he revelled in the scene before him.

Untethered, their mounts began to graze. The saddles remained strapped on and the horses flicked at flies with their uncombed tails. They moved away, still grazing. Rifles poked from the holsters on the saddlebags, but the men seemed uninterested in the weapons. Did they think Clem was on her own and an easy make?

Keeping her distance, Princess Albert huddled and whimpered.

Clem's eyes flashed with fright as, letting out a grunt, she clawed and scratched and attempted to sink her teeth into the trooper's arm. From the corner of his eye, Yann saw Cyrano make a move: stomach low, he slunk past the British bulldog.

Unsure if he could take on two men and win, Yann removed the dagger from his mouth. He grasped the handle with slippery fingers. The tow-haired trooper wrangled Clemency Holmes-Lacy to the ground and a feeling of horror flooded through Yann. The trooper yanked up her skirt, ran his grubby fingers across her thigh. Clem struggled to release the trooper's grasp.

"Get away from me, you oaf!" She wrenched at the handkerchief covering the trooper's face but was unable to get a grip.

Finally, she managed to yank the fabric off to reveal the man's face, sharp and mean as a fox. "I do like to see young lasses with a bit o' spirit!" he said, ogling her.

"*Salaud!*" Yann breathed. He saw that the horses were too far away for him to grab one of the rifles, and wished he owned a firearm. "Bastard! I'll get you for this! If I had a gun you would be dead!"

Brandishing his dagger he began to run. Growling and spitting, Cyrano shot past him. The cat hurtled towards the tow-haired trooper while Princess Albert, now frothing at the mouth, let out a menacing bark. The animals rushed in tandem across the scrubby grass. As they launched themselves, Yann heard a pounding of hooves and looked up. The horses had bolted.

Nathaniel Clovis yelled, "Eh, me nag's gone" and took off.

Cyrano's claws ripped at the tow-haired trooper's skin. The trooper flung his arms across his face to protect himself. Blood filled a gash on the lawman's hand as he attempted to push the yowling Cyrano away. Yann lifted his dagger to stab.

"No, Yann!" Clem twisted her head around. "I will deal with this wretched excuse for a human being!"

Leaping up, she aimed at the man's side and kicked. Kicked again. She kicked once more, aiming at his trouser leg now clenched in Princess Albert's jaws.

"Oooouch. Oh, my Gawd!" The trooper's cry pierced the air. He rolled over and, with difficulty, managed to push the snarling dog away and stagger to his feet. "Jesus Christ!" Clutching himself, he stumbled off.

"Oi, oi, Neddy!" hollered Clovis in the distance. "Come back!"

Clouds of dust billowed up.

"Eh, wait for me!" The tow-haired trooper limped after Clovis and the horses. "A wild marsupial tore me to shreds! A mad dog's bitten me, and that slut destroyed my manhood. Heeeelp, don't leave!"

Yann rushed to Clemency's side. Tears slid from her eyes, washing trails of clean skin through the dust smeared across her face. Choking back sobs, she adjusted her smock.

"He nearly had his way with me." She shivered. "His breath coming through that filthy rag was as foul as I have ever smelled."

"You was very, very courageous, Clem."

Yann placed his arm around her and held on tight until he felt her body tremors begin to slow.

"Well, I had one small victory." She gave a brief, sardonic giggle. "I think I got him in the cods!"

"*Oui*. You did." A grin split Yann's face. "'E is in much pain."

"Serve me right for coming without my rifle today. I suppose I am lucky they didn't push a gun barrel into my chest." Her mouth was a grim line as she tucked her smock back roughly into her skirt. "I hate this place! I hate the greed, the drunkenness. I hate the dirt. I hate the children dying. I hate the way people pack up and move on before you really get to know them. I hate it, hate it, HATE the stinky smell of Forest Creek, loathe the entire Diggings!"

Yann shrugged. "I am not 'appy, too."

Her eyes were bleak. "So, now I have got to know you, I suppose *you* will be moving on as well?" Her voice quavered.

Yann shrugged again.

"Even they will be parted now they have found one another." She indicated Princess Albert and Cyrano, now licking each other on the snout.

About to swear he would never leave Clem, Yann knew he could not do so. Finding his father was the reason he had come to Australia and he would be moving on as soon as he had enough money.

He bit back the words. "But, but …"

"See, you will be off like all the rest." She lowered her gaze and then clapped her hands and pointed. "Or maybe not!"

"Wh-what?" Yann looked down, seeing nothing.

"Look! Look!"

"What ees it?"

She swooped on the toe of his boot. "Don't move, Yann. Do not move an inch! Stay exactly as you are!"

"Wh-wh …" His mouth dropped open. Had Clem discovered a poisonous creature on his footwear? Was this another jockey spider? He examined the grimy leather for a black belly with a red stripe but saw nothing.

Clem rose. She lifted a not-so-steady finger to show the tip sparkling in the sunshine. "Eureka! I think, if I am not mistaken and I'm rarely wrong about such things, we have found colour."

"Gold on my b-b-boot?"

"Yes, right there, gold on your boot!" Her topaz eyes bored through him. "You have apparently carried it from the mine without realising."

His laugh was weak. "I sink you 'ave discovered a poisonous spider."

"A poisonous spider? What a pessimist you are! Concern yourself with making your fortune, not with miserable arachnids." She held her head on an angle and the dimples showed in her cheeks. "Get back down into the mine this instant!"

Dumbstruck, Yann continued to gawp. Despite the gunk on her face, he couldn't help thinking how beautiful Clem looked.

"Whatever are you waiting for, Yann? Git!"

38

In the gathering darkness, the cicadas still chirped. Weary but content, Yann headed towards the hut, dodging barking dogs and miners drunk from a day spent in law-enforced idleness. Some cleaned their guns, slow and bored, as if itching to get back to their claims and start digging.

Without warning, a rifle went off. Then another … and another. Soon the bush echoed with gunfire, drowning out the cicada song.

Smoke rose from the slab hut chimney and Yann wondered what Magali had cooked the Brisket family for lunch while he was at Chinaman's Bend toiling in an abandoned claim without a licence. Couscous? Or one of the dishes Monsieur Brisket had suggested? A marrow roast?

Yann went over the events of that day. Had the troopers, preoccupied with attempting to molest Clemency, even noticed his presence? If Nathaniel Clovis had clapped eyes on him surely he would have returned, with or without his horse. Clovis would have held a rifle to his temple, arrested him and chained him to a log.

Yann let out a sigh. He was glad to be free. Not only was he free, but he had recovered approximately three pennyweights of gold worth about twelve shillings. He was satisfied to have achieved a day's work for fair gain. His hands were a mass of blisters, huge bubbles filled with fluid, and so close together they had almost joined to become one complete blister. But it was worth it

Clem had insisted Yann turn the other way while she changed back into her moleskins. She had twisted her hair up so tight that not a single bit could be seen and then jammed the leather cap, now covered in dust, onto her head. She had refused to let Yann clean the dirt off her face.

Clem had said maybe he now understood why it was safer for her to dress as a man.

"Everybody will ignore me if I look like a digger. They will leave me to my own devices. They will let me be and I will be free to do as I wish."

Yann, tempted to tell Clem no man was as '*jolie*' as she was, decided to say nothing.

She had shrugged off her struggle with the trooper. "One must accept these things on the Diggings, troopers and miners from all over the world determined to take whatever they want without asking—*and* too few ladies residing at Forest Creek to be a civilising influence."

Were *demoiselles* in the Colony of Victoria made of sterner stuff than those in France? Yann wondered. Clem hadn't even wept, not really. Apparently unafraid of being attacked again, she had simply gritted her teeth and traipsed all the way back to Pennyweight Flat for the shovel she had seen earlier. While on the slopes, she had also discovered a discarded bucket. On her return, she had sifted the shoals of tailings with the holey tin pan and even climbed down into the mine with Yann. She estimated that about two feet of rich gravel lay on the pipeclay bottom.

At the end of the afternoon she had made damper from flour, salt and water. She had wrapped the dough around a stick, and then cooked it in the coals of an open fire. While waiting for the damper to be ready, they'd divvied up the takings. Yann had six shillings worth of gold to keep, Clem the same amount.

She said she needed to build up a stash, just in case…

"Why you need money, Clem?" he had asked.

"I don't know what for, I simply have a feeling." The expression in her eyes had been thoughtful as she tapped on the damper to check for the hollow sound—indicating the mixture was cooked through.

Chewing on the bush bread, Yann had been surprised to find that he enjoyed the smoky flavour, the eucalypt taste. He had briefly stopped munching and asked if Silas Holmes-Lacy hit her often.

"*Il vous tape souvent?*"

"You mean does Da strike me? Only if I have been wilfully disobedient." She had abruptly changed the subject. "I have some golden syrup here." She had rummaged around in her carpetbag. "Would you like some syrup with your meal? The diggers call it 'cocky's joy' and it tastes wonderful."

The damper laced with golden syrup had tasted better than wonderful, and Yann pondered: *Will Silas Holmes-Lacy think you have been wilfully disobedient, spending the day on the Diggings rather than help prepare the important Sunday dinner?* Rather than ask the question, he had continued to chew on the gooey sweetness. Was it any of his business? As soon as he had enough money he would be moving on. Did he need to know how Clem's parents treated her?

Clem had interrupted his thoughts. "Sorry, I have no billy tea for us. I forgot to bring the billy as well. Can you believe that? I am such an addle-brain. I really am not myself today."

"It is no matter. I prefer coffee."

"Coffee? You like coffee?" She had stared, shaken her head. "Oh no, I like English tea, strong and bitter!"

Clem had even managed to discover oil in the bottom of her voluminous carpetbag and had topped up his lamp for him. They had left the tin pan and shovel below, covered up the mine with the matted grass, packed up and set off home.

Cyrano thrashed his tail and growled at the snake's head—still tacked to the outside wall of the hut.

"*Chut!*" Yann suppressed a yawn. "Be quiet! You will arouse the curiosity of Dora and Bethany. And then I will have to pretend to be Asian and I'm too tired to be bothered."

His bones were aching. His lids were heavy. At the first chance, he planned to ask Magali for some salve to smear on his blisters. It was not often Yann craved the curative properties of his mentor's herbs. Even simple honey would do.

He put his lamp down. Rolling up the canvas window, he prepared to hoist his body in through the gap. He paused, eyes widening. His bed was already occupied—by a scrawny child with long fair hair. Wearing a tuck-pleated chemise, she lay on the mattress with her arms thrown back behind her head. Her cheeks were flushed. Every now and then a rasping cough interrupted her feeble snores. She coughed some more, rolled over and mumbled in her sleep. Tear tracks marked the side of her face.

"*Sacré bleu!*" he breathed.

Was Dora in his bed? Or was this Bethany? Or had Magali brought some other waif into their home? At this rate, his mentor would be housing all the children of Forest Creek in their small slab hut.

Perched on Yann's shoulder, Cyrano wiggled his haunches. He flexed his claws and prepared to leap inside.

Yann was barely able to make a fist. Grimacing, he grabbed the Tonkinese. "Stop! We must find somewhere else to lie tonight."

He winced. He felt a mixture of pity for the child, laced with resentment at having had his bed taken from him. The excitement of his gold discovery faded. He dropped to the ground.

39

Yann fumbled about until he hit upon the chaff bag. He hauled a reluctant Cyrano behind him and lifted the fabric. Using his knee to push his lamp along, he crawled under the dwelling and scratched around for somewhere to doss down for the night.

He set about creating a makeshift bed by heaping leaves and twigs into a cushiony pile, before flattening his hat to create a pillow. He wriggled his body into position in an effort to get comfortable.

Apparently uninterested in sleeping, Cyrano wove his way around Yann. Should he sling him in the butcher's cage? Yann wondered. Or let him roam free? No longer inebriated from the absinthe, Cyrano pounced on insects, alternately bounding and crunching and making satisfied grunts. Finally, he settled into the crook of his master's elbow.

Yann's eyelids began to droop. The tinkle of a piano drifted from the Red Boulder Hotel. Balls clicked on the Bagatelle table. The plaintive sound of a mouth organ could be heard from a nearby tent: 'Hard Times Come Again No More'.

Horses and drays clopped along Mount Alexander Road. A bullock driver's whip cracked in the distance. A child coughed overhead and, strangely, these sounds were comforting. The smells of pipe tobacco, gunpowder and gum leaves no longer seemed so foreign. Even the Cousin Jacks brawling with a wild Irishman didn't bother Yann as his mind went back to a more refined time.

To Le Meurice in Paris…

Yann used to lunch with his parents at Le Meurice in rue de Rivoli, particularly on Sundays. There, beneath glittering chandeliers, diners wore lace jabots and spoke English. Yann ate hard-boiled partridge eggs, and sometimes swan eggs. He would pull a face when his father persuaded him to wash down the meal with the bitter brown beer they served at the hotel. Jean-Paul Sauvage said beer was good for him, that it would make a man of him, and that his son should learn to appreciate the Anglo-Saxon culture. All the while, Jean-Paul sipped from his glass of calvados. Kings and queens from all over the world stayed at Le Meurice.

After lunch, the family would stroll in the Tuileries, taking the central alley of the famous gardens. His *maman*, Madeleine, wearing feathers in her hair and a dress edged in lace, would chat about her friend Magali, and how she envied Magali's exotic life in Algeria. The buttons on Jean-Paul's uniform gleamed and he hung upon every word his wife uttered. He promised to show her this North African country one day—it was a place he knew well. They nattered about the Casbah, couscous and *tadjine*, camel races, the succulent figs which grew on the hillsides, the grand white houses owned by the Pied-Noir settlers overlooking the Mediterranean. The cool internal courtyards.

They talked about how Magali had been secretly engaged to marry an Arab and how her parents had forbidden her to have anything to do with him. Soon after, the man was killed by a French soldier, sliced through with a bayonet. So it didn't matter in the end. But sometimes he heard his parents whispering about it, his mother murmuring, "You knew, you knew …"

Bored with the talk, Yann would toss lumps of white quartz into the huge Octagonal Basin, watching the stones etch rainbow-coloured ripples on the surface of the water.

Plop! Plop! Plop!

"*Arrête*, Yann!" Madeleine scolded him. "Where are your manners?"

Jean-Paul looked on indulgently, saying nothing, as if he was proud to see his son showing some spirit.

Crash!

The sound of splintering glass filtered into Yann's mind, waking him from his reverie.

Plop! Plop! Plop!

He heard Magali's muffled tones overhead. "Oh, what have you done, Dora? You've broken it!"

He sat bolt upright, bumping his head on the floor beams.

"Cyrano!" he called, running his fingers over his brow.

There was no sign of the cat, just this dampness. Just these drips coming from above and landing on his forehead.

A child complained. Was that Dora? Or Bethany?

"Do as I say!" The boards shook under the weight of Magali's footsteps. "And be quiet, Bethany. Eleanor needs her rest. She is extremely unwell and you are not helping."

Who is Eleanor? he asked himself.

"'Tis a folly to cry for spilt milk." That was definitely Monsieur Brisket.

Had Dora spilled some milk? Although milk was hard to come by on the Diggings, so it was unlikely the Brisket children were drinking it.

Yann ran his hand over his brow again. His skin was sticky, slimy. He scrabbled around for a match, swiped it across his leather vest and, holding his breath to avoid inhaling the fumes, lit his lamp with trembling fingers. In the flickering light, his eyes made out no milky white colour. Only red. Puzzled, Yann realised his skin was smeared with blood.

In the dusty shadows he spied Cyrano, not far from the butcher's cage, devouring a bush rat with relish. At least the cat hadn't run away again. Had the blood come from the rat he was eating? It made no sense.

A slimy fat shape caught his side vision. His eyes snagged on a creature attached to his skin. Shimmering in the lamplight, it oozed and wriggled just above his wrist. Oddly, he felt no pain.

With a start, he realised what this gooey thing was. "*Aïe! Aïe! Une sangsue!*" A leech was gorging on Yann's blood.

His first instinct was to rip it off, but he held back. The bloodsucker swelled before his eyes. Gore ran over his wrist, and Yann wondered if he were about to die. What to do? His eyes rotated, his heart thumped and he could feel the hairs on his arm stand up. His sight narrowed into a tunnel. His mouth became dry.

"*Merde! Merde! Merde!*"

Cyrano, hearing him swear, glanced up fleetingly. Uninterested in Yann's problem, he continued chewing on his bush rat. He clamped a paw on his prey and tore at the flesh, purring as he ate.

Yann's heart slowed. Where had the leech come from? Had he transported it from the mine on his clothing? The mine was alongside the creek and leeches lived in water. But … this fluid dripping through the boards: where was that from? He gazed at the leech again. His hand still itched to rip the fat worm off but, in the back of his mind, he recalled Magali saying the bloodsucker would vomit if you did that, fill your veins with poison and make you ill. Had anybody ever died from being attacked by a leech? Oh, *Mon Dieu!* He was so tired. He needed sleep to able to rise early and return to the mine before the cradles started roaring.

His befuddled brain finally recalled the solution to his problem. Salt. If he sprinkled salt over the leech, it would drop off. Or fire? Leeches backed away from fire. He could use a lighted match to lift it off. But a match would burn his skin. The blisters on his hands were excruciating enough without adding the pain of burns to his woes.

135

Only one thing for it. He decided to crawl out from under the hut, scratch at the front door and ask Magali for the salt she used in her cooking. But what if one of the Briskets opened up? Dora? Bethany? Or the new child, Eleanor?

"*Je suis idiot!*" Of course, he should steal the salt.

Lately, he had been nicking things almost without giving it a second thought. Clem, too, seemed to have few qualms about taking stray items left lying about. He could simply nab what he wanted from a nearby tent, raid another digger's supplies. But what if he were caught stealing? He could end up with a litany of thieving misdemeanours. He was in enough trouble as it was.

Taking care not to swipe the leech off his arm, Yann grabbed his hat and jammed it on his head. Using his elbows, he wriggled out from his hiding place. He pushed himself up and, keeping the brim low over his eyes, slunk around looking for abandoned supplies. The Diggings were quiet. No music came from the Red Boulder Hotel. The wind rustled in the bushes, there was a chill in the air and Yann could smell rain. Heavy drops began falling from the sky, plopping into the ground beside him, sending up spurts of dust. Corrugations formed in the earth.

Ignoring the wet, Yann prowled around, trying to find a tent without a leashed dog keeping guard. His head began to swirl with dizziness. Shadows lunged, and he felt like vomiting. He desperately needed to lie down before he keeled over. But he also needed to keep going until he discovered some way of removing this slimy worm gorging on his blood.

He stumbled on, tripping over tent pegs and pickaxes. He went around and around in circles, until he was almost back at the hut. Abruptly, his mind cleared. He had the answer. He would head for the Holmes-Lacy General Store and Post Office, wake Clem. Clem would know what to do.

As he set off for Mount Alexander Road, a voice behind him spoke.

"Stop! I need to talk to you!"

40

Yann swung around. Drizzle swirled in the air and Magali stood there.

"What are you doing wandering about in the middle of the night, Yann?" she asked in French, and before he could answer added, "And where have you been all day? The cards tell me you are heading for troubled waters."

Thinking he was already in troubled waters, and not about to admit he had been panning for gold illegally on a Sunday, he locked his gaze with hers. "My bed is occupied. I had nowhere to go, no place to sleep save under our hut." He frowned. "Who is the child I saw lying on my mattress?"

"The child is Eleanor. She is gravely ill and all the other beds were occupied, so I had no option but to give her yours."

"And who is Eleanor?"

"She is a poor child I tended once. Her mother is a gold digger." Magali's voice was etched with weariness. "The woman … I shall not call her a lady … ran off to Melbourne with a man twice her age who struck it rich."

"And her father, why can't he care for her?"

"Her father believes Eleanor has typhoid and wants nothing to do with her. He has taken up with a fancy lady in Fryerstown, the proprietor of a coffee shop, newly opened, and wants no sick child to impede him."

"What you *really* mean is his fancy lady runs an illegal grog shop?"

Magali's shawl was dotted with fine beads of moisture. "Yes, something of that nature." Her fingers trembled slightly as she adjusted the grey wool around her shoulders. "Put simply, Eleanor has been abandoned. She is ill. She has a nervous fever, and I have no option but to take her in. The weather is turning bad and I have no tempest prognosticator to tell me what to anticipate for tomorrow. By then she might have passed and off to a cold grave in Pennyweight Flat Cemetery."

"But it is my bed!" Yann protested, feeling angry and yet awash with guilt at the same time for being uncharitable.

Magali studied her feet for a moment and added in a low voice. "I am sorry, Yann. I had little choice in the matter."

"And why have you no barometer?" he asked, confused.

She gave an exasperated sigh. "Dora knocked it flying and the glass shattered, leaving liquid all over the floor and, in all the fuss, my hysterical aquatic bloodsucker disappeared."

Did that explain the liquid oozing through the boards onto his forehead, the leech on his wrist?

"Do you plan to take in *all* the children on the Diggings who need help?" .

"The good Lord would expect it of me." Wet wisps of hair clung to her cheeks. "I plan to start up a school when I have enough money."

"So, you have given up any idea of seeking my father on the goldfields?"

Magali let out another sigh. "Reflect on it, Yann. Look at all the tents around you, the comings and goings, the people who pitch canvas for a day, collapse their abodes and move on, prompted by the merest hint of gossip concerning a new strike elsewhere in Victoria. What are the chances of success in finding Jean-Paul Sauvage among all these thousands of persons?" She averted her gaze. "Everybody looks alike. Rumours abound, and I have yet to get to the bottom of any of it."

"I will find *Papa* then, on my own!" He noted her glance slide and knew she was hiding something. "You don't *want* to find him, do you? You have no intention of looking for my father. We are here under false pretences!"

"That is not true. I owe it to my dear friend, Madeleine, to do the right thing by her husband and son. You have an overactive imagination, Yann."

"It's Monsieur Brisket, isn't it? You have fallen under the miner's … and I cannot imagine why … dubious charms."

"Mr Brisket is a good man who is bravely coping with the loss of his wife." She hesitated. "And after all I have been through, the death of my fiancé in Algeria … by the most horrible means imaginable … I, at last, have a chance of personal happiness."

Tempted to uncover more details of Magali's fiancé's death, Yann decided not to tell her the little he knew about the liaison. Instead, he said in frustration, "Well, I am not concerned whether you wish to find *Papa* or not. If I am forced to travel throughout the entire Colony of Victoria to do so, I will!"

He saw her eyes widen. Was she about to reveal her reasons for being reluctant to find Jean-Paul Sauvage? Jean-Paul had served as an officer in Algeria. *Had he been involved with Magali's fiancé's death?*

Instead she pounced on Yann's wrist, grasped it and held it in the air. "Aha!" she shouted. "That is my leech! Do not move! If the parasite drops off, do *not* lose it. The phial is broken, so I must find something else in which to house him. Do not move a muscle until I see if I can discover a new home where he will be as content."

"New home?"

"A jar will suffice, as long as it is properly clean!"

"How do you know it's *your* leech and not a leech from …?" About to mention Chinaman's Bend, he bit off the words.

"Oh, I would recognise him anywhere! Alphonse has a special curl to his tail, right beside the oral sucker, like no other hermaphroditic parasite I have ever known."

"Alphonse!" Yann muttered beneath his breath. "She calls it Alphonse. Whoever names their leech?"

Magali gave an excited giggle. "Oh, what joy! I have my tempest prognosticator back!" She strode off towards the slab hut, humming, and with a flurry of skirts disappeared inside.

The rain eased, turned to a fine mist and faded with the breeze. Yann stood stock still. He watched the blood continue to ooze until it streamed over his wrist. Drops of water dripped from the brim of his hat, making it look worse than it was. He felt dizzy, telling himself that if he remained like this for much longer he would faint like a Parisian society *demoiselle*, sink into the ground and pass out from the bleeding.

Magali seemed to be taking forever to find her jar. In the meantime, Alphonse kept gorging away. The leech was becoming more and more bloated by the minute. Just as Yann thought he would collapse Magali was by his side again, clutching an empty pickle jar.

"You have forgotten the salt!"

"Salt? Oh no, one doesn't use salt! We must wait until the annelid has had its fill and drops off naturally." She led him towards a fallen tree trunk. "If we force Alphonse off, he will regurgitate into the wound and could give you far more grief than from the wound itself. You could become quite unwell."

Yann blew out a heavy sigh. "And how long will this process take?"

"Alphonse appears rather plump, definitely swollen, so he should be finished soon." She sat down beside him and took a long look at the leech. "Of course the wound will continue to bleed quite profusely due to the anticoagulant it uses to facilitate the flow of blood …" Her voice hardened. "What is this?"

"What is what?" He tensed up at the thought: *Had the leech vomited, sending poison into his bloodstream?* "Is something the matter?"

Magali picked up his other hand, examined it. "These are terrible blisters, Yann. Where did you get them?" She paused. "There is only one way I can think of. I believe you have been keeping something from me."

"I have been keeping nothing from you," he lied.

"Then how did these pockets of fluid on your hand come about?"

He didn't confess that he had been mining illegally, but the knowledge hung there between them.

41

Yann's wrist still seeped from the leech bite. He re-read the note left by Clem beneath the gravestone at Pennyweight Flat Cemetery:

Yann, this is not the morning for you to venture into the mine. I have heard rumours. C

He folded the note carefully. He could see no reason why he should not continue, given his digging had so far been fruitful. He jabbed at the soil with his pickaxe. His lamp, balanced on a chock of wood in the mine wall, flickered fitfully as he worked. Still light-headed from the blood he had lost, he recalled how he had finally admitted to Magali that he'd been mining in an abandoned Chinese claim without a licence, and on the Sabbath.

Surprised, he had heard her murmur, "I wondered when you would take things into your own hands."

"You are not annoyed?"

"Pfft. Life is different here. The lines of virtue become blurred in a place like the Diggings and one does what one has to in order to get by." Then she had added, "A murdered Chinaman has been discovered, no doubt slaughtered for his gold. His headless body was found not far from the slopes of Pennyweight Flat, rather decomposed, it is rumoured. The authorities haven't fallen upon the head yet. He was taken …" Pause. "Well, I should say his torso and limbs were taken to the Red Boulder Hotel where William Bass will organise an autopsy, due to be carried out this morning I believe. They have reached the conclusion that the slain man was Chinese by the colour of his skin, and by the garments he was wearing."

Yann had adjusted the snake pelt at his waist and said nothing.

Magali had tapped her teeth thoughtfully with her fingernail. "There is a move afoot to expel the Chinese from the Diggings. They say a meeting is being organised … all hush-hush at this stage. I wonder if the proposed anti-Chinese meeting has something to do with the Chinaman's death."

Yann had shrugged and examined his blisters.

"Racism is an ugly thing. It blighted my life in Algeria." And then, expressing aloud Yann's own fears, she had said, "I also wonder if you are toiling in a dead man's claim." She had abruptly changed the subject. "I do not see Cyrano. He is always by your side. Where is he?"

Yann had pretended he did not know. Under no circumstances, would he allow Magali to dose Cyrano with absinthe again. The cat had been through enough torment.

Yann went back to chipping with renewed vigour. A shiver went through him at the thought of a headless body having been discovered on the Diggings. Was he really toiling in a dead man's claim?

The blisters on his palms were hardening, thanks to a salve of herbs and unguents Magali had smeared across the wounds. Although his hands were tender, the pain was tolerable. It was important for him to find gold as quickly as possible. When he had enough, he would have the means to find his father.

The religious symbol at his neck swayed on its chain. Cyrano, sitting on a stone, watched him swing the pick. Gouging and yanking, Yann gradually moved along towards the cross passage. Slinging the pointy end, he soon created a decent pile to be panned. He began to shovel the wash dirt into his bucket. Overhead, he could hear the rain pounding down. A flash of lightning lit the tunnel for a second. The ground beneath his feet was becoming sloppy with water, which rose up the sides of his boots, leaving spreading maps of wet on the leather.

Glancing upwards, he saw the pre-dawn sky had lightened. A tinge of rose filled the gloom. Soon it would be time to leave. He knew the Forest Creek diggers would be undeterred by bad weather. He would head off as soon as the first cradle started up.

A voice echoed down the mine shaft. "Are you there?" someone called.

Wary, Yann remained silent.

"If you *are* there … and I left you a note telling you *not* to be there! … I can do some panning, but only for a short while."

Yann eased himself from the cross passage. He tilted his head to see Clem peering down at him from beneath a pink umbrella.

"Do you need any help? I felt I should check on you. I can sift the dirt for you if you like, which will save you climbing up and down the shaft." A skittish curl tumbled over her forehead. "When Mama asked me what I was doing up so early in the morning, I told her I was off to visit the cemetery and I planned to pick a bunch of wildflowers for little Silas. I gathered Emu Bush, Turkey Bush and some Poverty Bush, but of course the stench at Pennyweight Flat Cemetery is so bad that one needs flowers to counter the odour … worse than usual lately, it seems. And the crows are making a terrible racket!"

"*Oui*, I 'ear them and zey frighten me a little."

She brushed the tress away. "I think Da was suspicious of my motives, and then he said I should become *used* to rising in the early morning dark once the bakehouse lease has been signed. Oh, heaven forbid!" She gave a groan. "I pray every night the bakery agreement will fall through."

"I cannot imagine you working as a *boulangère*, Clem." Yann hauled the laden bucket to the rope and slid the hook beneath the handle until it held firm. "I 'ave a load for taking to surface. Is it too much raining for you to pan?"

"Oh, it is never too wet on the Diggings for panning!"

"And your clothes will not be destroyed?" At Yann's feet, Cyrano tossed a dead dragonfly into the air, caught it and began to chew.

"Never fear. I am clad in my trusty moleskins!" Raindrops trailed down her cheeks like tears.

Thinking how suspicious a pink umbrella must appear when held by someone wearing moleskins, he shouted, "Bucket is ready, Clem!"

"I shall bring it to the surface then!"

The windlass squeaked and groaned. The rope, more frayed than ever, snarled in protest. The rain continued to sheet down, sluicing over the walls of the mine shaft. Yann could feel the water inching up the sides of his boots.

Clem ceased winching. "I can see blood on the bucket. Are you injured, Yann?" she called.

"*Non, ça va.*" He decided not to launch into an explanation about the escaped leech called Alphonse.

"Does that mean you are in robust health and able to continue?"

"*Oui.*"

"Very well, I shall start panning now! The weather is turning bad, so the rain may well do the washing for me. I might not be forced to lug this wash dirt down to Forest Creek."

"Do not become ill wis pneumonia, Clem," he said, but his words slipped to nothing in the din.

About to repeat his warning for her to take care, he was distracted by a bright blob floating nearby.

Gold never floats, he told himself. He knew gold was heavier than water, which was why the ore sat in the bottom of the tin pan or long tom after the washing and puddling had been done. He bent to pick up the object; it was a gilt button. He ran the pad of his callused finger over the surface of the button. Was that the Imperial Eagle, like the one on the uniforms of the soldiers in the French army of Napoleon III, like the eagle on his dagger? What an odd thing to discover inside a mine in the Colony of Victoria.

Yann knew the regimental button could not be from his grandfather's army. Those had been made of tin and had famously contributed to Napoleon Bonaparte's defeat. In Russia, the Grand Army had been reduced to a starving rabble after the retreat from its disastrous siege of Moscow in 1812. On that occasion, the buttons had turned from white to grey and then become powdery before disintegrating. French soldiers had fought with their sword in one hand whilst holding up their trousers with the other.

"How is it going down there, Yann? Are you all right?" Clem was back.

"*Oui. Ça va!*"

A wry smile came to Yann's face. Fancy your empire crumbling, all because of buttons which had become infested with tin pest. Logic told him that the button in his hand must be from the uniform of an officer in Napoleon III's army. He inhaled sharply. Did this mean Jean-Paul Sauvage had been here, digging in this very spot? If so, he was getting closer to his goal.

He stuffed the precious find in his pocket. Knowing he was in the same place his father had been, Yann began to work even harder. He yanked his dagger from its sheath and, hair flopping over his brow, scraped at the mine walls.

Soon he had found a number of gold particles, together with smaller specks of gold dust. He carefully folded the colour into a kerchief and pushed it into his pocket, beside the button.

"It's on its way!" Clem wound the empty bucket down for Yann to refill with wash dirt.

"*Merci!*" he called.

"Sorry, I must go …"

Yann glanced up. Clem was no longer there. The sky was bruised with clouds. In the distance, he could hear the sound of a cradle rocking. If Clem had left, he would also leave. In a moment.

The water on the mine floor kept rising. With a frightened squawk, Cyrano scrambled onto his shoulder. Mud and slime clogged Yann's palm.

Dobs of gravel covered his forearms, glued on by the mud. He attempted to lift Cyrano off his shoulder so he could make a final foray into the cross passage. The cat's claws became tangled in the weave of Yann's shirt, as if Cyrano were reluctant to let go.

"*Ça va, mon pote,*" he murmured. "It is all right, my friend. We will be departing soon and you can sleep under the hut right next to the warm chimney. We'll find a dry spot there."

Managing to extricate Cyrano, he positioned the cat on the broadest chock of wood he could find on the mine wall. Tail thrashing, Cyrano gave a low growl but remained in position while Yann stooped beneath the overhang of the cross passage.

Water splashed into his face as he swung the pickaxe. Clumps of stinging stones spackled his skin, leaving grime which adhered no matter how his body slewed and twisted. He wiped his eyes clear with the back of his hand, reluctant to leave. One last blow of the pick and he would be out of there. Just one last blow.

With a start, he felt clods of clay and bits of dirt thump at his shoulders. Sludge rained down and onto the brim of his battered hat. The mine shuddered and creaked. The ledge, only inches above his head, began to break up. The muck slid, oozed over his body until it settled over his limbs.

Yann turned to flee, but his legs were pinned. No matter how hard he levered and tugged, he was unable to pull them out. He was stuck fast. And the water was rising.

42

Pinned down and helpless, Yann watched the mud ooze around the clumps of fallen quartz and clay.

He had replaced his dagger in its sheath. Fumbling, he eased the blade out with icy fingers and attempted to push back the slime. He would slice it away if he had to. He would slice off his legs if that was what it took to save his life.

From the main shaft, he heard a yowl and then a splash. Had Cyrano slipped and fallen? Did the cat know how to swim? Cyrano's blue eyes had been huge with terror during much of the voyage to Australia. He had studiously avoided the ship's deck.

A resounding second splash and Yann managed to swivel his neck. He was just able to make out the rim of the bucket bobbing and swilling in the bottom of the shaft. The rope from the windlass hung loose.

No sign of Cyrano. No sound. Only Yann's own breathing, rapid and hoarse.

"Clem!" he hollered. "*Au secours!* Help me!" As if in a bad dream, his voice came out in a squeak.

No reply.

Yann was hemmed in by a wall of silence, of slipping and slopping muddiness. In the distance, the rain drumming against the windlass made a pinging noise. Yann wielded his dagger. He slammed away, shoved and heaved as the mud inched up his chest. Death was creeping towards him. The true horror of his situation exploded in his head. At this rate, his nostrils would soon be clogged with sludge and he would be unable to breathe.

From the rear of the cross passage, a round object rolled over the toe of his boot. Was that the missing human skull Magali had talked about?

"*Oh, mon Dieu!*"

Yann suppressed a scream. His heart fluttered like a moth battering at a windowpane, desperate and powerless.

Appalled, he felt sudden warmth around his thighs. Had he urinated into his moleskins? With all the water around him, it was hard to tell. And did it matter anyway? The smell of slain cattle from the butcher's shamble had seeped into the mine. The reek was so overpowering it made his head swirl.

His lamp sputtered and faded, leaving him in total blackness. The gunk remained halfway up his chest and he lay there, unable to see anything, unable to hear anything. Save this soft slurping. He was alone but for a human skull, deep in the heart of darkness. Was the skull at his feet the Chinaman's, or someone else's? Was this place cursed? Were the diggers terrified? Was that the reason the dig had been abandoned? Had Clem known a man died here, but not told him in case he was too much of a coward to work the claim? Questions eddied in his mind like the muck.

The blackness was playing tricks with his imagination. He trusted Clem. Why should he not trust her? She had joined him in the bottom of the mine, apparently unafraid of stumbling upon dead bodies, dead heads, dead limbs or dead animals. Uncontrollable tremors ran through him.

Sour mud swilled around him and he shook from the cold. The hairs on his neck bristled. A vein in his temple pulsed. His teeth chattered so hard he could feel his jaw jerk up and down against his collarbone like a pestle pulverising skeletal remains into the mortar.

A thread of resignation fleetingly ran through his thoughts. So was this it? Was this what it felt like to pass over to the other side, into the world of the dead? Was this his destiny, that he should take his last breath inside a filthy gold mine? He berated himself for grubbing about in ground halfway around the globe, for having quit the place where he was born. He should have stayed in France. Jean-Paul Sauvage would have returned in the end. He had come on a fool's errand.

A pinpoint of an idea jabbed into Yann's mind. Apart from Clem, nobody knew he was there. How long would she wait before she alerted the authorities? Would Silas Holmes-Lacy prevent her from leaving the store to help save him? Yann knew the storekeeper scorned him, looked upon him with contempt.

Would it be days … weeks? If the latter were the case, his body would be one with the soil and filth. How he hated the filth of Forest Creek, detested the stench of Pennyweight Flat, loathed the cemetery where tots lay uncoffined and unregistered, where the fortunate ones were buried in discarded grocery boxes. What a hideous place he had come to.

Yann's head rocked with images. The suffocating dampness clothed him like torturous velvet. He was exhausted from the struggle. His eyelids drooped. He forced them apart, knowing he should stay awake or he would surely die.

Minutes passed. Hours passed. He counted, *"Un, deux, trois, quatre…"* until he reached a thousand, and then a million. He counted backwards. He counted forwards. He multiplied numbers in his head, vast figures which came to nought. He tried to wiggle his toes, but his feet had no feeling. He thrashed, but nothing happened. He felt hungry. He felt sick. He retched, but only a small amount of bile came up. The contents of his stomach ran over his chin, joining with the slop on his chest.

He began to sing: *"Frère Jacques"*. He got to the second verse, and then switched to a croaky rendition of *"Sur le pont d'Avignon, on y danse…"*

He stopped singing. He would never dance again. He would never see Avignon again. Sobs wrenched at him, gulps of self-pity. He took a breath and forced himself to change tunes. *"Alouette, gentille alouette…"* His mind wandered. If only he were a lark, or, even better, a mopoke. He liked the sound of the mopoke on the Diggings, liked its yellow eyes and ooh-ooh call. Oh, to be a bird! He would fly away.

If only he had his accordion with him. Just the feel of it would bring him comfort. The daguerreotypes of his parents? He'd never thought to carry their images about on his person.

He could feel the Imperial Eagle on the regimental button digging into his thigh. At least he would die with something from France, with part of his father's uniform by his side. He prayed the button had belonged to Jean-Paul Sauvage. *Non*, he *knew* it belonged to his father. Hot tears coursed over his cheeks. He had farewelled his mother into her cold grave at the Cimetière du Père-Lachaise, but he would never get to see his father again, never see his dashing *Papa*, whose eyes were almost as blue as Cyrano's.

A shudder ran through him. Death possessed his spirit.

Was Cyrano also dead, entombed only feet away inside the rocks and clay, the gravel and the wash dirt? Cave-in? He had never thought about a cave-in. The idea of a mine collapsing had never presented itself when he embarked on this mad scheme to make his fortune.

A small pocket of air enabled him to breathe. His breathing was shallow. His body was trapped inside this hell, but his soul meandered through fields of flowers. He admired the marguerites, the rows of poplars, the sweet-smelling stacks of hay. The sun always shone, but the countryside he knew was never too hot. It rarely rained and yet it remained always green, always perfect.

The minutes passed. Hours passed. Yann moved in and out of reality. He could no longer feel his body but he no longer cared. He was free. Peasants cut crops with their scythes, blades sharp and glinting. These men's voices were deep, kindly. He was at peace. They even called him by his first name. Everyone seemed to know the name of Napoleon Bonaparte's grandson.

"Yann …"

"*Oui*," he said, in a trance-like state. "*Je suis là*. I am here. Where else would I be?"

The voices got louder.

"Yann, lad, are ye there? Please answer us if ye're alive. Give us a sign!"

The sharp sound of a shovel broke his delirium.

43

When they finally lugged Yann to the surface, the sun hit him like a malevolent furnace. He cringed from the heat. He flung his claggy arm across his face, wishing the white-hot orb would go away. His eyes were red-rimmed, sore from having strained to see so long in the dark. He took in deep, exhausted breaths.

A crowd stood around the stretcher made of flour bags. A string of curious onlookers pointed and made comments. "'E's the survivor of that cave-in", "Yeah, he's the Frenchie with the monkey cat", "No, Asian, somethin' foreign anyway". One man puffed on a cheroot and said nothing.

Yann lay there. From his side vision he could see Clemency Holmes-Lacy, in a crinoline, standing back from the others. The straw bonnet she wore was tied under her chin and she sobbed into a lace handkerchief. Her nose was as pink as her outfit.

Through slitted lids, he also saw Magali's nose redden as she took an almighty sniff and enveloped him in a suffocating hug. He didn't mind being suffocated this time. He found himself wrapped in a comforting waft of herbs and enjoyed the sudden feeling of security. He was elated to be back in the land of the living, intoxicated by the sight of tents, cradles, puddlers and tin pans, the long toms and never-ending whir of activity. Even the dirty green eucalypts and spiky bits of scrub seemed like Paradise.

Nearby, skinny Mr Brisket leant on his shovel. He dragged his left sleeve across his brow, wiping away the perspiration. His lank hair poked out from beneath the brim of his hat, a sort of mousy brown fringe with an overlay of dust.

He pulled out his pipe, chewed on the stem and murmured, "Well done, lad. Ye've been very courageous to survive such an ordeal. I imagine ye must be ravenous. The best sauce in the world is hunger!"

For once, Brisket mouthing one of his well-worn proverbs was the most wonderful sound. And, yes, Yann was hungry. He cautiously wiggled his toes. His feet tingled. He flexed his muscles and stretched, to find his body ached but remained unbroken. .

A thin girl, dressed in a pin-tucked white calico smock with a matching bow in her fair hair, jabbed a finger. "'E stinks, Maggie. I can smell 'im from 'ere."

"But we don't care, Dora, do we?" Magali turned her head. "Disagreeable odours are of no real importance. We are simply grateful to have Ya … ah, our boarder … back with us and with no bones broken."

Dora twirled a strand of hair around her forefinger.

Magali leant down and whispered in Yann's ear. "Are you in pain?"

"I hurt, but it is bearable."

"That is as well. Johnnie Lee is … is currently unable to provide opium. This will have to do." She pulled a flask of whisky from her apron pocket and held it out.

The alcohol sent a jolt through his body and he resisted the urge to cough

"I wanna have a geek at the mucky stuff down there, where there is lots and lots of gold and people can get really, really rich. Can we go down into the dis-*gus*ting mine, Maggie?" demanded the girl beside Dora. She was not quite as thin, but was dressed in a similar calico smock.

"No, Bethany. The mine is far too dangerous without shaft support timbers and, anyway, you would soil your beautiful new clothes."

One child stood slightly to one side. Also fair-haired, but frailer than the Brisket children, she sucked vigorously on her thumb. She removed her thumb and gave a rasping cough. Was that Eleanor, the child Yann had last seen in his bed?

"How long was I down there?" he whispered to Magali in French.

"A little more than two days, I believe. I thought you had departed the Forest Creek Diggings at first and was not concerned. Then Silas Holmes-Lacy's daughter knocked on our door and gave the alarm. So Mr Brisket in his resourcefulness gathered together this wonderful group of miners."

Three men, also leaning on shovels, raised their ragged hats. Two of them grinned, showing nicotine-stained teeth. The third, through a mouthful of gaps, said, "Seek and ye shall find!" Their moleskins and flannel shirts were almost as muddy as the ones Yann was wearing.

"Maggie did a lot of prayin' for a heathen. I mean for *her* bein' a heathen," interrupted Brisket, "and her prayin' *for* a heathen." He gave a sprightly wink.

Yann gathered that Monsieur Brisket was playing along with the belief he was Chinese, keeping up the pretence for the children's sake and for his—Yann's—own protection from the trooper who was after him.

"Cyrano was with me when the mine caved in!" Yann said in French to Magali, pushing himself up on one elbow. "Did they discover his body? Did they find him? Is he dead?"

Magali straightened. Tall and imposing, she made Brisket seem even shorter and skinnier. She tucked wisps back into the tortoiseshell comb holding her hair aloft. "No animal was unearthed in the mine, Yann. I am sorry if Cyrano has passed." She shrugged. "Perhaps it is for the best."

"I'll look for Cyrano myself then!" Yann attempted to stand, but stumbled backwards onto the makeshift stretcher.

"You should rest. Lie here for a moment until you have regained your strength," she said.

"I have been lying on my back for two days or more! I have had enough rest!" He heaved his body up until he stood, swaying. He drew cautious breaths, determined to remain upright.

Clem pushed the onlookers aside and ran towards Yann. Grabbing him by the arm so hard he almost lost his balance, she reached up and whispered in his ear, "Cyrano escaped! He managed to scramble up the shaft and is with Princess Albert as we speak. They are having a lovely time together, playing among the boxes in the store." Her voice caught. "Your monkey cat was the one who saved you, Yann. He scratched on my window and warned me of your plight. Cyrano saved your life!"

She began to sob again and Yann wondered why she was so upset. He understood that she was glad he'd survived, but he sensed there was something else, something she wasn't telling him.

The clop of horse's hooves, slow and relentless, impinged on his thoughts. A trooper came into view and, deep in the pit of his stomach, Yann knew who it was. Even before he saw the black patch over the trooper's eye, and the food-splotched uniform, he knew the man swinging down from his horse was Nathaniel Clovis.

The crowd began to break up and drift away. Some scurried off as if they were certain trouble was afoot, or were afraid of being arrested for mining without a licence. Or were they guilty of having carried out some other dire deed?

Hand in hand, the Brisket children skipped down towards the creek. One couple remained planted to the spot and Yann stared, trying to work out where he had seen these people before. The pair was familiar. The man wore a threadbare smock, but didn't half the men on the Diggings dress like that? So why did he feel he had met them?

Beside him, Magali flinched. Her hands were pressed against her abdomen as if she were in pain.

Mr Brisket's pupils flared. He hissed, "Make a run for it, lad, while the goin' is good! This mad trooper is after yer blood, for no good reason that I can make out. Git! Go on, git!"

On wobbly legs, Yann turned to flee.

44

Yann had taken only a few halting steps when he felt the barrel of a gun between his shoulders.

He heard the words, "Ye've run out of luck this time, Frenchie!"

Magali drew herself to her full height. "I can vouch for this young man, sir. Yann Bonaparte Sauvage abides with me and is of impeccable lineage and superb character. He is the Great General's grandson. What a ridiculous notion that he should have done anything underhand!"

A tremor went through Yann. He lifted his hands in a defensive gesture. "It is not my fault if my cat puts your eye out, *monsieur*. 'E is only an animal and does not know much better."

"Oh, I am not concerned with yer rabid monkey hybrid anymore!" Trooper Clovis's voice crackled with menace. "Nor am I concerned with the boots ye've stolen from under Barnaby's nose."

Yann saw Magali's lips purse at the mention of the stolen boots.

Clemency Holmes-Lacy's topaz eyes were huge and Yann briefly wondered if she had informed on him, taken money for revealing his whereabouts to the lawman. Was that why the trooper had turned up? Did it explain her distraught weeping? Was she overcome with guilt? He no longer knew who to trust.

"I have no interest in paltry misdemeanours," the trooper continued, "nor of chargin' ye with mining without a licence, *and* on the Sabbath." He shoved the rifle harder again into Yann's back until he almost fell over. "No, sir, I am chargin' ye with *murder*!"

Magali inhaled sharply. Mr Brisket chewed furiously on his pipe stem.

At Clemency's renewed sobbing a kookaburra started up its maniacal laugh in a nearby gum tree. Cicadas poured out a torrent of sound.

The couple in the raggedy garments still stood there, smirks on their faces. The man's nose dripped. He made no effort to wipe it. Yann suddenly remembered where he'd seen these people before. He had watched them bury their infant. The digger's wife had lined the grave with pages of the Argus newspaper before placing the chaff bag containing their child deep inside. She had done it lovingly, as if putting the mite to sleep in a crib. She had even crossed herself before her husband set about shovelling soil into the hole.

Yann took a long look at the miner's smock. He remembered it had been stained, badly stained. And now, although still threadbare, it was relatively clean. The crows had circled the grave, and Cyrano had shown an unnatural interest in the plot after the couple had left. "To 'rock another sort of cradle'", wasn't that what the digger had said? His wife had complained that Jonas—yes, she had called him Jonas—shouted at her. It was coming back to him. But why should they accuse him, Yann, of the crime of—murder?

"Murder!" The word exploded from Yann's mouth. He had never killed anyone in his life, never thought of killing anyone.

"This honest hardworking man and his wife will attest to the fact that you were behavin' in a suspicious manner, loiterin' in Pennyweight Flat Cemetery during their time of grief."

"But ze only skull I see is in mine." Yann pointed to the collapsed mine shaft. "And, and I did not do it." Sweat streamed from his hairline. "I swear." His legs threatened to buckle under him.

"Well, well, that's a double murder now. It seems ye've carried out the heinous act of homicide at least once previous to this occasion."

"*Mon Dieu, non, non!*"

His whole body ached from the injustice.

The trooper intoned, "Ye will be taken to Melbourne to be tried." The words came out, flat and unemotional, as if he had uttered them many times before. And maybe he had. Murder on the goldfields was not uncommon.

"Mel-bourne? Oh, no, you can't send him to Melbourne!" Yann heard Clem cry out. "Yann has done nothing wrong!" Her voice was like that of a wren, high and twittery. "He could *never* do anything evil."

"If found guilty you will be hanged by the neck until you are dead!"

"Hanged!" Magali gasped and crossed herself. "Please forgive me, Madeleine. They know not what they do."

The lawman wrenched Yann's arms behind his back. Yann winced as the manacle snapped around his wrists. He was so sore, so tired, and his mind was filled with despair that his newfound freedom had been so brief. Imprisoned in Melbourne? He would never feel Jean-Paul Sauvage's comforting presence again, either here or in France.

The cicadas' screech was deafening now.

Through the din, Silas Holmes-Lacy could be heard. "Daughter, where are you? You are needed in the store," he called, making his way along Forest Creek,

"Oh, no, it's Da!" Clem gathered up her skirts. "I must leave!" Her ankle boots threw up dust as she took to her heels.

Silas Holmes-Lacy thrashed the reeds with a stick, back and forth along the bank. "Where are you, Clemency?"

No response. Was Clem taking another route, hoping to reach the Holmes-Lacy General Store and Post Office before her father? Yann prayed she would make it.

"There is an animal with unusual markings among the cartons of food recently arrived on the Cobb & Co. coach and our bulldog is behaving strangely, as if bewitched by it." The storekeeper emerged from the rushes. "Do, do you know anything about that ..." The words petered out. His cold eyes stared at the scene with disapproval.

No one spoke.

Silas Holmes-Lacy turned on his heels and retraced his steps, still thrashing the reeds with his stick. "Clemency!"

His voice receded. Everyone turned to look at Yann.

45

Barefoot and shackled, Yann stumbled down the steps, prodded along until he had descended into the bowels of the Red Boulder Hotel.

Another prisoner dressed in rags, chains clanking, shuffled past in the other direction. In the narrow passageway, water dripped. The candle flickered in the alcove carved into the sandstone wall. The flame flared and danced. Yann floundered along.

The trooper shoved him into the cell and whipped Yann's dagger from its sheath.

He examined the carved eagle on the handle for a moment. "Hmmmm," he murmured, adjusting his eye patch. "This must've cost a bit. I can see youse is not short of a shillin' or two, eh?"

He slotted the dagger into his belt and clanked the door shut. The key grated in the lock and Yann was left, bewildered to find himself in this nightmare. Why had Jonas, the man with the dripping nose, accused him of committing murder? As soon as he had asked himself the question, he knew the answer. Jonas must be connected to the Saint-Simonians. Had the Comte de Corbeau paid him money to denounce Yann?

Yann had happened to be in Pennyweight Flat Cemetery at the opportune time. After he was hanged, the Saint-Simonians would have no fear that he would inherit anything from Napoleon III. Rights of inheritance? Once Yann was dead, the Comte de Corbeau would have accomplished his mission.

Who had made the gruesome discovery at Pennyweight Flat? Had it been the smell, the sweet aroma of freshly spilt blood? Had the crows given warning, announced the death by cawing louder than usual? Cyrano had guessed, and Yann had shooed him away. A thousand thoughts swirled in Yann's mind. He knew one thing. The Saint-Simonians had set him up.

Nathaniel Clovis was standing outside the door, clipping the key back into the fat bunch on his belt.

"Ze man who is killed, what was 'is name, *monsieur*?" asked Yann.

The trooper looked up. A tiny smile showed in his good eye and Yann thought: *It's as if he is delighted to have caught me at last.*

"You *know* 'is name, Frenchie." He drawled out the words. "It were Johnnie Lee-eeee, café proprietor of the highest quality, respected in Forest Creek among the yeller people and the Europeans alike."

"And, and wh-why would I kill zis man?" Yann stammered.

"Per'aps he had a yen for yer rabid monkey hybrid?" Saliva speckled the trooper's mouth. "Animal would've made a luverly stew when cooked with Mr Lee's home-grown spring onions!" Giving out a sneering laugh, he strode off.

A feeling of dread ran through Yann. Was the trooper now on his way to the Holmes-Lacy General Store and Post Office to kill Cyrano? Thanks to Silas Holmes-Lacy, everybody knew the cat was there. Would Clem have the presence of mind to hide the Tonkinese somewhere safe?

He heard the trooper's footsteps mount the stairs, before making a right into the bar of the hotel. Hopefully he would down a whisky or three and forget about Cyrano.

Still weak from the leech having gorged on his blood, dizzy from not having eaten, Yann slumped onto the wooden bench running along the southern wall of the lockup. He placed his chin in his hands. Overhead he could hear a fiddler sawing, people shouting, the clink of glasses. The click of cue on ball as patrons played Bagatelle.

He shivered from the dankness, from the packed earth floor beneath his feet. One thing gave him comfort. The Napoleonic button in his pocket sat snug beside the stash of gold wrapped up in his kerchief. Part of his father was right next to his body. At least he would die with that knowledge.

Someone whistled in the passage outside the lockup. Barnaby appeared, a snigger hovering at the corners of his mouth as if he also were delighted to find Yann in trouble.

"Here are some victuals to keep yer strength up, Frenchie." He shoved a bowl of soup beneath the door. "I have to congratulate ye. I never thought ye had it in ye to commit murder!"

Yann yearned to punch the barman. He tossed his raven hair back defiantly. Leaping from the wooden bench, he planted his foot into the bowl and, almost losing his balance, sent it crashing against the door. The watery substance missed its mark. Goo seeped across the floor of the cell.

Barnaby clicked his tongue. "Temper, temper, Frenchie!" His footsteps receded as he padded back along the passage.

"*Salaud!*" Yann rubbed his ankle where the shackle pressed into his flesh. "You are bastard!"

Yann could smell salt in the air, sweat, horse manure and a hint of old straw entwined with the sharpness of urine. His own urine from his time spent trapped in the mine? The urine of prisoners trapped in the lockup? He could even detect vomit, rancid and rum-filled.

The light was dim now. Yann could barely see his hand in front of his face. He hankered for someone to talk to. He desperately needed to speak to Clem. He ached to confide in his new friend, smell the lavender perfume she sometimes wore. At this moment, even the company of Cyrano would not suffice. He needed to talk to a human being, one he could confide in.

He could hear voices and muffled footsteps moving up and down the passage leading to the lockup. Each time he thought he was about to have company in his cell, it was a digger who stopped short and turned into the vault where William Bass stored the gold. There the colour would remain until the next Gold Escort travelled to Melbourne. The government escort or the private operator, Studs de Wolf, would then carry the gold directly to the big banks in the city. Sometimes they would travel the long way round, calling in at other goldfields.

The thumps, clangs and clunks of the miners wove through the walls as they left their haul for safekeeping. From time to time, Yann heard arguments in the vault, William Bass's voice raised in anger.

"Parcels of gold, deposited for escort, must be limited to two hundred and fifty ounces!"

A loud whining complaint.

"I am sorry, sir! The Gold Office stipulates this, and the dimensions of those containing cash are five inches by five inches by four inches."

Another complaint.

"A shilling an ounce to have your gold escorted, and that's final, sir!"

Sometimes Yann heard whispers. The sickly smell of death from bodies in the morgue on the far side of the vault filtered into his nostrils. Was the headless restaurateur Johnnie Lee lying there waiting for the post-mortem? How did he die? Was his head lopped off, severed, carved, sawed … removed with a quick slash of the axe? Or with a swift twist of a length of wire? There were many options for a beheading.

He remembered the guillotine in Paris. He had gone once, snuck out at dawn to join the crowd in a public square near the Santé Prison. The long heavy blade had descended. The head had rolled into the basket and the seated ghouls had cheered. "*Bravo*, Madame La Guillotine!"

Women knitted as they watched, screeching—"*Bravo!* Encore! Encore! *Encore!*"—and men in brown leathers dragged the next man up.

He had been close enough to hear the prisoner hyperventilate as the executioner, Sanson, prepared to chop off his head. Did the man really have blood on his hands? Or had he been innocent, as Yann now was? The blade had shot down onto the man's quivering neck. Clunk!

A fellow onlooker had told Yann the poll continued to live, that the mind watched all this happening. Yann had returned home and stayed in his room for days, unable to wipe it from his thoughts. His mother had called the doctor, who'd told her Yann had a simple fever.

La dignité humaine? There had been no human dignity. And there would be none for him if they did the same. Would the authorities really punish him for a crime he had not committed? They would, but not in the same way. In the Colony of Victoria, they hanged people. In a few weeks' time, Yann told himself, he would be dangling from a rope in the Melbourne Gaol, dropped through a trapdoor and executed for … for having done what? For being Napoleon's grandson?

"*Non!*" Yann banged and banged on the sandstone wall of the cell until his knuckles were scraped and sore. "*Je suis innocent! Je suis innocent!* I am innocent! *Laissez-moi sortir!* Let me out of here!" His heart hammered in time with his fists.

The hammering slowed. Defeated, Yann realised that it was obvious that people of Anglo-Celtic origin in Forest Creek would suspect him. He was French. In the country of his birth, the death penalty was carried out by decapitation. .

His breath came in tiny, rhythmic gasps. Was this how Magali's fiancé had felt before being stabbed with a bayonet? Had he been indignant at the injustice of it all? Or had his death come about in the heat of battle? Yann was aware that his father had been involved in some way. "You knew, you knew …" He remembered Madeleine's words in the Tuileries as clearly as if she had said them that morning.

His breathing calmed. Somewhere he heard music, a sawing sound, discordant. Like a cow in pain. Was he sick in the mind, driven insane by having been locked up unjustly? He had heard music like this before, one time on the footpath outside Le Meurice when he and his parents arrived for lunch. The musician had worn a strange costume, a skirt, just below the knees.

Jean-Paul Sauvage had smiled, tossed a few sous into the man's cap and said, "*Merci, monsieur.*"

Yann had winced, thinking the tune harsh and ugly when compared with his own sweet accordion.

"This person is from Scotland and he wears a kilt," Jean-Paul had murmured in Yann's ear. "Are not the bagpipes the most wonderful sound in the world?"

Yann had screwed up his brow. "Can we go into the hotel? I am hungry for some hard-boiled swan's eggs. The kilt looks ridiculous and the noise from the bagpipes gives me a headache."

That same sound drilled through the pub din. Was he really going mad?

46

Upstairs, the chink of glasses faded. The fiddler no longer played. The piano fell silent, and the click of balls on cue stopped. Yann wondered if he should attempt to dig his way out while everyone was asleep, using his cut-throat razor as a tool. The sandstone walls were three feet thick, at least. He felt the walls of the prison close in on him, but forced his shoulders back, inhaled and decided to try anyway.

At first, the stink from the hole in the ground which did duty as a toilet made him gag. He swallowed back the bile, and moved from the north-west corner of the cell to the southern end. If there was a gap in the foundations, he reasoned, he could tunnel underneath and crawl out.

He edged the cut-throat razor from his pocket and opened it wide. The shackles bruised and lacerated his ankles as, chains rattling, he began to scratch around in the dark. He ignored the putrid earth beneath his feet and soon detected the sweet smell of fresh soil. He continued on and managed to create a hole, only small, but a hole nevertheless.

He inserted his fingers into the gap and felt around. Was that another wall to the rear? He could detect no draught. Did the cell join the Assembly Hall? If the aperture became large enough, he could wriggle through and let himself out the door exiting onto Mount Alexander Road. Once on the highway, he could head for the scrub. He could exist in the scrub indefinitely, eating wild berries and other native foods. He could collect dew for clean drinking water.

Maybe he could even befriend a newcomer to the Diggings? In this constantly fluctuating community, it would be easy to enlist aid. He could hitch a ride on a dray to somewhere, anywhere. As long as he got away safely before they tried to hang him.

Feverishly he continued to dig. His hands were so raw he could barely feel them and he paused to shake the circulation back. While flexing his joints, he heard footsteps. Heavy and measured. A light flickered through the darkness. Someone was approaching. Were the authorities coming to take him away to Melbourne in the middle of the night so they could hang him sooner? he wondered. Even without trial? Was he to be hanged quickly, before any evidence of his innocence had emerged?

Yann's body dripped with sweat. His heart seemed to cease functioning. He hastily folded the razor and pushed it back into his pocket, numbed and trembling, praying this was not the police.

"You will never dig your way out of *this* lockup!" boomed a voice. "The cell in which you are incarcerated is the most secure in the entire Colony of Victoria! I reckoned from the start there would be vagabonds aplenty on the Diggings. So I designed the place m'self. No one can escape!"

William Bass wore a chartreuse velvet frockcoat and a shirt with a white lace jabot, as though he had been socialising. He stood there with a beaming smile on his face. His whiskers were neatly combed. He held a lamp and a platter of cheese and grapes, together with a bottle of wine and a glass.

Yann felt the saliva surge into his mouth. He couldn't remember when he had last eaten and briefly regretted not having accepted Barnaby's offer of soup.

He eyed the food hungrily. "*N-non, monsieur.* B-but I never, never do any-sing wrong."

It was as if he had never spoken.

William Bass made no comment. The tone of his voice was jovial as he continued, "My barman says you were not too appreciative of our cook's soup … and, I have to say, at moments I would agree with you, especially when his wife is unable to do duty as kitchen hand and the chappie is in his cups. So I thought you might enjoy some fresh cheese, arrived on the Cobb & Co. coach just this morning. All European fellers like cheeses, don't they?"

Not waiting for an answer, the innkeeper continued, "I have some camembert, all the way from Normandy together with a few grapes. I considered offering you our house liqueur, then decided on this superb Beaujolais." He waved the bottle of red.

Yann gaped.

"You do enjoy camembert, I assume?" William Bass pushed the platter under the cell door with his blunt forefinger, and then poked the wine and the glass between the bars.

Yann could feel his mouth drop open even further.

Was he dreaming? Had he really gone insane this time?

"*Oui, je-je, oui, oui, monsieur,*" he stuttered, his mind scrabbling for some way to explain the hotelkeeper's unexpected largesse. "I-I am, I am sorry I not find your chapbook. I even see zis man one more time … on ze night of Gala Ball. But 'e disappear before I can do anysing."

And, after that, Yann reminded himself, the Comte de Corbeau had paid Jonas to denounce him. The reason he was in this predicament.

"Forget about my errant slim volume! You have done the movement an even greater service, an act of supreme courage. Well done, young man."

Yann's mind whirled. Movement? What movement? The Saint-Simonian movement? None of this made sense.

"You have shown fortitude in adversity. I shall put in a good word for you!" The gold fob chain on William Bass's ample stomach gleamed in the dim light. "Don't you worry about a solitary thing!" His eyes shone with approval. "Now we know you are on our side, we will look after you."

"B-b-but."

"*Bon appétit!*" He turned on his heels.

"*Merci, monsieur.*"

The hotelkeeper's footsteps receded.

Yann pounced. He stuffed the food into his mouth, barely even tasting the camembert. Creamy goo clung to his tongue. The grapes exploded onto his palate. The delicious cheese mixed with spittle and ran down his chin. This was food of the gods, ambrosia, better than any meal he had ever eaten at Le Meurice. Far superior to the hard-boiled partridge eggs he had so enjoyed, and to the swans' eggs washed down with the not so enjoyable bitter brown beer.

Ignoring the stemmed glass, Yann snatched up the bottle of wine. He tilted his head and swigged, wiped his mouth with the back of his hand and swigged again. Never had French wine tasted so good. He drank until every drop was drained, then curled his tongue around the neck of the bottle. Replete, he slumped back onto the bench that stretched along the south wall of the lockup.

A mangy cat with yellow eyes slunk into his cell. Another cat arrived. Their coarse tongues licked at the remnants of runny cheese on the platter. Yann ignored them. Apart from Cyrano, he disliked cats, believing them to be cold and calculating. The Tonkinese was different: not only high-bred, but also sympathetic.

Yann prayed Cyrano was safe. His eyelids drooped. He ran his hands over his stomach. He would rest awhile before resuming his attempt to dig his way out of the lockup. He was sure William Bass was wrong. There must be a way out of here.

Shapes moved and swung. One of the cats snuffled at his feet, extending its tongue to lick his skin. Yann kicked the animal away. His shackles struck a sideways blow and the cat yowled and spat before slinking back beneath the bars of the lockup.

He was tired. So very, very tired.

And yet he needed to stay awake.

47

Yann lurched awake from a dreamless sleep. He clutched his head in his hands. His skull was pounding. Even his hair, flopping darkly over his brow, hurt.

The bagpipe player was approaching the lockup, making a terrible racket and Yann could hardly think for the noise and the pain. He shook his hair from his eyes. Closer and closer the squawking sound came until an officer of the Native Police appeared, pushing the kilt-clad man before him.

The lawman rattled a bunch of keys, opened the door and manhandled the resisting Scotsman into the lockup, where he continued to blow and squeeze the musical instrument. Yann felt his eyes spin from the agony. This piper was worse than the one outside Le Meurice. Or was his brain giving him false information, like an absinthe-infused fantasy?

And then he remembered. William Bass had come to visit him in the dead of night. His recollection of the event was hazy. Had the innkeeper really given him a bottle of French wine, which he had swigged until he passed out? And, if so, what had possessed William Bass to do such a thing?

Yann glanced around, unable to see any sign of the cheese platter, or the empty bottle. His gaze was diverted by the policeman's boot brushing against some grape stalks, sending stems skittering across the earthen floor. Yann spied some pips, those he had managed to spit out between jamming handfuls of food down his throat. Had someone removed all sign of the innkeeper's unexpected kindness? Had he been so drunk he had slept through that, and not heard a thing?

"Excuse me, *monsieur*. We are at what time of day … or night?" he asked. "'Ow long 'ave I been 'ere?"

The policeman gave a broad white smile and shrugged. He locked the door and strode off. Did the native not speak English, or was Yann's accent so bad the man was unable to fully understand? Sometimes Yann's poor grasp of English made him feel inferior. He promised himself to improve his language skills if ever he were freed. First he had to prove his innocence. But how?

Splinters of thought ran through him as the Scotsman continued to blow into his goatskin bag. The musician had small red eyes and a ginger beard. He wore a pilled brown tunic with his checked kilt, and his legs, bristling with ginger hair above tartan socks, were encrusted with dried mud. His breath reeked of whisky.

Yann felt a wave of nausea pass through his gut. He was tempted to pull out his cut-throat razor and slash the bag in two. Anything to stop that atrocious din.

As if reading his thoughts, the piper stopped playing. He lowered himself onto the bench beside Yann, removed his cap and rolled it between his hands. He then opened the fabric wide and began to fan his face, now beaded with sweat. His hair rose from his head in sprigs of curls.

"And what have ye done to be incarcerated, mon? Have ye mined without a licence, eh?" he asked with a half-smile.

Yann noted that not only did the man stink of whisky, he also smelled of sweat and blood pudding. He shook his head, murmuring, "Zey 'ave accused me of 'aving slain a Chinaman."

The piper scuttled backwards in a crablike movement to the far end of the bench seat. "Murrr-der?" His red eyes flared; his cracked lips narrowed. "Murrrr-derrrr!" His horsy teeth sputtered as he spoke. "Aye, mon, that's a veeeery serious off-ence!"

"But I not do it! I not cut off ze Chinaman's head which find itself in Pennyweight Flat, ah, *cimetière!*"

"Cemetery? Cut off his *head*, mon?" His voice rose to a hysterical squeak. "Ye must have a strongerrr stomach than I! How coooo-uld ye?" The Scotsman positioned the bagpipes firmly between them, as if that would help prevent Yann from slitting his throat right there in the cramped cell.

"But you no unnerstand. I not do it!"

"I believe ye, I believe ye." Then, in a more subdued voice, the piper added, "But there be thousands wouldn't." His little eyes darted from Yann's shackles to his own boots, as if assessing which of them would win if it came to a tussle.

Yann thought for a moment. "*Pardon, monsieur?* Ah, excuse me?"

"Aye, what is it ye be wantin', mon?" He rolled his cap between his hands again, round and around and around.

"Do you know anysing about h-h-hanging, *monsieur?* What 'appens? Where do zey carry zis out?"

"Me name is Scotty and noooo, I bain't seen any hangin', mon. I would rather have a bullet in me back while tryin' to escape than dangle at the end of a rope." He sighed, carefully unrolled his headgear and pushed it back down over his matted ginger hair.

"Ze jury, will zey be merchants of Melbourne who not know anysing about life on Diggings, or, or …" Yann's throat grated as he took a breath. "Does rope ever break, *monsieur*?" He had so many questions to ask. "And if ze trapdoor not work do zey let one go out into freedom?"

The Scotsman shook his head and remained mute. He clasped his hands, unlaced them and moved them back and forth in a washing motion. He frowned, and stopped what he was doing.

"Been eating grapes, mon?" He picked up a discarded stalk and twirled it.

Yann ran his tongue over his teeth, feeling their furriness.

"Aye, it's a lucky feller who eats the fruit of the vine, the food of the gods when locked up in prison, eh, mon?" Scotty gave a nervous laugh.

Yann decided it was better to say nothing. They sat there in silence, and Yann regretted not having read up on death by hanging before he came to Australia. He had known the laws were different here but he knew nothing of the law which most concerned him.

As he pondered, a sudden din broke out, yelling and screaming. Men and women, for the most part drunk, were being prodded down the passage towards the lockup. They hooted and complained in slurred and angry voices. They screamed abuse, using words Yann had never heard before.

"I never mined wif no licence", "I sell coffee, not ruuuum!", "Never served one drop of alcohol in me soup", "This is calumny, sir", "Wrongful arrest!", "Oi am not a strumpet! Oi am a respectable lady-eeee", "I don't wanna be shut up near no dead people!"

Phrases flung around the walls. The door squealed open. Two officers of the Native Police stuffed people, protesting, inside the cell.

One woman in a scarlet crinoline continued to announce her fear at being incarcerated near the morgue. "I don't wanna be shut up near no souls who've passed. I can smell 'em!" she wailed. "I can smell dead people in 'ere!"

Diggers dressed in soiled clothing milled, shoved one another, and soon there was only room to stand. Yann and the Scotsman became separated in the crush.

Nathaniel Clovis elbowed his way through, carrying manacles and a long chain.

"Youse is comin' with me, Frenchie," he snarled.

A hush fell over the other prisoners.

"*Ne me touche pas!*" yelled Yann. "Do not *touch* me!" In vain, he tried to ward off the trooper.

The eyes of the detainees widened as the trooper snapped the irons around Yann's wrists, attached the long chain to the links between the manacles, and turned the key. Checking to make sure the cell door was secured Nathaniel Clovis hauled Yann behind him up the passage, past the flickering candle in the alcove.

A new candle had been placed in the niche and a solitary tear of wax ran down one side, like a ghost weeping. Water dripped off the sandstone as Yann stumbled towards the stairs. Chains clanking, he inched his way up the steps, one foot at a time. Splinters pricked at his skin. Pebbles and river sand left by the miners going down below to deposit their gold dug into the soles of his feet.

The afternoon sun blasted into his face and Yann's eyes filled with tears, making it difficult for him to see. His heart ricocheted so hard he thought it would shatter into a thousand pieces. So already they were taking him to Melbourne to be tried for the murder of a Chinaman he barely knew?

Diggers trudging up Mount Alexander Road gave sideways glances, briefly paused, muttered into their beards, and then moved on. The trooper led Yann to a sturdy log on the opposite side of the highway to the Red Boulder Hotel.

"Ye can wait here, Frenchie."

"Am-am-am I going to Melbourne, *monsieur*?" stammered Yann. "Will zey be coming for me 'ere?"

No reply.

"B-b-but I am innocent!"

The trooper propped his rifle against the log and pushed Yann down into a sitting position before winding the long chain around a side branch at one end.

"Ye won't be goin' too far at all now! Not of yer own volition." He spat at the ground. "Even yer animal cunning, yer apish ruses can't help ye … ye influence peddler wiv grandiose ideas! The Little Corporal's grandson? A likely story!" He pulled a nail from his pocket and hammered the chain into place with the butt of his rifle. "Youse has crawled out of the gutters of Paris, I'll be bound."

Adjusting his patch, the trooper swaggered back across the road and into the bar of the Red Boulder Hotel.

The sound of horses' hooves rang out. A Cobb & Co. coach crested the hill.

48

Passengers descended from the coach. A band of fear constricted Yann's throat and he had difficulty breathing. He mumbled the Lord's Prayer in a low voice: *Pater noster, qui es in caelis, sanctificetur nomen tuum ...* Tremors ran through his body as he waited to be released from the log and taken aboard. But his fevered gaze could see no rifle-wielding lawman. Even Trooper Clovis failed to reappear.

No one came near him. William Bass's sister was the only person to mount. Francis Angus handed her valise to the coachman to stow, waved farewell and went back inside the Red Boulder Hotel.

With a shout and a sharp crack of the whip over the heads of the straining horse team, the driver set the vehicle in motion. The carriage wheels crunched, sending stones flying as the conveyance disappeared over the hill in the direction of Melbourne.

Yann exhaled. His body seemed to melt with relief.

The sun beat down. The shackles and manacles, heated by the rays, scorched his skin. Yann's feet, pale from having been encased in boots, soon became inflamed. Chinese diggers, carrying their possessions at the end of long, curved poles balanced on their shoulders, passed without a sideways glance. Diggers pushing barrows, and their trailing dogs, barely looked. The tinker hurried by, whistling, but said nothing. A cart covered in a bulging canvas tarpaulin, like a risen pudding, swayed along the road throwing up clouds of dust.

The Gold Escort team pulled up in front of the Red Boulder Hotel and Studs de Wolf jumped down from the driver's seat. Giving a brief, uninterested glance at Yann chained to the log on the other side of the highway, he turned and went into the bar.

But then one man edged up and murmured to him, "Well done, young man." The digger tipped his waterbag over Yann's head before moving on.

Another whispered, "Welcome to the movement", before cutting through tents and scrub on his way to Forest Creek.

A third spat in his face and hissed, "Human life is sacred, no matter what colour or creed!"

Yann listened to the talk filtering around him, much of it complaints about the Chinese presence on the Diggings. A groom scurried out of the Red Boulder Hotel. The carrot-haired lad unhitched the Gold Escort horses and led them away to the stables at the rear of the inn. A gypsy caravan, daubed with vivid carnations on a sun-bleached yellow background, trundled along. An urchin jumped from the back and wove his way through the passers-by, fingers darting into pockets as he extracted pieces of gold, silver watches, trinkets, charms and gleaming fob chains. A bowler-hatted gentleman yelled, "Hey, stop! Thief!", and waddled after the urchin.

The pickpocket vaulted back into the caravan and the bright wagon disappeared over the hill in the direction of Castlemaine.

The driver of a cart piled high with wooden boxes filled with cackling chickens pulled up and leapt down from his perch. He examined the shaft and found it was broken. He jogged off down the road to the blacksmith. When the driver tapped him on the shoulder, the smithy handed him the bellows and set him to work.

A digger pushed a wheelbarrow made from pine cases, loaded with bedding, two picks and a shovel. A box-cart joggled along the centre of the road, carrying a lady flourishing a green parasol and with a multicoloured parrot beside her. A large dog, harnessed to a small two-wheeled cart, clattered along with three ragged children in the tray.

Bathed in traffic dirt, Yann wondered how long he would have to remain in the sweltering sun. Would they send him to Castlemaine? Or would the Commissioner decide to have him tried in the Court of Petty Sessions held in the Red Boulder Hotel? Would he be committed for trial at the next General Sessions? He was exhausted by the heat and the waiting.

His eyelids began to close. If only another passer-by would stop and tip a waterbag over his head. He felt an unexpected breeze in his face. He could smell sage and rosemary.

49

Yann coaxed his lids open. Magali stood there, waving a plaited fan and holding a man's straw hat. His accordion was tucked under her arm. Her eyes were puffy and red-rimmed.

"Oh, Yann," she said in French. "I cannot imagine what they are saying is true. Madeleine would be so distressed ... is so distressed." The accordion squawked as she placed it on the ground and pointed upwards. "Knowing her beautiful boy has been accused of the terrible crime of slaying a Chinaman."

"But I did not do it!"

She smoothed his hair back from his brow and plunked the straw hat down on his head. "Oh, I understand. It is not your fault. Gold drives men mad."

"You do *not* understand. I did not, I repeat, did *not* do it!" The chain between the manacles clattered and rubbed as he attempted to gesticulate.

Magali looked distracted. Tears began to stream down her face and Yann remembered the Scotsman saying he believed him but thousands wouldn't. Did Magali also not believe him?

"Do you not trust me?"

Her tears turned to howling sobs and Yann was gratified to know she cared so much about him.

"O Lord, give us strength and succour! My plants have failed me! I was unable to cure the child," she moaned, "and now she is gone to Pennyweight Flat Cemetery and I with not enough to buy her a decent headstone. Mr Brisket consoled me, saying the Lord is not concerned with fancy gravestones, but the ground is so hard in the children's cemetery, so unforgiving!" She wailed anew.

"Who has gone to Pennyweight Flat?" Yann asked, confused. "Did Dora pass, Bethany?" Although he found them obnoxious, he would not have wished this fate on either of them.

Magali did not respond.

"Tell me!"

She continued to ramble on. "I recited the 23rd Psalm all day and night. The Lord is my Shepherd is a psalm about living, not dying, and yet she still passed! When she came to me, her clothes were laced with typhoid. But I was wrong in my diagnosis. Her rash had turned to pustules at the end, poor infant. I pray it was not the pox and the Brisket children are not infected."

Yann frowned, trying to concentrate. His head was pounding and he was having difficulty following Magali's tale.

She waved the fan across her now swollen face. "I *had* to take her in, you see. I simply had to!" Locks of hair broke loose from the bonnet tied beneath her chin; she tucked them back under. "I had no option, you understand. She was so frail, so very very frail."

By this time, Yann had realised that Eleanor was the child who had passed. Had Eleanor infused his mattress with a terrible contagion? Or did it not matter? Would he ever sleep in his bed again? Here he was, drowning in dust and heat, and with little prospect of surviving this terrifying predicament.

His shoulders sagged. "I have gold in my pocket. Take it and buy a proper gravestone for Eleanor. I won't need it where I am going."

"O Lord, give us strength and succour!" Magali repeated the mantra. "O Lord, please help Madeleine's son to bear the pain he suffers."

A woman in a blue gingham pinafore crossed herself as she walked by, but for the most part, diggers wheeling barrows and trailing dogs ignored Magali's weeping and hand wringing. A dray trundled past, hauling a load of timber. The bullocky gave a bloodcurdling oath as he urged the team on. The sound of the whip, a thong of bullock hide, was like a gunshot. Magali started. The sudden sharp noise seemed to restore her composure.

"Buy a gravestone for Eleanor, did you say?" She gave a quick sniff. "How generous, Yann! How kind of you to be cognisant of the misfortunes of others when in such an onerous situation yourself! Madeleine would be so very proud."

Yann deliberated, before saying, "You could even buy her a marble slab, like the ones in Cimetière du Père-Lachaise, to mark her grave. Like the one *Maman* has."

"No, that would be too much and *quite* unnecessary for Pennyweight Flat Cemetery." Magali snaked her fingers into his pocket, searching for the gold, and pulled out his kerchief. As she did, the Napoleonic button fell out. "*Wherever* did you find this?" she gasped. "This reminds me, but surely not …"

"I discovered the button in the mine, before the cave-in. It was, oh, I think it was floating in the water."

"Does this mean, is this, could this really be …?" Magali's gaze, now dry-eyed, locked with his.

"That *Papa* had worked the very same claim, has been in the very same mine as I was? I have no other explanation for the find. An amazing coincidence if it is true, and I believe it is!"

"Why, that is wonderful! You are coming ever closer to finding Jean-Paul Sauvage." Leaving a small amount of gold for his use should he need it, she folded the button into the fabric and pushed the kerchief back into his pocket.

"But I will never see him now, so it is of no importance whether *Papa* worked the same mine as I did."

"Of course you will see Jean-Paul!" She straightened. "Your father has connections. He will have you released from this terrible charge in no time." She rummaged in her purse. "I have brought with me the images of your parents to give you comfort while you wait." She poked the daguerreotypes in beside his kerchief.

"First, he needs to know I have been accused." The chains rattled. "Second, you cannot be so sure he will have me released, or you would not have brought my parents' likenesses for me to carry to wherever I am headed." He drew a breath. "Third, this will not happen if the Saint-Simonians have their way."

Magali's brows drew together, as if she were thinking.

Yann added, "At any rate, I am certain Le Comte de Corbeau planned the whole sorry episode!"

"Pfft!" Magali was back to her old self. "It would have been easier for him to shoot you than run the risk of a judge perhaps letting you off the charge of murder and setting you free. No, I have decided it is all a misunderstanding."

"Then why am I sitting here, chained to a log? Tell me that. Explain my arrest if you can!"

She abruptly changed the subject. "I am starting up a school for young gels, that is my plan. I will set up a ladies' seminary on the goldfields."

Yann stared at her as if she had gone mad.

"The Diggings needs a school," she continued. "The respectable portion of Forest Creek residents complains of the scenes of gross … yes, gross! … debauchery constantly witnessed in the neighbourhood. *Repugnant* spectacles by day are succeeded by riotous behaviour at night."

Yann shuffled his feet, trying to get comfortable.

Her voice was awash with righteousness. "A whole host of sly grog shops operate in the vicinity." She pointed down the highway. "They receive the most disreputable characters on the Diggings long after the Red Boulder Hotel and others are closed. The profligate and indecent conduct of some of these people is said to be past endurance."

"They are simply homesick, as I am," he murmured.

Her eyes flashed with anger. "A remedy to help stop the nuisance is education, Yann! Education is a civilising factor. And not only is Mr Brisket supportive of my scheme … William Bass has indicated he is prepared to chip in, hold a benefit for the wellbeing of the young who are lost in this town of canvas tents, starvation, disease and depredation. Mr Francis Angus has promised to pull his weight by conducting quadrille classes, and has also agreed to design the building for my new school *plus* provide the labour. Isn't that wonderful?"

"What about me?" Yann burst out. "You have all these plans. I am to be hanged for a crime I did not commit and you are concerning yourself with the lives of others."

"They will not hang you!"

"Of course they will hang me! That is what they do in the Colony of Victoria! The penalty for murder is death at the end of a rope!"

"I wouldn't be so sure, Yann, not so sure at all." Magali lowered her voice and said, "This is a very racist place we live in! The Chinese, although a gentle people, do not help their cause by sending the gold back home. There are many who would be sympathetic to your actions, ascribing them to a simple case of sunstroke."

"But they were not my actions!" he fumed. "Even if Johnnie Lee did plan to buy Cyrano from the butcher, I did *not* kill him!"

"I believe you, Yann. And … ahem! … I now plan to retrieve your boots, which the cards tell me have been dishonestly taken." She touched him on the shoulder. "Mr Bass will give the footwear to me, I am certain. I doubt he will agree to return your dagger, but at least your feet will be more at ease."

The sun was now low in the sky.

Magali's form assumed a golden glow as, regal and upright, she crossed the road and disappeared through the front door of the Red Boulder Hotel.

50

Still perched on the log, Yann eyed the boots beside his now stockinged feet. These boots had caused him so much trouble. He longed to wear them but, hampered by the shackles, he was unable to put them on.

William Bass, meeting with Forest Creek businessmen inside his private sitting room, had sent a lackey to fetch Yann's footwear, according to Magali. However, he had refused to arrange for the removal of the irons. Magali had gone on to say the trooper was inside the bar, too drunk to be capable of uttering one word which made sense, and was of no use to anyone.

"Nathaniel Clovis is an ex-convict from Van Diemen's Land and completely unprincipled. The bigger the fine the more money he makes … I understand he gets fifty percent. *And* he will be the beneficiary of an even greater windfall for having captured a murderer."

"But I am *not* an assassin!"

"I know, I know, but there are those who think otherwise." Magali had then tried to wedge the boots on so they sat beneath the constraints. "Mr Brisket is constantly saying, 'The Lord moves in mysterious ways', and I believe he is correct in his assessment of this situation.".

Yann had clamped his teeth together and said nothing.

After wiggling the footwear unsuccessfully, Magali had blown out a sigh and pushed herself up. "I must leave. I have to prepare a supper of galettes for when Mr Brisket returns." Her cheeks turned a rosy shade of pink. "And the children, too, of course, are with him and all will be ravenous after the day spent panning on Forest Creek!"

Yann was too depressed to reply.

After giving him a moist kiss on the forehead, Magali had rushed off. "Eleanor will be grateful." She had pointed upwards again. "Grateful for your thoughtful gift of a gravestone befitting a life cut short in such a terrible fashion."

Yann squirmed within the constraints, realising he would never get to see Eleanor's gravestone. His own life was about to be cut short, and he would have been ecstatic to spend the day panning on Forest Creek, rather than be chained and waiting to be formally charged with murder. His mouth filled with saliva at the thought of eating galettes, the food he had taken for granted. Dark sweat oozed through his flannel shirt, sticking the fabric to his back. His braces were digging grooves into his shoulders and he attempted to slip out of them, but the manacles kept getting in the way. He squiggled about in a vain attempt to make himself comfortable.

Twilight had set in. Carriages continued to pass. Diggers mooched by with spades slung over their shoulders. Some headed for their tents and supper, some for the sly grog outlets and others, with more gold in their pockets, for the bar of the Red Boulder Hotel.

One man laughed. "Ye will be sittin' there until ye pay yer fine, lad," he chortled, hitching up his moleskins.

If only it were that simple.

Yann saw Clemency Holmes-Lacy passing on the opposite side of the road. Dressed in a mauve crinoline with a white pinafore tied at her waist, she carried a basket of produce slung over her arm. Princess Albert, on a leash, snuffled along behind her.

Yann attempted to whistle, but only a rush of air came out.

"Eh, Clem!" he shouted in a croaky voice, anxious to know if Cyrano was still safe, but his words were drowned by an Indian merchant, trailing a pair of miniature horses and banging on a drum.

Without giving the slightest glance in Yann's direction, Clem wound Princess Albert's leash around the hitching post. She turned and entered the hotel, disappearing into the dimness with her basket.

Princess Albert began licking. The dog stopped to chew on a flea and then licked again, ceased what it was doing, sniffed and peered myopically across the road. Excited yelps rang out. Did he really smell so bad that the animal was able to detect him by odour from the opposite side of the busy highway? Yann asked himself.

The dog continued to yelp. Studs de Wolf emerged from the bar into the street. Yann held his breath, expecting the Gold Escort operator to give the animal a swift kick. Ignoring Princess Albert, Studs de Wolf strode off down Mount Alexander Road, hair flying as he made for the Holmes-Lacy General Store and Post Office. Was he collecting his mail, Yann wondered, or was he stocking up for another Gold Escort expedition? The British bulldog continued to yelp and turn circles, tying the lead in knots around the hitching post.

Clem came out of the hotel. "Oh, Princess Albert, what have you *done*?" She busied herself untangling the leash, still not looking in Yann's direction.

Why did Clem refuse to acknowledge his existence? Yann was bewildered. Had something happened to Cyrano and she was too afraid to let him know? Or did she believe he had murdered the Chinaman and want nothing more to do with him?

He yelled again. "Eh, Clem! I am 'ere, on ze ozzer side of ze street."

This time Yann's voice carried, and he knew it. Still she ignored him. Her cheeks were fiery. Blonde curls bobbed from her bonnet and her fingers jiggled at the leash until finally Princess Albert was free. Her button-up boots threw out puffs of dust as she hurried off down the street, heading for the Holmes-Lacy General Store and Post Office. Princess Albert alternatively barked, growled and yelped in her wake. Globules of foam and frothy frustration flew into the air. The dog's eyes bulged.

Princess Albert kept looking back at Yann, and hauling against the lead, but Clem's gaze remained steadfast. She never gave a sign, never wished Yann good luck. Again, Yann began to doubt Clemency Holmes-Lacy. Was she really his friend through thick or thin, or was she only a fair-weather friend? Had his original assessment of Clemency Holmes-Lacy—that she was arrogant and thought him no better than the dirt beneath her feet—been correct,?

Darkness descended over the Diggings. Fires burned beside the tents. Yann could hear snatches of conversation coming from the dwellings. The scent of smouldering leaves was heady and he took deep breaths. Still no one came near him.

The piano started up in the Red Boulder Hotel, a tinkly Irish tune. He could hear shouting from the bar, raucous laughter, tales being spun about the gold which had turned out to be nothing but fool's gold. A patron belted out a rendition of 'My Old Kentucky Home'. Bearded diggers stood at the doorway smoking pipes and bidding one another drawn-out farewells before heading off to their canvas tents, slab homes and pug dwellings. Did they feel as homesick as he, as cut off and lonely? If they did, they hid their feelings well.

Yann's rear end was numb. It felt as though he had become one with the log he sat on. Carriages passed, their lighted lamps flashing. Men on horseback clipped by. Drays rumbled along the highway.

A phaeton pulled up at the Red Boulder Hotel and two ladies in satin crinolines descended. They wore fascinators in their hair, black net scattered with silken flowers. They lifted their skirts and, bowing and smiling, passed through the front door. Were these women singers? Were they part of the English Opera Company William Bass had advertised as soon to perform in his Concert and Assembly Hall? Or were they ladies of the night, like the courtesans Yann had seen descending from gilded carriages in France? Like the women who had hung on Napoleon Ш's arm before he married the beautiful Spanish noblewoman, the Countess of Teba?

Did fancy ladies frequent William Bass's establishment? Yann wondered. He didn't believe so. Rumour had it that the innkeeper would be marrying his respectable lady friend, who resided in Melbourne, and bringing her back to Forest Creek.

Farther down the road a quarrel broke out. People were handing around drink in buckets. Men dipped mugs in the alcohol, swigged and, inebriated, punched one another. A man pulled out his gun and waved it. Soon the evening ritual of firing into the air began, and the sky filled with stuttering lights which blotted out the stars above.

During the kerfuffle, flames burst heavenwards. Forks of fire began to lick at the roof of the Empire Inn further down the road. Was this a riot by anti-Chinese miners on his behalf, similar to the one which had taken place in Ballarat? Would this diversion help him to escape?

Windows exploded. The hotel turned into a blaze of burning rafters, flaming eaves and falling walls. People jumped for their lives, two men naked from the waist down. One woman ran down the middle of the road in a lace corset and stockings, stumbling and screaming. She smelled of cheap perfume and singed fabric. Men burst from the bar of the Red Boulder Hotel. Feathers of sparks rained down. The fireman's cart rattled down the road, the barrel filled with swamp water, swaying and rocking as the horses picked up pace.

William Bass stood in the doorway of the Red Boulder Hotel with a glass of port in his hand, surveying the scene. He looked across at Yann chained to his log.

He raised the drink and called, "Keep your pecker up, young man!" then turned and went back in.

Cinders clogged Yann's nostrils. He coughed, spat sooty phlegm onto the ground and tugged at his chains. He bunched his fingers into a long narrow shape. If he managed to slip off his restraints, no one would notice in all the fuss. Except maybe the hotelkeeper. And William Bass had indicated that he was on Yann's side.

Diggers scrambled out of their tents, rushing along Mount Alexander Road to gawp. It was as if Yann was invisible. This was his chance.

51

Exhausted, Yann lay sprawled sideways on the log. His efforts had come to nothing. His wrists were bruised, his ankles lacerated, and he was still chained. The crackle of the fire had died down, the roar of the flames extinguished.

Quietness had settled over the Diggings. A single scream rang out as someone staggered, probably drunk, into the wrong tent. Acrid smoke still hung in the air and the charred ruins of the Empire Inn etched chaotic spikes against the navy-blue sky.

Yann dozed fitfully. Starting at the call of a mopoke, he was lulled back to sleep by the rattle of possums and the other nocturnal creatures around him. More and more, they seemed to give him comfort. His dreams became vivid. Something poked at his arm? A snake? A lizard? Yann was too exhausted to care.

A furry object clamped itself on his neck. He was wrapped in pelt and saliva. Pins pricked his skin. His left hand clinked and fidgeted, as if shaken by an alien being. A rasping filtered into his imaginings. Shivers ran through his body. The strange jangling continued and he opened his eyes.

"I am sorry, Yann, but we have little time to waste. Am I hurting you?" a voice murmured.

Yann jerked his left shoulder to edge away the weight. And then he realised it was Cyrano seated on his neck, purring and dribbling, pinning him down.

"*Salut, toi!*" Yann said, grinning. "Hello, you!"

Straining to lift his head, he saw Clem, wearing moleskins and with her hair tucked under her leather cap, kneeling on the ground beside him. The saw she wielded grated against the metal. She clacked and scraped, grunting as she worked. Normally Clem would have chatted, come out with words of encouragement, words he had come to depend upon. But this time it was different. Her hand moved with urgency.

Yann elbowed his way up. Cyrano, now on his shoulder, jumped down. The Tonkinese perched on one end of the log and settled to watch.

The tool vibrated and shivered until Yann heard a crack. A chunk of metal plopped into the soil beneath his feet. Clem hissed through her teeth and kept on sawing. The chain between the manacles rattled against the nail driven into the log. In the distance a dog barked, whined and then began to yelp. A howl echoed through the night, high and piercing and almost hysterical.

Cyrano's fur rose. He made a strange twittering noise.

"Whose dog is that?" asked Yann.

"Princess Albert," Clem responded, not looking up. "Poor darling, she misses your monkey cat already."

Cyrano stalked back and forth along the log, purring and flexing his claws.

"Why did you not wish to talk to me zis afternoon?" Yann's knuckles tensed. "I call to you and you not reply."

She shrugged and kept filing. "If I had crossed the road and spoken to you, I would be the first person to be accused after your escape from Forest Creek. I could not afford to jeopardise your chance of liberty. Now no one will be able to name the one who set you free. Even Da will not suspect."

"But you make me very unhappy. I need to speak wis you and you do not answer me."

Clem did not reply this time, merely complaining about the tool she was using. "This amputation saw is really quite blunt. I believe it is something to do with the tapering style of the instrument." She grated the blade across the metal.

"Amputation?" Yann felt a pinpoint of panic.

"Don't worry. I shall do my best to avoid severing your hand!" He saw the dimple curve into her cheek and then fade. "The sawbones who ordered this surgeon's tool never thought to collect it from our store. He was too concerned with making his fortune through colour and, following a rumour, fled to Wombat Flat." She gave a final swipe. "There we are! One manacle gone!"

Part of the constraint dropped to the ground, freeing his left hand. Yann felt like whooping with joy. Without saying a word, Clem passed him her waterbag.

Yann's hand shook as he tipped the water into his mouth. "*Merci!*" He gulped the cool fluid.

"Here you are, take this." Clem passed him a finger saw with a cross-hatched ebony handle. "You can do the right manacle while I attend to the shackles. You will be able to put your boots on in no time."

Tides of warm night air washed over them and, as they worked, a lone rider clipped along the highway. The horse whinnied. The clop of hooves sounded.

"A person is coming!" Yann, rasping at the metal bracelet on his right hand, felt sweat break out across his upper lip.

"Do not be concerned. It is only Studs de Wolf preparing to leave. He has agreed to take you with him. He needs an extra hand to drive the supply wagon. You do know how to handle a dray, I assume?"

Yann, who was used to riding horses in France, but had never driven a dray, looked down. "*Oui*," he said in a low voice.

"Good. Then you will be leaving with the Gold Escort before dawn, off to the goldfields at Ballarat."

"Ballarat? But I do not wish to go to Ballarat goldfields!"

"I understand your concerns. There is unrest in those Diggings. The Ballarat Reform League has been formed with a view to abolish licences, and their aim is also to have the miners who were imprisoned for burning down Bentley's Eureka Hotel released. But you will be free there, Yann. No one will *know* you on those Diggings. With all the comings and goings, you will blend in and maybe discover enough gold to purchase a ticket back to your country." Her voice caught. "I wish I could say otherwise, that you will remain in Forest Creek. But you have no other option, unless you prefer to be hanged for something … for something you did not do."

The shackle on Yann's right foot dropped away. Before he had succeeded in severing the manacle on his right hand, the shackle on his left foot parted. Yann still sawed while Clem pushed his feet into the boots and laced them.

"There is something in here!" She poked the toe of each boot.

"Ze boots are too big. Magali puts bandages inside so zey will fit my foots."

"Oh, I see."

Yann still struggled to cut through the right manacle. "*Merde! Merde!*" he muttered. "I am sorreee. I am *droitier*, so zis is not easy for me."

"Of course, you are right-handed," she sighed. "How silly of me! I should have done the right manacle first." She picked up the amputation saw and began to whittle the metal.

Snap. The lock of the Red Boulder Hotel front door clicked open.

"Quick! Lie down as you were," hissed Clem.

The accordion beeped as she vaulted the log and threw herself lengthwise on the ground. William Bass poked his head out the front door.

He whistled, long and low, waited for a moment and retreated back inside. He clicked the bolt back into place.

Yann turned and peered down at Clem. "Why does 'e whistle?"

"Oh, Studs de Wolf prefers to take the bullion from the back of the hotel." She pushed herself up. "Mr de Wolf always chooses a different hour of the night to leave. He warns Mr Bass in advance so he can bring the gold up from the vault in the hotel." She brushed the dust off her clothing. "He was just giving the all-clear."

"It make sense."

She pulled him upright. "Now you only have to wait. Mr de Wolf will let you know when he is ready."

"I can take Cyrano wis me?"

"Of course!" Clem's voice trembled. "Did you imagine otherwise? I know how much your monkey cat means to you."

Yann eased his fingers from her grasp.

"And Magali? She will be quite worried when she sees I 'ave disappeared." He placed his hands on either side of Clem's neck, feeling the softness of her skin. "She will sink I have been taken to Melbourne for trial."

"I shall tell her after you have gone. I will not say *where* you have gone, just let her know you are safe."

Yann inhaled a scent of vanilla and starched calico. As he reached to say good bye, his heart paddled. He hesitated.

And then, "I will say '*Au revoir*' in ze French fashion, a *bise* we call it in France."

She leaned into him and he kissed Clem on each cheek, slowly.

"*Merci*," he breathed, noticing the wetness of her tears, tasting their saltiness on his lips. "*Merci beaucoup* for every-sing you 'ave done for me."

Clem did not reply. Breaking free, she fled down Mount Alexander Road.

Feeling hollow inside, Yann tapped his shoulder. "*Allez viens*, Cyrano!"

The cat jumped up.

52

Yann placed the rifle on the seat beside his accordion. He was unsure how to use the weapon should he be forced to. He had fired his father's silver-handled pistol, but that was in France. He had not been in a situation where he'd had to defend himself then. How would he react under pressure?

"Ye may need it, ye may not." Studs de Wolf, his hair now tied at the nape, adjusted the two guns jammed into his belt. "It depends on whether there be rapacious strangers abroad. However, don't let any man come near ye. Challenge at fifty yards and warn 'em to stand off."

"And what if zey still come on?"

"Fire, lad!" The cartridges slotted into his leather vest were like long shiny slugs. "Any closer than fifty yards, fire!"

"'Ow do I know if I am on right direction for Ballarat?"

The Gold Escort operator suppressed a sigh. "Annabel knows the way. She won't mislead ye." He ran his fingers through the horse's mane, and then gave her a resounding slap.

Yann tensed up, expecting the draught horse to bolt. Annabel merely flicked her tail.

Behind Yann, Cyrano crouched on a mound of loose onions. The cat narrowed his eyes, but remained passive. In fact, Cyrano was purring. Which was odd. Yann tried to concentrate on Studs de Wolf's instructions.

"Just crack the whip to get her goin' and follow the highway, lad. The road is rough and, bearin' in mind this is the land of the Dja Dja Wurrung tribe, ye'll only manage about two miles in the hour … less than me."

"Will zey shoot spears at me?"

"Who's gunna shoot what spears?"

"Dja Dja Wurrung people."

"Reckon ye'll have more problems when ye get to Ballarat. They pretty stirred up about licences at the moment, even settin' up a stockade on the Eureka Lead." Studs de Wolf squinted. "Naw, the pastoral runs established here in the 1840s was called 'Yarrayne' afore that by the blackfellers." He spurted a wad of tobacco to the ground, where it left an ochre blob in the dust. "They's friendly enough as natives go. Ye'll know you're on the right track when ye see the big tree at the intersection."

"Big tree?"

"Red gum! *River* Red Gum, hundreds of years old with a generous umbrage and vast height. Ye cannot miss it." He sank his hand into his beard and scratched thoughtfully. "And then ye'll pass a large encampment of Chinese, upwards of six thousand, gathered along Campbell's Creek. Tents, Joss houses, opium dens, herbalists, even a circus. Ye can't go wrong! Biggest cluster of Chinese ye ever did see."

"Are zey dangerous?" Goose bumps pricked Yann's arm.

"Naw, they be too busy protectin' themselves. They even go to lengths of mining together, not as individuals, like, but in a type o' co-operative, using a new-fangled system of open-cut mining along Campbells Creek." Studs de Wolf grinned sourly. "They *knows* they's not pop'lar. A mob of diggers come down to Guildford, pinched their ounces and shot at least one of 'em." He wedged his thumbnail between his teeth, extracted a sliver of gristle and examined it. "I hear ye don't fancy the Asians yerself?"

"I did not …" Yann's words petered out to nothing. He knew it was no use protesting his innocence. The residents of Forest Creek had decided he'd beheaded the Chinaman, Johnnie Lee, and he could do little about it.

"Well, we should get back to the job at hand. Aim for the Bank of Victoria, Ballarat south side … look for an iron pot, a timber frame." Pause. "It were robbed by bushrangers for a sum of eighteen thousand pound last October … ye cannot miss it." He spat on the palm of his hand and they shook. "My iron-banded box is not necessarily what it seems, ye know. The colour may be stored somewhere different from what you, or anybody else, might expect. So keep yer firearm at the ready!"

Yann nodded.

Studs de Wolf turned to climb onto the seat of his wagon, patted the waiting brown dog, and then said over his shoulder, "I'll be changin' me horses at staging posts in the ten mile towns that service Gold Escorts. But you should have no need of that. Annabel will see you to the end, and this is where we part. I have a couple of fellers to accompany me through to Melbourne town." He flicked the reins.

The Gold Escort horses—one black, one white—clipped off, taking the road south.

Yann soon adjusted to the rocking motion of his supply wagon. On the seat beside him the lamp cast a wavering light on his accordion. Eucalypt fumes veiled the air like impregnated gauze and he inhaled the pungency.

It felt good to be free, although Yann missed Clem already. He was almost tempted to turn back, but knew he could not.

Through the darkness, in a distant valley, Yann heard boughs and branches falling as miners felled trees in the night for lining mine shafts as soon as the sun was up. The moon was bright and, from the stumps on either side of the road, Yann could tell that the Diggings had once been a forest.

The spread of tents that was Forest Creek receded. Wisps of cloud floated across the moon, leaving Yann with only the feeble flicker of the lamp beside him. The dray rattled over tree corrugations. The roads had been corduroyed; saplings and trunks had been laid to provide a firm footing for the horses towing the wagons.

A blacksmith's hut—dark and with no sign of life—on the side of the road advertised 'Farrier Supplies and Hand Wrought Iron Shoes'. A tent with 'Soups' on the roof made Yann feel hungry, but the lights were out there too. The empty bottles scattered among the tussocky grass and bare earth told him the soup was really alcohol. This was another sly grog shop.

Annabel jerked the bridle. Yann guided her around a dead horse and then a fallen bullock. He steered her through the debris of abandoned vehicles. More dead horses. More bullocks. Feral dogs ripped at decaying flesh.

"*Ça va!*" he murmured, surprised the horse was not spooked. "It's all right."

On the side of the road, salt-stained furniture had been abandoned in the wheat grass. A few solitary graves edged the roadside, their wooden crosses like wonky teeth. High above a far-flung valley, lightning lit up the sky. Eucalypts and box trees stretching upwards were ghostly and black-limbed. Soil dug from holes made shapes like lumps of coal plopped about by a drunken fuel merchant.

Stray boots and discarded picks showed gold fever had driven the diggers mad, making them discard everything that slowed them.

Thunder rumbled. Studs de Wolf had faded into the distance long ago and Yann was becoming edgy. What if a bushranger leapt from the undergrowth and waved a gun at him? He was uneasy at the thought of killing a man, even in self-defence. Then again, his wagon was filled with onions, sacks of flour, sugar bags, salt, tea, candlesticks, potatoes and pit props. Stock hardly worth fighting for. Unless a digger was starving, or low on support timbers for his mine, he would have no interest in murdering Yann for his load.

A mopoke hooted. Ground fog swirled around him and Yann's thoughts were drawn to France. When he told his Parisian friends he had worked as a Gold Escort driver, would they understand? Or care? Would they be more interested in their own partridge shooting, their visits to the tailor to be measured for elegant redingotes?

Again, he found himself missing Clem. There were so many things he wanted to ask her. He yearned for her down-to-earth advice, her sense of humour, the wholesome smell of her. He was free, though, and that would have to be enough.

Behind him, Cyrano sneezed.

"*Allez viens!*" Yann patted the seat beside him.

The cat remained on the pile of onions.

Well, Cyrano had saved his life, Yann reasoned. If not for him, he would probably be dead by now, interred within the mine. If Cyrano missed Princess Albert and wished to sulk, so be it.

53

A frisson ran through Yann. The constant snuffling in the undergrowth, the movement of the nocturnal creatures, set his nerves on edge. Possums peered down, their eyes red orbs of curiosity. Bush rats scuttled past. An owl swooped overhead, as pale and graceful as an angel. Everywhere he looked, eyes shone in the dark.

He spotted an unidentifiable mass of dark fur clumped within the branches of a roadside gum and his mind turned to the one person determined to make him suffer. What if the trooper woke from his drunken stupor and discovered his prisoner was no longer chained to the log? Would he follow, chase the supply dray all the way to Ballarat? The trooper's horse, although mangy, could outrace Annabel. Yann would have no chance of escaping a second time.

Except now the object of the trooper's hatred, Yann Bonaparte Sauvage, was armed with a rifle. Yann's cut-throat razor, although blunt from his attempt to dig his way out of the Red Boulder Hotel lockup, could also be handy if the need to fight to the death arose. The military button in his pocket reassured him. While he had that part of his father with him, he felt protected.

An inky darkness filled the heavens, indicating that dawn was not far off. An object lay by the roadside, fleshy and pulverised. Was that a human foot? Or road kill, a dead marsupial crushed by a passing coach laden with miners?

Yann's gaze lit on smashed whisky bottles, crockery, tinware and an old boot. He saw an axe-head, a leather bucket held together with metal studs and a frayed length of rope knotted into a noose. Had a digger attempted to hang himself—the very thing from which Yann was fleeing?

His side vision made out a pair of bellows, a rusted griddle iron and a crocheted milk jug cover fringed with glass beads. The spokes in the wheel of a discarded barrow were splayed at odd angles. Animals darted among these objects. The glowing eyes of spiders stood out in the bush like tiny yellow diamonds. Hollow logs and nests in trees, even holes in the ground, were a hive of night-time activity.

Cyrano was unmoved by the racket in the scrub. He seemed completely uninterested in this journey. Normally he would have been alongside Yann, keeping him company, speaking to him, responding to his queries, watching, sending out signals if strangers were abroad.

The air was cooler now and Yann felt an icy chill run through his veins. He had a bad feeling, and hunkered down into his waistcoat.

Soon kookaburras began to chortle in the surrounding trees. The pre-dawn light etched the horizon pink. The reins, moist with dew, slipped through his fingers, forcing him to secure the leather around his hand. He could see a mighty tree taking shape in the morning mist.

Was this 'The Big Tree'?

A cock crowed. Yann saw calico tents with narrow thoroughfares running this way and that between them, as Studs de Wolf had described. He noted the joss houses, tea-houses, boarding houses, tailors, apothecaries and gambling establishments. Inside opium dens, men slouched over wooden benches as though they had spent the night there. Some played mah-jong outside in the street, seated at small square tables. Yann spied a herbalist and a barber. Was that massive tent a theatre, or a circus?

A tiger paced back and forth inside a bamboo cage, telling him the canvas construction was indeed a circus, a big top.

Chinese miners stirred, emerging with poles slung across their shoulders. They made for the creek to begin fossicking in a long open cut area. The men took little notice of him, barely glancing in his direction from under their wide-brimmed hats. The cradles started roaring. Yann saw the puddling machines and windsails and felt ill at ease. What if these people recognised him, knew about his alleged crime? Would they come after him, believing he had killed one of their own?

A sign said Pennyweight Flat. Another ground of little value? Yann thought of the Pennyweight Flat Cemetery in Forest Creek. If his small contribution meant Eleanor would have a decent headstone, he would have achieved one good thing in this country.

Annabel hauled the dray past a building marked Cobb & Co., the staging post for coaches on their way to Melbourne. The Guildford Arms Hotel was next. A horse tied to the hitching post gave a lazy swish of its uncombed tail. A groom dozed on a bench nearby.

The sky, heavy with dryness, filled with an opaque glow. The scabby mined area, riddled with potholes and putrid heaps of soil, receded. Cyrano, still curled up on the onions, sneezed again.

"*Allez viens, mon pote!*" Again, Yann patted the seat beside him. "Come here, mate! I need someone to talk to."

The cat changed position, but made no effort to join him.

Yann saw fewer dead horses and bullocks during this part of the journey. Bits and pieces of abandoned luggage and shredded clothing lay by the roadside. He took deep breaths of fresh air. It was good to be free. He had nothing left to worry about—apart from finding Jean-Paul Sauvage.

In his bones, Yann was sure this had been his lucky break. Before being arrested for murder, Yann would never have considered leaving Forest Creek so soon. Now, with his father's military button secure in his pocket, he knew he would come across his father somewhere—*somewhere*.

A horse whinnied and he started, catching a glimpse of riders moving through the undergrowth a few yards in from the road. He suppressed the urge to make Annabel pick up pace. He counted in French: *un, deux, trois, quatre, cinq, six, sept, huit* … telling himself it was important to remain calm.

The horsemen disappeared and Yann relaxed. The road became hilly. The dray moved on, making for the next town: Wombat Flat. In the distance, kangaroos thumped across the paddocks. Again the roadside became littered with dead dogs, the flyblown corpses of fallen horses, bullocks' heads and even more abandoned luggage.

From the highway, Yann made out a bark hut. Beside it, a group of natives roasted a goanna over an open fire. Thin and black, they wore animal skins. Were they members of the Dja Dja Wurrung tribe? Would they throw a spear at him? He felt uneasy, but they looked peaceful enough. The undergrowth thickened again. A whipbird cracked. Willy-wagtails landed on Annabel's hindquarters. The birds skittered up and down her rump before flying off again.

Yann decided it was time to stretch his legs. He took a swig from the water bottle and jumped down. He tied the reins loosely and walked around in circles, stamping his feet on the tussocky ground. He could feel the bush's moodiness, the oppressive isolation of the countryside. Sweat soaked his flannel shirt and he couldn't remember when he'd last had a bath.

Cyrano, still in the back of the dray, sneezed again. Why was the cat, still crouched upon the onions, behaving so strangely? Was he miffed at being separated from Princess Albert? Was he sulky and annoyed with Yann for taking him away from Forest Creek?

While pondering this, Yann heard the clatter of an approaching vehicle. A Cobb & Co. coach packed with Chinese miners rattled over the hill. Hats and calico bundles dangled from the rear. The fortune hunters, dressed warmly for this time of year in jackets and scarves, huddled on the roof or inside the carriage. The coachman flayed the horses whose flanks were spackled with dried mud. The team of six blew and strained as they hauled the diggers on to Ballarat.

Wondering if he should give Annabel a rest from the shafts, Yann leaned down and plucked a piece of wallaby grass. He brushed off the seeds, retied his hair, pushed his hat back down on his head and prepared to release the mare.

At that moment, the sound of tree felling rent the air. Branches cracked. Gunshots split the silence and two horsemen galloped out of the undergrowth. Were these men bushrangers, intent on holding up the Cobb & Co. coach in order to rip gold and other possessions from the Chinese miners? Crows, cawing and swooping, settled in a nearby box tree.

The horses wheeled around. Yann's heart pumped.

The vagabonds headed in his direction.

54

The rifles gleamed in their holsters. The morning light hovered over the saddlebags. Sparks flickered off the metal of the gun barrel and Yann's eyes latched onto the black patch, the grog-blotched countenance of Nathaniel Clovis. He froze. He felt dizzy. His mouth went dry. Worse, his nemesis was accompanied by the tow-haired trooper. The latter's uniform was as ragged as ever and a dirty kerchief covered his face as he spurred the knock-kneed nag on.

The angle of the sun threw out long shadows, making the men appear taller. Twigs cracked. They towered, looming through the grasses and scrub. A mangy dog with brown and black stripes on its back trotted along beside them, sniffing the ground, its tail between its legs. *Had they been following all the while?* Yann asked himself.

The horses' nostrils flared and steamed. The sound reverberated through Yann's belly until he felt like throwing up. Two against one! He had no chance. His rifle, still on the seat of the dray, was beyond his reach.

"*Merde!*" he cursed. An icy determination washed through his body. "Fire!" Studs de Wolf had said. *Mon Dieu*, but it was not so easy.

"Halt!" he shouted.

A hot northerly wind picked up, moaning, and as Yann spoke a torrent of rain burst over the landscape. Ropes of moisture blew sideways, blurring the troopers with gold-seared streaks of water. Annabel whinnied, pushed backwards into the shafts and attempted to rear. Hooves hit the ground again.

The wagon shimmied, and in his peripheral vision, Yann saw Cyrano creep towards the front of the dray. The cat remained crouched, teeth bared for a moment. Guttural growling came from deep within his throat and he leapt in one bound, darted across the scrubby earth and up a nearby tree.

"Haaaallittt!" Yann bellowed for a second time.

The troopers kept on coming, slowly advancing. The bush creaked with their movement.

Yann felt anger at his inadequacy, at his poor language skills, at the fact that he had neglected to take the gun off the dray and carry it with him. His brain scrambled for an answer to this predicament. His cut-throat razor rubbed against his thigh. Not enough. He could never defend himself from two men with such an instrument, he told himself. His breath came in pants.

The water, streaming down from an apparently clear blue sky, stopped as suddenly as it had begun. Without warning, the onions in the dray erupted. Flakes of onion skin flew into the air, papery brown. The accordion pinged and bounced. The fat potatoes beside the onions flipped off the dray and puttered along the ground. A cloud of flour flew upwards, coating everything around it in sticky white powder.

Yann's eyes popped. Had he gone insane from too many hours in the sun? Turned lunatic from the stress of his ordeal? Had his arrest for murder, his burial in the mine, unhinged him? "*Merde!*" What was happening? He really had gone crazy, this time.

He could feel the bars of the asylum close around him, but then he saw Clem surging upwards. He knew then who'd been sneezing during the trip. It had been Clem, underneath the onions. Not Cyrano.

Clem threw her moleskin-clad body lengthwise onto the seat he had vacated. She snatched up Yann's rifle and began pumping bullets onto the ground around the troopers. The horses skittered, pitched upwards. The tow-haired trooper yanked the reins of his steed.

Nathaniel Clovis wheeled about, retreating to more than fifty yards away. He sat astride his nag watching, assessing the situation.

"There's another gun among the onions, Yann!" yelled Clem.

Her leather cap flew off. Her flaxen curls tumbled down and the tow-haired trooper knew for certain the young woman shooting at him was Clemency Holmes-Lacy—except, on this occasion, Clem was dressed as a man. His eyes glittered. Was he recalling the time Cyrano, Princess Albert and Clem had fought off his unwelcome advances? Was he remembering the storekeeper's daughter kicking him so hard in the groin he'd had trouble walking for days afterwards?

Yann knew he must do something or they both would die. He crept along the side of the wagon. Vaulting into the back, he kept his head low. Brandy bottles packed inside the flour had exploded and the dray was slippery with the gunk. The fumes from the illegally-stowed cargo stopped his breath. Gasping, he scrabbled around until he found the second rifle.

Annabel, agitated, shied but remained between the shafts. The dray slewed and rocked and Yann found it hard to maintain his balance. He slithered towards Clem.

The tow-haired trooper brought his horse under control and kept moving forward. Clem took aim. A screech rent the air. The mangy dog yelped and yelped, like a wolf baying at the moon.

"Oooh, nooo," moaned Clem. "I shot the poor dog!"

As Yann was about to fire at the advancing trooper, Cyrano launched himself from the tree. Aiming for the tow head he shafted his claws into the man's scalp, scratching and biting. He gouged at eyes and neck and ears, flying about like a whirling dervish. As if his life depended on saving Clem.

The tow-haired trooper screamed in pain. His horse bucked and reared. Hooves pawed the air and the lawman slipped sideways. He clung desperately to the saddle, like an acrobat rider from the Chinese circus. He kept slithering down, down, down. Slowly. Inexorably. As he went, he hauled on the steed's neck.

Cyrano, having leapt to safety, watched from a distance as the horse shuddered and flipped over. The tow-haired trooper's body slipped beneath the heaving torso. The animal rolled over and over, crushing the man's arms and legs. The man's ribs made a sickening, snapping noise as the horse struggled upwards, rolled back, and finally managed to right itself. Standing on four trembling legs, the steed snorted, gave a feeble whinny and cantered into the bush beside the highway.

The tow-haired trooper lay still, like a stranded starfish out of its natural environment. The kerchief had fallen from his now slack-jawed face. A trickle of blood ran from the corner of his mouth. His limbs were awry, raggedy and broken. The mangy dog continued to howl.

Nathaniel Clovis, his face twisted with rage, lifted his gun and made as if to shoot the dog. Thinking better of it, he slotted his rifle back into the holster on his saddlebag. He galloped off at high speed, firing a pistol into the air. He slowed, took aim at a kangaroo. The flailing marsupial fell to the ground, twitching until its eyes glazed over. The trooper careered off into the distance. Puffs of mud and dust flew into the air until the one-eyed man faded from view.

Cyrano leapt back into the dray. He perched beside Clem and began to lick his paws in long strokes, concentrating as he worked. His tongue was bright pink, his eyes two black-edged azure slits. His tail was like a bottlebrush, the only sign of any agitation. He continued to clean himself.

Clem made a choking sound.

Averting her head, she called to Yann in a shaky voice, "Pick up the tiger dog and put him inside the dray!" A shuddering breath. "Please, please, Yann, before it is too late! At least we can save the dog!"

Yann saw sticky marks on the dray seat. He saw a trail of blood. Did the blood belong to the dead trooper? Or was Cyrano injured? His heart rose in his throat and he could hardly breathe. Or had Clem been hit by a stray bullet?

55

Relief flooded through Yann when he found that both Clem and Cyrano, apart from minor lacerations, were free of injuries.

He scooped up the mutt, lifted it onto the seat of the dray and examined the spot where Clem's bullet had grazed the animal's left shoulder. Blood oozed from the wound and Yann scratched his head. How to stem the bleeding?

Clem, ecstatic to know the dog might live, cried, "You have bandages in your boots, Yann! We could use *those* to fix up ... what shall we call him ... what about, yes, let's call him Tiger!"

"Ees not very original name." Yann fumbled with the clogged laces of his boots. "Why not we call 'im Tabby?"

"Oh, no, that would be too silly. Only cats are called Tabby."

"Per'aps you like Cheetah?"

"No, he's more stripy than spotty."

Yann reefed the curled, grey bandages out from the toes of his boots while Clem cleaned the dog's wound with brandy. This created a spate of ear-splitting yelping. Clem cradled the stripy mongrel while Yann bound the damaged shoulder as best he could.

"Zere is a big mess."

"Oh, the wound is not too bad. I am horrified to think I could have killed this very evidently abused poor creature."

"*Non*, I mean ..." Straightening, Yann indicated the burst flour bags which had spread a claggy paste across the supplies he was carrying.

"I am so ashamed," Clem said in a low voice.

Yann raised a dark eyebrow. "Of what you are ashamed?" He gave a Gallic shrug. "Is it ze cognac?"

"Does cognac mean brandy?"

He nodded.

"Yes, well, I am mortified that my Da stowed brandy in the flour bags. It's illegal, you know, and he could be fined. Apart from the licensed bars in the taverns, the Diggings are meant to be alcohol free."

Yann gave a short laugh. The Diggings were awash with grog and he had seen far worse crimes committed during his time here than Silas Holmes-Lacy's attempt to smuggle alcohol. He re-stacked the dray while Clem comforted the whimpering dog.

"I sink we will call him Belle," he announced, rubbing a dirty rag over the supplies in an effort to remove the soupy muck, "because 'e is so ugly!"

"We can't name him Belle! He's a boy dog. Only girls are called Belle."

"Ze name of your girl dog is Princess Albert. Albert is boy name, *non*?"

Cyrano made chattering noises at the mention of the British bulldog's name and a soft smile came over Clem's face. "Princess Albert was so fat when she was born, rolls and rolls of fat." Her face turned a rosy shade of pink. "We thought she was a boy dog and named her Prince Albert. When she grew a little older and leaner, we realised, ahem, that she lacked, um, and we decided to change her name to Princess." She cleared her throat. "I *know*, let's call the dog Hollyhock!"

Yann groaned.

"What? Is the name too flowery, even for a boy dog?" Clem's topaz eyes were shining again, two jewels in her dust-smeared face. Only her moist eyelashes told Yann how terrified she had been.

"H-h-h-holleeey-h-h-h-hock is impossible to say when you are French! Many 'h' sounds."

Clem gurgled with laughter. "I could teach you while we travel!"

Yann gave a cautious smile.

Clem's laughter died. "What shall we do with *him*?" She pointed at the body of the tow-haired trooper. "The crows are hovering. Shall we bury him? Or at the very least, hide him in the bushes?"

Gun smoke hung in the air. Yann slowly shook his head. "We must tell *gendarmes* in Wombat Flat."

"No! You cannot inform the police!" Clem's shoulders began to shake. "You will be arrested all over again!"

"But we not kill zis trooper!"

"They don't know that! Anything we did was purely in self-defence, but they may not believe us. You cannot go to the police!"

Yann sighed, thinking they should get a move on before another conveyance came rattling along the highway.

"*D'accord.* Very well, I do as you suggest," he said, giving a reluctant shrug.

Yann dragged the body into the scrub and hastily raked leaves and twigs over the dead trooper to keep the crows off.

Clem was pale faced and quiet when they resumed their journey.

"I am very surprised when you jump out. Why do you hide?" Yann jabbed a finger over his left shoulder, indicating the supplies on the back of the dray. "You wish to come to Ballarat wis me?"

"Oh, I-I-I, well, you see," she stammered, "Da has signed the bakery contract and, and, I refuse, *refuse* to be a baker." Her words came out in a rush. "So I decided the only thing to do was stow away."

He twitched an eyebrow.

She averted her gaze and Yann knew she was lying when she added, "And, and, I was suspicious that Da was transporting alcohol through the Colony of Victoria, a terrible crime, and I *had* to be certain."

A grin crept across Yann's face. "An' I miss you, too!"

"Oh, yes, and of course I *missed* you. But I never would have done what you suggested. I am not lacking in virtue." She gulped in a breath. "Let's call him Ock!"

Yann turned and stared at Clem. Her face was flushed and a sprinkle of freckles dotted the bridge of her neat little nose. Dirt and gunpowder smeared her skin and his fingers itched to touch her.

"*Quoi?*"

"Does that mean 'what'? The tiger dog, we shall call him Ock!" she repeated, bringing him to his senses. "And then you won't have to worry about all those nasty '*h*' sounds."

Cyrano jumped up, settled into the curve of Yann's neck and began spitting at the mongrel.

"*Arrête!*" said Yann. "Stop! Ock is our friend now."

Cockatoos arced overhead. The birds folded and swayed like newspaper pages caught in an updraught and Yann felt as happy as he had been since arriving in the Colony of Victoria. Clem had run away to be with him. He was so elated that he briefly forgot he was still wanted for the murder of Johnnie Lee.

Beside him Clem chatted about the River Ock, near the village of Little Coxwell where Viola Holmes-Lacy had been born. Clem said her grandfather had worked for the Canal Company and the weather had been cold and damp in that part of England.

"Quite different from here," she breathed.

"And your parents meet 'ow?"

A spring cart clipped past along the highway, spattering their clothing with even more dust and mud.

"Mama and Da met on the ship," Clem continued. "They went first to Adelaide, but life became difficult in South Australia after the gold rush. Men walked off the farms, heading to the Victorian goldfields.

Few people were left to harvest the crops and look after the sheep so Da, like other shopkeepers and merchants, shut up shop." She picked dirt off her moleskins, one piece at a time. "Everything closed, everywhere! Newspapers no longer printed. Government employees were dismissed from their jobs." She sighed. "So Da decided to leave us and make his fortune by becoming a miner in Victoria."

"And?" Yann flicked the reins, urging Annabel around a clag of fallen branches and discarded rubbish.

"Da drew ten pounds from the bank. He purchased food, a tent, shovel, pick and other mining equipment and walked all the way to Forest Creek. The route was long and there were no permanent water supplies." She inhaled a ragged breath. "He was lucky not to perish, but he finally made it to the Diggings. First, he mined at Quartz Hill, south of Castlemaine … north of the rich Red Hill … where the gold ran in seams through white rock. He used to break off lumps of the quartz and roast it to make it brittle, and then smash the quartz with hammers to free the gold."

"Zis is veeery hard work?"

"Oh, yes! Da used to grind the gold in dolly pots, like a mortar and pestle." She cleared her throat. "I was much younger of course, but back home, Mama and I had a terrible time fending for ourselves. We still had some money in the bank. Mama decided to follow Da and she purchased a passage on a packet to Melbourne for two pounds ten shillings. The trip was rough and I remember being very afraid, regurgitating over the ship's rail and soiling my best dress. It was horrid."

"I also 'ave memories like zis," Yann murmured.

"I'm sure you do. And we had even provided ourselves with a few boxes of Dr Graham's anti-bilious and digestive pills. But despite the good doctor's assurance of safety and certainty as to beneficial results, I was still violently ill … and dizzy too, if I remember rightly."

"So you were very 'appy to arrive in Forest Creek?"

She screwed up her nose. "Yes, but by that time, Da had realised that the people who made money on the Diggings were the ones who sold the picks and shovels. So he pitched a canvas tent, small at first, and erected a sign which read 'Holmes-Lacy General Store'. The post office followed and we continued to grow. Now the Holmes-Lacy General Store and Post Office is the biggest in all of Forest Creek."

"And *voilà*, as we say in France!"

"What does that mean?"

"It means 'zere you are'."

"There you are," she corrected.

Cautiously, Yann poked his tongue between his teeth. "Th-there you are."

"*Voilà!*" she cried.

He laughed.

Clem went on, "Apart from the bakery, Da is interested in purchasing a freehold property at Forest Creek, a mortgagee auction on ground, Argus Hill. The land has a frontage to the Main Road to Melbourne and, upon it, is erected … according to Da … a first-rate weatherboard building containing a large store and four extra rooms, lately occupied."

"So you will become very rich one day?"

"Oh heavens no! With so much hard work I fear we will all perish before our allotted span, and for what?"

Without warning, the tow-haired trooper's horse erupted from the wilderness of streaked grasses and eucalypts. The nag charged across the road in front of them and thrashed off through the scrub. Annabel whinnied and set off.

Yann hauled on the reins. "Whoa!" he cried. "*Arrête!* Stopppp!"

Annabel continued to gallop, with surprising speed.

"Make her stop!" cried Clem. "She will damage a fetlock and we will be left without a horse to carry us to Ballarat!"

A mix of soil and water flew up. Cyrano jumped, and landed, spitting and hissing, on the flour bags. The conveyance fishtailed to a halt.

"Oh, no, we are stuck in mud!" groaned Clem.

56

The sun was now a molten ball. Hot rays seared through Yann's straw hat and speared into Clem's leather cap. Perspiration ran down their faces in fine brown rivulets. Splinters gouged at their hands. Onions stung the cuts in their fingers as they unstacked the dray. They heaped supplies on the roadside in untidy piles in their effort to lighten the load so they could continue their journey.

Ock lay in the wheat grass, whimpering. From time to time, Clem ceased what she was doing and gave the dog a comforting pat. Cyrano, seemingly impervious to the mongrel's pain, watched nearby and occasionally leapt onto sacks and bags as if indicating which were the heaviest and most important to take off.

"Could we try now, Yann, see if the wagon will move?" Clem took a long swig from the canvas waterbag and wiped her mouth with her fingers.

"*D'accord.*" Yann clambered up into the driver's seat, planted his feet and flicked the reins. Cracking his whip, he urged Annabel on, bellowing, "*Allez! Allez! Allez!*"

The vehicle remained stuck.

"It's no use. Try speaking to Annabel in English!" Clem shouted over the puffs and rumbles of the straining draught horse. "She might understand better."

"Go! Go! Go!" Yann yelled.

Mud and clogged particles spurted from the wheels, but the dray stayed firm. Clem shaded her eyes with her hand. She gazed into the distance, praying for a passer-by to appear, someone who might be able to help. But no one came along the winding road.

"It's no use, Yann. We have to unload everything, absolutely everything."

With a sigh, she reached into the dray and hoisted a pit prop onto her shoulder. Yellow soldier beetles and shiny dung beetles clung and scrambled as she tossed the prop onto the growing heap. She swiped ants and insects off her small, but deceptively strong, hands. Together they unloaded the dray until there was nothing left to unload but still Annabel was unable to shift the wheels from the sludgy ground.

"We will have to use the shovel and dig our way out. I can see nothing else for it." Clem brushed flies from her sweat-stained cheeks. "I shall gather branches to give the wheels something to grip on while you use the spade."

As Yann shafted in the blade, he mulled over Clem's resourcefulness. Her pluck never ceased to amaze him. He couldn't imagine any of the French girls he had known doing anything other than complain about the heat and the discomfort.

Clem reappeared with an armful of twiggy scrub and small logs. Alongside Yann, she kicked the branches under the wheels with her boots. Yann's right boot, looser without the bandages inside, flew off and sank into the mud. He dug it out, shoved it on his foot and pulled the laces tight.

Eventually, there was enough traction and he jumped back onto the seat. "Go! Goooo!" he yelled.

This time, Annabel inched the dray, bit by bit, out of the gloop.

Manoeuvring the horse further up the road, where the terrain was firmer, he said, "Now we must load again."

The shadows lengthened as they worked. By the time they had reloaded the dray, it was twilight.

"If you move the vehicle to one side of the road, I will make damper for our tea," said Clem. "It's as safe a place as any for us to rest. Perhaps we could spend the night here?"

"But we 'ave no tent!"

"No tent?" She gave him a weary glance. "We shall sleep beneath the wagon, just as everyone else does when travelling through the goldfields."

Yann protested a second time, "But my lamp 'as very little fuel left, and I 'ave seen no more among ze supplies." He rummaged around in the back of the dray for lamp oil, cursing as he did so.

"No matter," said Clem. "Whisky usually suffices … although I have seen none of that either." Pause. "What about using some of Da's grog?" She gave a brief laugh. "Having seen him flame our Christmas pudding over the years, I am certain it will do for giving us light." Longer pause. "Do the French eat Christmas pudding during the festive season?"

Yann, slitting open a sack of flour with his cut-throat razor, stopped what he was doing and said with a half-smile, "*Non*, we eat *bûche de Noël*."

"And is that nice?"

"If you like *chocolat*!"

"Doesn't *everybody* like chocolate?"

Yann extracted a brandy bottle. He opened it with his teeth, tipped a dash into the lamp and struck a match. Blue flames shot out, spreading a waft of aromatic fumes into the evening.

"*Voilà*," he said. "Now we are able to see."

Clem used plenty of salt when making the dough for the damper. She added a dash of the illicit alcohol to enhance the taste and, although unlaced with golden syrup, the crusty bush bread was mouth-wateringly delicious. They sat on the side of the road, chatting and chewing. Even Ock ate at a small portion of damper.

Cyrano took a disdainful nibble, then curled up before the fire to sleep. One eye flicked open from time to time at the pattering in the surrounding trees. Yann knew that, if the Tonkinese was truly hungry, he would chase down a marsupial.

"Tell me, Yann, what was your mother like?" Clem tossed a handful of tea into the boiling billy.

Yann delved into his moleskins, edged the daguerreotype out carefully and handed it to her.

"Oh, how *beautiful* she was, exotically beautiful!" Clem wiped her hands on her trouser legs and ran her forefinger over the lustrous raven hair, the dark gaze, the enigmatic smile.

"*Oui*," murmured Yann. "*Elle était belle.*"

"And you are so like her in appearance … your face, your colouring." Clem's topaz eyes gleamed in the firelight. "You resemble your mother a great deal." She cleared her throat and blushed when she realised what she had said. "I mean, I mean … and was your father also handsome?"

Yann snaked his fingers into his pocket and produced the photo of Jean-Paul Sauvage.

Clem peered. "Oh, your father has fair hair and blue eyes. He is very dashing in his uniform, but not so much like you."

"*Non*," murmured Yann. "I 'ave my muzzer's Corsican mien … and *caractère*." A feeling of shame washed through him as he remembered the day he had almost thrown a stone at Clemency Holmes-Lacy. "I 'ave a bad temper and I sometimes do not 'ave such good control when I become angry."

They sat, lost in the warmth of the fire, until Clem broke the silence.

"You must miss your parents."

Yann exhaled. "I do since, ah, *Maman est morte*."

"Yes, you told me she had passed."

"*Oui*, but one day I find *Papa*. I will not leave zis country, I will continue wis my search until I find 'im."

"You are still planning to return to France?"

Yann stared at Clem. He had never considered remaining in Australia. France was his home.

"Well, if Jean-Paul Sauvage is somewhere in the Colony of Victoria, you are bound to come across him sooner or later, as long as you keep looking. It won't be easy with all the comings and goings, with diggers folding up their tents to chase every new rumour, but ..." Her voice trailed off.

They gazed into the coals. Any concerns about their future were lulled by the glowing embers and, for the moment, they felt safe.

"I have an idea!" Clem burst out. "It is too tricky for you right now as you are still a wanted man, and, anyway, you will need to stay with the dray and mind the supplies." She drew in an excited breath. "But now I am aware of your father's likeness, *I* could ask diggers at Wombat Flat!"

"Will it not be dangerous?"

"Not at all. They will think I am a boy." Her eyes shone. "And, if I have no luck there, I could ask at Creswick if they have come across a Frenchman who might answer to his descript ..." She stopped short.

A crashing resounded through the scrub. Branches snapped. Hooves pounded.

They looked up and saw it was the dead trooper's horse. Again.

57

Yann, with Clem's help, heaped leaves, grass and soft branches beneath the wagon. They attempted to sleep, but whenever they nodded off the riderless horse came back. Hooves churned up the ground, thundering back and forth. Up and down. Around and around again. The steed's flanks gleamed silver in the moonlight. Plumes of steam erupted from its nostrils, wisps of white fog churned into the cool night air and the earth shook. Doing his best to ignore the unsettling sound, Yann turned over and wriggled into as comfortable a position as he could.

Goose bumps rippled across Clem's skin. Little shudders ran through her and the hairs on her arms stood up. She ran her fingers over Ock's snout to calm the dog's terrified quivering.

"That nag is trying to tell us something," she hissed, prodding Yann in the side. "Even Cyrano looks concerned, and he usually takes things in his stride."

"Per'aps ze *gendarme* is not … not dead?" he mumbled.

"Oh, how awful! But he must be! He certainly looked dead! *Surely* you checked for a pulse before you covered his body?"

"*Oui*, but now I am not so certain." Yann pushed himself up, leaned on one elbow and looked down at her. "I must go back. I must find out if he is truly *mort* or I will never sleep in my life again."

"How will you get there? You'll never find your way in the dark and Annabel will expire from exhaustion if we retrace our steps. If we keep unloading and reloading the dray we will never reach Ballarat and Mr de Wolf will be wondering where his supplies are!"

"'E will take me back."

"Who will take you back, Mr de Wolf?"

"*Non*," he sighed with impatience. "Ze horse."

"How will you catch it?" Clem gasped in a breath. "And, if you do, it no longer has any saddle." She thought for a moment. "Someone must have stolen it. Or it fell off when the horse rolled. Or, I don't know … do you think the trooper is still alive?"

"I do not need saddle." Yann stuck out his jaw.

"Well, at least you must put on your boots. You cannot go barefoot. Your feet will be trampled, and then where will we be?" Her voice was threaded with panic.

"I do not need boots!"

Clem comforted the quaking Ock while Yann grabbed a piece of rope. He eased his body out from under the wagon, knotted the rope into a noose and moved stealthily through the scrub. The trooper's nag continued to gallop in circles, harrumphing and snorting and bucking.

"Whoa," Yann swung the rope gently between his fingers, ready to sling it. "Whoooaaa!"

Sweat streamed over the horse's coat and it continued to turn in circles.

"*Allez viens!*" Yann's whisper was low and long. "*Allez viens!* Come wis me. Coo-ome wis me. "

The steed calmed a little. The whites of its eyes showed and it tossed its mane, thicker and glossier than before. The moon gave its coat a sheen which had not been evident in the full light of day. Even its gait seemed less knock-kneed.

Yann approached, step by cautious step. He cursed that he had no apple, no food to entice the poor creature, whose legs were encrusted with mud, spotted with burrs and lacerated with ragged cuts. Its huge eyes rolled like two lumps of blackened quartz.

"*Chut!*" Yann whispered, moving closer. "Shush! Ssssshhh."

He clicked with his cheek and tongue. His feet made no sound in the grass as the rope spun from his fingers. The twine swirled over the neck of the steed and Yann hauled it tight, dragging the sidestepping animal towards him.

"*Ça va,*" he murmured. "Everything will be all right."

Snatching at the bridle, he leapt on. The horse reared at first, whinnying, but Yann dug in his heels and they galloped, pounding over the ground, returning to the place where he had hidden the trooper's body. His mount neighed and grunted, sucked in and gave a blustery blow, jerking its head as if afraid.

They waded into the scrub, Yann checking for danger. Squealing with its mouth shut, the horse attempted to shy away as Yann swung his leg down.

"Whoa! Whoooooaaaa!"

Yann prayed no snakes were abroad that night. Swishing aside twigs, he searched for the trooper. He broke off a branch, brushed it backwards and forwards until the stick nudged a long, inanimate object. Shoving aside the bushes he saw the body and reeled back, drawing in a horrified gasp. The lawman's face was so disfigured as to be almost unrecognisable. Worms crawled inside the blackened sockets where his eyes had been. Yann had never seen such a gruesome sight.

The trooper was indeed dead. Clem had nothing more to fear.

The horse waited, trembling, blowing through distended nostrils. Winding his hand through the mane, Yann vaulted back on. He headed back up the highway to the dray, where Clem, tresses loose and spread across her shoulders, waited with Ock. Cyrano sat on her shoulder, curled into her neck as if he, too, were afraid.

"*Ça va aller*," murmured Yann, swinging off the horse. "It will be all right. 'E will never 'arm you, never anymore."

He slapped the nag on the rump, put his arm around Clem and they watched it thunder off into the distance.

Back beneath the wagon, Yann drew Clem to him and clung hard until she ceased jittering. For the remainder of the long night, they lay in a tangle of human legs, cat's legs and dog's legs. But the horse kept coming back, galloping around the wagon, circling, circling, nickering and whinnying.

They were still awake when the kookaburras cackled, but the trooper's steed had left. The pre-dawn washed the horizon pink. Clem backed Annabel into the shafts for the next leg of the journey.

58

A raptor circled above as they headed up the hill towards Wombat Flat. Yann hoped it wasn't an omen.

He gave Clem the reins, picked up his accordion and began to sing:

Frère Jacques,
Frère Jacques
Dormez-vous?
Dormez-vous?

Clem chimed in:

Are you sleeping?
Are you sleeping?
Brother John,
Brother John?

Yann pushed the instrument in and out, squeezing, creating the melody familiar to them both. He sang, even louder:

Sonnez les matines.
Sonnez les matines.
Ding, ding, dong.
Ding, ding, dong.

Clem, eyeing the eagle, bellowed in response:

Morning bells are ringing.
Morning bells are ringing.
Ding, dong, ding.
Ding, dong, ding.

Each time the bird of prey circled anew, they sang louder, until they were no longer singing. They were shouting now, happy to be alive and not rotting in the bush like the tow-haired trooper.

Ock ceased whimpering and nosed the bandage off his wound. He began to lick the bullet graze clean. Cyrano, curled up again on the onions, ignored the rollicking sound of laughter and pretended to sleep.

Clem stopped singing and murmured, "Sometimes, when I think about it … which I mostly try not to … I feel sorry for the poor man."

"*Non*, 'e deserve to die." Yann's voice was harsh with bitterness for what the trooper had put them through. He added, "Even more than other *gendarme*, Trooper Clovis."

They began to sing again, softly at first and then building up to a crescendo. They were making such a din that they failed to hear the Cobb & Co. coach approaching from behind. The American-built conveyance travelled over the ruts at great speed, but the sound that alerted them was the squawking of bagpipes—it was so loud that it drowned out their song.

Yann whipped his head around to see a man on top of the coach. The Scotsman, in the same pilled brown tunic and checked kilt that Yann remembered, puffed and blew and squeezed. Other passengers seated on the roof clapped and whistled in time.

"*Aïe! Aïe!*" The accordion dropped from Yann's grasp with a clang.

He clutched his head.

"Don't you like the bagpipes, Yann?" asked Clem.

He jabbed his fists into his ears as the coach swayed alongside. "What terrible noise, *affreux!*"

The piper stopped playing. He spied Yann and yelled, "I'm free, mon! I am free! Can ye believe that? And so are you, mon, so are yooooou! We are both free as birds, mon! Free as biirrrrds!"

"Do you know this man?" Clem eased Annabel across to the edge of the road, dodging fallen branches and gluggy mud holes, to allow the coach to pass.

"It is Scotty!" Yann gave a reluctant grin. "We were in lockup together, and 'e drive me *mad* wis 'is noise. I am like a *fou*, insane!"

"Well, Scotty says you are free, too. Is that true? *Are* you free?" Clem's eyes bored into Yann. "What does he mean by that?"

"Pfft! My friend drinks too much whisky. '*E* may be free, but, *non*, I am still a wanted man."

"But what if …"

"*Non*, not true." Shaking his head, Yann reached across and squeezed Clem's hand. "I do not believe in fairytale."

The Cobb & Co. coach rocked off into the distance. A sea of tents, windsails, puddling machines, long toms and canvas dwellings told them they had reached the outskirts of Wombat Flat. They pulled up and Clem jumped to the ground.

"I shall ask around, see if Jean-Paul Sauvage is here, or has been seen here." She pulled her cap down over her brow. "You can guard the dray."

Yann gave her the photo of Jean-Paul Sauvage. She hitched up her braces and strode off with purpose, leaving him to watch over the supplies.

Diggers passed, wheeling barrows or lugging possessions in cloth-covered bundles. Some stopped and begged for handouts, whining to Yann that they hadn't eaten in days. And, from the rags they wore, Yann believed them. But the goods were not his to hand out.

"I do not own zese sings," Yann said over and over, lifting his rifle to prevent anyone from snatching even a potato.

A human shape, clad in a nightshirt, lay stretched among the clumps of grass and Yann wondered if it was a body. Without warning, the miner jumped up and jabbed a finger at him.

"You are cursed!" the man cried, eyes wild. "When the full moon rises you will be plagued for the rest of your days, and the gods will have their vengeance!"

Although he was not superstitious, Yann felt uneasy, and edged the dray further up the road while the drunken digger subsided back into his tussocky bed. Tired of waiting, he was beginning to think this had not been such a good idea when he saw Clem returning. Circling windsails, puddling machines, pug dwellings and barking dogs on leashes, she made her way to the dray.

"Wombat Flat is filled with Italians and Swiss working over the soil," she said, clambering aboard. "I heard a great deal of French spoken, but none of them seem to have seen your father. Perhaps it would have been preferable if you'd been present to speak to them in their language?" She spread her hands. "Of course, nobody stays too long in these towns."

"So you 'ave no luck?"

"No, no luck. But, for a place to dig, it is not so bad. I even saw some springs there. Diggers were lolling about in muddy water, claiming their aches and pains were cured by the amazing waters." She brushed ants off her moleskins and added, "I saw Scotty again, too, but had no time to quiz him about his newfound freedom. The Cobb & Co. coach changed horses and left. So, apart from some who were violently ill from motion sickness and decided to stay in Wombat Flat, they are all on their way to Ballarat."

"Per'aps we will see Scotty when we arrive zere." Yann heaved in a breath. "Or is 'e on his way to Melbourne?"

"I do not know. There are a thousand rumours in this town. They say riots are threatening in Ballarat. There is extreme anger about the Miners'

Licences. Diggers are armed. The place where we are headed could be dangerous."

Yann shrugged. "But Monster Meeting at Golden Point, Forest Creek, in 1851 ... twenty thousand miners ... come to nothing."

"Maybe this time it will be different?"

He stuffed Jean-Paul Sauvage's image back in his pocket and steered Annabel back onto the highway.

"People were also saying there are plans afoot in Forest Creek to get rid of the Chinese." She paused. "But they were not specific about the details."

"Per'aps true? Not too many people are unhappy to find a Chinaman's head buried at Pennyweight Flat."

"I fear the Chinese do not have an easy time on the Diggings." Clem turned to pat Ock, who was now standing and sniffing the breeze. "Did you know we are now entering the land of the Wemba-Wemba people?"

Yann made no comment. The Dja Dja Wurrung natives had been peaceful. He had no reason to believe this tribe would be any different.

Clem continued, "The Creswick brothers established a large sheep station twelve years ago in the next place where we are headed, but I fear it has changed since they surveyed for a town site this year. In Wombat Flat miners I spoke to told me there are upwards of twenty-five thousand people camped in Creswick while they dig, almost as many as in Forest Creek."

"Monsieur Holmes-Lacy could set up a store in ze next town and you will become very, very rich."

"Do not even suggest it!"

As they crested a hill, heading for Creswick, Yann saw a long shiny object on the side of the road. The sharp blade pointed south. Was this his confiscated weapon?

He squinted. A Napoleonic eagle glinted in the sunshine. He was certain the dagger had been put there deliberately. Was Trooper Clovis sending a message, warning him not to venture any further?

59

Another mud hole grabbed at the wheels, bogging the wagon. Willy-wagtails bounced along a fallen log by the roadside as they unloaded and reloaded the dray. Annabel flicked flies away with her tail. Cyrano perched on the horse's rump while Ock worked at his wound with long tongue strokes.

"*Voilà!*" Yann handed a pit prop up to Clem. "We are almost finished."

Her brow gleamed with perspiration as she stacked the straight poles in piles alongside the rest of the supplies. She blew a stray wisp of hair from her eyes. "Oh, my hands are so rough now. They're blistered like a miner's!"

Yann smiled to himself. He had never heard Clem complain about her appearance before, never thought she concerned herself with being feminine. And yet, despite the moleskins and flannel shirt she wore, she was alluring. Sometimes he had to push away the urge to discover the taste of her lips.

"Whoever would have thought we could be stuck in the mud again, and on a day as warm as this?" Her brows drew together as she reached down for the next length of wood.

Yann grunted and sighed, "*Oui.*" He hoisted the next shaft support timber.

A whipbird cracked. A choir of kookaburras started up, like laughter in the bar of the Red Boulder Hotel when someone had told a bawdy joke. Another choir, farther away, joined in and then stopped.

"At least you have your weapon back." Clem stifled a yawn. "Do you think Trooper Clovis put your dagger in that exact spot so we would become wedged and our journey become even more arduous?"

"*Oui*, per'aps." Yann glanced up at her. "But I still do not understand why he not arrest me." His eyes swept the trees on either side of the road. Vistas of forest opened up in every direction. "It would be easy for 'im to lie in wait and maybe put a bullet into my brain."

"Perhaps he has taken pity on you at last?"

Handing over the final prop, Yann shook his head. "But I am still wanted for a crime I not commit." He adjusted the dagger at his waist. "It is very strange."

A feeling of isolation and uncertainty surrounded him like a cloak. He clambered back into the dray, picked up the loosely tied reins and gave a brief crack of the whip to urge the horse forward. The kookaburras started their chorus anew, then fell silent. Beside him, Clem was also silent. Ock, upright, pricked his ears. Back on the dray, Cyrano propped on all fours, stiff and unmoving.

Annabel picked up pace. Her ears slanted backwards and she lengthened her stride. In the bush, no animals stirred. Sap dripped from a nearby eucalypt. The sound of dripping faded and Yann breathed in. He could smell no smoke, no hint of bushfire. But this silence was unsettling.

As the reins rippled over Annabel's neck, Yann's gaze fastened on a snake, like the one he had killed on the slopes of Pennyweight Flat. Blending with the leather, it slithered along the harness. This one was smaller, but he knew it would be just as venomous.

Nudging Clem, Yann pointed to the snake and to the rifle. She shook her head. He wondered why. Clem was an accomplished shot. Was she worried she might misjudge and shoot the horse? But what if the snake sank its fangs into Annabel? They would all be at the mercy of the lawman then.

"Wait," she whispered.

Her eyes were huge as pennies as she watched the snake slither along the reins. Its tongue was flicking as it headed for the horse's rump. Cyrano made soft noises but remained rigid. No birds sang. The bush was eerily quiet.

A vee shape suddenly blurred downwards. A streak of brown and white plumage flashed back up, in a hum of streamlined feathers.

"The snake's gone!" hissed Clem.

The bush echoed with a sharp crack. From the kookaburra's beak hung a jagged shape, the dead reptile blending with the branches. The bird choir started up again. Animals went about their business, scrabbling through the scrub. Dragonflies flitted over the spiky grass and Annabel resumed her customary plod.

"Ouf!" The tension ebbed from Yann's body.

Clem placed her hand on his shoulder and gently squeezed. "Isn't the Australian bush incredible?" she breathed. "There is so much danger and yet so much to marvel at. It's as if God counterpointed evil with goodness when he created this place. I have grown to love it. Have you grown to love it too, Yann?"

He chewed his lip. "I do not *love* it, not yet, but maybe one day."

"One day? But you will be gone as soon as you find your father. Won't you, Yann? You will be returning to France and back to your life of shiny carriages and boulevards and clothing made from fine silk?"

A breeze had sprung up, drying the sweat on his face and tightening his skin. He made no comment.

"Although, you know, one day there will be boulevards in the Colony of Victoria, too. Melbourne will have the widest streets in the world. There will be grand buildings and elegant shops. I am certain of it!"

Yann shrugged. Watching the reins move in waves across Annabel's back, he was simply glad the horse had survived, for all their sakes. He was growing to respect and admire the Australian bush, but would he want to spend the rest of his days here? He doubted it.

Emerging from the dappled light of the forest, tents and shanties shone in the sunshine. A few dwellings had mud brick chimneys, a sign of optimism and permanence. Diggers cut slabs from the soil on either side of the wide road leading led into Creswick.

Clem, stiff-backed, held out her hand for the daguerreotype.

"If you pull over," she said, "I shall take his image with me and see if any miner has come across Jean-Paul Sauvage."

60

Yann, having nodded off in the hot sun, woke in a lather of perspiration. Footsteps crunched. Bits of gravel from the side of the road pinged against the dray wheel. He pushed himself upright and fumbled his hat back on his head. Clem's topaz eyes shone up at him, brimming with excitement. She slipped the chaff bag up and over Annabel's neck and tossed it in the rear of the dray. Dust flew from her boots as she clambered aboard.

"Your father has been seen in Creswick!" she said, breathless. "I spoke to a man they call the 'Welshman', Jones I think his name is. He is from Liverpool and he travelled all the way to San Francisco during the rush in America. He's a forty-niner and he ran a hotel in San Francisco and the great earthquake struck and the building was flattened!" Her eyes grew rounder as her tale progressed.

Yann wondered if, in her excitement at meeting a man who had survived an earthquake, she had forgotten to discover the details about his father. "An' you ask about Jean-Paul Sauvage?"

"Can you believe such an amazing story?" She pulled the leather cap off her head and fanned herself.

"*Oui*, but Mr Jones ... 'e spoke to my *Papa*?"

"Well, yes, the Welshman said a Frenchman whose name was Sauvage ... apparently they call him the French Lieutenant ... but he wasn't certain if it was the *same* Sauvage, has been involved in the movements for reform on the goldfields."

"But 'e is no longer in Creswick." Yann's voice went flat.

"No." She crooked her forefinger and pushed it against her temple as she thought. "There is also another Frenchman, which makes it very confusing."

"Is other Frenchman Le Comte de Corbeau, Saint-Simonian who steals William Bass's leeetle book of poetry and maybe arranges for me to be accused of murder?"

"I think so, but it's easy to become muddled up with so many people from your country on the Diggings."

"Two … plus *moi* … is not so many Frrrrenchmen!" His voice rose in indignation.

Cyrano, back on Annabel's rump, stopped licking and looked at them with narrowed gaze. Ock, snoring on the potatoes, opened a lazy yellow eye and resumed sleeping.

"Stop interrupting, Yann!" Clem poked him in the side. "As I was saying, Mr Jones thinks either one or both men may have left Creswick, but he's not sure when. However, a man called Sauvage is certainly assisting the miners to protest against the licence fee, and the ten pound fine, and being chained to a log until the fine is paid, *and* he believes this is unfair and the police are corrupt … but we already know that!" She gasped in a breath. "Mr Jones is so inspiring when he talks. He tells of at least four hundred men marching on Ballarat as we speak. Today, the first day of December, is an auspicious date for rebelling against the military and police troops." Her voice rose to a squeak. "Isn't it exciting?"

"And is my father wis them?"

"Mr Jones is not sure, but yes, Jean-Paul Sauvage could well be with these men. He says there is a whole French contingent revolting against the licences, not to mention Swedes and Germans and Irish and Vandemonians." She snatched the whip from Yann's fingers, drew it back and cracked the leather thong. "We must hurry! Your father may well be on the road at this very moment, heading for Ballarat!"

The dray jerked forward. Cyrano leapt onto the front seat.

They passed through the broad, curved main street of Creswick and were on the road leading to Ballarat. Clem, in her frustration at Annabel's slow plod, kept whipping the draught horse.

"*Arrête!*" Yann placed his hand over hers. "Stop! You will kill ze 'orse. And we will be in very much trouble."

"But we need to catch up with the marching miners! It's only ten miles to Ballarat, and if they get there before we do, they will disperse and we will never find your father!" The flecks in her irises shone gold in the afternoon sun as she turned to look at him. "The Welshman said there is a large crowd and great unrest in that town, particularly since the hotelkeeper, Bentley, was acquitted of murdering that poor digger, James Scobie. Wasn't that his name?"

"*Oui*, I believe it was 'is name, but we need Annabel!" Yann insisted. "She will die if you keep whipping 'er."

"It doesn't matter if she can't continue! We can leave the dray behind and walk! The distance is not far."

"*Non!*" Yann's eyes became burnished steel. "I do not wish to be taken away by *gendarmes* for a new crime of stealing supplies which belong to *Monsieur* de Wolf. 'E is depending on me."

"Oh, you are so tiresome, Yann!" Clem folded her arms and sat in silence.

The wheels thumped over the ruts. They swayed along the track, passing primitive three-wheeled carts and men pushing barrows. Clem pulled her cap down and slouched while Yann scanned the horizon. He was relieved that they were travelling south-east. The sun was behind them, but the air was humid and he felt thick-headed. Unable to see any marching miners, he was almost ready to dismiss Clem's story as fanciful.

The dray rumbled up a hill. As they descended, Yann saw a crowd ahead. Miners were ranged three abreast in the middle of the road. At the forefront, a band played the 'Marseillaise'.

The leader waved a sword and sang:
Allons enfants de la Patrie
Le jour de gloire est arrivé!
Contre nous de la tyrannie
L'étendard sanglant est levé ...

"There they are, exactly as Mr Jones said!" Clem nudged him in the side. "And the man leading them is Mr Thomas Kennedy."

"But why is 'e singing the song of my country?" Yann looked at her, confused.

"Because they are *rebelling*, Yann, rebelling against the licences and the corrupt police and, in Creswick, they say they are even agitating for a republic, *rebelling* as the poor did in France."

Yann's jaw slackened in amazement.

The rows of men went on and on, like soldiers going to war. The rifles slung over their shoulders gleamed in the afternoon light. Some carried makeshift weapons, pikes and lances. Others pickaxes and shovels. The dray drew alongside and Yann noted the faces smudged with dirt and grimy with purpose. These men looked as angry as any he had ever seen. Pushed to the end of their tether doing backbreaking work often for no reward, forced to pay licence fees whether they struck gold or not.

"No taxation without representation!" chanted one man.

"Wipe out police corruption!" shouted another.

This was followed by: "Put an end to digger hunting!" and then, "When do we want an end to digger hunting?" "Now!" came the resounding cry.

Yann pushed the reins into Clem's hand. He vaulted from the dray and ran back and forth along the lines of protesters, scanning their faces. Most had beards or bushy mutton chop whiskers. Clenching unlit pipes between stained teeth, they smelled of sweat and tobacco. All the men looked identical and Yann's heart beat hard as he moved through their ranks. He looked each person up and down, checking for a sign of awareness. He flourished the daguerreotype of his father. They shoved the photo away. "Don't bother us, lad!"

And then Yann remembered the Napoleonic button. He pulled the kerchief from his trousers and, unwrapping it, ran from one to the other. None of these diggers looked like the father he knew, but the button could well jog someone's memory.

Still they pushed him away. Some kindly. Some roughly.

One broke ranks with his friends, took the memento, rested the butt of his rifle on the ground and held the button up in the afternoon light to better inspect it. Yann's heart lurched in his throat. He had trouble breathing. Could this be the link to his father? The digger turned, and Yann had never seen such anger before.

"This button is from a uniform worn by Napoleon Bonaparte's assassins, murderin' cohorts. Hell-raisers they were," he roared, "until the Russians found their measure!"

"But, but zis is button of Napoléon Ⅲ."

"This piece of metal most certainly is *not* from a soldier of the current regime! The First Empire eagle is more awkwardly posed. The Second Empire button has more sharply defined feathers and a shorter neck, is more majestic in appearance."

"But, but …"

The digger's face took on a purple hue. "I know better than *you*, young man. Me grandfather and his three brothers were *slaughtered* at the Battle of Austerlitz. They lie in a cold grave and I *spit* on the soldier who wore this!" A glob of ochre-coloured saliva landed fair in the middle of the button. The digger ground the keepsake into the dirt with his boot.

The band still played the 'Marseillaise' and Yann's mind swirled. He was not about to admit that his father, Jean-Paul Sauvage was a deserter from Napoleon Ⅲ's army. That could raise the ire of the digger even more.

"But, *monsieur*, you are very much mistaken," he said. "Zis is not button of my *grandfather*'s army …"

"Ye say Napoleon was yer grandfaaaaather!" The digger's beard bristled. His face was livid.

Yann backed away from the digger's anger as the marching miners continued on down the highway, singing:

Aux armes, citoyens,
Formez vos bataillons ...

The digger growled and clenched his fist. A sideways blur.
Everything faded to black.

61

Yann felt a rough tongue licking his hand, over and over, backwards and forwards and sideways. *Was that Cyrano?* He groaned and tried to move, but found he could not. Pinpricks of hot and cold rippled across his skin. His head throbbed as if a thousand tom toms were beating inside it. He tried to heave himself up but his vision swirled and he slumped back. Rancid lumps, smelling of onions, dug into his shoulder blades.

"*Aïe, aïe, aïe.*"

Yann's right eye was gummed up and weeping. He had never felt such pain before and he was unable to recall what had happened. He made a second attempt to lift his head. His hair, now loose, clung to his skin like seaweed and his braces grooved into his shoulders, unaccountably hurting him.

"Clem?" His voice came out in a strained whisper.

No answer. He made a third effort to push himself up. His elbow slipped on an onion skin. Potatoes bounded to the other side of the dray, releasing a flurry of dust. Yann was sure vehicles had gone past, but it seemed no one had bothered to stop and offer assistance. Had passers-by thought him out to it from having drunk too much?

At his next try, Yann managed to creak into a sitting position. He was alone. Only Cyrano, who kept licking his hand, was there. His boots, still on his feet, faced the front of the dray. The shafts of the wagon rested on the ground. There was no Annabel. No Clem. No dog called Ock. He felt for his dagger, found it still at his waist and exhaled a sigh of relief.

Where had everyone gone?

A wagon clunked along the road, but Yann was unable to see more than a yard in front of his face. The sun, glowing through the dust, was a low ball in the sky and he shaded his eyes with his hand. Night was fast approaching, and fragments of memory began returning. The men marching down Melbourne Road to the tune of the Marseillaise while making for Ballarat to protest against the Diggings licence fee. The angry digger who'd been so certain Yann's button had belonged to a soldier in

Napoleon Bonaparte's army, not Napoleon Ш's army. Disappointment washed over him to know the button had not been Jean-Paul Sauvage's. Would he ever discover his father?

Shivers of apprehension clenched at Yann's mind. Where was Clem? Had they realised she was a girl and decided to kidnap her? What about Annabel? Had they stolen her ? he wondered. And Ock—why would anyone wish to steal the ugliest dog in the universe? Or had Ock died? Then again, the dog's wound was almost healed. Unless … was the trooper still alive? Had he simply imagined, nay hoped, the decomposing body belonged to the lawman?

"*Non, non, non.*" His head reeled and swayed. "*Aïe!* Ouch!"

A thousand scenarios roared through his mind and he paused, noticing that his clothes were covered in flour. The whole dray was covered in flour. Burst sacks lay everywhere. From a shattered bottle of brandy, shards sparked in the light of the disappearing sun. It seemed someone had known about the contraband brandy. Had the marching diggers stolen the drink to give them courage for the battle ahead?

Yann took a deep breath and looked around. The supplies were now seriously depleted. Some of the shaft support timbers were gone. Nicked for firewood? There were fewer potatoes. In fact, the dray contained less of everything. The rifles were no longer there. It seemed passers-by had been helping themselves while he was unconscious. Even if he could find another horse to move the wagon on to Ballarat, Studs de Wolf would not be pleased to find a portion of his goods stolen. Heat lightning flashed. What to do? Should he leave, hunt for a horse? Then again, he could well find, when he returned, that every single thing had disappeared. How would he explain that to the Gold Escort operator?

A digger pushing a wheelbarrow piled high with his possessions, and accompanied by a stringy dog, gave him a sideways glance. Yann peered. Was the dog Ock? He was unable to make out any stripes. And, anyway, Ock would have wagged his tail or shown some other sign of recognition. He sighed. There were so many mangy dogs on the goldfields and most, apart from Princess Albert, seemed alarmingly similar.

The man trudged down the road, the wheel of his barrow squealing, spraying out dust and stones as he went.

Yann took a swig from his waterbag. His accordion squawked and he winced as he heaved himself out of the wagon and shook out his moleskins. Thank heavens, his legs still worked. With his head still aching, he prowled through the wallaby and kangaroo grass, seeking some sign which would point him towards Clem. Had she, watching his dispute with the digger, become disgusted with his behaviour and begged a ride back to Forest Creek?

As he scoured the roadside scrub, Yann saw Cyrano dart under the dray. The cat gave out a low miaow and, re-emerging, pranced across the grassy spikes to Yann. He placed his paws on Yann's knee, turned and scooted back under the wagon. He remained there, making the same strident sounds. Yann's heart tumbled. Was Clem wounded? Or worse, had she been murdered? Feeling sick in the pit of his stomach, he crawled beneath the dray. He glanced around and saw the barrel of his rifle, gleaming softly, secured by rope to a crossbeam. Only one person could have done that … Clem. His fingers fiddled with the knots to release the gun.

Footsteps scrunched the roadside gravel and Yann made out moleskin-clad legs, scungy boots. He slithered out, expecting to see Clem.

An old digger in a battered hat was scooping up potatoes.

"Stop!" shouted Yann, waving his rifle. "Or I shoot!"

The raggedy man scurried off down the highway.

The northerly wind picked up, moaning in the trees. Yann tried to figure out a way of moving the conveyance the last few miles to Ballarat. Diggers passed. Some stopped to ask if they could purchase pit props, or onions, potatoes or sugar. There was precious little flour left. Yann said no to them all.

He set about tidying up, pondering whether he should light a fire and make some damper with the remaining flour. As he tidied, he heard a horse in the scrub, a familiar nickering. Hooves rustled in the undergrowth, getting closer. Cyrano leapt off the dray, flew into the bush and disappeared.

Yann lifted his rifle. First, Ock emerged. Then the trooper's knock-kneed nag appeared. Convinced the lawman was, against all odds, still alive, Yann was preparing to fire when he heard Clem's voice.

"Oh, Yann, I am exhausted," she said. "I have walked *miles*, calling, looking for this horse." Pushing her way through the undergrowth, she trudged towards him. "Eventually he galloped up, and he was pleased to see me. I was so grateful. I managed to clamber onto his back, but after a mile or so I was unable to tolerate the discomfort. I jumped off and walked the rest of the way." She propped the rifle she carried against the dray's shaft, blew wisps of hair from her face and added, "So you are awake at last! That was a fine punch the digger landed. I thought he might have killed you!"

"So you leave me to die on my own, and I wonder where you are and if you 'ave been kidnapped!" His voice was filled with relief, mixed with indignation.

"You weren't completely alone! You had Cyrano to keep you company." She patted the cat, now winding around her legs. "I was forced to take the dog with me in case I was waylaid by vagabonds."

"And Annabel? Where 'as our horse gone?"

"Well, a digger ... not he who punched you ... took pity on us and helped me lie you down in the dray. With all the excitement, I needed to ... you know! So I went into the bushes and when, after mere moments, I returned to the wagon, Annabel was gone, *stolen* by the very same Samaritan who helped me!"

Yann gaped.

"He," she went on, waving a finger at the knock-kneed nag, "was our one hope." She eyed the bay horse doubtfully. "Do you think he is capable of pulling a dray?"

62

Yann spared the whip, urging the horse on with his voice. With Clem helping, he practised his 'th' sounds. "Th-th-th," he repeated, sticking his tongue between his teeth. The dray rumbled past market gardens, gullies and shanties and into Ballarat. The town was set above a basin with, beyond, a belt of unbroken forest. Lights shone like jewels through the tents.

"This is a city in comparison to Forest Creek," Clem breathed.

"*Oui*," murmured Yann, telling himself it was nothing compared with Paris.

The Main Road looked onto the Bakery Hill area, where stores and mines crowded together. A navy-blue flag with a long white cross and five stars hung from a flagpole.

"What an unusual flag," said Clem. "I believe it is meant to represent the Southern Cross and freedom from tyrannical rule." And then, "Storekeepers must be making their fortune in this place, doing far better than the miners if those other flags are any indication." She pointed at the shelters over the claims where the American Stars and Stripes flew. "But the hotels seem to be closed. It is a fine night. Why are they not open?"

They passed a stockade in the process of being hammered together. Old carts turned on their sides jostled with slab walls. Within the defensive fortification, people were doing drill with weapons. At the centre, a blacksmith forged crude pikes while his offsider worked the bellows. Sparks of flaming metal drifted up, climbing into the warm night air.

"*Regardez!*" Flabbergasted by these signs of imminent war Yann lapsed into French.

"In Creswick, they said the stockade is on the Eureka Lead," whispered Clem.

They clipped past a Commissioner's camp to their right. It was seething with action as soldiers and police entered and left the compound. A wall of sandbags resting against the mess tent was riddled with bullet holes. Concerned with delivering the supplies to Studs de Wolf, and even more unnerved by the police presence than he was by the Eureka Stockade, Yann shook his head.

As they passed mounted troopers and foot soldiers with fixed bayonets, his skin crawled. The air was awash with animosity. Men stood in clusters, muttering and shaking their fists at the lawmen patrolling the Main Road.

"Licence hunts twice weekly!", "Digger huntin' must stop!", "We've burned our licences, what more do ye want?", "Do ye want blood?", "Commissioner Rede, the enforcer, will go to hell for acquitting the 'otelkeeper!", "Retribution!", "Yeah, Scobie were an honest digger!", "We want democracy, an end to class privilege!", "We swear by the Southern Cross to stand truly by each other …", "and fight to defend our rights and liberties …"

People shouted in different tongues, different accents. Yann heard French, German, Dutch, Irish, Scottish, Polish, the twang of the Americas. These were all sounds he had heard in Forest Creek, but not at this magnitude. Here was a wall of multicultural sound, of angry international sound, of menace.

"Where do we meet Mr de Wolf?" Clem interrupted his thoughts.

"We meet 'im at the bank."

"You said 'the' correctly, without thinking!" she said, doing her best to sound cheerful.

A surge of pride ran through Yann.

"Everything is closed," she continued, turning her head to view the locked doors of a music hall. "Will the bank not be closed, too?" She gave a brief frown. "Or does Mr de Wolf have an arrangement with the Gold Receiver?"

"I 'ave no idea."

They passed the remains of a building at Eureka South. Blackened bones of beams thrust skywards.

"That must be Bentley's Hotel," she whispered, "the place they set fire to in retribution for the innkeeper and his cohorts murdering the digger Scobie."

At the edge of his side vision Yann saw the trooper with the black patch, Nathaniel Clovis, watching over the crowd. The trooper recognised him but made no move.

"Trooper Clovis 'as seen us but does nothing." Yann's heart clamoured in his chest. "Why does 'e not arrest me?"

Clem twisted in her seat. "You are right. He is looking at us. Perhaps he knows where we are heading and is waiting until we have delivered the supplies to Mr de Wolf." She grabbed him by the arm. "I couldn't stand it if you were thrown into gaol here!"

The iron pot building hove into view. Beneath the flaming torches outside the bank, Studs de Wolf stamped his feet and chewed tobacco. A man in rimless spectacles and a grey frockcoat stood beside him, together with two hulking men. Their eyes darted from left to right. Their faces were etched with anxiety.

Yann spied Annabel. The draught horse, tied to a nearby hitching post, ignored the police activity and the shouting men and lazily flicked mosquitoes away with her tail.

Studs de Wolf's eyes lit on the dray and he waved his arms about. "Where've ye *been*?" he yelled. "Me horse turns up and no supply wagon!"

"Whoa!" Yann yanked on the reins. "Your horse, *monsieur*, was stolen by a digger who is marching to Ballarat and …"

"And where did ye get that shiner, man? I hired ye to bring me dray to Ballarat, not to have a brawlin' time enjoyin' yerself." Studs de Wolf eyed Clem. "Who's this with ye?"

Yann's mind scrambled for an answer. "Zis boy ask me to give 'im a ride to Ballarat."

Clambering down from the dray, Clem hitched up her braces.

"That horse looks like a trooper's nag." Studs de Wolf glared. "Did ye *pinch* it?"

"It-it threw its rider and r-r-rolled on 'im," Yann stuttered, "and it is very lonely, so we think it will be all right to use it."

"Yeah, well." Studs de Wolf chewed thoughtfully. "See the VR brand? I cannot keep it." He tied the horse next to Annabel at the hitching post. "Okay, lads. Leave the shaft support timbers on the side of the road to be taken to the Eureka Stockade later. Ye can unload the colour first!"

"I am sorry, *monsieur.* We are late because we become stuck in mud, and, and, some of the goods 'ave also been stolen."

"I'm not concerned about the *supplies*, young man! I'm only interested in the gold ye've been carryin'!"

"Gold?" Yann stared.

Studs de Wolf grabbed his rifle from the seat of the dray. The beefy assistants with him dumped the supplies on the road, before turning the wagon on its side. Swinging hammers, they undid bolts and screws. Releasing the rear wheel, carved from a tree trunk, they staggered into the bank behind the Gold Receiver.

"But where is gold escort box?" asked Yann, relieved not to have known he had been carrying precious metal.

"Me gold escort box is empty, this time!"

"You mean …" Sweat oozed from Yann's body.

"It's *you* who've been carryin' the gold. I took a gamble, thought I'd lost and ye'd been waylaid by vagabonds with the lot gone!" Studs de Wolf spat a yellow blob on the ground where it was swallowed by the dust. "I was held up by vagabonds me'self. I shot one in the arm and they ran off." He dropped a gold coin in Yann's palm. "Here's yer money."

He stomped into the Bank of Victoria and slammed the door shut. An assistant reappeared and stood guarding the wagon which was now leaning perilously.

Clem exhaled. "Well, now that's done, should we look for somewhere to sleep?"

They walked away, Clem with Ock sniffing the ground beside her and Yann with Cyrano perched on his shoulder.

"*Oui*, and I would like something to eat."

"Very well, we will dine first." Then she exclaimed, "Oh, look! There is a wonderful women's outfitter." She dragged him to a taped-up window, behind which shawls and bonnets and crinolines trimmed with pink bullion roses were arrayed. "Are they not beautiful?"

Yann saw the dimples curve in her cheeks and held up his gold coin. "I will buy you a new dress, tomorrow, when the shop is open."

"That's adorable of you to offer, but I have money of my own. I saw Chinamen sweeping the dust off the roads in Forest Creek and washing it and this gave me food for thought. The next time I passed a heap of road metal opposite the Red Boulder Hotel I spied a handsome specimen in the quartz and picked it out. The Chinese are very shrewd."

"*Non*, I wish to buy it for you."

The noise of bagpipes split the air. "Listen! There are the bagpipes you hate so much!"

Diggers parted to let Scotty through. Still blowing his pipes, he advanced towards Yann and Clem.

"You're *free*, mon, as am I. Have ye and yer friend come to join the Eureka Stockade, as I have, to fight the good fight against the licence huntin'?" The ginger hairs on his legs bristled. "Did ye know there was a licence hunt on the Gravel Pits Lead just yesterday, nearest the Camp and *eight* defaulters were arrested? It were a large and angry crowd indeed."

"Why you keep telling me I am free, Scotty?"

"Well, ye are, mon. The digger Jonas, what slaughtered Johnnie Lee and buried 'is noggin at Pennyweight Flat, was fool enough to brag about it to William Bass, thinkin' he would get a pat on the back for muuurrrder-in' an Asian."

Yann shuddered. "I see 'is wife cradle Johnnie Lee's head and think it is just one more poor little baby."

"As ye can imagine, the hotelkeeper, though no lover of the Chinese, was enraged. He summoned the Native Police and they marched Jonas off to the Forest Creek Camp!" Scotty gave a delighted squeeze of his bagpipe.

Relieved to know why Clovis had not arrested him as he drove past, Yann clamped his hands over his ears. "*Arrêtez!*" He grinned. "Stop! Please stop!"

Scotty ceased playing and began to outline his views on the need to grant suffrage to all men, not just the wealthy. Half-listening, Yann saw a box cart go past with three people crammed inside, one of whom was Le Comte de Corbeau. The count wore a striped maillot and a red kerchief at his neck. In his hand, he carried a slim magenta-coloured volume.

William Bass's chapbook?

63

Cyrano streaked ahead as Yann pushed people aside in his effort to catch up with Le Comte de Corbeau. His hat flew off and he zigzagged along the road, searching through the gloom. It was important for him to find William Bass's chapbook, for the theft of this was reason he had lost his job at the Red Boulder Hotel, and thus the cause of his struggles ever since. If the poetry book had not been snatched, he would still be working as a rouseabout at the Red Boulder Hotel and saving his pennies to purchase a licence to fossick—legally.

Yann wanted nothing to do with the struggle for miners' rights, the violence taking place in Ballarat. He had no desire to become involved with the birth of democracy in the Colony of Victoria. All he wanted was to recover the chapbook and find his father. In and out, he sped, sometimes stopping to ask passers-by if they had seen the Frenchman. "*Monsieur*, 'ave you seen a man in a striped maillot …"

But every digger he asked looked at him as if he were mad. So many people had come to the town of Ballarat to support the burning of the licences. Aggrieved miners were gathered in groups everywhere, and from every country imaginable. The threat of martial law and the unjust treatment of the diggers by Commissioner Rede were more important to them than the needs of one young man with a foreign accent.

A coach rumbled past. Yann leapt onto the back. He clung on and peered ahead, straining to see if he could make out the box cart. Dust flew into his eyes and he struggled to blink it away.

And then he spied Le Comte de Corbeau. This time he was chatting with another digger, waving the magenta-coloured book as he did so. The man he was speaking to wore scuffed boots and the standard navy-blue shirt and moleskins. Yann swung down from the carriage. *How to deal with this?* He took a breath and did his best to compose himself. Should he snatch the hotelkeeper's book of poetry and run? Or should he try to reason with the Saint-Simonian, a man who believed the rights of inheritance should be abolished? As Napoleon Bonaparte's grandson, Yann was convinced the count wished to assassinate him.

Perhaps he *should* seize the book?

He took a second deep breath to slow his heart. His palms were sweaty and he was finding it difficult to breathe. Then he noticed that Cyrano was standing on his hind legs. The digger Le Comte de Corbeau was talking to stroked the cat's ears, picked up Cyrano, said something, placed the cat on the ground again and went on talking. Cyrano stretched his claws on the digger's trouser leg again, and the digger picked him up once more.

Le Comte de Corbeau reached to pat the cat. The men laughed.

The digger, whose shirt was badly frayed, resumed stroking Cyrano's ears and his face as if he had met the cat before. He slung the Tonkinese onto his shoulders and continued with his conversation.

Seeing Cyrano behave in such a friendly manner, and apparently not bothered by Le Comte de Corbeau's presence, meant grabbing the chapbook and making himself scarce would be difficult. Yann cleared his throat and approached. Perhaps the count would not recognise him?

"Pardon, *monsieur*," he said in French, ignoring the digger who was singing the praises of the Irish leader Peter Lalor, "but I believe you have my employer William Bass's book of poetry." He held out his hand. "Poetry cannot be so important to you that you would deprive the hotelkeeper of his innocent pleasure. May I 'ave it, please?"

The Saint-Simonian turned to him with a look of surprise. "Poetry, young man? You say this book contains *poetry*?"

"*Oui, monsieur*, you have in your hand a simple book of verse."

"Verse? I think *not*! This book contains the names of people who plan to evict the Chinese from the goldfields, send them packing when they have done no wrong, save be industrious and good at what they do."

Cyrano, still on the shoulders of the digger, purred loudly and delightedly.

The digger in the frayed shirt spoke. "What the count says is correct. Names are listed in that book, names of people who would throw out the Asians. What Le Comte de Corbeau has done is delay the racist movement just that little bit longer. A massive anti-Chinese meeting is planned in Forest Creek. Are you really so against the Chinese, Yann, that you would go along with this abhorrent behaviour?"

Yann froze. How come the digger knew his name? Had they met at Forest Creek? Was this a trap? He turned. He had never seen this man before. The digger's beard was uncombed. His blue eyes were washed out and weary. His crow's feet were like knife cuts. His nails, with a groove of dirt beneath each one, needed cutting. But the voice sent an electric shock through him. He knew that voice!

"*Papa!*" Yann found himself strangled in a bear hug. "*Papa! Papa!*"

Jean-Paul Sauvage's arms were strong and muscled and smelled of sweat and honest labour. Yann felt the dampness of tears within his father's rough beard. He barely noticed Cyrano disentangle himself and jump to the ground.

They continued to hug and weep, unashamed to weep, too choked to speak. The handsome soldier in the glittering uniform was gone. Yann's *Papa* was now a simple digger, fighting for the rights of his fellow man. As if in a wild dream, he found himself being introduced to Victor, Le Comte de Corbeau.

"Victor," said Jean-Paul Sauvage, "I would like to present my son. Is he not handsome? He's the image of his mother. Apart from his bruised eye, he is the very image of his mother."

64

The four of them sat in a little French cafe on the Main Road. They chatted, spooning tasty *pot-au-feu* into their mouths. The conversation swung between French and English, with the two older men speaking the latter language almost without accent.

"In the country regions of France the saucepan is never removed from the fire," Jean-Paul Sauvage, tearing off a hunk of bread and dunking it in the stew, explained to Clem. "You may well be supping on meat which has been reclining at the bottom of the pot for six months!"

Clem made a face. She picked a piece of beef from her plate and passed it to Ock beneath the table, then passed another to Cyrano, who sat on a nearby chair. They talked of Pennyweight Flat Cemetery, how Yann had been unjustly accused of having murdered a Chinaman and burying his head in one of the graves.

"Pennyweight Flat? The saddest burial ground I have ever seen," murmured Jean-Paul Sauvage. He took a swig of his beer.

"A Chinaman was murdered, you say?" Le Comte de Corbeau chewed as he spoke. "I'm not surprised. There is a hotbed of unrest on the Diggings, a dislike of all things Asian. Constable Thomas Cooke single-handedly stopped an anti-Chinese riot at Forest Creek just recently and the potential rioters eventually went on their way. This took place about a mile south of the Commissioner's Camp in Gully Road. Did you know that, Yann?"

Unwilling to admit he had lately spent much of his time in hiding, either down a mine shaft or incarcerated, Yann shook his head.

"People worry that the gold which the locals, including the natives, believe to be rightfully theirs will be shipped to China rather than being spent to boost the local economy. And, of course," the count added, "the Chinese make excellent miners. We may well employ them when spreading our railway network throughout the Colony of Victoria and, indeed, the whole of Australia." The patch of hair the size of a shilling on the crown of his head gleamed white in the firelight. "Unless the Anglo-Saxons chase them from these shores, I say why not?"

A map spread open in the centre of the table became spattered with a multitude of food stains when he stabbed his fork in the air.

"You see, Yann," said Jean-Paul Sauvage. "Victor has moved on from his crusade against the rights of inheritance, so you can relax. Oh, and he did not sell your cat to the Forest Creek butcher!"

Le Comte de Corbeau spluttered, "I am not so indigent, yet!"

"Victor now plans to connect all points of this vast continent of Australia with his railway tracks," continued Jean-Paul, "if Governor Hotham creates no further obstacles."

The count, recovered, gave a slow smile. "Yes, and we have plans to place the Forest Creek Station on Wattle Flat. This appears to be the most suitable site, notwithstanding any engineering difficulties we may encounter *or* the wishes of the inhabitants." He waved a crust of bread. "Wattle Flat is the most central place to be reached with ease and will, we hope, gratify the great bulk of the population."

Clem placed her hand over her mouth, suppressed a yawn and reached down to pat Ock.

Jean-Paul Sauvage grabbed Yann by the collar and pulled him close, whispering in French, "Do you not think it unwise to be seen consorting with this pretty young boy? People might get the wrong idea!"

"Clem is a girl!" Yann hissed in his father's ear.

"Then why does she not wear a dress?"

"Clem has difficulties with men on the Diggings trying to molest her."

Jean-Paul Sauvage indicated the firearm resting against the wall. "Is not the rifle she carries rather an overreaction?"

"She likes shooting. Clem is a good shot!"

Jean-Paul Sauvage's faded blue eyes crinkled at the corners. "Well, if you must hold hands with her, do so in private … until she dons a dress!" He threw back his head and roared with laughter.

For the first time, Yann saw how much grey was in his father's formerly lustrous fair hair and a sense of time lost wedged in his consciousness.

"Good evening, French Lieutenant!" A waitress in a low cut dress smiled at Jean-Paul flirtatiously. "Has the day been good to ye?"

Jean-Paul nodded. "Very good!"

"Ye have found gold?"

"Better than gold!"

"Is anythin' better than gold?"

"Yes, indeed. I have found my son!"

"Oh, get away with ye. You're not old enough to have a son!" She winked and swished off to the next table.

Yann felt a stab of resentment. "Have you met someone else, another woman?" he asked when she had moved on.

The reciprocated smile faded from his father's face. "I have human needs like everyone else, Yann, but no, I shall never remarry. There will never be another Madeleine. That part of my life is finished."

Yann glanced at Le Comte de Corbeau, who was locked in conversation with Clem about his vision for railways in Australia.

"Did the Saint-Simonians kill *Maman*?" he said in a low voice.

"Do you really think I would be supping with Victor if I believed such a thing?" Jean-Paul Sauvage's face flushed red. "I know there was talk, but the reality is Madeleine died of consumption. And so quickly, so quickly …" His voice caught. "I could not remain within Napoléon Ш's army after that. I had to get as far away as possible." He let out a heavy sigh.

Silence fell between them.

"And where are your lodgings?" asked Jean-Paul.

"I hadn't thought about it."

"Well, you won't find anything in Ballarat at this late stage. Every man and his mistress are here." Pause. "I have a tent, within the Eureka Stockade, if you are interested. It's only small but …" He indicated Clem. "I think the three of us would fit comfortably."

Clem fell asleep almost instantly, with Ock at her feet.

Yann and his father lay alongside one another. Wrapped in rough blankets, they talked through the night. Diggers on watch outside hefted their arms and marched back and forth.

"Does this stockade mean the beginning of civil war?" asked Yann, pushing Cyrano off his feet. "And all because of a mining licence fee?"

"The miners cannot afford to pay thirty shillings a month, and the government wishes the penalty to be even harsher. I'll wager you aimed to pan for gold … and were you able to afford a licence fee?"

Yann shook his head no. "But we did not come to the Colony of Victoria for that, we came to find you." Pause. "And then I got the strangest feeling Magali did not wish to find you, something about her fiancé, all those years ago."

"Magali always was a fine-looking woman, and headstrong. The fellow was an Arab. Oh, he may have looked exotic in his flowing robes and on a white horse, but she should have known he would be unsuitable as a husband."

"Did you assassinate Magali's fiancé?"

Jean-Paul Sauvage pushed himself up on one elbow and looked down at him with a frown. "Do you *really* believe that, Yann?"

"You knew something. I heard *Maman* say that you knew."

Jean-Paul sank back and couched his head on his folded arms. "I was in Algeria and knew the order had gone out to the French commissariat to 'take care' of the situation."

"Magali has never forgiven you."

"I cannot be responsible for that."

"She has a new man now, Mr Brisket. He is a widower, is the size of a bean sprout and quite plain in appearance. His wife died in a tent fire and left him behind with his daughters, Bethany and Dora. The Briskets call her Maggie and, lately, she talks of opening a school for young ladies in Forest Creek." Yann stifled a yawn. "Magali also took in an abandoned child, Eleanor, who passed and is buried at Pennyweight Flat Cemetery. I wouldn't be surprised if she has taken in others since I left."

His father gave a quiet chuckle. "She sounds as resourceful as ever, but Magali need have no fear. This egalitarian country is very different from France. I will not be blighting her, ah, her ... new relationship ..." His voice trailed off and soon he was snoring.

The stripy dog's ears pricked up. Ock crept to the doorway of the tent, his tail between his legs.

65

Ballarat, Saturday 2nd December 1854

By morning, the heightened mood in the Eureka Stockade had dissipated to languor. The flag of the Southern Cross swooped and swayed overhead in the warm breeze when Jean-Paul Sauvage met up with Victor, Le Comte de Corbeau in the stockade. They righted a wheelbarrow, placed a plank of wood across it and spread open maps of Victoria to discuss railway stations, sidings, sleepers and the laying of tracks.

Yann and Clem, with Cyrano, pushed past the makeshift wall encircling almost an acre of ground. They negotiated shaft support timbers set in the ground and roped together, and dodged around overturned carts. Ock refused to accompany them. Trembling, he remained at the French Lieutenant's tent with his tail between his legs.

Despite the growing military presence, they strolled down the Main Road. The knock-kneed nag had gone from the hitching post. Yann surreptitiously eyed the mounted patrols lining the street. Would the tension and ill-feeling escalate to civil war? he wondered, and then noted that diggers from within the stockade were already carousing in the grog shops and hotel bars. The miners seemed unconcerned. Tomorrow was Sunday, a day of rest, and everyone knew they could sleep off their hangovers.

Clem expressed her surprise at the number of women she had counted within the stockade. "Are they not afraid?" she said.

Yann took her rifle and guided her into the women's outfitter. "I believe it is now safe for you to wear a dress in Ballarat!"

Clem had trouble deciding between the pink striped gingham and a creamy silk crinoline embroidered with pink bullion roses. After lengthy deliberation, she chose the cream silk and a straw bonnet to go with it, plus a frilled pinafore to keep the dress clean.

Crunching on barley sugar and licking toffee apples, they ambled to the gum tree holding Buchanan the jeweller's clock, one of the local sights.

"When I marry, I shall have an At Home at least every six weeks, and leave calling cards with the influential ladies of the district. I will have aromatic plants and bee plants in my garden …"

"You are wishing to marry already?" Yann stroked Cyrano, perched on his shoulder. "You 'ave told me your Da 'as plans for you to be a baker?"

"Oh no, I will not return to Forest Creek. I shall either remain in Ballarat or take the coach to Melbourne … I have an aunt in Fitzroy. She has a large garden and her guests take tea from four to five o'clock in the formal manner."

"And will you 'ave shooting competitions after you finish your tea?" He burst out laughing.

"Silly!" She gave him a playful shove and lifted her skirts to step over a patch of muddy ground. "You must be so glad to have found your *Papa*."

"*Oui*," he said simply. Clem could never comprehend the joy in his heart.

Everywhere they went they heard people extolling the virtues of Peter Lalor, the Irishman who had inspired the diggers on Bakery Hill. They even saw his image in the window as they passed the *Ballarat Times* newspaper office. They halted at the saddler and looked at the bridles and bits, spurs and riding crops he had for sale. Yann admired a pocket-knife and considered purchasing a hand-plaited belt.

"You still have that old snake pelt at your waist. You could do with a new belt," said Clem.

Recalling his battle with the serpent, the struggle to the death followed by the smelly skinning, Yann decided to continue wearing his snakeskin waistband. They passed the Post Office, the clockmaker and the apothecary, slowing at the butcher's shamble where legs of lamb hung from chunky hooks.

"I know, let's purchase a leg of lamb!" said Clem. "We will make a fire and I will cook it beneath the soil of the Eureka Stockade."

That night, they lit a biggish fire in their pit and let it burn down to coals. Yann inserted his dagger down to the bone and Clem stuffed the cavity with rosemary and garlic. She rubbed the outside of the leg with crushed rosemary, butter and a sprinkling of salt and pepper. She wrapped the leg in fifteen layers of paper, placed the lamb on the coals and covered the pit with an earth lid.

Three hours later, the lamb was cooked, pink and tender. She gave it a quick brown on the fire and Jean-Paul divided the meat up with his knife. Juice dribbled down their chins. They ate until they could eat no more, then washed the meal down with beer and billy tea. Yann played his accordion. They sang French songs, chatted, and watched diggers half-heartedly patrolling the perimeter armed with pikes and rifles. Jean-Paul was the first to turn in, followed by Clem. Then Yann and Cyrano.

Ock remained on watch at the tent opening, tail still between his legs.

66

Ballarat, Sunday 3rd December 1854

A choir of kookaburras started up and then stopped. Clutching their blankets to them, Yann, Clem and Jean-Paul rolled over and continued sleeping.

Without warning, the sound of horses' hooves fractured the silence. Gunfire broke out. Yann reeled from his dreams to hear ammunition whining. Explosions split the air. After a quick succession of volleys, upwards of three hundred troopers swept aside the barrows and pit props to storm the Eureka Stockade.

The French Lieutenant was the first to react to the wild firing, the thundering steeds. He leapt to his feet, pulled his gun from its holster and rushed into the compound. Cyrano streaked across the ground to the nearest tree. Clem, cursing the dress she wore, lifted her rifle and began shooting.

Ock remained inside the tent, whimpering.

Horses whinnied. Tents were set on fire. Flaming canvas spiralled into the early dawn. Dirt and stones spat from the horses' hooves and Jean-Paul pulled Yann along with him. He pushed a gun into Yann's hand, the silver-handled pistol he recalled having used in Paris. In his right hand, Yann wielded his dagger with the Napoleonic eagle carved into its handle.

With slitted gaze, Yann took aim with his left hand. He clipped a trooper on the thigh and the trooper's yawps of pain seared his mind. He swallowed, gritted his teeth and followed his father. The suffocating smell of gunpowder clogged the air. Horses screamed with fear. Eyes rolling, they reared in the air and the ground throbbed with their pounding. Through the haze, women howled and ran for cover. Diggers dropped to their knees, writhing in agony. Blood seeped across the Eureka Stockade.

"Peter Lalor's been shot!" The shout went across the compound.

Jean-Paul Sauvage gunned down another trooper. The lawman slid from his saddle and lay prostrate.

"Watch out!" shrieked Clem.

Yann whipped around to see Trooper Clovis bearing down on him. He took aim. Missed. Clovis fired back. Yann fired again.

Trooper Clovis lifted his weapon and pulled the trigger a second time, but Yann did not receive the bullet. He did not tumble to the ground. An unbearable horror scorched through him as he watched Jean-Paul Sauvage sink back, almost without resistance. No writhing. No struggle. His beloved *Papa* lay there without moving.

The trooper swung down from his horse and raised his gun to finish off the French Lieutenant, to make sure he was truly dead. A scream broke from Yann's throat as if from someone else, from someone he'd never known, from outside of him. He lunged at the trooper, stabbing with his dagger. Stabbing. Stabbing. Trooper Clovis had slaughtered his father when they had just been reunited. He would not rest until he had killed him. He would see this man into his grave.

The firing continued around Yann. The wails of the diggers' wives and children went on, but he barely heard them. Sounds of desperation, of failure, of a cause lost filled the countryside. A ripple of despair rang through the entire Diggings, through every field, claim and lead.

Bodies lay sprawled like broken rag dolls, their life force seeping out within an agony of miscarried justice. Slipping on gore, Yann chased his adversary across the stockade. When he reached the boundary distant from the Main Road, the trooper pulled the trigger again and Yann heard the impotent click. He knew victory was his, was within his grasp. The dagger was an extension of him, and he kept slashing and slashing until finally Nathaniel Clovis lost his footing. The trooper stumbled, attempted to right himself, and began to push rearwards with his hands and knees. Like a toxic jockey spider.

"I killed yer father, Frenchie! An eye for an eye? Nah, an eye for an old man, a dirty deserter!"

Awash with fury and loss, Yann jabbed his dagger at the trooper's belly. The blade missed but the lawman's boot slipped on a discarded coffee tin. Not seeing the deep lead behind him, he fell backwards. Arms and legs flailing, he seemed to drift down to the bottom of the mine. Almost in slow motion. As if in a mad dream, Yann heard the crack of the trooper's neck. He knew his nemesis was dead, but he felt as though he wasn't properly there. His victory was suddenly without meaning.

Heavy with a sense of helplessness and streaming with sweat, Yann turned. He threaded his way through the bodies strewn across the Eureka Stockade. He saw soldiers haul down the flag of the Southern Cross. They carried it around the ground, waving the hand-sewn symbol of unity, crowing and whooping. Around and around they went. Flames flickered and flounced among the slain.

Yann had only one thing left to do. After that, he would quit this vile place for good.

As he wondered where to bury his father, he heard a voice cry, "Yann! Yann! Are you all right?"

In a sullen daze, he saw Clem pop her head up from behind an upturned cart. Rifle in hand, she waved and called his name.

"Over here!" she shrieked. "Quick, Yann! Military reinforcements are on their way! We need your help!"

67

Ballarat, Monday 11ᵗʰ December 1854

They stood beside the coach. Yann gave Clem a French *bise*, a kiss on each cheek, and then a third and a fourth. She'd had a bath that morning and she tasted delicious.

"You will be 'appy in Melbourne?" he finally asked.

"Oh, yes. I have had enough of death. I could not stand to remain here and I could not stand to return to Forest Creek and keep burying my brothers and sisters, taking flowers to the cemetery each Sunday." She touched the skin around Yann's eye where the bruise had changed from purple to green. "I wish to be in a safe place, a happier place than the Diggings, with all its greed and anger and corruption."

She patted Cyrano farewell.

Jean-Paul Sauvage's *bise* was more formal, one on each side of her face, before he handed her into the carriage. "Victor was wise not to spend Saturday night within the stockade." He clutched the sleeve of his new flannel shirt, groaning, "Lalor may have lost his arm, but *I* am not used to being wounded!"

"You mean officers never go into the field of battle?" A smile quivered on Clem's lips.

Beside the French Lieutenant, Ock wagged his tail. The driver cracked his whip and the coach to Melbourne moved off, crunching over the stones.

Clem leaned from the window, waved and called, "Oh, Yann, don't forget to tell Princess Albert I haven't forgotten her."

"'Ow do you know what I plan to do?"

"Oh, I know!" She pulled her head back inside the coach.

Veiled in a cloud of dust, the coach rattled off down the highway and a sense of emptiness ran through Yann.

"Well, Clemency Holmes-Lacy saved my life," murmured Jean-Paul Sauvage. "And, of course, I am an expert at playing dead. Twenty-two diggers fatally wounded, plus five troops, martial law, and gunned down stockaders heaped into a common grave … a common grave, I ask you. Is this the birth of democracy?" He pushed Cyrano aside and hung his good arm around Yann's neck. "And what are your plans, *mon fils*? Will you return to France? Or will you remain with me to help set up a railway system in Victoria and visit marvellous Melbourne from time to time?"

Yann tilted his head and let the hot sun caress his face. He had grown accustomed to the vaulted sky, the warm-smelling earth. The bush had wormed its way into his soul. Thanks to Eureka Stockade, Australia was part of him now. He jiggled the last of the gold in his pocket. He had other business to attend to, apart from helping his father and checking on Princess Albert and Magali.

And, yes, he was looking forward to taking tea with Clem in Melbourne.